MAC's D

CW00343526

by

Susie Baggaley

Copyright

Mac's Dilemma
(Impossible Choices)
Copyright Susie Baggaley 2022

The right of Susie Baggaley to be identified as author of this work has been asserted in accordance with Sections 77 and 78 of the Copyright, Design and Patents Act 1988.

No reproduction, copy or transmission of this publication may be made without written permission.

This is a work of fiction. Names, characters, companies, places and incidents originate from the writer's imagination. Any resemblance to actual persons, living or dead is purely coincidental.

Published by
Baggatelle Publishers Ltd
ISBN: 978-1-7391408-0-9

Licence Notes

This book is licensed for your personal enjoyment only. This book may not be resold or given away to other people. If you would like to share this book with another person, please purchase an additional copy for each recipient. If you are reading this book and did not purchase it, or it was not purchased for your use only, then please return to your favourite book retailer and purchase your own copy. Thank you for respecting the hard work of the author.

Table of Contents

MAC's Trilogy

BOOK 3

MAC's Dilemma
(Impossible Choices)

Prologue

I had to face it. My actions during the late summer in Simla had put paid to any chance I had of completing my Ph.D at the Calcutta School of Tropical Medicine. Without the college's funding, my research into mother and infant mortality was impossible and made my presence in India meaningless. I had attacked the establishment in a fit of pique, and I was now being punished which, on reflection, seemed inevitable. Englishmen of the British Colonial Service, once threatened, did what they had done for decades. They closed ranks against their opponent, in this instance me, and defended their position like any well-trained army unit. It didn't matter that I was trying to right a wrong or expose racial prejudice, one simply did not criticise one's peers.

"It is not the done thing, Old Boy!"

Being young, female, and a thorn in the Indian Medical Service's side, I was being quietly removed using the simple tactic of cancelling fifty percent of my Ph.D funding.

I smacked my clenched fist against the desk and groaned. 'How could I have been so stupid?'

It was a reasonable question with little in the way of an answer. Perhaps, having been awarded an Empire Gallantry Medal by the Viceroy of India at his summer garden party had given me aspirations above my station, or my innate sense of injustice had overridden my professional judgement, or, more likely, I was just full of self-righteous hubris. Whatever the reason, I was now well and truly hoisted by my own petard and unable to rectify the situation. My Indian adventure had run its course and I had only myself to blame.

'Damn you, Mac, why are you so headstrong and stubborn?' I screwed the Calcutta School of Tropical Medicine's termination letter into a ball and threw it in the bin, recalling Pa's constant complaints about these same character traits listed in my annual year-end school reports.

'A leopard cannot change its spots,' I groaned, trying to justify myself, but it didn't help. I was out of my depth in India and had to accept that it would take a better woman than me to alter the status quo within the Indian Medical Service.

It had been a long, tense and fractious year, with many highs and lows along the way, but it was now over. I had to pack my bags and return home, all my grand ideas dashed, and ambitions foiled.

'Well, Elizabeth, look on the bright side,' announced Aunt Karr inside my head, *'at least you're no longer naïve.'*

That much was true. My colonial adventure had certainly made a woman of me, but this was not necessarily going to be of much use in an English provincial backwater like my home village of Riveldene. How I was ever to settle back into village life after the exotic sights and sounds of India was beyond me, but settle I would, come hell or high water . . .

Chapter One

T he slow, undulating swell of the India Ocean barely registered on deck as the P&O steamship, ss Ranchi, cruised at seventeen knots towards Aden on that January day in 1931.

Seated in a steamer chair watching the malachite-coloured sea rise and fall in never-ending waves, my legs wrapped in a ship's blanket and a cup of steaming beef tea in my hand, I tried to enthuse about returning to my life as a resident GP in Northumbria. I failed miserably. Too much water had passed under the bridge since I had departed for foreign shores some fifteen months earlier and I baulked at having to return to the staid, predictable world of home. I grunted and returned to Rudyard Kipling's *"The Man who would be King".*

After reading the same paragraph three times without taking in one word I gave up, closed the leather-bound novel and stared vacantly at the vast liquid horizon, my mind recycling recent events like a cracked record.

Since the day my character assassination of Sir Charles Ponsonby-Pritchard had appeared in the Delhi Times, I had been on an emotional roller-coaster. My article had attacked this Senior Surgeon of the India Medical Service for failing to attend a sphincteroplasty operation on a thirteen-year-old Muslim girl trapped in a child marriage, preferring instead to spend his evening playing poker with his colleagues, and by implication, I had accused him of being racially prejudiced. I was now mentally exhausted, both grieving for my lost research post and irritated at how events had worked out.

To add to my distress, the very idea of being seen as one of the Fishing Fleet's *"Returned Empty"* girls gave me collywobbles, and I knew no rebuttal by me would alter the opinion of Riveldene's parishioners. To them my trip to India had really been about finding a husband and, having failed miserably, I was returning home still single and past my prime.

'Christ,' I groaned. 'If only they knew the truth.'

A zephyr of sea breeze ruffled my hair as I adjusted my seat into a reclining position. My eyelids felt heavy after another sleepless night on board and the rhythmic sounds of the sea gurgling along the waterline were soporific. Resting my head on the chairback's cushion, my mind tracked back to Simla and that fateful September morning when Ruby and I were enjoying breakfast at Mallards, on the Ridge . . .

My telephone call from the Calcutta School of Tropical Medicine, telling me my Ph.D funding had been prematurely withdrawn, was a bolt out of the blue, but Vijay's early morning cable from Jhalanpur, announcing the sudden death of his father, was like a meteorite smacking into the earth's crust.

Ruby and I were both speechless as we stood at the entrance to Mallards hours later, watching the new Maharaja of Jhalanpur limp on crutches towards his limousine then disappear through the imposing entrance gates with his physician and chaprassi in tow, heading for his palace in the Rajputana desert.

Ruby's future was now precarious. As Vijay's mistress her status would be called into question by his family and she faced the possibility of being cast adrift, far from home, without financial support. The very idea caused her to shake violently.

'Where will I go, Mac?' she implored, as we walked back into the villa, her strong veneer visibly crumbling before my eyes. 'What shall I do without Vijay's protection?'

Fear brought on one of her severe asthma attacks, and as her airways constricted she turned puce and began to gasp for breath.

'Relax, Ruby,' I demanded, as she gripped her throat and wheezed, bending double as her chest heaved, struggling against suffocation. 'Where's your nebulizer?'

'In the . . .' She gasped again and shook her head, pointing to the ceiling. '. . . bathroom.'

I took the stairs three at a time, slid across the tiled floor of her bedroom in my stocking feet and threw open the bathroom door. The nebuliser was sitting in its box on a shelf above the washstand. I grabbed it and raced back down as panic began to set in. Ruby's lips were now turning blue.

'Here.' I rammed the mouthpiece between her teeth and began hand pumping the rubber bulb, pushing oxygen and atomised epinephrine into her lungs while trying to keep her calm.

'Deep breaths, Ruby. Deep breaths. Now don't stop.'

I couldn't help remembering another occasion when I had tried to keep her alive after she suffered carbon monoxide poisoning on board ship. Zapping the memory from my thoughts, I concentrated on the present, gritted my teeth and pumped for all I was worth. It seemed to take for ever, but eventually her colour returned and her bronchial tubes began to expand. Finally, she was able to breathe alone.

'Jesus, Ruby, don't do that to me.'

She coughed, pushed the nebuliser away from her face and took a deep breath. 'It's a good job you're a medic . . . or I'd be breathing my last.'

'Rubbish.' I checked her pulse. 'Now stay there while I fetch my stethoscope.

Two minutes later I was listening to her chest through the bell cup and could hear air wheezing in her lungs. Well, at least she's still upright, I thought, wiping the nebulizer mouthpiece with an antiseptic pad and returning it to its box.

She eased herself out of the hall chair and headed for the drawing room, slumping onto one of the sofas, resting her head in her hands. 'What the hell do I do now, Mac?'

My sigh spoke volumes. 'Ruby, I've no idea, but you must hang onto the fact that Vijay loves you and is unlikely to cast you aside just because he's become a Maharaja.' I joined her on the sofa trying to be positive.

'What about you?' Despite her own sudden change of fortune, she managed to think of mine.

'Goodness knows.' I rubbed my forehead trying not to think about my future, but it didn't work. 'I imagine Agnes Scott will ask me to remain in the Women's Medical Service as a permanent doctor, but the idea of spending my days in one of the Countess of Dufferin's hospitals doesn't appeal and was certainly not what I had intended when I came to India.'

'But at least you would have an income. I can't imagine what the hell I could do to stay afloat. There's not much call

11

for an aging Soho stripper here in Delhi.' Ruby was having difficulty keeping her hands still.

'Then don't think about it. Nothing is going to change immediately for either of us, so I suggest we stay calm, let the dust settle, and concentrate on our options.'

'. . . Memsahib. Memsahib, wake up.'

I felt someone shaking my arm. Slowly I opened my eyes and stared into the pockmarked Asian face of a ship's steward, his white, pleated turban inches from my nose.

'Your chai, Memsahib, it spill over.'

I shot up, feeling a damp sensation spreading across my groin. 'Oh, damnation!' I leapt from the chair, flicking excess beef tea from the large round wet patch on my linen skirt as my novel bounced onto the floor and slid along the starboard deck. I quickly scooped it up, threw the sodden blanket onto the steamer chair and made my way aft, wondering if the beef stain would come out in the wash.

I dunked my skirt in cold water, scrubbed it vigorously with carbolic soap and hung it on a hanger behind the cabin door. The stain was still evident as a pale brown ring embedded in the beige material. 'Drat!'

I stood by the porthole, half naked from the waist down, and watched other passengers taking the morning air. A young couple sauntered by, arms linked, heads drawn together, chatting amiably as they promenaded along the deck on their morning constitutional, adding to my angst as a wave of nostalgia enveloped me like a shroud.

Tom Wallace and I had looked just like that, I thought, as vivid memories of our daily strolls around the deck on the ss

12

Narkunda came sharply to mind, our bodies almost touching as we discussed the latest cases from his morning clinic.

I dragged my trunk from under my bed and rummaged through my clothes for something else to wear. A tear dripped onto my cheek and I brushed it away like a pesky fly, frustration replacing remorse over what might have been.

'What the hell am I doing here?' I groaned, as I dropped onto my bed and pushed my legs into a pair of white linen trousers which needed ironing, then lay back and fiddled with the rubber buttons, trying to fasten the fly front.

While my fingers battled the minute buttonholes, unwanted images tore at my heartstrings. Tom carefully bandaging my wounds after the ship's fire; making love to me in the Taj Mahal Hotel; announcing he was married during our picnic on the slopes of Karnala Fort above the Bhor Pass. When an image of him handing me his gift of a malachite and ivory bracelet as I boarded the train for Calcutta came to mind, I thumped the mattress with my fist.

'Damn it!' I swore. It helped vent my anger but left me wondering if I would ever get over this shipboard romance.

'Elizabeth, stop being pathetic and do something useful.'

I sat up and shook my head to get rid of Aunt Karr's voice. She was my opinionated spinster aunt, now retired from her post as a psychology professor at St Andrew's University and living in Peebles in her dotage, who I had always loved and respected. But her no-nonsense attitude never failed to impinge on my emotions at the most inopportune moments.

I checked my watch. It was still only eleven-thirty and the day stretched ahead of me in a series of endless, monotonous hours. I pulled my camera from the trunk and searched for some spare Kodak film, intent on spending the rest of the morning photographing passenger life aboard ship.

'At least I can record my experiences at sea to show the family,' I muttered, pushing my writing case to one side. Something made me pause and I opened the flap. There, lodged in the side pocket, was a small black and white photograph taken by one of my closest friends, Frances.

It was of the Lady Reading Women's Hospital in Simla, my young patient Lamis Abbas and I sitting in the grounds, my protective arm around her shoulders as dappled sunlight cast shadows across the lawn. Lamis was giggling as Frances shouted '*Sadaqah*', and my camera clicked, recording the moment for posterity.

'What does *Sadaqah* mean?' I remembered asking.

'Smile in Urdu,' replied Frances, handing over my camera. 'At least I think that's what it means. It's one of the words that Lamis has taught me.'

'*Sadaqah*,' I now whispered, as I placed my lips to the picture and thought back to the events that had followed . . .

I had been in Doctor Agnes Scott's office at the Lady Hardinge Medical College in Delhi and, as I had predicted to Ruby, she and Sir Peter Bonham-Cavendish, my joint supervisors for my Ph.D, were trying their best to persuade me to remain in India despite the repercussions of my newspaper article.

Their argument certainly had some merit, and the Women's Medical Service certainly needed every female clinician they could get their hands on, but the knowledge that I would be constantly snubbed by my male colleagues in the Indian

Medical Service for lambasting their boss was something I simply could not stomach.

My intransigence had only deepened after I learned that the militant fanatics in both The Congress Party and the Muslim League were using my Delhi Times article, about racial prejudice in the corridors of power, as another means to fuel unrest in their ongoing fight against direct rule. Civil riots had broken out in the Old Delhi suburbs leaving Lord Irwin, the Viceroy of India, no choice but to act. Days later, Sir Charles Ponsonby-Pritchard announced his retirement as Surgeon-General of the IMS on medical grounds and left for England on the next available passenger liner with his family.

Deciding to keep a low profile, I had concentrated on working out my notice at the Lady Hardinge by taking over Lamis's nursing care when she arrived back from Simla, monitoring her recovery from her now infamous rectal reconstruction surgery.

I had discovered her months earlier, sitting on a flea-infested, soiled mattress in a windowless back room of a hovel in Old Delhi during one of my house-calls. Illegally married off at thirteen by her father, she had been physically and mentally abused by her illiterate, forty-three-year-old husband, Jusuf Abbas, who had inflicted violent and appalling sexual injuries on her small, malnourished body. By the time I found her, these injuries were festering and she was in excruciating pain. If I had been a vet, and she had been a badly injured animal, I would have put her down.

Newspaper hacks and radical activists who heard she was back in Delhi were determined to turn her into a Muslim victim of racial injustice, so protecting her from these journalists had proved to be no easy task. I found reporters, clad in medical attire, with cameras slung around their necks, hiding in linen cupboards or behind hospital screens and had to instruct orderlies to evict them and confiscated their camera film.

Meanwhile, Agnes Scott had to severely reprimand hospital nurses and students when it became clear that some were receiving payments for passing on titbits about Lamis's medical progress.

The operation to reverse her temporary colostomy to allow her digestive system to function normally once more was scheduled for late December, and I was determined to be Agnes's Assistant Surgeon at this procedure before I packed my bags for good and followed the ousted ex-Surgeon-General back to England. Lamis would be joining Frances in Poona early in the New Year where she would be safe from prying eyes and be given one-to-one tuition in the confines of St Saviour's School for Girls.

All was arranged, except that my patient had no idea about any of this or that I was leaving India permanently. Being responsible for shattering her world again was killing me because she saw me as her surrogate mother. Trying to find the courage to tell her was becoming harder each day.

One mid-December morning as Agnes and I were walking across the quadrangle on our way to lunch, my supervisor appeared to read my mind. 'You'll have to tell Lamis at some point, Elizabeth. Better to get it over with now than have it hanging over your head.'

I clenched my fists and stuffed them inside my laboratory coat pockets. 'The question is, Agnes, what do I say? She will never understand the politics of all this, even if I could explain it to her. On the other hand, without knowing the truth, she will think I'm abandoning her for no good reason.'

Agnes stopped in her tracks. 'Elizabeth, you only have yourself to blame for this. I warned you months ago not to get too emotionally involved with Lamis, and this is the reason why.'

'I know,' I said, walking on, 'and I can assure you, I will not make the same mistake a second time.' I held opened the refectory door then followed Agnes into the canteen, 'though I'm hardly likely to find a case like Lamis's amongst Pa's parishioners in Riveldene.'

'Maybe not, but right now you have to be cruel to be kind. You must tell Lamis when you are leaving and under no circumstances give her any hope that you'll be coming back.'

I could hear the bitterness in Agnes's words and realised that she too was having difficulty coming to terms with my departure.

'Do not give her any false hope, Elizabeth. The poor child deserves better than that.'

Gritting my teeth, I found Lamis in the college library, her shoulders hunched over the desk as she practised copying the English alphabet onto a large notepad, the tip of her tongue trapped between her teeth and her chewed pencil producing clear letters along the lined paper. I waited quietly until she had finished then tapped her on the shoulder.

'Hello, Umi,' she said, her face lighting up the room.

'Hello, Lamis.' I paused, trying to find the right words. 'I . . . need to tell you something . . . important.'

She frowned, sensing something was wrong but unsure of my words. I repeated them in broken Hindi and knelt by her side, taking her hands in mine and squeezing them tightly. 'I have to go home to England.'

Her bottom lip quivered and she slowly shook her head. 'Why?'

'Because my family needs me,' I lied, hoping this would pacify her.

'When you come back?'

I hesitated, hating myself for what I was about to do to this child. 'I cannot come back, dear. It's not possible.'

There was a pause as my words infiltrated her brain, then she wailed, her cries echoing off the wooden panelling. 'No, Umi. No, please, you not go from Lamis.'

I pulled her into my arms and stroked her black shiny hair, rocking her back and forth, wishing I could make it all better. 'I have no choice, Lamis. I must go home.'

Her little body shook, her violent sobs piercing my heart like steel pins.

'You have to be strong,' I said, raising her head and brushing away her tears with my thumbs. 'Dr Scott and Dr Joshi will be here to look after you until you are better, then Miss Frances will take my place and become your new "Umi" in Poona. You will love living in Poona, Lamis, and I know Miss Frances will take very great care of you.'

The child's kohl black eyes searched my face as her brain slowly interpreted my words. 'No. I stay with you, not Miss Frances.'

My shoulders slumped under the weight of my guilt knowing that no-one could ever replace me in Lamis's mind. I had been the one who had rescued her from that hovel in Old Delhi and saved her from an early death. To this little girl, I was her saviour and protector, and she would never understand why I was abandoning her now. She had been to hell and back in her young life and the thought of casting her adrift was beginning to crucify me.

'I promise, Lamis, I will write every month and send photographs of my home and family. You will like that, won't you?' My words sounded hollow.

She put her hands over her ears trying to block me out. 'Why you no like Lamis?' Her tears dripped onto my skirt. 'Am I bad girl?'

'NO. Don't ever think that.' I shook her shoulders gently. 'You are perfect.' Now I was crying.

'Umi, please, you no go away. I try harder to be good girl.' She was now squeezing me tightly around the waist and sobbing in hiccups.

At that moment, I would have given anything to gather her up and take her with me, but I knew that such action was impossible and my hatred for Sir Charles Ponsonby-Pritchard now knew no bounds. I closed my eyes and prayed that he would be struck down dead for the pain he was causing this innocent child.

'One day,' I had whispered, my emotions in tatters, 'I hope you will be a great doctor here in India, and I will be so proud of you.' My lips brushed the top of her head. 'God willing, Lamis, we will meet again one day.'

I would never forget this extraordinary child, or her ability to smile despite so much trauma. All I could hope, as the ss Ranchi carried me towards Aden, was that she would slowly forget me and find true happiness with people of her own kind. We had bonded in the strangest of circumstances and the photograph now resting in my hand would always remind me of her struggle against adversity and my part in providing her with a better future.

'Take care, dear Lamis,' I said, as I placed it back into my writing case. 'Become a beacon of light for Indian girls everywhere and show them the way to a better future. *Inshallah.*'

I loaded my camera with film and went out on deck feeling drained. The young couple I had seen earlier were walking towards me along the port deck looking as if they didn't have a care in the world. The young man's India Civil Service uniform was impeccably pressed, and the girl's frilly lace parasol coyly hide her face from the sun.

'Beautiful day,' he announced, raising his government issue topi in salute as they approached. 'A great improvement on the fetid air from the unwashed rabble of India, wouldn't you say?'

'Oh, I don't know,' I replied, raising my camera, and bringing them both into focus. 'If it weren't for the unwashed rabble of India, Sir, I imagine you would be out of a job. Now smile.' The camera clicked and I continued along the deck, leaving him standing there open-mouthed.

'Bloody Colonial British,' I muttered.

Chapter Two

T he jolly boat bounced against the stone steps of the dock wall at Steamer Point in Aden, and I gingerly stepped ashore, trying to keep my footing on treacherous slimy green algae as I climbed to the wharf. Once safely on dry land, I scanned the harbour buildings for the Crescent Hotel and located it standing imposingly at one end of the harbour. Crossing the busy thoroughfare with traffic constantly in motion, I made my way along the bleached promenade with the sun beating down on my head.

I was to meet the British Resident's wife, Lady Stewart-Symes, for morning coffee, and hoped the perspiration dripping down my neck and gathering under my armpits wouldn't stain my freshly laundered lemon organza short-sleeved dress before I reached the shade of the hotel's veranda.

Geraldine and I had met once before, when the ss Narkunda had docked in Aden on its way to Bombay. At the time, I was trying to keep Prince Vijay Kumar Singh II's wife from miscarrying and thought a trip ashore would do her good after being cooped up in the Jhalanpur suite for weeks on end. Vijay happened to mention that he was to pay his respects to Sir George Stewart-Symes on behalf of the Princely States of India, so I suggested that Princess Dashwanabai and her aunt should accompany him. He agreed on the condition that I went along too, overriding my plans to see the sites of Aden with Frances and Ruby. It had been hard to agree as I had already missed out on my trip to Giza and Cairo earlier in the voyage, but I had become the Princess's personal doctor and I knew she would refuse to go anywhere without me. Reluctantly I had changed into my best day dress and accompanied the royal entourage, spending five cool, peaceful hours in the seclusion of Government House while Geraldine hosted a delightful lunch. She also gave me some sound advice on dealing with the misogynistic men of the Calcutta School of Tropical Medicine who were to fund my Ph.D research. Funny, I thought, as I walked through the Crescent Hotel entrance, I was now prematurely back in Aden having fallen foul of those very same men.

'I'm to meet Lady Stewart-Symes for coffee,' I announced to the hotel receptionist as I approached the desk. 'Is she here yet?'

'No, Memsahib. She no here. Please you go to terrace and I tell her you waiting there.'

I wandered through the restaurant, the electric ceiling fans whirring quietly above my head creating a welcome mechanical breeze from the heat of Aden outside. Catching sight of the ladies lavatory on my right, I deviated towards it, extracting my lace-edged hankie from my bag. For the next five minutes I rinsed my face and neck in tepid, rust-coloured water before checking my reflexion in the chipped washstand mirror, adding more soft pink lipstick and running my fingers through my cropped auburn hair.

'You'll do, Mac, so stop preening,' I chided, and made my way to the terrace.

'Doctor,' called out Geraldine from across the pillared expanse, 'what a lovely surprise to get your telegram and to learn of your unexpected visit.'

We shook hands, made ourselves comfortable at a circular wicker table, far enough away from other hotel guests to maintain some privacy, and ordered coffee and cakes.

'Now, dear, I want to know all about your time in India, and what's all this about you giving up your Ph.D?'

We spent a pleasant hour as I recounted my experiences working with the Women's Medical Service, my impressions of Calcutta and Delhi, and my adventures with the Indian Army on the Northwest Frontier, the latter proving to be highly entertaining.

'Sir George will be fascinated, Elizabeth. He fought on the Frontier under Major General Edgerton's command during the Mahsud Waziri blockade, and he will love your story of Captain James Squid arresting a drunken oak tree outside the Officers' Mess at Landi Kotal.'

Geraldine's laughter was infectious, and for the first time in days I began to relax, enjoying the company of a lady who reminded me so much of my dear Aunt Karr.

'Did Princess Dashwanabai manage to go the full term with her pregnancy?' she asked.

'I'm afraid not. She lost the child during the ship's fire. I assume Sir George received a full account of the disaster.'

Geraldine nodded, instantly serious. 'Indeed, he did. As Aden is a Province of British India, he receives Government reports from Delhi on a weekly basis. What a dreadful tragedy. Do fill me in on the details.'

The waiter poured more coffee while I described what had happened. 'Sadly, the Princess was in fear of her life having been badly burned as a child. Her experience created huge stress which was too much for the foetus and she aborted the following day. I have to say Geraldine, the memory of it constantly haunts my dreams.'

'I bet it does, and that young woman must have been distraught. Such a lovely girl. Have you kept in touch?'

'No, unfortunately not, although I am a close friend and medical adviser to her husband, Vijay. He was later thrown from his horse in a polo match at the Gymkhana Club in Bombay and suffered life-changing injuries.'

'Good Lord. What sort of injuries?'

'Compound fracture of the femur, concussion, loss of sight in one eye and a permanent limp.'

Geraldine sat back and dabbed her lips with her linen napkin. 'And now you're going to tell me that you were also there to witness that accident.'

'Yes, I was. In fact, I ended up nursing him throughout his summer convalescence in Simla and was even present when he received the news that his father had died of a heart attack.'

'Elizabeth Stuart-MacKenzie, it's no wonder your Ph.D has suffered. I doubt you have had time to sleep let alone carry out research on tropical diseases.'

'Oh, I don't know. I did save a young Muslim child-bride from a fate worse than death in Old Delhi and I also discovered a calcified stone baby in the abdomen of a Mrs Banajee in Poona.'

'Let's adjourn to the lounge and continue this conversation in more comfortable surroundings.' She called the waiter over and ordered a jug of freshly chilled lemonade, then led the way to the interior.

Settling into matching brown leather, wing-backed chairs, with panoramic views of Steamer Point visible through two large box-framed windows alongside, we waited for the juice to arrive.

'Now, dear, I was not born yesterday, and I can see that you're doing your best to steer the conversation away from the real reason you are returning to England, but I must tell you that, in addition to receiving regular Government reports, Sir George gets weekly copies of the Delhi Times.' I shuffled in my seat. 'We both read the article about the Surgeon-General's poker game and I have a sneaking suspicion that your reason for rushing back to Northumbria with your tail between your legs may have something to do with it. Am I right?' She stared at me from under raised eyebrows, expecting a truthful answer.

Silence was not going to cut it, so I filled her in on all the ghastly details, hating myself for indulging Geraldine in such scandalous gossip.

'If it makes you feel any better, Elizabeth, I found Sir Charles Ponsonby-Pritchard to be a pompous old fool who should have been put out to grass years ago.'

I was shocked. 'Forgive me, Geraldine, I had no idea you knew him.'

'I didn't, not personally.' Her nose wrinkled. 'I met him when we hosted an impromptu lunch for the Ponsonby-Pritchard's as they passed through Aden on their way back to England. My father-in-law and Sir Charles's father served in the same regiment and there is some tenuous connection between their two families down through the ages.'

There would be, I thought, reminding myself that Geraldine was also part of our interbred aristocracy.

'I must say it was a rather strained affair, and that daughter of his. Evadne or Ethel?' Tramlines appeared on her forehead.

'Edith,' I interjected. 'Lady Edith Postlethwaite. Daughter-in-law of the Governor of Madras and the apple of her father's eye.'

'That's right. Edith. What a stuck-up, over-bearing, patronising and conceited female she turned out to be.' Geraldine certainly didn't mince her words. 'If her inflated ego had been any higher, Elizabeth, she would have been airborne.'

I burst out laughing, my fertile mind picturing Edith being shot out of a cannon like some heavily moustachioed circus entertainer, never to be seen again. 'I imagine she was rather scathing about me too?'

'Actually, she never mentioned you by name, but your article was severely castigated, and I had great difficulty keeping tight-lipped on the subject.' She poured lemonade into two tumblers. 'India really doesn't need the likes of Edith Postlethwaite,' she handed me a glass, 'or men of Sir Charles's calibre. Aging, arrogant aristocrats are no longer relevant in today's post-war world, and if the Foreign Office mandarins in Whitehall don't replace them with some younger blood soon, George V will lose India to the likes of Mahatma Ghandi and Jawaharlal Nehru.'

'You seem very exercised on the subject, Geraldine. Perhaps you should ask Lord Irwin to appoint you as his political agent.' I was joking.

'If I thought it would do any good, dear, I would.'

Obviously, Geraldine was not. 'Sadly, women of my generation were rarely given the opportunity to rise to such dizzying heights, but that is not the case today, and the old guard know it. That's why they fear young women like you.'

'Seriously?' I had difficulty believing this statement.

'Of course, Elizabeth. Why do you think the Governors of the CSTM cancelled your funding?'

I had to pinch myself, remembering that this was the British Resident's wife giving forth with her views, not my Aunt Karr on her soap box.

'Take it from one who knows, dear. The top brass at the Indian Medical Service were hell bent on seeing you gone because you had the audacity to question their authority. No-one is allowed to do that, especially not a woman, and as you are sitting here today, I assume they were successful.'

Her words cut to the quick. 'What else could I do, Geraldine? Men like Sir Charles are too powerful, and much as I've grown to love the country and its people, I couldn't face being lambasted and ostracized by bigoted physicians, born with silver spoons in their mouths, who were determined to undermine me at every turn.'

'And nor should you. But don't underestimate what you achieved. With one stroke of the pen, one simple newspaper article, you exposed the Surgeon-General for what he was. A racially prejudiced member of the British nobility. Whether you like it or not, you have brought to light a level of ethnic discrimination which runs through the core of the British

Imperial Government and thanks to you, both the Muslim League and The Congress Party are using it to their advantage.'

'I know. That's another reason I decided to leave.'

Geraldine reached across the coffee table and took my hand in hers. 'No one is blaming you for choosing to go home, Elizabeth. No woman wants to spend her days battling with intransigent and self-righteous pedagogues with their heads in the sand, but just think what you might have achieved if you had stayed. Your departure is India's loss, my dear, and it could be years before the sub-continent finds another feisty, determined Boadicea to come to its aid.' She patted the back of my hand and sat back. 'But enough of my lecturing. I suggest we return to Government House for a spot of lunch, and you can tell Sir George all about your time with the Khyber Rifles.'

She signed for our refreshments and called for the car. 'Incidentally, do you know who is to be the new Surgeon-General at the IMS?'

'No, I've no idea. Probably another grey-haired, chinless wonder with a smell under his nose and a total disregard for the unwashed rabble of India.'

'Then you're probably making the right decision to go home.' I followed her into the lobby. 'With luck, you'll marry some gentleman farmer with a passion for bullocks, have a brood of children, and grow old gracefully, spending your days dreaming of the Taj Mahal.'

'The Monument or the Hotel?' I quipped, thinking of my erotic nights in the Taj Mahal Hotel in Bombay, and nodded to the concierge as he held open the lobby door.

I was still mulling over Geraldine's words when I stepped back aboard the ss Ranchi. It was four-thirty and the second-class passengers were taking tiffin in the lounge bar. I was in no mood to indulge in polite conversation so made my way aft intending to spend a quiet hour writing to Ma and Pa about my day. I was passing the Purser's office when I heard him call my name.

'Doctor Stuart-MacKenzie, a telegram arrived for you from the Steamer Point Post Office at lunchtime.' He rummaged through his desk papers and handed over a pale brown envelope.

'Thank you, Ernie.' I checked the name and carefully opened the flap.

Doctor E Stuart-MacKenzie stop ss Ranchi Steamer Point Aden stop Just promoted to Surgeon-General IMS by Lord Irwin stop Meeting with the All-India Institute of Hygiene and Public Health on 29th inst to discuss new department for trained female health workers stop Need you to argue case and become head if approved stop SS Mulbera departing Aden for Calcutta on 12th inst stop Be on it stop Sir Peter B-C

'Are you alright, Doctor? You've gone quite pale.'

I read the telegram once more trying to get my head around Sir Peter's news. 'Yes, Ernie. I'm fine, just a bit shocked. I've been called back to Calcutta urgently.'

'Then you'd better get a move on, Miss, 'cause we cast off as soon as the tide turns.'

'When will that be, Ernie?'

He looked up to the wall clock behind him. 'Within the hour, Miss.'

'Crikey, that doesn't leave me long then, does it?' I stuffed the telegram into my pocket. 'Right, tell the steward to collect my baggage from the cabin in thirty minutes, and Ernie . . .'

'Yes, Miss,'

'I'll need a room at the Crescent Hotel for two nights and a berth on the ss Mulbera leaving for Calcutta on Sunday.'

'Very well, Miss, leave it to me. Two nights at the Crescent and a berth on the Mulbera.'

Twenty minutes later my trunk was packed, my medical bag, Afghan Rifle box and valise were stacked by the cabin door and I was anxious to depart.

I staggered into my room at the Crescent Hotel and flopped onto the bed, kicking off my shoes as I looked out through the tall bedroom window at the stern lights of the ss Ranchi as she cast off her lines and moved sedately towards the harbour entrance before fading into the night on the next leg of her journey through the Red Sea to Suez.

I felt lightheaded, as if I'd had too much sherry, and kept repeating over and over that Sir Peter Bonham-Cavendish, the thirty-seven-year-old Head of Immunology, and my ex-supervisor, was now in charge of the Indian Medical Service. His promotion significantly altered my prospects in India and I couldn't wait to get back to Calcutta. As to the thought that my public health dream might actually become reality, I was cock-a-hoop with happiness.

The idea had formed part of my quarterly report on improving the survival rates of women and infants throughout India, an idea which I had discussed in depth with Agnes and Sir Peter before leaving Delhi. Sir Peter had thought my proposal fanciful and with little chance of Governmental support, but with his unexpected rise to power, he appeared to have changed his mind and not only wanted me to present the case to the Institute Board but wanted me to run the project as well. I couldn't believe my luck at this change in my fortunes and recalled Geraldine's words earlier that day.

'Men like Sir Charles are no longer relevant in today's post-war world, and if the Foreign Office mandarins in Whitehall don't start replacing them with some young blood soon, King George V will lose his hold on India to political heavyweights like Mahatma Ghandi and Jawaharlal Nehru.'

'Well,' I announced, as the ss Ranchi disappeared from view, 'the decision-makers in Whitehall must have read her mind.'

I returned to the lobby and pushed the telephone cubicle's concertina glass doors aside and stepped inside. Picking up the handset I waited for the hotel's telephonist to answer.

'I'd like to be put through to Lady Stewart-Symes at Government House please.'

'Hold the line, Memsahib.' I tapped my fingers on the wooden shelf as empty seconds ticked by.

'Government House, who is calling? . . . Just one moment Doctor Stuart-MacKenzie, I'll see if her Ladyship is free.'

'Elizabeth, shouldn't you be on your way to Suez?'

'Not anymore, Geraldine. I'm back at the Crescent Hotel and have some wonderful news. You were asking earlier if I knew who had replaced Sir Charles. Well, now I do. It's my ex-supervisor, Sir Peter Bonham-Cavendish, and he wants me back in India to argue the case for a national cohort of female health workers. If I'm successful, the WMS will get a brand-new division and I'm being offered the chance to run it.'

'Excellent, dear. That's the best news I've heard all day. When do you leave?'

'Sunday, on the ss Mulbera. My presentation to the All-India Institute of Hygiene and Public Health is scheduled for the twenty-ninth in Calcutta.'

'Then give them hell, dear. Knowing Peter, you will get all the backing you need.'

'I hope so.' I had my fingers crossed. 'Is Sir Peter a friend of the family?'

'More than a friend, Elizabeth, he's my husband's nephew twice removed and spent many summer holidays with us in Kerala as a youngster.'

'Of course he did,' I replied, wondering if Geraldine happened to be related to King George V as well. 'Then I'll pass on your regards when I see him later in the week.'

'You do that, dear, and Elizabeth, this time don't let those toffee-nosed, chinless wonders push you around.'

Chapter Three

'Doctor Stuart-MacKenzie, you have given us much to think about regarding the need for female health workers throughout India and your arguments have been both succinct and well researched. We will now consider all aspects of this proposal and reach a conclusion by the end of the day.' The Chairman of the Institute addressed Sir Peter sitting by my side. 'I suggest we reconvene at four-thirty this afternoon.' Sir Peter nodded. 'Thank you both for bringing the matter to our attention. Good morning.'

Another brush-off, I thought, as I examined the blank expressions around the long mahogany boardroom table and felt a knot in the pit of my stomach. Sir Peter, however, was having none of it. He stood, gathered his papers together and, towering over his august fellow associates, addressed them in an assertive manner.

'Gentlemen, as you can see, Doctor Stuart-MacKenzie is horrified that these appalling statistics have been ignored by His Majesty's Imperial Government for so long. The Women's Medical Service has been struggling for decades to get its voice heard on the subject, but as with many female issues these grievances have fallen on deaf ears.' He stepped to the side and walked to the head of the table, peering down at the aging group of departmental heads as he went. 'This cannot go on, gentlemen. India is now entering a new phase in its development, and we must rise to the challenge to help it move into the twentieth century. We can no longer rely on some

God-given right to be here, and the sooner we face up to that fact the better. Recent civil unrest in the countryside is a warning none of us should ignore. If we do, we will surely be kicked out of India sooner rather than later.'

There was a general shuffling of backsides on seats and the shaking of heads as Peter continued. 'Indian women have as much right to medical, sanitary and healthcare services as their British counterparts and Doctor Stuart-MacKenzie's proposal is a simple, economic and practical way for us to achieve this.'

'That's all very laudable, Sir Peter, but funding for such a project will be enormous and other priorities, such as the defence of our Empire, must take precedence.' That was Lieutenant Colonel Townsend, the aging, monocled, ex-army Director of Public Health, who was too full of self-righteous pomposity to see any threat from local uprisings.

Sir Peter's jaw stiffened. 'Reginald, a body of local female health workers would do more for the defence of India than the whole of the British Indian Army put together.' His words dripped sarcasm. 'This proposal would bring paid employment to a number of women in the community and improve death rates substantially.'

'Leaving us with even more mouths to feed,' muttered Reginald Townsend under his breath.

Sir Peter refused to be humiliated. 'An added bonus to this female army is their ability to collate dependable statistics on population levels throughout the provinces, making it much easier for you to budget for their Public Health needs.' He looked straight across at the Head of Statistics whose job it was to maintain such information. The man visibly shrank in his chair.

My respect for Sir Peter rose by leaps and bounds as he strode purposefully down the length of the room berating his older peers, rather like a headmaster lambasting his pupils at morning assembly, and letting the impact of his words reverberate around the room. He turned at the door. 'Be under no illusion, gentlemen, funding such a project could mean the difference between us remaining in India or losing the country altogether, which is exactly what I said to the Foreign Secretary in despatches.' A collective intake of breath sucked oxygen from the atmosphere. 'I have no doubt Arthur Henderson will agree with me. We must be seen to provide proper healthcare to all the King's subjects, including Indian women and children, and I am convinced such care will prove highly beneficial in stemming the growing tide of protest towards British direct rule. Good day, gentlemen.'

I leapt to my feet and followed him out of the room. 'Crikey,' I exclaimed as we left the building and made our way across the Maidan. 'You don't believe in sugar-coating your words, do you?'

'Mac, if there's one thing I have learned living in India, it's that you don't get anywhere pussyfooting around power. These men need to be reminded that their privileged positions are not guaranteed.' He balled his fists in anger. 'The facts are plain to see, Mac. We are a mere twenty-thousand men ruling a population of three-hundred million. You do the maths.'

Striding into the Bengal Club with me two steps behind, he signed the visitor's book and led me through to the lounge where another of my close friends, Jonathon Harrington-Davies, was awaiting our arrival. I beamed at the sight of this familiar freckle-faced, clean-shaven, young man, realising how indebted I was to him for introducing me to his Godparents, James and Victoria Cottesmore, when I first arrived in Calcutta. Their niece, Henriette, had needed a doctor to cure her of syphilis and Jonathon had suggested me as the ideal candidate. Without this introduction, my stay in India would have been curtailed before it had even begun.

'How did the meeting go, Mac?' he asked, leaping to his feet and pulling out my chair.

'Lord only knows, Jonathon, but I'm not holding my breath.' I dropped my bag on the floor and sat. 'We will find out at four-thirty, but if the Director of Public Health has anything to do with it, my plan will be rejected out of hand. Reginald Townsend spent the whole time with a bad smell under his nose.'

'Don't take it personally, he always looks like that,' replied Jonathon.

'Maybe, but if it hadn't been for our new Surgeon-General here using some underhand tactics, India's Director of Public Health would now be holding sway.'

'Underhand?' Jonathon waited for Sir Peter to respond but my boss ignored both of us and studied the club's lunch menu.

I arched one eyebrow and continued. 'Do you recall a certain covert operation by Lord Cottesmore and Sir Peter when I was trying to get funding for my Ph.D?'

'How could I forget?'

'Then it won't surprise you to hear that Sir Peter casually dropped into the discussion details of a report he'd sent to the Foreign Secretary in London recommending my project as a means of quelling civil unrest. Personally, Jonathon, I thought it a bit farfetched, but it certainly got the attention of the board.'

'Crikey.' Jonathon peered at the large brown leather menu masking Sir Peter's face. 'Have you?'

'Have I what?'

'Written to Arthur Henderson?'

'Yes.'

We both looked sceptical.

'And the report?'

'Is sitting on my desk.' His eyebrows twitched. 'Once I get the green light to run Mac's project, the letter will be on its way to London in the next diplomatic bag.'

'See.' I winked at Jonathon. 'Another covert tactic.'

'Hardly.' Sir Peter's chest expanded. 'I wasn't lying, Mac, when I said my report existed, I just failed to mention exactly where it was.'

'Or what it says.'

'Exactly what does it say?' asked Jonathon.

My future boss cleared his throat. 'Simply that I have unilaterally created a new army of female community health workers to improve women's living standards, which will combat simmering unrest amongst the masses and severely undermine their political activists.'

'Damn you, Peter Bonham-Cavendish.' Other club members looked around, shocked. I quickly lowered my voice and continued. 'You have the audacity to pinch my idea, paraphrase it in military jargon and present it to London as if you're Sir Francis Drake coming to the defence of Tudor England.'

'Not a bad ruse, if I do say so myself.'

'You would, but where does that leave me?' I was hopping mad.

'Mac, stop griping. In one master stroke, I have set a precedent on how the Indian Medical Service will prioritise women's medical needs in the future and provide the resources to put them into effect. What could be better than that?'

'ME getting some of the credit for MY project?'

'Never fear, Mac, you will also be mentioned in despatches. Now, can we order lunch?' The menu was thrust into my hand.

'Well,' remarked Jonathon, peering over my shoulder, 'I know two people who will be delighted to hear that Mac is back in useful employment. I can't wait to tell my future in-laws.'

'They already know.' Sir Peter raised his finger to attract the head waiter. 'As it happens, this ruse was Lord Cottesmore's idea.'

'Why am I getting a sense of déjà vu here?' I studied the dishes on offer as my head caught up with Jonathon's last comment. 'Your future in-laws, Jonathon?'

'Yes, Mac. Henriette and I are to be married in the autumn.'

I leapt up and smothered him in kisses then turned to Sir Peter. 'When were you planning to tell me this?'

'Sorry, Mac,' he tapped his nose three times. 'Hettie swore me to secrecy, and the engagement could well be off when she hears that her intended has let the cat out of the bag.' Jonathon instantly resembled a ripe pomegranate.

'Ooops! When is it to be announced?'

'This weekend at the Governor's Ball.' Jonathon ordered the chicken korma.

'And the wedding?'

'St Peter's Church, here in Fort William. We've been given permission by Field Marshall Childers.' Jonathon squeezed my arm. 'But, Mac, you didn't hear that from me.'

'Well, we'll have to see about that.'

He choked on his response. 'Oh, come on, you wouldn't betray me, would you?'

'Quid pro quo, Jonathon. If I'm to save your bacon, the least you can do is save mine.' I appeared to be staring into the face of a miscreant deckhand about to be lashed.

'By doing what?'

'By getting yourself seconded to my civilian army as our Chief Sanitary Inspector.'

'You've got to be joking?'

Sir Peter chuckled. 'A fair exchange in my opinion. Having insisted on starting at the bottom in the Indian Sanitary Department and working your way up the seniority list, Jonathon, Mac is now giving you the opportunity to do just that.'

'But the ICS would never agree to promoting me to such an elevated position at my age.'

'That never stopped Sir Peter,' I quipped. 'And with Lord Cottesmore adding weight to your application, how could you possibly fail?'

'Can we please order lunch before I expire?'

'I'll have the beef,' I replied as an aside, and returned to the matter in hand. 'If I'm to improve the lives of all these pregnant women, mothers and infants, Jonathon, I'll need better sanitation in the rural villages and a decent supply of fresh potable water.'

'And you want me to persuade the various District Commissioners of Public Works to cough up the money, manpower and equipment?'

'Exactly. As the Governor of Bengal's nephew-in-law, you will have enormous influence amongst your ICS colleagues and can demand things I could only dream about. As sanitation is your speciality, you're the ideal person for the job.'

Sir Peter tapped me on the knee. 'Aren't you being a bit premature, Madam? I haven't offered you the job yet.'

'But you will, or I'll be back on a P&O passenger liner heading for Tilbury and you'll be paying for my passage.'

'Time out,' cut in Jonathon, sounding like a boxing match referee. 'Perhaps we could continue this conversation when you both know if the Institute has agreed to your plan? Meanwhile, Mac, where do you imagine I'd be based?'

'Somewhere in the Punjab?'

Sir Peter's raucous laugh rattled the club chandeliers. 'I'm sure Hettie is going to love that idea!'

'Oh, hell!' exclaimed Jonathon, grabbing my arm and propelling me towards the restaurant. 'Perhaps that's another secret we can keep to ourselves until after the wedding.'

We were back at the Institute as the belfry clock chimed the half hour and sat impatiently in the lobby waiting to be called.

'Why the Punjab?' Sir Peter asked, skimming through the Calcutta Chronicle.

'Actually, a few districts of the Punjab. There is no way I could cover the whole province in one year. However, the Punjab is not too far from Delhi, it has a mix of Hindu, Muslim and Sikh communities, it's agricultural rather than urban and has one of the highest obstetric death rates.'

'Is that all?'

'Well, you did ask, and anyway I'll need Agnes Scott's help in supplying suitably trained midwives form the Lady Hardinge Medical College to teach my health workers what to do.'

'And where do you imagine this army of health workers will come from?'

'One step at a time, Sir Peter. There are certain doctors in the WMS who I have to get onside first.' I grimaced, picturing Gloria Hodgson's horrified reaction when I announced to the world that India's indigenous *dais* were to be re-trained to run village health clinics.

'Sir Peter.' We both turned as a member of staff, standing at the top of the central staircase caught our attention. 'Your presence is requested in the boardroom.'

'Right, I'm on my way.'

'Shall I stay here?' I asked, feeling my knees knocking together.

'Of course not, but leave the talking to me. If we're to get this project off the ground, then diplomacy will be the order of the day and we both know that diplomacy is not one of your better traits.'

I grunted but knew that he was right and clamped my mouth shut as we entered the boardroom.

'Sir Peter, Doctor Stuart-MacKenzie, please be seated.' The Chairman was standing, his hands in his trouser pockets, a sheaf of voting papers in front of him on the table. 'We have finally come to a decision.' He glared at Reginald Townsend who glared back. 'By majority vote, we have agreed to fund this project of yours but with two specific caveats.'

My heart sank as I waited for the bombshell to drop.

'Firstly, it is to start as a pilot project until we have proof of its success.' We both nodded. 'And secondly, Reginald has insisted that the department falls within his Public Health remit of supervision, not yourself at the IMS.'

My mouth opened, Sir Peter's hand grabbed my arm, and an ominous smirk crossed the face of our nemesis.

'In regard to the pilot scheme,' announced my companion-in-arms, leaning forward and smiling at the Chairman, 'I think this caveat is an excellent idea. In fact, Doctor Stuart-MacKenzie has already suggested to me that the best place to begin this work would be in districts of the Punjab Province where the worst death rates occur amongst women and children.'

There was a general muttering of approval around the table.

'As to who should supervise the project, might I suggest we postpone that decision until we have approached Lady Irwin, in her capacity as the President of the Countess of Dufferin's Fund. Our Vicereine has been instrumental in raising funds for female medical care within the WMS for many years and her expertise in this field is extensive.' He turned to eyeball

Townsend. 'I am sure she will agree that we men have little understanding of female health issues or needs, and we already have our hands full dealing with our current workload.' Townsend resembled a pit bull terrier eyeing up its opponent. 'It is my opinion, gentlemen, that the project would be far better served with a female senior clinician supervising it.' He sat back and twiddled his thumbs.

The Chairman was rather lost for words and slumped onto his seat.

'What do you think, Doctor Stuart-MacKenzie?' asked the Inspector General of Civil Hospitals.

Sir Peter dug his fingers into my arm, and I waited for him to answer for me, but the Chairman beat him to it.

'Yes, Doctor. As a female clinician, what is your view on the matter?'

I eased my arm from Sir Peter's grip, slowly inflated my lungs and tried to muster as much diplomacy as I could.

'My Lord,' I nodded to the Chairman, 'and gentlemen of this Institute, may I answer by posing three questions to you all?'

I scanned the room but received no answer. 'Can any of you tell me what *bal-golis* is?' You could have heard a pin drop. 'Or when *conjee* is used?' No answer from the floor. 'Or what happens to mothers in a zenana during the first forty days after giving birth?' By now some were fidgeting with their papers. 'As I suspected, gentlemen, although you are highly knowledgeable about the needs of the men under your command, you are oblivious to the needs of women. Indeed, in all cases, you would not be allowed entry into a zenana to see the problem first-hand. Therefore, in my experienced view, all matters relating to female public health should be run entirely by women, for women, and I respectfully suggest that this should be under the auspices of the Women's Medical Service.'

'Well said, Mac,' whispered Sir Peter as Reginald Townsend grunted.

'Doctor, exactly what is this *bal-goli*?' asked the Commissioner for Sanitation.

'Opium, Commissioner. Tiny balls of opium given to babies to stop them crying.'

'Good God!'

The Chairman cleared his throat and stood once more. 'I think the Doctor has clearly demonstrated her point and I would like a show of hands on placing this pilot project within the jurisdiction of the WMS.' He raised his hand in the air and looked at his contemporaries. Slowly other hands rose until only Reginald Townsend remained with his hands firmly resting on his lap, his lips clamped together turning white. 'Then, we appear to have a majority for the proposal. Sir Peter, you will receive our decision in writing later today. Perhaps you will advise Lady Irwin of what has transpired here.'

'It will be my pleasure, Lord Montgomery.'

'Very well. If there is nothing else to discuss I propose we adjourn the meeting forthwith.'

My comrade-in-arms held the car door open for me and I climbed into the back seat.

'So, are you going to offer me the job now?'

'Maybe.' I ignored the twinkle in his eye.

'If you don't, I will send my report on female health workers to the Foreign Secretary in the diplomatic bag which, you may recall, pre-dates yours by months.'

'Elizabeth Stuart-MacKenzie, that is below the belt.'

'Then stop beating about the bush and get on with it.'

'You sound like Geraldine Stewart-Symes.'

'Oh, I almost forgot. She sends her congratulations on your new appointment.'

Sir Peter lowered the car window as he made himself comfortable and loosened his collar. 'I know, I received a telegram from Sir George last week. It's a pity women like Geraldine are not running this country. We'd get a damned sight more done if she were in charge.'

'I agree. She certainly doesn't suffer fools easily and I imagine she would make mincemeat of Reginald Townsend.'

'To say nothing of the rest of the Indian Civil Service.' He paused, mulling something over in his head. 'Perhaps I should ask her to be the Honorary President of the Women's Community Health Service once Sir George concludes his term in Aden?'

'Now that, boss, is the best suggestion you've had all day. Just don't forget to include it in your report to the Foreign Secretary.'

Chapter Four

My feet didn't touch the ground over the next few weeks. Meetings with Agnes Scott and Lady Irwin in Delhi, visits to outlying clinics, presentations to WMS female surgeons in the Punjab and burning the midnight oil writing reports, left me little time to eat, let alone sleep. I was having a ball and sent regular updates to Frances and Aunt Karr about the project as it blossomed into reality.

I asked Agnes's permission to offer Fatima Patel the chance to head my training programme for local *dais* and was delighted when the college's star midwife accepted. Fatima and I had been through a lot together over the past months and I knew she would be an asset to the WCHS. Agnes was sad to see her go from the Lady Hardinge but agreed that she was the ideal person for the job as she spoke Hindi, Urdu and English and was well liked amongst her peers.

As I sat on the terrace of Ruby's Delhi mansion congratulating myself on getting this talented girl onto my team, Sanjay appeared at my side with a cable from Jonathon.

Dear Mac,

Guess who is your new Chief Sanitary Inspector at the WCHS starting first inst? (covert tactics by Lord Cottesmore notwithstanding.) Hettie delighted as we will be based in Delhi. Ring me soonest.

Jonathon.

'YES!' I yelled, as I rushed into Ruby's bedroom and thrust the cable into her hand. 'Sir Peter and Lord Cottesmore have done it again. All I need now is to get Gloria Hodgson onside and I'll be all set.'

'Who's Gloria Hodgson?' asked Ruby, trying to keep the cable from damaging her newly applied nail varnish.

'Only the best American obstetrics doctor in Bombay, that's who.'

'Oh, really? And why would she leave Bombay to join you in the depths of the Punjab?' Ruby's nose wrinkled.

'Because I'm going to ask her to be my deputy. I can't be everywhere, and Gloria is the obvious choice. She's respected by every female Senior Surgeon in India and has extensive knowledge of the subject. With the two of us running the project, Punjab's Public Health Commissioner will wonder what has hit him.'

'So, why have you got your fingers crossed?' Ruby handed back the cable and blew on her fingernails.

'Gloria will refuse to have anything to do with training *dais*.' Ruby's eyebrows locked together.

'Indigenous birthing attendants.' Her eyes now glazed over. 'Uneducated local midwives to you and me. They need re-training to become useful community health workers and they'll get paid into the bargain.' I sat on the end of the bed. 'Gloria Hodgson, however, believes that they are beyond the pale and no better than witch doctors who wouldn't know a birth canal from a back passage.' Ruby's lipstick was adding the final touches to her make-up as I remembered Gloria's lurid examples of village midwifery when we had first met. '*Dais* firmly believe that childbirth should be quick and easy and have been known to pull the limbs off babies as they try to yank them from their mothers' wombs.'

A cerise red line shot across Ruby's chin. 'Damn it, Mac, do you have to be so graphic?' She marched off into the bathroom muttering expletives.

'Sorry,' I shouted. 'I forgot how sensitive your stomach was.'

'It's not my stomach that's the problem,' she countered, reappearing with bland coloured lips, 'it's your inability to gloss over the gore.' She looked at her Cartier watch. 'Christ, Vijay will be here any minute and I'm not even dressed.'

'I doubt that will bother him. Where's he been anyway?'

'At a meeting with Lord Irwin on some Jhalanpur matters-of-state. Something to do with his twenty-one-gun salute.'

'Why, is the noise damaging his hearing?' I was rather amused by my quip.

'Very droll, MacKenzie.' She rubbed her freshly painted lips together and examined the result in the mirror.

'How's he coping as the new Maharaja of Jhalanpur, anyway?'

'Badly. He hates all the pomp and protocol that goes with it, and is constantly arguing with his mother about me.'

'Because?'

'Because she wants me gone and is doing everything she can to oust me from his life.'

'Well, you did say his family would object to the affair once he became Maharaja.'

'I know, but I didn't realise how desperate the Rajmata is. She wants Vijay to take a second royal wife to give him an heir.'

Ruby picked up her silver-backed hairbrush and attacked her golden, crimped locks with gusto. 'He's having none of it, of course, and is now insisting that we spend the summer on the French Riviera to get away from her constant nagging.'

'Nice.' I folded Jonathon's cable and stuffed it in my skirt pocket. 'Can I assume Princess Dashwanabai has not managed to get pregnant again after the miscarriage?'

Ruby studied her hands. 'No, and I'm beginning to think she's barren.'

'That's ridiculous, Ruby. You can't be barren if you've been pregnant before.' I paused, searching my brain for information on infertility. 'That said, it could be Vijay who's the problem.'

Ruby's eyes doubled in size. 'God alive, don't tell him that. He's already like a bear with a sore head over his polo injuries, without being told he's sterile.'

'All I'm saying is that it's a possibility and he should get it checked out. Only the other day, I was reading there are now laboratory tests that can verify sperm counts in men.'

'Ugh, do stop it.' Ruby looked as if she had swallowed something rancid. 'Anyway, what's the point? He's the one who got her pregnant in the first place.'

'True, but that was before his accident. Since then he has suffered severe neurological trauma, and the brain is a very sensitive instrument.'

Ruby was now pushing her head through an emerald silk, long-sleeved dress. 'Are you telling me that he could have become sterile because he banged his head.'

50

'Possibly. After all, he did do it twice and lost sight in one eye in the process. Who's to say it hasn't affected other bodily functions?'

'Me, for one,' she announced confidently, tying the emerald silk belt at her waist.

My expression was pure Aunt Karr. 'Just because he ejaculates, Ruby, doesn't mean he's capable of fathering a child.'

'Jesus, Mac, what is it with you and your medical terms?'

'All I'm trying to point out is that it would be ridiculous for him to marry again to produce an heir if he's the one with the problem.'

'Fine, then you can be the one to tell him, because I'm not going near the subject.' She slipped her feet into gold and emerald silk pumps, checked her reflection in the dressing-table mirror and breezed out of the room, shouting over her shoulder, 'Are you coming down to dinner or are you going to sit there all night examining your navel?'

I was still mulling over the infertility question when Vijay appeared on the terrace. I hadn't seen him in months and even with a patch over his left eye he was as handsome as ever, his Saville Row twill trousers, cream silk shirt and navy-blue blazer giving him the air of a British aristocrat rather than an Indian Maharaja. He strode towards me minus a limp, and I beamed with delight.

'Your Highness, it's a joy to see you looking so well.' I rose from the sofa and held out my hand.

'Likewise, Mac.' He leant in and brushed his warm lips against my fingers. 'I couldn't believe it when I heard that you'd left for England without saying goodbye.'

'I'm sorry about that, but you were deep in the Rajputana desert at the time, and if it hadn't been for Sir Peter, I would now be blue with cold and spending my days dispensing medicines to the sick and needy of Northumbria.'

'Well, I'm very glad that you are not and that my country will continue to benefit from your medical knowledge.'

'You seem to have lost your limp.'

He lifted his right foot and wiggled the deep amber leather brogue shoe. 'Had this specially made in Italy. My uncle suggested having the sole built up to compensate for my uneven leg length, and it worked. See.' He paced along the length of the extensive veranda with a perfect gait.

'Wonderful,' I said, pleased that my correspondence with his uncle, Prince Kapoor Dhawan, had born fruit. My fears of Vijay being left with one leg shorter than the other after his compound fracture were correct, but an article in the Lancet on shoe prosthetics for polio sufferers had given me an idea. Obviously, it had worked. 'How is your sight? Has there been any improvement there?'

Vijay sat down beside me and removed his eye patch. 'My left eye is still blurred but the ophthalmologist here in Delhi is working with me and is confident it will improve with time, although it will never be perfect.' His deep sigh spoke volumes.

I rested my hand on his arm. 'You do know, Your Highness, that it could have been a lot worse?'

'Mac, stop being so formal. Being a Maharaja hasn't changed anything between us. The name's Vijay.'

I chuckled at his reference to me demanding to be called Mac on the ss Narkunda.

'As for my accident, yes I do know, but it doesn't stop me getting depressed about it at times.'

'Like when?' My professional interest sprang to the fore.

'Mostly when I have to watch my team play polo or cricket from the side-lines.' The melancholy in his voice darkened my mood. 'I know I should count my blessings, Mac, and it's amazing how well my right eye has compensated for the other eye, but I still can't forget what used to be.'

'And the headaches and migraines? Do they still bother you?'

'Occasionally, particularly when I'm stressed about something.'

I immediately thought of his mother. 'Then don't stress, Vijay. That's an order.'

'Easier said than done, Mac, especially since my father died. I'm afraid my carefree days as a Prince are well and truly over.'

'Nothing lasts for ever, Vijay.'

He relaxed back on the sofa cushion and stared longingly out at the night, but I refused to allow him to wallow in self-pity.

'Playing polo or cricket may be out of the question, Vijay, but surely you can still ride?'

'Yes, I can. In fact, I ride every morning with Duncan Fitzpatrick when I'm in Jhalanpur, but losing the ability to play sport is really hard for me.' He slowly turned to face me. 'I

Mac's Dilemma

haven't thanked you for introducing me to Fitzpatrick. He's proving to be a real asset in Jhalanpur and I'm not sure what I would have done without him over the past few months.'

I kept my opinion of my ex-lover from my university days firmly under wraps. 'That's good to know. He's a highly qualified vet and a consummate professional when it comes to his work.'

'He certainly knows his stuff when it comes to horses, Mac, and he's very popular at court.'

A twinge of concern rippled down my spine, knowing Duncan's penchant for womanising. 'Is he here with you in Delhi?'

'No, I've sent him to Bombay to cast his eye over some new bloodstock.' I quietly exhaled. 'He should be back at the end of the week.' My breath caught in my throat.

'Who should?' asked Ruby, as she sauntered onto the terrace looking as if she had just walked off a Hollywood film set.

'A certain veterinary surgeon from the Emerald Isles,' I replied, raising one eyebrow.

'That news should have the young ladies of the Fishing Fleet abuzz with excitement.' She winked at me.

Vijay chuckled. 'The young ladies of the Fishing Fleet have about as much chance of landing Duncan Fitzpatrick as landing a blue marlin in the River Thames,' he said, rising from the sofa and wandering over to her side.

'Oh really? And what makes you so sure?'

54

'Ruby, Duncan Fitzpatrick has only two interests in his life and neither include the debutantes of the Fishing Fleet.' He suddenly had my undivided attention.

'I'm intrigued.' Ruby kissed him on the cheek and locked eyes with me across the terrace. 'What would they be then?'

Vijay wrapped his arm around her waist and looked in my direction. 'Maintaining his highly respected reputation as a veterinary surgeon, and waxing lyrically about his relationship with Mac.' Vijay's words were left hanging in the air as he turned and disappeared into the drawing room.

'Close your mouth, Mac, you're catching flies,' whispered Ruby.

My jaw clamped shut, I shot to my feet and spoke through gritted teeth. 'What the hell has that Irish horse doctor been saying to Vijay behind my back?'

Ruby shrugged.

'Damn it,' I dragged my fingers through my carefully coiffured locks in frustration as the penny dropped. 'That ungrateful leprechaun. He knows that Vijay respects me, and by suggesting that we're in some long-distance relationship, he'd hope to impress his boss.' I punctured the air with my index finger. 'Jesus, Ruby, that man lies with impunity and believe me, he can be very persuasive.'

'Calm down, Mac, Vijay is not stupid.'

'Maybe not, but it's my reputation we're talking about here, and I will not have it sullied.' My hands shot to my cheeks. 'You do realise that this could get straight back to Sir Peter?' I must have resembled Edvard Munch's painting of *The Scream*.'

'If Vijay tells Sir Peter that I'm having an affair with his Irish veterinary surgeon in Rajputana, I'll be out of the WCHS before you can say gynaecology.' I pressed Ruby's hands in mine. 'For God's sake, find out what Vijay actually knows and make it clear that Duncan Fitzpatrick is ancient history.'

Ruby's fingers curled around mine. 'Leave it to me. Your ex-lover is not the only one who has Vijay's ear and I know which one of us has the most influence.'

Her assurance didn't help. What I needed was her asthma nebulizer. 'If that narcissist has spun this story to bolster his own ego, I promise you, Ruby, I will personally remove his genitals.'

'Not a good idea, Mac.' Ruby linked her arm in mine as she manoeuvred me towards the dining-room. 'As a eunuch, he'll gain access to Jhalanpur's zenana.'

'God forbid!' We crossed the marbled hall. 'Still,' I mused, regaining my sense of humour, 'a fat lot of good it would do him, if he did.'

My pulse rate didn't return to normal until we were well past the main course, but Vijay's description of royal life at the Jhalanpur Palace was a revelation and it gradually distracted me from my thoughts. He was halfway through describing his father's state funeral when he took me completely by surprise.

'Have you ever ridden an elephant, Mac?'

'No, Vijay, I can't say that I have.' I recalled my childhood rides along the windswept Arisaig beach of Morar on a rather cloth-eared donkey and giggled. 'Elephants are rather few and far between in the Highlands.'

'Then it's high time you did.' Vijay looked so much younger with laughter lines around his eyes. 'Sanjay.' His butler appeared at the dining room door and bowed. 'There's to be a tiger shoot in Jhalanpur in October. Tell my chaprassi to organise it.' He turned and addressed me directly. 'Doctor Stuart-MacKenzie will be my guest of honour.' Sanjay backed away, bending double.

'I . . . I don't know what to say to that.'

'No need to say anything, just don't forget your rifle.'

'Just think, Mac,' remarked Ruby, twiddling her dessert spoon. 'A tiger's head above the mantlepiece in your Ma's front parlour at Riveldene would certainly add opulence to the Vicarage. Far better than that flea-ridden rhino head in Gentleman's Accessories you couldn't take your eyes off at Simon Arzt departmental store in Port Said.'

'Maybe, but I'm not sure it would quite go with her aspidistras,' I countered, 'and Ma would refuse point blank to dust it, glass eyes or not.' I pictured my mother in her flowery apron holding a feather duster up to its nose and tickling around its ears.

'You have to kill it first,' remarked Vijay, clapping his hands.

Sanjay reappeared with the dessert. A froth of vanilla souffle garnished with crushed pistachio nuts and flaked almonds was placed on the table. I waited for him to depart.

'Ruby tells me you're planning to spend the summer in Europe.'

'Yes we are, Mac. I need a break from the politics in Jhalanpur and a few months enjoying the Mediterranean air on the French Riviera with the odd shopping trip to London, Paris or Rome should set us up nicely for the winter.' He gazed lovingly at Ruby. 'Hopefully, by the time we are back, the WCHS will be a well-organised, efficiently run Punjab project and you can take some time out to join us in the desert.'

'That would be wonderful, Vijay.' I was now imagining myself riding on the back of an elephant dressed in my bush jacket and topi with my Afghan rifle balanced on the edge of a wooden howdah.

'Us?' cut-in Ruby.

'Yes, us, Miss Tavener.'

I was all ears.

'It's high time we made a home together in Jhalanpur, so I've decided to move out of the palace and make Puttakar Lodge our home.'

I watched my friend's complexion drain.

'You will love it, Ruby,' he continued. 'The lodge sits on an elevated promontory overlooking Puttakar Lake with extensive views across the plain to the distant Aravalli hills. While we're in Europe we can search for furniture to turn the interior into a home suitable for our modern tastes.'

'But Vijay . . .' She was now stuttering.

'No buts, Ruby. Being separated for weeks at a time has to stop. I need you with me in Rajputana. We will live there while I carry out my official duties at the palace, and for the rest we'll remain here in Delhi, summer in Simla, or travel extensively overseas.'

I was green with envy.

'But what will the Rajmata say to all this?' Ruby's voice sounded strangled.

Vijay's voice dropped like a stone, chilling my dessert. 'My mother must learn to face reality. I will not live without you, Ruby. She won't like it, but my word is final. I am done with her scheming, and by moving to Puttakar Lodge our privacy will be assured and I will have distanced myself from the machinations of court. If my mother tries to interfere, she will be making a very big mistake.'

Icy fingers rippled down my spine, Ruby's spoon rattled against her dessert bowl and Vijay helped himself to more vanilla souffle. Obviously, the subject was closed.

'Mac, do you know how I can contact Tom Wallace?'

I suddenly lost my appetite. 'I . . . I have . . . no idea, Vijay.' The sudden mention of Tom's name absolutely floored me, and my eyes pleaded with Ruby for support.

'Wouldn't P&O be able to put you in touch with him?' she suggested, fielding the question.

'No, sadly they can't. Apparently, he left P&O late last year and they don't have a forwarding address.'

'Then try contacting Jim Hamilton. He might know. Isn't that right, Mac?'

I nodded. 'Jim would know,' I stuttered. 'They have been close friends and work colleagues for years.' I clenched my fingers together in my lap.

'Good thinking. Perhaps you can let me have Jim's address, Mac?' Vijay had no idea what he was doing to my sanity.

'It may be quicker to send Jim a cable at the Bombay Port Authority,' I replied, now fingering my wrist trying covertly to check my pulse. Its speed would have powered a Bugatti sports car.

'Why do you want to find Tom anyway, Vijay?' Ruby poured me more wine.

'Because I need his medical advice on my plans.' He placed his dessert spoon on his plate, leant on both elbows, placed his hands in prayer against his lips, and kept his eyes firmly on my face. 'Last year, Mac, I promised you that one day I would do something to honour my deceased son and regain your respect. Do you remember?'

I slowly nodded, recalling our conversation in the Bombay Gymkhana Club before his disastrous polo-match.

'Well, as the Maharaja of Jhalanpur, I can now fulfil that promise.'

'By doing what?' Ruby was intrigued.

'By building a modern hospital in Jhalanpur for my subjects. It will be called the Dhyan Kumar Singh General, after my son and will be the envy of all India.'

I looked back at Vijay and my heart swelled with pride. 'I can think of no finer way to honour your child, Vijay. But why do you need Tom Wallace? Surely, there are any number of qualified surgeons in the IMS who could advise you on planning a hospital.'

His lips parted in a smile; his eyes still locked on mine. 'I'm sure there are, Mac, but showing favouritism to one will only offend all the rest.' He continued with his dessert. 'No, I need someone who is outside the IMS but knows a great deal about India and its medical needs. Tom Wallace fits the bill perfectly. He has extensive medical experience in hospitals such as St Thomas's in London where he still has many useful contacts. He also worked with Colonel Grafton-Young and his team at

St George's Hospital in Bombay after the ship's fire. By the way, the Colonel highly respects him as a surgeon. And finally, he has extensive knowledge of tropical diseases. If that was not enough, he also honed his leadership skills setting up field hospitals in France during the war.'

Vijay was right, of course, but that did nothing for my equilibrium. 'I'm sure he will be up for the challenge if you can find him,' I said, wiping my lips on my napkin. 'As for the politics inside the IMS, your diplomacy is commendable.'

'I thought you'd agree.'

My mind was swirling around the possibility of Tom working in India and I paid scant interest as Vijay continued.

'However, the DKS hospital is not all. My female subjects deserve their own state-of-the-art hospital, fully staffed with female clinicians. Is that not correct, Mac?'

I snapped to attention recalling our nightly discussions in Vijay's bedroom in Simla during his convalescence, where I complained, ad nauseum, at the lack of female hospitals throughout India. 'Indeed, it is, Vijay.'

'So, I plan to build one in Jhalanpur alongside the General Hospital, and with your permission, I intend to name it the Stuart-MacKenzie Zenana Hospital. Hopefully, when you come to Jhalanpur in October, you can lay the first stone.'

I was stunned and struggled to comprehend what he had just said. This man, this Prince, this Maharaja of Jhalanpur, was actually suggested naming a hospital after me. It was surreal. I shook my head in disbelief. How could a thirty-year-old GP from Northumbria with aspirations above her station, have her name emblazoned across a Women's Hospital in the middle of the Rajputana desert, all because she had tried to save the life of a royal son and heir on board a P&O passenger liner? Never in a million years had I expected to hear these words and I had no way of processing them.

Vijay sat waiting for my response. 'Mac, did you hear me? Do I have your permission?'

I was like a stuffed dummy, incapable of movement, my vocal cords frozen.

'Oh, for the love of God, Vijay, of course she agrees.' Ruby was standing behind my chair, her hands on my shoulders, her fingers pressing into my flesh. 'Don't you, Mac?'

I felt my head rock on my spinal cord and could hardly see Vijay through the prism of water in my eyes. 'Vijay, this is unbelievable. I'm just a doctor. My job is to save life without fear or favour, as you well know. Naming the zenana hospital after me is beyond comprehension.'

'Rubbish.' Ruby was back in her seat. 'I think it's a splendid idea, and well deserved.'

'Thank you, Ruby.' Vijay was not going to take no for an answer.

'Is this really what you want?'

'Yes, Mac. It is.'

'Then, I am honoured to have my name associated throughout India with a place of excellence for all Jhalanpur women and their children. You make me very proud.'

Vijay left his seat and came to stand at my side, gently lifting me onto my feet and turning me to face him. 'Mac, do you remember what you said to me that day at the Bombay Gymkhana Club?'

I saw myself reflected in his eyes. 'I'm sure you're going to remind me.'

'You said that without respect there could be no friendship.'

My lips quivered at the memory.

'Well, I must ask you now. Have I earned your respect Doctor Stuart-MacKenzie?'

Chapter Five

I left Vijay and Ruby deep in conversation about their future plans and retired to my room. I wanted to let Frances know what had transpired and as I was leaving for Ludhiana the following evening there was no time like the present to put pen to paper.

Dear Frances,

I have so much to tell you I don't know where to begin. Today has been the most astonishing day of my life. At dinner this evening, Vijay firstly announced that Ruby was to go live in Jhalanpur with him, then said he wanted to find Tom as he needs his advice urgently, and finally told me he is planning to name a new Women's Zenana Hospital after me! I can tell you; I'm reeling from it all.

Perhaps I should calm down and stick to the main purpose of this urgent letter which is twofold.

a) Please tell Jim that Vijay will be contacting him to find out where Tom is right now. Apparently, our shipboard doctor has disappeared. He left P&O late last year and the shipping company do not have a forwarding address. Is there something I should know on that front? Please write soonest with any news. I'm off to Ludhiana for two days but will be back in Delhi by the weekend.

b) Have you said anything to Lamis about me being back in India yet? How is she and do you think it is better to say nothing at all? I miss her so much, but I have no idea when I could get down to Poona and I don't want to muddy the waters in this regard. I rely on your good judgement on this matter. If she does know, then send her my fondest love and tell her she is always in my thoughts.

I will write further regarding the rest while I'm travelling north, but suffice to say, Ruby is shell-shocked and scared out of her wits at the idea of taking up residence in Jhalanpur and I'm convinced I will wake up to find that this idea of a Stuart-MacKenzie Zenana Hospital is all a fantastic dream . . . Where is Aunt Karr's sherry when it's needed???

Much love

Mac

x

The second-class carriage was packed, and I was crammed into the corner by the window being buffeted from left to right as the North-Western State Railway train made the one-hundred-and-fifty-seven-mile journey from Delhi to Patiala where I planned to spend the night in a dak bungalow.

I was on my way to a meeting with Gloria Hodgson in Ludhiana where she was giving a series of lectures, and I could only hope that the second phase of my journey would be a great deal more comfortable than this one.

It was late, I was exhausted, and having missed dinner, I was starving. Perhaps I would find some food on the platform at Panipat Junction, I thought, and looked at my watch. It was nine-thirty in the evening and still another forty-five minutes to go to our next stop.

I watched the rotund, middle-aged gentleman opposite me bite into a samosa and the aroma from the hot spicy filling caused my stomach to rumble loudly. He looked up, realised I was salivating, peered into the brown paper bag on his lap and offered to share his dinner.

I shook my head, feeling embarrassed at being caught out. 'No thank you. Very kind I'm sure but I'll buy something at Panipat Junction.'

'Nonsense, Lassie,' he replied, his accent giving me goosebumps. 'You look done-in, dear, and my wife would never forgive me if I let a fellow traveller starve to death while I stuffed my belly with victuals.' He patted his expanded waistline.

While I vacillated, my hand made a unilateral decision to dive into the bag and extract a crisp triangular samosa, then ram it into my mouth as if my life depended on it.

'Gosh, that tastes good,' I sighed, letting my tastebuds savour the mix of soft potato, peas, and spiced crushed cumin, fennel and coriander seeds. 'Doctor Elizabeth Stuart-MacKenzie,' I announced, as the last of the delicacy slid down my throat. My arm stretched across the carriage once more and we shook hands, my knuckle bones cracking under the force of his grip.

'Alastair Galbraith,' he replied, offering another samosa.

'Nice to meet you, Mr Galbraith, and where in Scotland do you hail from?'

'Near Loch Lomond, Lass. Crianlarich to be precise, but it's a wee while since I set eyes on that village.'

'You've been in India for many years then?'

'Aye, I have that. Thirty-two to be precise, and I'm still trying to get the pompous, bungling elite out here to change their inefficient ways.'

I had to smile, realising that I was not the only one battling with authority. 'What line of business are you in?'

'Mining,' he said, 'I'm a mining engineer.'

No wonder his hands are so rough, I thought. 'Are there many mines here in the Punjab?'

He chuckled. 'You could say that. The Khewra Salt Mine in Jhelum is the second largest in the world and is renowned for its pink salt crystals.'

'Gosh, I had no idea. How long have they been mining salt there?' I was fascinated.

'Since Alexander the Great's troops discovered it back in 320 BC when their horses kept licking the stones.'

'Good Lord!' My outburst shocked the other occupants of the carriage, and I shrank back into my seat feeling foolish.

Mr Galbraith was highly amused. 'That's what my good wife said when she found out. Anyway, enough about me. What brings you to this neck of the woods?'

I leant forward and spoke in more measured tones. 'I'm heading a new medical department for the WMS called the Women's Community Health Service. We're running a pilot project in several Punjab districts to help indigenous mothers and infants get better health advice and support in their local areas. If it's successful it will be replicated throughout India.'

He slapped his thigh with gusto. 'Well, good for you. It's high time women in this country were treated like human beings instead of animals.'

'You seem to be talking from experience, Mr Galbraith.'

He scanned the carriage of men, his eyes settling on an Indian gentleman reading the Delhi Times. 'Doctor MacKenzie, when you've witnessed the horrific sight of heavily pregnant women bent double in the salt mines shovelling salt crystals into wagons for hours on end, you begin to despair at man's inhumanity to man. Or should I say woman?'

My jaw dropped to my chest. 'But that's terrible. Can't the government do something about it?'

'They could, but they don't. Britain's wealth has been made on the backs of low caste men, women and children for decades. Why change a habit of a lifetime?'

He sounded like Gloria Hodgson bemoaning the state of midwifery. 'What happens if the women go into premature labour?'

He coughed to clear his throat. 'They go behind a rocky outcrop and let nature takes its course.'

I had now turned green and swallowed hard before asking the next question. 'Do any survive?'

'Not many, but life is cheap in the mines and there is no shortage of women to replace them. As I said, they are treated no better than animals.'

'Then we at the WCHS must do something to improve it.'

'Well said, Lassie, and I suggest you start at the top. Ask for a meeting with the Governor of Punjab, Sir Geoffrey Fitzhervey de Montmorency. He's based in Lahore.'

I made a note of the name and decided to have Jonathon with me if the meeting went ahead. 'Perhaps I should see the conditions in the salt mines for myself before I tackle the likes of Punjab's Governor. Is that possible?'

'I don't see why not. The next time you are going up to Simla let me know and I'll take you to a local salt mine myself. Here, let me write down my contact details on that bit of paper.'

I handed over my notebook and stared out of the carriage window at the black night sky imagining what these women's lives were like. 'I'm not sure when that will be, Mr Galbraith, but be assured, I will be in contact with you at that time.'

Screeching brakes announced our arrival in Panipat Junction.

'Now you stay right there, Doctor and I'll go and get you some food. What do you fancy?'

'Anything hot please. Vegetable curry perhaps, and some chai.'

'I'll be back in two shakes. No, put your money away. This is my treat.' He squeezed passed the other passengers and disappeared through the compartment door as I laid my bag down on the bulkhead table and pulled open the window to get more air into the fetid interior. My eyelids drooped and I was dozing in seconds.

'LASSIE, WATCH OUT!'

Shocked out of my nap, I followed my handbag as it rose up the window glass, pulled aloft by an old wooden walking stick hooked around the handle. Without thinking, I grabbed the stick and pulled for all I was worth then watched with shock as a small, emaciated body dropped, headfirst, to the ground.

'OH NO!' I threw the window wide open and leant out, screaming for someone to come to the child's assistance. Seeing no-one moving, I rushed from the compartment, jumped from the platform onto the track and gathered the child into my arms.

'Is he dead?' asked Mr Galbraith standing over me, my curry still steaming from a tin dish in his hands.

'I can't tell. Please help me get him onto the platform where there's more light.'

My curry was abandoned as we lifted the boy carefully and laid him on the rough concrete, my hands holding his head level with his spine. I looked up through choking steam and dim platform lighting and saw a group of black-haired heads peering nervously down at me from the top of the train's roof.

'Goodness, there are hordes of them up there,' I muttered, as a masculine arm stretched down and pulled me up over the crumbling edge, snubbing my toes and snagging my skirt. I placed my hand on the child's chest, praying for a sign of life. There was nothing. What have I done? I thought, fearing the worst, as I leant over his mouth in the hope of feeling warm breath on my cheek. The rancid smell of stale curry rose up my nostrils making me gag, but I refused to give in. Swiftly placing my fine cotton hankie over his small mouth, I blew air into his lungs, willing this small skeletal infant to release me from becoming a murderer as my fingers checked his neck for a pulse.

'It's no good, Lassie, the little chap has gone to his maker.'

'No,' I groaned. 'Please God, no.'

Large hands pulled at my shoulders dragging me from the body and I heard myself wail like a wounded animal as the stationmaster bent low, gathered the limp body into his arms and pushed his way through the throng of onlookers towards the platform exit.

I wriggled free and tried to run after him, my arms outstretched in a gesture of anguish and despair, but it was no use, the crowd closed in around me, blocking my progress, and the last I saw of my victim were his tiny, blackened, bare feet, banging against the bodies of others as he was carried away.

I sank to me knees and sobbed, oblivious to my surroundings, guilt at what I had done holding my body in a vice-like grip.

'Come on, Doctor, you can't stay here.' Alastair Galbraith's gnarled fingers encircled my elbow as he pulled me to my feet and propelled me towards our carriage. 'You mustn't blame yourself, Lassie. Kiddies die all the time falling off trains. This is India. It's horrific, but it's the truth.'

'I didn't mean to kill him, Mr Galbraith.' I searched the mining engineers face, desperate for understanding. 'I was asleep. It was a panic reaction. If I'd known it was a child, I wouldn't have done it.'

'If the child had not been on the roof in the first place and intent on stealing your money, none of this would have happened. These kids know the risk and they face death on a daily basis. You can't hold yourself responsible. Now, up you go and let's get you to Patiala where you can report the incident to the police.'

I remembered very little of the rest of the journey, sitting crumpled in the compartment corner, wrapped in my pashmina, shaking like a leaf as my chai went cold and the retrieved vegetable curry congealed in its tin. I still had grease on my palms from the child's hair and the smell of his bad breath in my nostrils. I was in a nightmare and had no idea how

71

to deal with the situation, conscious that Ma and Pa would have been appalled.

On arrival in Patiala, I spent the remaining hours until midnight stuck at the local police station trying to report the death to an elderly uniformed Punjabi officer with a squint, who seemed to treat the whole incident as a mere bagatelle.

'Officer, the child fell on his head and is dead.'

'Yes, Memsahib. I write it down in ledger.'

'But he's dead. Don't you understand. I killed him.'

'No, Memsahib, you not guilty. You only pull stick. Child fall from train on head himself and poof, he gone to other world.' The man's hands flew into the air as his head rocked back and forth.

'But, Officer, if I hadn't pulled the walking stick, he would still be on the roof. I killed him. It was my fault.'

He sighed and scratched his scrotum. 'Memsahib, you not know he was at other end of stick?'

'Well, no, not exactly.'

'Then you not responsible, Memsahib.'

'Of course I'm responsible and it's your job to arrest me.'

His sigh blew the candle out on his desk. 'Memsahib, it is, how you say? *Inshallah.*' A spark struck phosphorus and his obstinate features reappeared.

I couldn't believe what I was hearing. 'Inshallah had nothing to do with it,' I exclaimed, as he walked around the counter and bodily ushered me out of his police station, keen to close up for the night.

I stood alone outside the flat roofed, concrete building in a daze, and looked around for a tonga. India had, yet again, left me bereft and incredulous, just as I had felt when I found Lamis in that hovel in Old Delhi. I could not let this matter drop without doing something to assuage my guilt.

I arrived at the dak bungalow in the dead of night, mentally and physically exhausted and was shown to my room by a tutting housekeeper. The sound of rain hammering onto the corrugated iron roof made conversation impossible, so I gave up trying to apologise and dropped onto my bed, fully clothed, and fell into a deep, troubled slumber.

It must have been just before dawn when I woke to the sound of scratching on the bedroom's louvered veranda door. I lay there convinced someone was trying to enter the room and gently slid the palm of my hand across the surface of the bedside table until my fingers clamped onto a heavy brass candlestick. There it was again, like fingernails scraping down a kettle, raising goosebumps along my arms.

Counting to ten, I swallowed hard and quietly lowered my feet to the wooden floor then tiptoed across the room with my heart in my mouth. Under the pressure of my thumb and forefinger I felt the key turn in the lock until it disengaged. I thrust the candlestick aloft, yanked on the doorknob and threw the louvered barrier aside. Cold fingers immediately grabbed my neck and I screamed in the pitch-black night, smacking the offending appendage for all I was worth with the candlestick. A heavy thud hit the floor and I didn't hang around. Running out along the terrace resembling a demented Lady Macbeth, I slammed straight into the chest of a fellow guest.

'What the blazes is going on?' he demanded, cocking his pistol and pushing passed me.

'Someone's in my room,' I stuttered, convinced I had just murdered yet another local criminal.

'Stay where you are,' shouted my neighbour. I was rooted to the spot and could hear shuffling, then the glow of a candle flame followed by my neighbour's confident English voice.

'Madam, you appear to have single-handedly decapitated the miscreant.'

I returned to my room in trepidation and gingerly peered around the doorframe. My eyes scanned the interior but it was empty. I turned, confused, to find my neighbour standing in his striped nightshirt, a wry grin on his face and his pistol pointing down at his feet. I dropped my gaze to the floor where a dead monitor lizard lay motionless, spread-eagled across the frayed rush floor mat, its head caved in, its brown scaly body, long neck, elongated claws and powerful tail looking for all the world like a pulverised primeval alligator.

My hand shot to my mouth and I passed out.

Chapter Six

'Doctor, Memsahib, are you awake. Do you want chai?'
The woman's voice sounded distant, as if coming through
a fog as she tapped against the door. 'You miss your train if
you not wake-up.' She tapped again, more loudly this time.

'I'm awake,' I shouted and staggered to my feet, scanning
the bedroom. Had I been dreaming? I bent to examine the rush
mat by the veranda door but the blood splatters across the
reeds confirmed otherwise. 'What time is it?' I called out,
backing away from the offending object.

'Seven-thirty, Doctor, Memsahib. Your train to Ludhiana, it
leave at eight-fifteen.'

Ludhiana? Why am I going to Ludhiana? My brain refused
to function, then I gasped and grabbed my chest as the full
horror of the previous twenty-four hours hit me like a hammer
blow.

'Jesus, Mary and Joseph,' I blasphemed, taking a leaf out of
Duncan Fitzpatrick's book, as a shell-shocked expression
stared out at me from the dresser mirror. 'Christ, Mac, you look
as if you've been evacuated from the Western Front.'

I poured cold water from the jug into the ceramic basin and
doused my face until my cheeks turned pink. I still looked like a
walking cadaver but at least my brain was now functioning.
Ludhiana, I thought, remembering the reason for my trip as
Gloria Hodgson's image sprang to mind. 'She'll never believe
me when I tell her what's happened.'

I quickly changed, packed my valise and walked out into the
corridor.

'Good morning, Lassie,' said Alastair Galbraith, sitting at the long oak dining table with several other men. 'I hope you don't feel as bad as you look.'

I stared from one to the other as they collectively nodded and went back to their breakfast. 'Mr Galbraith, after yesterday, my whole world has turned upside-down. The police officer refused to arrest me last night and now I've annihilated an innocent monitor lizard.'

'I shouldn't worry about the monitor lizard,' he replied, standing and pulling out a chair. 'It'll be in tonight's curry if I'm not mistaken.' I clasped my stomach. 'As for the police officer, it would be more than his job's worth to arrest an English woman, no matter how insistent she was.'

I shook my head at the injustice of it all. 'But?'

'No buts, dear. Think of it all as a bad dream. Now, have some porridge and get yourself off to Ludhiana to that important meeting.'

The others, seemingly aware of what had transpired, all appeared to agree, and with no further ado, a bowl of steaming porridge was placed in front of me along with a jar of honey. It tasted wonderful on my empty stomach and I remained silent until the last spoonful had slid down my gullet.

'Mr Galbraith, gentlemen, I have to do something. That poor boy's family need to be compensated, and I'll never live with myself unless I . . .' I ran out of steam.

'Pay them blood money?' suggested the neighbour. 'Major Redfern,' he announced, now dressed from head to toe in khaki, who stretched across the table to shake my hand. 'Rum deal, last night with that critter, especially after the events at

Panipat Junction. I trust you didn't bump your head when you fainted?'

I rubbed my right temple. 'No, my head appears to be in one piece which is more than can be said for my conscience.'

'Doctor, listen to me, and listen well. What happened yesterday is a tragedy, an accident beyond your control, but you must put it to the back of your mind and get on with your work. Galbraith here, has told us all about the WCHS. Very commendable. An incident like this should not overshadow the good work you are doing and as sure as King George V is our sovereign, stealing from a train roof will not stop because one child fell off.'

'Hear, hear,' said a fellow officer lighting his pipe at the end of the table.

'If it would make you feel better, I'm travelling through Paniput Junction later today and can have a word with the stationmaster. He will know of the family and can arrange to pay them on your behalf. Be assured, the family will bless you for your kindness and generosity.'

I looked for support from Alastair Galbraith.

'Lassie, a few rupees will go a long way to feeding them. It may be called blood money, but that's by far the best solution. Believe me.'

I swallowed hard. 'But how sure are you that the family will get the money?'

'It would be more than the stationmaster's life to try swindling the British Army, Doctor.'

I dragged my purse from my bag recalling it slowly rising up the compartment window on a walking stick. 'What would be suitable blo . . . compensation?'

The matter was quickly discussed. 'Five rupees,' said the Major. 'Four for the family and one for the stationmaster's trouble.' I handed the blood money over to him, praying that my Pa never found out.

'Doctor, Memsahib.' I turned to face the housekeeper pointing to the wall clock. 'You go. Train will not wait.'

'Major,' I said rising. 'I am indebted to you for acting as my conscience in this matter, and from now on I promise to keep my handbag firmly below my seat when travelling around the subcontinent. Mr Galbraith, I will be in touch.'

With that, I was out of the door, into the waiting tonga and heading back to the railway station, vainly trying to consider the last twenty-four hours as a bad dream.

Gloria was waiting for me as I stepped from the train in Ludhiana and pointed at the taxi waiting to transport us to her lodgings.

'Mac,' she peered into my eyes and frowned. 'You look awful.'

'I know, Gloria, and with good reason. I've just been responsible for the death of a child.' I filled her in as we weaved our way between crowds of bicycles, tongas, rickshaws, wagons, bullocks and people, dust from the road creeping through every gap in the vehicle's chassis and turning my shoes a rusty brown colour.

'Jesus, Mac, that's awful, but you couldn't have known that it was a child at the other end of the walking stick. It was a terrible accident. Surely you can see that?'

'No, I can't. That child should never have been on the train's roof in the first place. Why doesn't the stationmaster put a stop to it?'

'Mac, this is the Punjab, not Hampshire or Virginia. You can't bring your British values of fair play into this country, it simply doesn't work, and the sooner you come to terms with that, the better.'

She was right, of course, but it didn't help my situation. I was searching for excuses to justify what happened and I would probably do so for many years to come.

'What you need, my girl, is to de-stress. A stiff drink and a long, hot bath is what's called for right now.' She waltzed me into a dak bungalow in the Civil Lines and instructed the housekeeper to produce some sandwiches and a jug of iced lemonade. While we waited, she poured two large whiskies from the sideboard and flopped into a faded wing-backed fireside chair.

'You can't change what happened, Mac, but by paying blood money you have given the parents a chance to keep their other kids fed and less likely to steal from passing trains.'

'But where is the justice in all this?'

'Justice is for the rich, Mac. In this country, many children are maimed by their own families and sent out to beg on the streets. That is their justice. Yesterday, here in Ludhiana, a man sold his infant daughter as a child bride for cash. Where's the justice in that?'

I buried my head in my hands. 'God alive, Gloria, will we ever manage to put a stop to these practices. It's like walking through molasses.'

'All we can do is try, Mac. One day all our efforts will have an effect, believe me. Now, drink your whisky and tell me what has been happening to you since that article of yours appeared in the Delhi Times.'

It all seemed so irrelevant now. I sighed, recalled my telephone conversation with the Deputy Director of the CSTM regarding my cancelled Ph.D funding, and spent the next half-hour recounting the whole sorry saga from start to finish.

It was cathartic to be sharing it with Gloria. As a female surgeon, she could identify with my viewpoint and even burst out laughing when I repeated Geraldine Stewart-Symes's unflattering impression of Sir Charles in Aden.'

'Good riddance is what I say, and well done you. But how on earth did Peter Bonham-Cavendish manage to worm his way into Ponsonby-Pritchard's job at his age?'

Being American, Gloria never saw the need to use honorary titles. 'Better you don't know,' I said, drawing a line across my lips with my fingers. 'Suffice to say, Sir Peter will make an excellent Surgeon-General of the IMS and he's a great supporter of the Women's Medical Service.'

'And not before time.' Her remark dripped acid as she bit into an egg and cress sandwich, her fitted herringbone suit and white blouse looking pristine against my rather dishevelled cream linen skirt and jacket.

'How did your lectures go here in Ludhiana?' I asked, lifting the chilled glass jug and pouring us both some lemonade.

'Ever more boring.' She put down her plate. 'You know, Mac, there are times when teaching student midwives the latest obstetric techniques really begins to pall. I must have given the lecture on MVA abortion procedures hundreds of times over the years.'

I shuddered at the reference to manual vacuum aspirators and subconsciously rubbed my abdomen. 'Well, if you give me an hour to go and freshen up, we can talk about work over tea.'

I lay in the cast-iron bath, wallowing in lavender bath salts, and searched for the right way to approach Gloria over the subject of becoming my deputy. It was not going to be easy, especially as she had been working in India a lot longer than me and was equally qualified.

Born and educated in America, she didn't suffer fools easily and had a natural authority over her peers and patients. She was full of grit and determination which was a breath of fresh air in the colonial world of female subservience. We had unexpectedly met over dinner, travelling by train from Bombay to Calcutta back in November 1929. At the time, she was on her way to a gynaecology conference and I was just off the boat from England. I was mesmerised by her account of life in the WMS and sickened by her descriptions of local birthing practices throughout India. On numerous occasions since then she had complained bitterly about the indigenous birthing attendants, as I had explained to Ruby.

Convincing her that I could retrain them for the WCHS was going to be an uphill battle, but I had one ace up my sleeve in the shape of Jonathon Davies. Gloria had argued constantly that without proper sanitation and clean water in the towns and villages, no amount of hygiene training would be worth a jot. Sadly, those in the Public Health Department who should have listened were deaf to her arguments, but with Jonathon as my Chief Sanitary Inspector, this situation was about to change.

I slipped into a fresh, pale grey cotton dress with white collar and cuffs, rummaged in my valise for my cream espadrilles, applied soft beige lipstick to my mouth and, grabbing my WCHS file, returned to the lounge. Gloria hadn't moved and was engrossed in reading Lahore's latest edition of *Punch* magazine in Urdu.

'Anything interesting?' I asked as I poured myself some Darjeeling tea.

'A detailed account of Mahatma Ghandi's Salt March,' she replied.

'Funny you should mention that. I've been invited to visit a salt mine on my way to Simla in the summer.'

Gloria looked up from the magazine. 'Who from?'

'Alastair Galbraith. The man on the train. He's a mining engineer and was telling me of the appalling conditions the lower caste women have to work in at the salt mines. Some even go into labour and end up having their babies out in the open, behind rocky outcrops.'

'With no-one there to assist them?'

'Apparently.' I went to sit on the bay window seat. 'If you're around, perhaps you'd like to join me.'

'Just try stopping me. I tell you, Mac, the more I hear, the more my skin crawls. It's high time we had some way of getting these women proper care.'

This was my chance.

'We have, Gloria. It's called the Women's Community Health Service. Sir Peter helped me get approval for it from the Institute Board in Calcutta. It has its own funding; it falls under the umbrella of the WMS and I'm running it.'

'Is that why Bonham-Cavendish called you back from Aden?'

'Yes. It was my idea originally. I had recommended it in my report to Sir Peter and Agnes late last summer. At the time he was sceptical, like all of the IMS, but once he got his hands on the levers of power, he decided to show his metal by taking up my cause.' I filled Gloria in on how the department came into being, and the pilot scheme in some of Punjab's districts.

'I even managed to get Jonathon Davies to work for me as my Chief Sanitary Inspector,' I nonchalantly said, helping myself to more tea. 'He's the Governor of Bengal's godson, you know, and soon to marry his niece.'

'Is he, indeed?' I could feel Gloria nibbling at my bait. 'Crikey, with connections like that, all sorts of doors could open in the Public Works Department.'

'My thoughts entirely, and as you've said more than once, without public health facilities, Indian women will continue to die like flies.'

'What did Agnes Scott say?'

'She was all for it and even allowed me to poach Fatima Patel from the Lady Hardinge to organise the health worker training courses.'

'Good God!' Gloria leapt from her chair. 'You've certainly not been resting on your laurels, have you?'

'No, I haven't, but to be honest, I think I've bitten off more than I can chew. Even a selection of Punjab's districts is one hell of an area to run this pilot scheme, and with only fifteen months to prove my case, I'm beginning to get cold feet.' I glanced at Gloria from the corner of my eye. She was now standing by the mantlepiece, tapping her foot on the fender. I could almost see the cogs turning in her brain.

'What you need, Mac, is help.' Exactly, I thought, and looked angelic. 'You can't let an opportunity like this go to waste. It's exactly what the WMS has been praying for.' She turned and threw out her hands, palms skyward. 'My God, Mac, do you realise what this could mean for women's health?' My bottom lip caught between my teeth and I nodded, feeling my toes crossing. 'You'll just have to find someone within the WMS to help you. Someone like me.'

'You?'

'Yes me. You need someone who can put your ideas into practise, someone with my organisation skills who won't take no for an answer. Someone who won't back down in a crisis.'

I've done it, I thought, I've landed my catch.

'Who would you suggest, Gloria?'

'Let me think about it. By the way, where are your health workers coming from?'

Here was the rub. I clenched my buttocks and dived in with both feet. 'I intend to utilise *dais* to get my message out across the towns and villages.

'*Dais?*'

'Yes, *dais*.' She took a step back. 'My plan is to train them as health workers and pay them a wage.'

'You've got to be joking?' Gloria paced the floor. 'You couldn't train that lot if your life depended on it.'

'How do you know, you've never tried.'

'I don't need to try, Mac. Most of them are nothing better than shamans and will not take kindly to you muscling in on their territory. Changing a habit of a lifetime will take more than bribing these women with a few annas.'

'I know that Gloria. That's why Jonathon is tasked with bringing clean water and good sanitation to the villages while I entice mothers into the clinics with the offer of free powdered baby milk.'

'Free baby milk?'

'Yes, my regular post-natal clinics will offer free baby milk to all the mothers who attend. Meanwhile, my young health workers will keep proper records of births and deaths, teach the women good hygiene and tell them which practises are bad for their babies. Like feeding them *bal-golis.*'

'And the older *dais,* what do you intend to do about them?'

My eyes dropped to the floor. 'Nothing. In time, they will become obsolete as more mothers realise the benefits of the baby clinics and our properly trained midwives.'

Gloria began to resemble Reginald Townsend and went for my jugular as her fervour crumbled before my eyes.

'Wishful thinking, Mac.' She stared down at me from her great height. 'You do realise you're insane. None of these women can read or write. Half of them don't even speak Hindi or Urdu. How the hell are you going to get your message across?'

My MacKenzie heckles began to rise at the slight and I went on the attack with gusto. 'Simple charts, Gloria. Diagrams about hygiene, childcare and feeding practises. The health workers can also demonstrate these practises using dummies. If the message is regularly repeated, the word will get out and more mothers will begin to see the benefits.' My voice was rising. 'These indigenous birthing attendants are a readymade workforce for this purpose and even though you think they are useless, I don't and I will prove it to you.' I could now be heard in the street.

'And you're expecting Fatima Patel to pull teams of these health workers together as if by magic, are you?'

'Yes, I am, but not by magic and she won't be alone. I have already got the backing of all the Punjab Mission Hospitals, who think it's a wonderful plan. They are going to help me set up the health clinics in their area and staff them until my workforce is in a position to take over.'

'And purdah? How will that work?' Gloria's lip curled.

'The clinics will be held in large tents away from male prying eyes. These are being donated by the local army units and their squaddies are putting up fifteen tents in local areas of Bathinda district as we sit here. Meanwhile, Jonathon is overseeing drill holes at each site to provide fresh water to the locals, and covered sewage ditches are being laid to remove waste from the lavatories. The tents will provide the women with an area to rest, to obtain important health advice and to feed their children and they will be sent home with copies of the charts to pin up as a reminder of what they have seen and heard. In time, the tents will be replaced with permanent buildings, but that's all for the future.'

We sat in silence, Gloria mulling over everything I'd said.

'All well and good,' she conceded, 'but how are the women supposed to get to these clinics?' There was a noticeable softening of her tone now.

'Collection points are being organised in a ten-mile radius of each clinic and the women will be driven to the clinics in canvas-covered, horse-drawn carts.'

'You seem to have put a lot of thought into this, Mac.' Gloria went back to her seat, sat and crossed her legs. 'The question is, will it work?'

I had run out of steam and felt demoralised. 'Only time will tell, and time is what I don't have.'

'When do you have to submit your results?'

'End of March next year.'

'So why have you travelled to Ludhiana to see me?'

I picked up my file and placed it on the occasional table at her side. 'I would like you to read my detailed plan. If you can make any constructive suggestions on improving it, or ways to save time, I would be interested to hear them.' Opening the cover, I lifted a buff-coloured envelope from the internal flap and placed it in her lap. 'As for this, I'll be waiting for your answer. Needless to say, I won't be holding my breath after the grilling you have just given me.'

Chapter Seven

I was never so pleased to see Delhi Junction as when the train pulled into the station. It had been a gruelling few days and I was relieved to be back on home turf, with or without a deputy.

Gloria had seen me off from the dak bungalow after breakfast with a promise that she would give my job offer serious consideration over the weekend. All I could do was wait and see.

A letter from Frances was waiting for me on Ruby's marble-topped armoire as I walked through the door. I dropped my valise, headed for the terrace and flopped onto my favourite ochre-coloured sofa where the cool air from the ceiling fan ruffled my hair. The temperature on the plains was beginning to build and with it, the arrival of those pesky mosquitoes. I ripped open the envelope and lay back, my feet resting on the glass coffee table and slowly read through Frances's news.

Dear Mac,

I hope your trip north was productive and that you are now back in Delhi with time to rest. All is very well here in Poona and Jim sends his love.

Lamis is in the rudest of health physically and never complains, even if she still suffers from minor problems with digestion and bowel. Agnes has called in to see her twice during her visits to Bombay and seems to be happy with her progress which I know will be a relief to you. As for Lamis's mental state, that is a more worrying question. Since arriving here, our young student appears to have lost her smile. She studies hard (she really is intelligent) and carries out all her duties efficiently, willingly and, as I said, without complaint, but something has died inside her. No matter what I do to try and bring her out of herself, she doggedly remains in a world beyond me. I checked in her bedroom yesterday morning to see if there was anything that would give me a clue to her malady and was shocked to find a hand-written calendar under her mattress, all the days since you left India crossed out in red crayon. She misses you, Mac, and I am now convinced that she always will. This is not what you want to hear, but you did ask.

No, I haven't told her that you have returned, and forgive me for bringing this up, but I think you promised to write to her every month and send photographs of your family and life in England. So far, she has received nothing from you apart from a P&O postcard from Aden.

My hand shot to my mouth and I let out an agonising wail.

Do you want me to tell her you are in Delhi? I know you are very busy with the WCHS, but a letter to Lamis would mean the world to her.

As for your query about Tom. I spoke to Jim, and he was as surprised as you are that Tom is no longer working for P&O. Jim is now sending a cable to Enid asking where he can be contacted, and I will let you know as soon as he gets an answer. It's all very strange, isn't it?

Perhaps we should talk on the telephone about Lamis. I so want to make life better for her and I am convinced that I can achieve this, if only I can get through this veil of apathy which hangs over her. I'll await your call, and news about Vijay, Ruby and what is going on in all your lives.

Much love

Frances

x

'How could you be so cruel, Mac?' I lamented, as severe guilt, like a punch to the stomach, caused my guts to ache.

Since posting that card from Aden, my promise to Lamis had gone completely out of my head. 'And you have the nerve to call Duncan Fitzpatrick an egotist. How dare you forget the one person who idealises you?'

'I sorry, Memsahib Doctor, did you want something?' Sanjay stood at the door, unsure whether to stay or go.

'No, Sanjay. Nothing, thank you.' I retrieved my valise from the hall and climbed the stairs. 'If Miss Tavener wants me, I'll be in my room.'

'Yes, Memsahib Doctor. I tell her when she here.'

Throwing my jacket onto the bed, I picked up the bedside phone and waited for the operator. 'Poona 5837,' I said and waited to be connected.

'St Saviour's School for Girls,' said a female voice at the other end.

'Good afternoon, may I speak with Miss Trotter please?'

'One moment, Madam.' The voice sounded strangely familiar.

'Miss Trotter speaking.'

'Frances, it's Mac. I've just read your letter.'

'One moment, please.'

I frowned, sat on the edge of the bed and heard low murmuring noises coming from the other end.

'Hello, Mac, are you there?'

'Yes, I'm here. What's going on?'

'That was Lamis answering the phone. I needed to send her out of earshot before we could continue.'

My heart leapt at this realisation. 'Her English is so . . . English, Frances.'

'I know. The child has taken to our language like a duck to water. Anyway, thanks for getting in touch. I hope you didn't take offence at me criticising you?'

'On the contrary, I have just thrashed myself with a lash for being so self-obsessed. I can't believe I forgot to write, and I have absolutely no excuse.'

'Well, what's done is done. The question is, what do we do now?'

'What you do Frances, is bring Lamis to the phone so I can talk to her myself, apologise for not contacting her sooner and telling her that I am back in India and longing to see her.'

'Are you sure, Mac. I hate to be a wet blanket, but I don't want you to raise her hopes and then have to disappoint her again. I'm not sure what that will do to her sanity.'

'I understand, and I have no intention of disappointing her again. In fact, before I speak to her, I want us to discuss what I have in mind for her future.' I kicked off my shoes and lay back on the bed. 'But first, answer these questions honestly, Frances. Would I make a good teacher for Lamis?'

'I guess that depends on what you plan to teach her,' she replied, sounding unsure.

'English, childcare and medicine.'

'Then the answer must be yes.'

'Good. Do you think I would be a good surrogate mother?'

Frances appeared to be having a coughing fit. 'Sorry, something went down the wrong way.'

'Liar. So obviously you don't think so?'

'Mac, you are about as maternal as a cuckoo. However, I'm sure Lamis could survive even you at a push.'

'Thank you, Miss Trotter, for those few reassuring words.'

'Don't mention it.' Frances sighed. 'Now what is all this about?'

I took a deep breathe, closed my eyes and explained what was on my mind. When I finished, Frances remained silent on the other end of the line. Seconds passed, then finally she spoke.

'Mac, I think it's a wonderful idea. Lamis will learn more in one month by your side than in a year here at St Saviour's with me, and she'll be an asset to you and to the women of her own culture.'

'Then I have your consent?'

'Yes, you do, whole-heartedly. When will you be here to collect her?'

'Next weekend. Is that too soon?'

'No. Come down on Good Friday. Jim will be here for the holidays and we can all enjoy Easter together.'

'Oh, heavens, is it Easter again?'

'Afraid so, Mac. Now, shall I call Lamis to the phone?'

Seven days later I stepped onto the platform at Poona and saw a small figure pushing through the crowds, her St Saviour's straw hat flying behind her and her green and white gingham dress getting crushed against the bodies of passengers going in the opposite direction. For a girl of fourteen years, she was still quite small and ran with a discernible offset gait.

'Umi,' she cried, her voice reaching the cast iron rafters of the train station. 'Umi, you come back.'

I lifted her off the ground and hugged her to me like a warm pashmina on a cold day. I would have spoken, but my throat wouldn't open, so I just held on tight to this small, tortured body and let the empty months without her fade away. When I did finally put her down, Frances and Jim were by my side and together we followed the throng out onto the concourse and into Jim's car.

Lamis would not let go of my hand as Jim eased the vehicle into the evening traffic, and his eardrums must have been aching from all the girly chatter by the time we reached the school gates.

'Lamis insists on showing you around the school, Mac,' said Frances stepping out of the car, 'so I suggest you let Jim take your bag, I'll go and see about supper, and you can pay your respects to Trotter.'

'Right.' I looked down at two kohl-black Indian eyes staring up at me and winked. 'Lead on, MacDuff.'

I was unceremoniously dragged into the hall and across to the common room where a group of girls, remaining at St Saviour's for the holidays, were playing dominoes.

'Good evening, Miss,' said one of the group, as they all stood to attention.

'Relax, girls,' I replied. 'No need to stand on ceremony at this time of night.'

They sat on cue. 'Is this your mother, Lamis?' asked another.

'Yes. This is my Umi.' Lamis's chest expanded like an aerated balloon, and she beamed from ear to ear.

'Actually, I'm her guardian angel,' I corrected, 'but we won't split hairs. Umi will do just fine.'

The school clock was chiming the hour as we returned to Frances's quarters and she immediately took charge, addressing my young companion.

'Lamis, bed. It's past ten o'clock and you've had enough excitement for one day.'

'Yes, Miss Frances.' I felt a tug on my skirt. 'Umi, please, you come too.'

'Lamis Abbas, your grammar is terrible, but I will forgive you this once. Now, off with you. We will both be up later to say goodnight.' With that her charge was gone, and I looked at my friend and shook my head.

'What's the matter?'

'How am I ever going to fill your shoes, Frances?'

'You'll learn,' quipped Jim, handing me a drink.

'Perhaps a crash course on child rearing over the weekend wouldn't go amiss.' I peered at the pinkish liquid in a tall, chilled tumbler. 'What's this?'

'A Singapore Sling,' Jim replied. 'Gin, cherry liquor, Cointreau, Benedictine, grenadine, pineapple juice, lime juice and Angostura bitters, in that order.'

'Crikey.' I took a sip. 'Bloody hell, Jim, this is strong enough to knock my head off.'

'Rubbish. You're just out of practice.' He handed Frances her cocktail then raised his own glass. 'Now, Ladies, as we are finally all together, I have an announcement to make, and on the basis that I can never get a word in edgeways when you two get together, I'll take advantage of the moment.'

I looked across at Frances who shrugged and duly sipped her gin sling. Settling into a fireside chair, I squeezed my lips together with my fingers and nodded to Jim. 'The floor is all yours, Mr Hamilton,' I squeaked through my clenched teeth.

'Thank you, Doctor Stuart-MacKenzie. 'Now, on this auspicious occasion, what I really need is a drum roll.'

I placed my glass on the low table and rapidly beat my fingers against the wooden arm. 'Will this do?'

'Excellent. Mac.' He paused, raised his glass, and addressed his audience of two. 'After much trial and error, it gives me great pleasure to announce that . . .

'Oh, do get on with it, Jim.'

'Fran, be quiet.'

I began to giggle.

'And that's enough from you, young lady. This is serious. Now where was I?'

'You were about to tell Mac that we are getting married,' replied Frances, trying to keep a straight face.

'Well, bugger me! You've just stolen my thunder Frances Trotter, and I thought I wore the trousers in this house.'

'You might wear the trousers, dear, but I rule the roost.'

By now, my sides were splitting which started off my hiccups. 'When is . . . hic . . . the wedding . . . hic?'

'This September, at Christ's Church in Simla,' fired off Jim, determined to have his moment of glory.

'And am I . . . hic . . . invited?'

'You're to be my Maid of Honour,' declared Frances, 'so you'd better be.' I felt her hand hammer my vertebrae as her left hip edged onto my chair arm. 'Mac, pinch your nose, hold your breath and count to ten.'

'I'm trying . . . hic . . . but I can't do all three . . . hic . . .at the same time.'

'Fran,' said Jim, as my diaphragm continued to jolt violently every three seconds, 'I suggest we finish our drinks and proceed to supper before your Maid of Honour expires before our eyes or sues us for grievous bodily harm.'

'As if I . . .hic . . . would?'

'I'd rather not find out if you don't mind.' Jim emptied his glass in one gulp. 'Hopefully, my future wife's oxtail soup will sooth your bronchial tubes sufficiently for us to receive your congratulations.'

I crept into Lamis's bedroom. She was fast asleep, her pert nose poking out above the pristine white cotton sheet and multi-coloured crocheted quilt, my postcard from Aden in pride of place, propped against her bedside lamp.

I kissed the top of her head and brushed her thick black locks away from her eyes. 'Sleep tight, child, and sweet dreams.'

Frances beckoned me to the door and switched off the light, dropping the latch very quietly. 'She's been a different girl since your phone call last week. She's come alive and reverted to the girl we all knew in Simla.'

'Thank goodness for that,' I replied, negotiating the stairs with care as the Singapore Sling attacked my legs. I stopped halfway down and turned. 'By the way, Frances, congratulations. Although I always knew you two would tie the knot at some point, it doesn't detract from my excitement at hearing this news, and Jim's attempt to announce it was just the best . . . hic.'

'He was rather amusing wasn't he?' She carried on down. 'I want Lamis to be my flower girl, Mac. Perhaps we can tell her tomorrow at breakfast.'

'Oh, she'll love that. I can see her now with flowers in her hair and a posy in her hand. She will look adorable.' My mind filled with the sight of Lamis crippled and in excruciating pain, kneeling on a flea-infested mattress.

'I'm hoping you'll help me decide what to wear while you're here in Poona. I'm rather hopeless as such matters.'

'And you think I'm not? Ruby is the wedding planner; you should ask her.'

'Heaven forbid. Ruby would have me walking down the aisle dressed as the Queen of Sheba. I'm not sure Jim would be too impressed.'

'Oh, I don't know. Men the world over have a penchant for the exotic.'

She chose to ignore that. 'You won't have a problem getting to Simla for the wedding, will you?' Frances pushed open the refectory swing doors and let me through.

'Absolutely not. As far as I'm concerned, hell could freeze over before I'd miss you getting married.'

She smiled and went to serve the soup.

'Penny for them?' asked Jim, as I joined him at the long pine table.

'I was thinking about the first day Frances and I met in the dining room on the ss Narkunda. She came over to tell me that Lady Wetherington was suffering from some noxious stomach disorder. Little did I know then that we would become such close friends. She is like a sister to me now and I thank my lucky stars that the voyage to India brought us together.'

'Me too, Mac. When you think about it, that crossing has a lot to answer for.'

I nodded and looked away, fiddling with my linen napkin.

'It would appear our guest's hiccups have stopped, Jim,' announced Frances, placing a steaming soup bowl in front of me.

'Well, praise the Lord for that, Fran. It must have been something I said.'

Chapter Eight

S weat was rolling down my back as I stood in front of a white wicket fence on Alipore Road in the Delhi Civil Lines a week later, looking at a gabled bungalow with pink and white roses growing in profusion around the veranda balustrade.

Having returned to the capital with Lamis, I had decided it was high time I had a home of my own. Whether this one fitted the bill depended on the state of the interior but, so far, it looked promising.

'You'll need a housekeeper,' declared Ruby, as she mounted the steps to the front door while I busily photographed the front elevation. 'How long is the lease?'

'Eighteen months, initially. The owners are on their travels in Australia and New Zealand before they return to England.' I followed her into the hall, the black and white diamond-patterned floor tiles and pea-green embossed wallpaper giving it a utilitarian appearance. The single ceiling light gave off little illumination in the passage but once we entered the drawing room, large glazed double doors to the rear filled the room with sunlight, while the deep bay window at the front cast shadows across the faded Kashmir carpet running along the whole length of the room.

'Well, this is spacious,' I said, aiming the camera at the view of the garden from my position beside the window seat.

'Can you redecorate?' Ruby was now picking at the corner of some dull yellow wallpaper above the mantlepiece.

'Yes, I think so.'

'Good, because this colour reminds me of the nicotine-stained walls of the Carpenters Arms pub my dad used to frequent in the back streets of Streatham.'

'Oh, come on, it's not that bad.'

'It's not good either.' She moved the wine-red leather fireside chair and a mouse ran under the skirting. 'Oh, nice.'

'For goodness's sake, Ruby, a small mouse won't kill you and you've probably seen far worse living in the East End of London.'

'Maybe, Mac, but this is not the East End and you're not a child. If you take this place on, it will need fumigating and a complete refurbishment.'

I walked past her into the kitchen at the end of the hall where yet more yellow walls faced me above green and yellow painted wooden kitchen units. 'Do you think the wife is colour blind?' I asked.

'Has to be. No-one with perfect eyesight could stand working in here for long.' Ruby pulled at the back door which squeaked alarmingly on its hinges. 'How long has this place been empty?'

I referred to the notes given to me by the Civil Lines rental officer. 'It says here that the owners left Delhi in November, so that would make it about six months.' I leant against the sink and sighed. 'It's a bit of a come down from your mansion, isn't it?'

'Mac, look on the bright side. The rental is within your means, the house appears to be structurally sound and the doors and windows are in good order.'

'Apart from the hinges.' I was not convinced.

'Assuming there are no leaks in the roof, all this,' she made an arc in the air with her hand, 'is simply cosmetic. Once it's had a Ruby Tavener make-over it will pass muster as one of Vijay's many guest quarters.'

'Is he seriously going to help fund this?'

Ruby batted the remark away with her hand. 'You know damned well he is. If he had his way, you would not be moving out at all, but since you are, he insists on making sure you're comfortable.'

'Then let's finish the grand tour, check out the garden, and depart for some lunch. After viewing eight properties this morning, I'm starving.'

'How's Lamis settling back into the student quarters at the workhouse?' asked Ruby, stabbing the exposed ceiling beams with her parasol.

I peered into the pantry where more mouse droppings peppered the marble shelving. 'She's enjoying being back with the other students, and as I've told you before, Ruby, the Lady Hardinge Medical College is not a workhouse.'

'As if you would know.' She poked the windowsill and broke a fingernail. 'Drat!'

'Next time use your hat pin.'

The sun was setting by the time I returned to the mansion that afternoon and I waved the signed lease contract in the air as I walked onto the terrace. 'All done and dusted. You are now looking at the new tenant of 208, Alipore Road.'

A round of applause ricocheted off the rafters. 'When do you take possession?'

'Next Monday. I thought I'd take Lamis to see it tomorrow and she can choose her own bedroom.'

'Then I'll come too and bring my interior designer along to give us some ideas on styles and timing.' Ruby disappeared. Seconds later I could hear her talking to someone on the telephone. 'Right,' she announced on her return. 'Madame du Bois will meet us there at nine-thirty.'

'Who the hell is Madame du Bois?'

'Only the most famous interior designer in India. She's French you know, from Paris.'

'I would never have guessed.'

Both Ruby's eyebrows touched her hairline. 'Not that you would know anything about it, but she's highly sought after here in Delhi. If we're going to do this, Mac, we're going to do it right and Madeleine du Bois is the best there is.'

'What happens if the owners don't like it when they return?'

'They'll just have to deal with Vijay. I doubt we'll hear any more from them once our Maharaja has had his say on the matter.'

'Very well, but let's get one thing straight right now. I'm not having 208, Alipore Road turned into some lookalike Parisienne brothel with tassels, drapes and wall-to-wall mirrors. Have you got that?'

'Loud and clear, Elizabeth, although I'm sure the odd velvet chaise longue would look good in the bay window.'

'RUBY!'

By the end of May, the neighbours in Alipore Road were green with envy. Number 208 had metamorphosised into a calm, pastel coloured chalet bungalow hidden amongst tall neem, mango and fig trees, with the climbing roses trimmed and trained to form an arch around the entrance steps, their scented buds cascading to the veranda floor like a rippling waterfall.

The house had three spacious bedrooms, a fully fitted marble bathroom, plus extra lavatory, a scullery and kitchen to die for, a dining alcove seating six with pale rattan furniture and a drawing room with stained and polished wooden floors covered in large cream rugs, harmonising with the soft cream walls. An open fireplace with alabaster surround took up most of one wall, while soft peach upholstered sofas and matching peach and duck-egg blue scatter cushions coordinated with the deep bay window seat, giving the room an ambience of quiet opulence and understated class. I had relented on the antique gilt mirror situated above the mantlepiece but other than that, there wasn't a sign of gold leaf anywhere in the place.

Lamis was in her element, and had chosen the attic bedroom as her own, spending hours up there studying at her small wooden desk where she could look out over the rear garden and small pond beyond.

Work was taking up all of my time, so Ruby had taken charge of the renovations and thoroughly enjoyed scouring the bazaars looking for china, glass and silverware, dressed as a downtrodden woman from the local Salvation Army Brigade, bartering the prices down to rock bottom. Meanwhile, Madame du Bois had ploughed through swatch after swatch of the latest European fabrics looking for the perfect patterns and tones to match her colour scheme.

Finally, Vijay appeared from Jhalanpur to give his seal of approval at my housewarming dinner, and we sat on the veranda as the sun set over the undulating hills of the Delhi Ridge, sipping aperitifs and catching up on news.

The doorbell rang as the last of the sun's rays caught the tops of the trees, and Gloria suddenly appeared on the rear veranda looking rather dishevelled from her train journey from Bombay.

'Mrs Appleby,' I called out to my new housekeeper, yet another of Ruby's amazing finds, 'Doctor Hodgson's luggage can go into the guest bedroom. Once she has had time to freshen up we will have dinner. Say twenty minutes?'

'Right you are, Doctor,' came the Northumbrian reply from the depths of the hall. I turned back to my guests.

'Gloria, allow me to introduce Prince Vijay Kumar Singh II, the Maharaja of Jhalanpur, and his charming partner and my very close friend, Miss Ruby Tavener.' Gloria nodded.

'Vijay, Ruby, this is Doctor Gloria Hodgson, one of America's distinguished female clinicians, who hails from Philadelphia and is highly respected throughout the WMS.'

Vijay jumped up from his chair, grabbed her by the hand, lowered her into his seat and handed her a glass of Pimm's.

'I understand you are joining Mac in her new venture, Doctor Hodgson?' He dragged another wicker chair from the end of the veranda and plonked himself down next to Ruby.

Gloria seemed unusually dumbstruck being in the presence of a Maharaja, so I answered for her. 'That she is, Vijay. I finally made her understand that my offer was too good to turn down. It was a close-run thing, but she eventually succumbed to my persuasion.'

'It's a pleasure to meet you, Gloria.' Ruby stretched across the veranda and shook her hand. 'Mac has told me so much about you and I understand that like her, you don't take prisoners.'

'A slight exaggeration, I'm afraid. Unlike Mac, I haven't yet managed to get the Surgeon-General of the IMS fired, although if this post turns out to be a failure, I might well follow suit and oust the current incumbent.'

'Be careful what you say about Sir Peter, Gloria. He happens to be one of Vijay's long-standing friends.'

'Oops.' She placed her fingers to her lips and shrugged. 'Sorry about that, Your Highness, but we Americans are not known for our diplomacy.'

'Nor is Mac,' replied Vijay, winking in my direction, 'so the chaps over at Viceroy's House had better watch their step.' His laughter was infectious. 'And please call me Vijay. All this grandstanding doesn't wash with me amongst friends.'

Gloria turned to me, the corner of her lip rising. Obviously, Vijay had risen in her estimation.

'So, Gloria, why did you change your mind?' asked Ruby.

'I had little choice in the matter. When my boss at the Cama Hospital received a telephone call from Sir Peter pointing out that this was an opportunity not to be missed, I was unceremoniously handed my severance pay and a train ticket to Delhi.'

I smiled over the rim of my glass. 'Perhaps I should withdraw my offer, as you seem genuinely aggrieved at leaving Bombay?'

'Don't you dare, Elizabeth Stuart-MacKenzie. After all, you made it quite clear in Ludhiana that without someone like me to help run the project, it would fail before it even got started.'

'Then I propose a toast.' Vijay rose to his feet. 'To the Director and Deputy Director of the Women's Community Health Service. Long may they succeed in the face of unimaginable adversity.'

'I'll drink to that,' added Ruby, and we all raised our glasses.

'Right, I had better check on Mrs Appleby while you all get acquainted. Ruby, please introduce Vijay and Gloria to Lamis when she appears to say goodnight, assuming I can winkle her from her desk.'

The evening was a huge success and for the next forty-eight hours, Gloria and I closeted ourselves in the dining alcove, its table spread with maps, work schedules, wall charts and teaching aids, while Mrs Appleby accompanied Lamis to and from the Lady Hardinge to continue her healthcare training.

Johnathon turned up on the second afternoon and updated us on developments with his sanitary and water installations. He had discovered an ingenious way of locating the best position for the WCHS tents by dowsing for water using coconuts.

'The technique had been used throughout India since ancient times,' he enthused, 'but our government pooh-poohed it as being fanciful. However, having seen it work with my own eyes, I disagree and now have a number of gnarled farmers and their coconuts trudging across the land at various sites. I'm pleased to report that nine out of ten drill holes have proved successful.'

'That's wonderful, Jonathon, but how does it work?' asked Gloria, fascinated.

'I'm not sure, but I believe it's something to do with electrical currents in the human body passing through the liquid in the coconut and reacting with electrical impulses given off by the water course. Not everyone can do it, but it really does works for those who can.'

'Goodness. How do they know when they've found water?' I was intrigued.

'It's incredible, Mac. A farmer will walk across a patch of parched earth with his coconut laid on its side in the palm of his hand. Suddenly, as he crosses a water course, the coconut rises up on its end like a jack-in-a-box.'

'You're kidding me,' exclaimed Gloria. 'This I have to see.'

'Well, it's certainly kept our costs down, I can tell you, and we have boreholes going over eighty feet down, right alongside our tents. Fresh water shoots out of the ground under natural pressure and once we've capped it off and channelled the water to our cisterns, we are up and running, if you'll excuse the pun.'

'And I imagine the local villagers are ecstatic too?'

'They are, Gloria.'

'So am I, Jonathon, and well done you, if you'll excuse the pun.'

By the evening we were all fully conversant with what needed to be achieved before the government's summer exodus to Simla and I went to my bed feeling positive that the WCHS was on its way to becoming a great success story.

Over the following weeks I took Lamis everywhere with me, insisting on us speaking Urdu during the morning, English in the afternoon and Hindi at night. My language skills improved rapidly and Lamis's infectious laugh could often be heard at the breakfast table when my attempt at Urdu left her in stitches.

All was going well until the day we arrived at Akbarpur in the Rajpura district of Patiala to attend the first post-natal clinic. There were no records regarding the population of the village, but a realistic guess put it at around five hundred, over eighty of which were women of child-bearing age.

Sister Agatha from the local Catholic Mission was there to greet us and led me through to where some young mothers were seated on metal chairs breast feeding their babies. I introduced myself and let Lamis take control of the toddlers who had their own area in the tent to play together.

I set myself up in a cubicle with one of our newly trained indigenous health workers and prepared to examine each mother and baby for myself. We were going along splendidly when Lamis tapped me on the arm and whispered in my ear.

'Umi, you must come and see this.'

I walked out into the main section and across to a young mother apparently having difficulty breast-feeding. I assumed she was too dehydrated to produce sufficient milk.

'What is the problem,' I asked Lamis in Hindi.

'The girl is Muslim, Umi, and the local *dai* insists the baby cord must not be cut.'

I immediately led the mother and baby into a second cubicle. Sitting her on the bed I asked for permission to unwrap her sari from around her chest and did a double take when I found the tiny baby's head rammed between the mother's breast and a terracotta jar the size of a funeral urn, the umbilical cord running from the child's belly into the pot.

Peering inside, I moved some ash with my surgical probe and found the mother's afterbirth lying, like a dead jelly fish, at the base.

'Sister Agatha,' I yelled.

'Yes, Doctor,' replied the nun appearing at my side.

'What in the world is this?' I held up the pot, being careful not to jerk the umbilical cord.

Sister Agatha stepped back, genuflecting. 'God preserve us, Doctor. I have no idea.'

'Lamis,' I said, turning, 'I want to know exactly when this baby was born and what the *dai* told this poor mother to do.'

'Yes, Umi.' She placed the pot back in the mother's arm and knelt by her side.

'Umi, the child was born about three weeks ago and the *dais* said the . . .' She hesitated, trying to find the word.

'Afterbirth.'

'Yes, afterbirth, must stay in the pot until it . . .' She pressed the palms of her hands together.

'Shrivels.'

'Yes, Umi. The local shaman says it is Allah's will.'

'To hell with Allah's will, Lamis.' I was beside myself with anger. 'This mother can't breast feed her baby while it's attached to a pot bigger than itself. Tell her I will be with her shortly and get antiseptic, two clamps, my surgical knife and a sterile bandage ready for my use. Make sure she knows that cutting the umbilical cord will not offend Allah.'

I handed the baby back to the mother after the procedure was completed and instructed her to return in seven days to have the bandage changed. I was trying to decide what to do with the offending pot when Sister Agatha reappeared.

'Doctor Mac, you are needed outside.' She held back the cubicle curtain and I walked out of the tent, still holding the terracotta jar. Standing some yards away were three Indians, two men and one woman, all shaking their fists.

'They are the village chief, the village shaman and the *dai*,' muttered Lamis, standing at my side.

'Right. 'What do they want?'

Lamis addressed the shaman in her native tongue but had some difficulty understanding his dialect.

'I am sorry, Umi, I do not understand well, but I think he is putting a spell on you unless you go away.'

'Is he indeed?' I thought back to the day Fatima Patel and I extracted Lamis from her hovel in Old Delhi and smiled. 'Very well, leave this to me.' I walked over to the shaman and glared down at this wizen old man leaning on a gnarled stick, his legs bowed, his nose and matted hair pierced with animal bones and vulture feathers, all sticking out like porcupine quills, his pockmark face and rheumy eyes showing evidence of past chickenpox and too much opium. I thrust the terracotta pot into his arms. He jumped back in terror, letting it fall at his feet where it smashed, the ashes, afterbirth and umbilical cord spilling out across the earth. I took my stethoscope from around my neck and held it aloft, pointing it at the *dai*.

'You, Madam,' I shouted in English, 'are a disgrace to my profession and a danger to local mothers.' I stepped forward.

'This abomination,' I kicked the pot towards the village elder, 'is nothing more than an old wives' tale, and if I witness such practices ever again, I will have you all arrested and sent to prison. Do you understand?' I glared at them as my words smacked the air. 'Lamis, translate what I've just said.'

She didn't hesitate and stepped in front of me. Her translation, made even more violent from her years of abuse by her evil Muslim father and husband, strafed the group just as surely as slaying them with a spray of bullets. The *dai* dropped to her knees, wailing, while the men shrank visibly in stature. Lamis, scarred for life, both physically and mentally, bent down, scooped up the abandoned afterbirth and rammed it into the *dai's* chest. The woman screamed, got to her feet and ran for her life, followed, a split-second later, by her male accomplices. Lamis stood her ground and visibly shook.

I had never felt so proud of a human being in my life and eased her back into the privacy of the tent where I held her in my arms as every muscle in her body quivered.

'It's alright, Lamis. I've got you. No-one will ever hurt you again. Let it go, child. Let all the pain and hurt out. You have no need for it anymore.'

She sobbed, and sobbed, and sobbed, the months and years of torture, deprivation and abuse by a man of her own culture leaching out from every pore as she exorcised her demons.

Sister Agatha touched my shoulder hesitantly. 'It's alright, Sister, this reaction is long overdue. Perhaps you would make us some tea.'

Hours later, Lamis tried to explain her reaction to me that day, but I already knew the answer. Pressure had been building for months in this traumatised girl as she learned how unjust her life had been before we met. When the dam finally burst, all the hatred and vitriol that had been bubbling within her surfaced, like magma, exploding in one cataclysmic eruption far beyond that deserved by the three antagonists of Akbarpur village.

We returned to Delhi in quiet contemplation, and for me, the day had been a salutary lesson. If we were to win the battle against outdated customs, traditions and male-dominated religious ideology, it was essential our health workers understood exactly why the WCHS was so important to women's welfare.

After Lamis went to bed, I sat on the terrace with Gloria enjoying a cup of hot chocolate and related the events of the day.

'Do you think the village elder will back down once he's considered his options?'

'Yes, I believe he will. I may not have understood all that Lamis said this morning, but it was obvious, even to me, that she put the fear of God into all three of them, and my new health worker told Sister Agatha that Lamis had achieved in five minutes what other women had failed to do in decades. She obliterated that *dai*, Gloria. The woman will never practice again in the Akbarpur region.'

'Then, what happened to Lamis in Jusuf Abbas's hovel in Old Delhi may have had a silver lining after all.'

'Maybe, but in the meantime, I've written to Mahatma Gandhi about her case, and asked him to find constitutional ways to stop child marriage in its tracks.'

Gloria's eyebrows knitted together. 'I thought it was illegal anyway?'

'It is, but our Imperial rulers are far too busy fighting border skirmishes to uphold the rights of Indian women. Gandhi, however, has no such handicap. He's a pacifist after all, and a lawyer. Hopefully he can make a difference.'

'Aren't you playing with fire?'

'Maybe, but girls like Lamis have to be educated if India is to modernise in the twentieth century, and Gandhi is probably the most high-profile person to influence this.'

'Then let's hope it works. But how do we get the message across in the meantime?'

'I've no idea, but we must do something or our clinics will be overrun by religious fanatics, intransigent *dais* and irritable village elders who believe their authority is being usurped.'

'I did warn you, Mac,'

'I know, and you were right, but they cannot be allowed to intimidate us.'

'Well, Lamis certainly put a stop to them today. Her action should be an example to all our health workers.'

'Exploiting Lamis's built-in hatred of Muslim men to set an example for others, Gloria, is not fair, and I won't allow it. She's still a child and mentally wounded from being married off to Jusuf Abbas. I cannot allow her to be used like some pawn for our benefit.'

'But I want to help, Umi.' My ward stood in the doorway in her cotton nightie, her bare feet misting the varnished floorboards.

'Lamis, what are you doing out of bed?'

'I could not sleep, and Doctor Hodgson is right. Muslim girls must learn from my story. It is powerful, and I can give them hope.'

'But Lamis, we have no right to use you for this purpose.'

She crossed to Gloria's side and stood her ground, her lopsided frame patently obvious beneath her knee-length shift. 'Why not?'

'Because you have been through enough and you're vulnerable.'

'What is vulnerable?'

Gloria wrapped her arm around Lamis's waist. 'Being in need of protection from others.'

Lamis puckered her bottom lip. 'I already have . . . prot . . . protection. I have Umi.'

'Who loves you and doesn't want you to get hurt again. But I know that you are a fighter. You proved that today,' Gloria ignored my pained expression. 'Your unique story will help other girls fight against out-dated and illegal traditions.'

'What is unique?'

'Very special,' replied Gloria, kissing her on the cheek. 'Now off to bed with you before we are both evicted from Alipore Road.'

'What is evicted?'

I had had enough. 'Lamis. Bed!'

By the following morning, Gloria was on a mission. Within days, leaflets were being printed in five languages and distributed to all our clinics and training courses around the Punjab, explaining Lamis's story and operations.

Professor Pandi, who lectured on Indian cultures, religions and languages at the Lady Hardinge, was approached by Gloria to assist in making the translations simple and clear for women to understand. He even added a footnote inviting Punjabi women to apply for training as health workers.

Missionary staff and midwives throughout the province were keen to spread the word, and Lamis quickly became a beacon of hope in India's male dominated world.

I was highly nervous about it all, but Lamis delighted in knowing that her story was having a positive effect on girls of her age. She never tired of appearing at training courses if Gloria asked her too and even more astonishing was her total lack of interest in her celebrity status. It didn't matter how often women wanted to cuddle her or give her praise, she remained the little girl I'd always known, and never failed to turn to me if she was worried about anything or needed reassurance.

We travelled the length and breadth of Punjab, going from clinic to clinic, with Lamis being feted while I checked on the staff, carried out clinical examinations, took photographs for my reports and undertook the odd minor operation, always making sure I paid my respects to the village elders to keep them onside before we left.

On our return to Alipore Road, Mrs Appleby was waiting at the door, a hot meal on the stove, a warm bath and bed for Lamis and a large gin and tonic for me before she departed to her own small house for the night. I burned the midnight oil recording my findings in my medical journal and making copious notes for the following day.

All in all, I thought, watching the peach muslin curtains waft in the evening breeze, life was proving to be productive and inspiring, but despite this, beneath my optimism at the progress we had made in the WCHS, constant self-doubt continued to keep me awake during the wee small hours.

Chapter Nine

An invitation to have lunch with Ruby was waiting for me on my arrival back at Alipore Road in late June.

Ruby and Gloria had become good friends during my absence, although I was oblivious to this as I walked into the lobby of the Metropolitan Hotel that Friday.

'Why on earth did you pick this hotel, Ruby?' She was seated in a lounge chair with a large aspidistra framing her emerald-green cloche hat.

'Why not, Mac? It has one of the best restaurants in Delhi and you've never eaten here since arriving in India.'

'With good reason.' I looked around the familiar lobby and recalled tripping through it disguised as Laura Henderson on my way to the third floor. 'You may recall we frequented Room 52 on the last occasion we were here,' I hissed through clenched teeth, 'with Fatima Patel carrying out a manual vacuum aspiration on me while you turned green.'

'How could I forget, but what has that got to do with anything? You're not staying there now and anyway; your abortion was over a year ago. You've been to Aden and back since then.'

I rubbed my forehead, failing to comprehend her logic and followed her to our table.

'Now, before we go any further, Gloria tells me you're becoming cantankerous.'

'Am I?'

'You know damned well you are.'

I shrugged. 'Well, maybe a little.'

'A little? When it comes to Lamis you're positively domineering. You're like a mother hen with an ailing chick.'

'I can't help it if I worry. You know I don't want her to get damaged, Ruby. Lamis has been through enough already.'

She removed her cloche hat and matching suede gloves and placed them on the table. 'Would you say that I looked damaged, Mac?'

'You?' I laughed. 'Good Lord, Ruby, nothing short of a cannon ball could damage you. You're like the Rock of Gibraltar.'

'Maybe, but growing up with an abusive father and an alcoholic mother was hardly a bed of roses.'

I realised where this was going and didn't like it one bit. 'No, of course not, but . . .'

'No buts. Have I survived intact?'

I pushed my spine into the back of the chair by ramming my hands against the table-top and bit into my cheek. 'Lamis is hardly you.'

'And you're not the Virgin Mary. For goodness's sake, Mac, let the child have her moment of glory. It's not as if she doesn't deserve it.'

'I know that Ruby, better than anyone.'

'Then what's wrong with you? Gloria tells me that you're like a bear with a sore head. Are you jealous that she is getting all the plaudits over her "Lamis" leaflets?'

'Damn you, Ruby Tavener, you know that's not true.'

'Then what in the world is making you so tetchy?'

I dropped my head into my hands. 'I'm scared.'

Ruby sent the waiter packing and leant towards me, lowering her voice. 'Scared?'

'Yes, Ruby, scared stiff. Lamis's name is getting noticed by powerful Indian politicians who want to kick us out of India. They care nothing for her wellbeing as long as her story can be used to inflame tensions amongst the rabble-rousers.'

'Well, that's choice coming from you.' Ruby was not mincing her words and if I was hoping for sympathy, I wasn't going to get it. 'Correct me if I'm wrong but weren't you the first one to use her situation to bring down Charles Ponsonby-Pritchard on a charge of racial prejudice.' She always sounded so like Aunt Karr when she was in this mood.

'That was different.' I felt cornered.

'No, it wasn't. Gloria's leaflets highlight female injustice in exactly the same way as your newspaper article did and from what Gloria tells me, the message is getting through loud and clear.'

'But at what price?'

'Mac, Gloria's no fool. She will be the first to stop if she suspects Lamis is under pressure from this promotion.'

'I hope you're right because from where I'm sitting, Gloria is on a mission to succeed just like those Indian politicians.'

'She's certainly strong-willed, I'll give you that, but so are you.' She sat back and crossed her arms. 'Look, Mac, stop worrying about Lamis and concentrate on running the WCHS. The child can always be sent back to Frances if necessary and if I know our headmistress, she will totally protect Lamis behind those high St Saviour walls.'

The thought of Frances taking charge again helped reduced my stress levels and Ruby was right. I was becoming paranoid about my unofficial ward, and probably a pain in the backside to all and sundry in the process. I caught the head waiter's attention and dived into the lunch menu.

We had just chosen from the dessert trolley when Ruby dropped her bombshell reason for our lunch.

'Mac, I need your advice.'

'On what, exactly?' My fig trifle melted like snow on my tongue.

She placed her hand on her clutch bag and fiddled with the clasp. 'When Vijay arrived back in Delhi for your house-warming dinner, he gave me this.' She flipped the clasp with her perfectly manicured fingers and pulled out a deep blue velvet box. You could have heard a pin drop as she opened the lid.

'WOW!' I mouthed, staring at a huge yellow diamond solitaire set in platinum.

I picked up the box and studied the beautiful Asscher-cut diamond as it twinkled in the sunlight and chuckled. 'I know exactly where this came from.'

Ruby's mouth puckered. 'I didn't realise you were an expert on diamonds, Mac?'

'I'm not, but I have it on good authority that the Maharani of Panajab has one just like it, and if I'm not mistaken, it was mined in South Africa.'

She retrieved the box and peered at the jewel more closely. 'Who told you that?'

'Agnes Scott. She was involved in the theft of the famous Panajab yellow diamond when she was working in Jind.'

'Agnes Scott? Don't be daft, Mac, she's never nicked anything in her life.'

'Of course she hasn't. That's not what I meant.' I recalled Agnes telling me about her being called as a witness in a court case years before and related the story of the Maharaja of Panajab's yellow diamond lying in the gut of his murdered agent when Agnes did the post-mortem, and the part the Great Indian Bustard bird had played in the subsequent court trial to convict his murderers. 'According to Agnes, the criminals were shot at dawn and the diamond was mounted in one of the Maharani of Panajab's tiaras.'

'I hope she cleaned it first,' declared Ruby, returning the ring box to her bag.

'So, what's the big occasion? Why has Vijay given you this magnificent ring?'

She fiddled with her cutlery. 'Because he wants to marry me. It's supposed to be an engagement ring.' Her enthusiasm was about as passionate as being told she had a dose of gonorrhoea. I, by contrast, was dumbfounded.

'Marry you?'

'Don't sound so surprised.'

'I'm sorry, but it really is a bolt from the blue,' I replied, adding salt to the wound. 'I mean . . . oh hell . . . What was your answer?'

'I'm still thinking about it.'

My eyebrows crossed. 'Thinking about it! Are you mad?'

'No, Mac, but definitely ambivalent, and I don't know how to let Vijay down gently.' She beckoned me closer, keeping her voice to a whisper. 'For a start, I'm not sure I want to be the second Maharani of Jhalanpur.'

'Why ever not?'

'Because I'll be stuck in the desert for the rest of my life trapped behind palace walls, surrounded by Hindu women who believe men are Gods.'

'Don't be ridiculous.'

'It's not ridiculous.' She resembled Lamis in one of her intransigent moods. 'Then there's the thorny problem of an heir and a spare. I've never been prize heifer material, as you well know, and even if I was, after that butcher of a backstreet abortionist my mother took me to at fourteen buggered up my chances of ever having children, I can't get pregnant so what's the point?'

Her lemon souffle was beginning to sink, postponing further discussion, but my head was reeling. As a Hindu, Vijay could take as many wives as he liked, but the main purpose of polygamy was to continue the bloodline. Choosing Ruby, therefore, seemed rather impractical, to say nothing of the repercussions an ex-stripper from the Windmill Theatre in Soho would have in the court of Jhalanpur.

'Could you see me bathing in asses milk?' she quipped, swallowing the last of her dessert.

Actually, I could, but I refrained from saying so.

'What I need from you is advice on how to persuade Vijay to provide me with a hefty Swiss bank account for my old age and to go marry someone else.'

'Oh, for goodness's sake, Ruby, that's about as likely to happen as Frances becoming a prostitute.' My frustration at her reticence was obvious. 'For pity's sake, girl, stop looking as if the world has come to an end. Nine months ago, you were in danger of dying from an asthma attack because you were terrified that Vijay would leave you. Now you're terrified because he wants to make you his wife.' I gritted my teeth and pushed my petulance to one side. 'Face it, Vijay is never going to live without you, and he certainly wouldn't dream of locking you away in the Jhalanpur zenana. He's already said as much by insisting on moving to Puttaker Lodge.'

'But what happens if he changes his mind?'

'He won't. He's already told you that you'll spend your summers travelling the world or relaxing in some fantastic villa on the shores of the Mediterranean, and your winters being feted by the great and good of India in Delhi and Bombay.'

'Do you honestly think so?' Ruby was not convinced.

'Yes, I do. I was there when he said it. Apart from anything else, Vijay would never get you to agree to wearing a *ghoonghat*.'

'What's a *ghoongha*t?' Ruby genuinely had no idea.

An image of Princess Dashwanabai and her entourage boarding the ss Narkunda in Marseille, their heads and faces covered in yards of silk material sprang to mind and was quickly erased as an example. 'Do you remember what I looked like as Scheherazade on the night of the ship's Gala Ball?'

'How could I forget. It's the first and only time you've managed to upstage me, which took some doing when I was wearing my gold-sequinned Cleopatra outfit.'

I ignored her sarcasm. 'Well, the *ghoonghat* is the head and face veil that stops men seeing a Hindu wife's features.'

'You're kidding?' Ruby sat bolt upright and puckered her lips. 'There's no way I'm wearing one of those, so Vijay can go to hell.' She was now stabbing the table with her finger. 'He'd have a bloody nerve if he tried, Mac, after ogling me naked at the Windmill Theatre back in the day.'

'But you weren't married to him then.'

'No, and I'm not now. If he thinks he's going to stop me showing my face to the world he's got another thing coming. I'm a bloody Protestant for God's sake, not a Hindu, and a lapsed Protestant at that.'

I had to smile. At least she was now considering the possibility of being his wife.

'Would I have to curtsey?' I was trying to lighten the mood.

'Probably,' she mumbled, deadly serious.

'Oh, Ruby, don't look so despondent. Vijay would never make you do anything against your will, and he'd be on a hiding to nothing if he tried. Believe me, I know from experience with you.'

She sniffed the air as she thrust up her chin.

'Don't you sniff at me. You know I'm right, and Vijay knows it too. If you really want some advice from me, then before you pack your bags and head to Zurich to collect your little nest egg, I suggest you read Elsie Thompson's biography of her life in India.'

'Elsie Thompson? Who's she?'

'A third-rate Australian actress who became the second wife of the Maharaja of Tikari. I'm sure you'll have no trouble relating to her life within the Princely States.'

'Did she end up wearing this goon-thingy?'

'*Ghoonghat.* I've never seen a photograph of her in a face veil, although I believe she did pay lip-service to Hinduism, and she did call herself Sita Devi. However, that didn't stop her blazing an infamous trail through British colonial society.'

'Crikey. I've never heard of her.'

'Then it's high time you found out.'

'Righto.' She tapped the hidden ring box. 'Will the bookshop in Connaught Place stock it?'

'Probably.'

'Then I'll buy a copy before I leave for France.'

'When do you sail?'

'Next Monday.'

The thought of losing her to Europe for three months depressed me, as did the fact that this was the third wedding proposal I had heard about in as many months and was doing nothing for my self-esteem.

'Can you order us some coffee in the lounge while I go to the lavatory? I'm about to wet myself.' She rushed away, leaving her clutch bag on the table. I picked it up and shook my head in disbelief.

At the dining room door she ground to a halt as if shot, saw me holding the bag in the air, then dashed back and grabbed it out of my hand.

'Jesus,' was all she said, as she rapidly thumped her breastbone.

'Ruby, either put that rock on your finger or get it into a bank vault without delay. If it gets stolen, Vijay will be within his rights to have you banished from India without a penny to your name, and I can guarantee that Agnes Scott's Great Indian Bustard will not be around to come to your rescue.'

I watched Ghalib drive her away in her Lincoln Sedan and felt strangely abandoned, realising that I wouldn't see this crazy friend again until we were all in Simla at the end of the summer for Frances's wedding. Cycling back to the office for a meeting with Gloria, I wondered whether I would survive India without her constant support. A lot could happen in three months, I thought, and knowing my luck, it would not all be plain sailing.

Chapter Ten

The night was hot and muggy and as usual, I couldn't sleep. Having tossed and turned for hours I got up, dressed in jodhpurs, a white aertex short-sleeved shirt and leather riding boots, grabbed my topi and quietly left the house, heading for the local stables. I hadn't ridden a horse since being up on the North-West Frontier with the Khyber Rifles during the Afridi uprising and I longed for a long-overdue trek through the hills to clear my head.

Dawn was breaking as I trotted down the lane on a piebald pony named Sandy, while Myna birds, chirruping in the trees, announced the start of the day. It felt good to have the breeze on my face as we left the urban sprawl behind and with the horse chomping at the bit I squeezed her flank and we cantered across the wide-open fields, picking up speed as the exhilaration of the gallop freed my mind of the stresses and strains of work.

I should have done this more often, I thought, as the contours of the city faded and we pounded the flat lands towards the undulating hills beyond New Delhi. We mounted the ridge and Sandy slowed, her lungs pumping from her exertion. I leant over and patted her neck, the rough texture of her mane tickling my cheek.

'Wow, girl, that's enough for now.' I released the reins and slid down off the saddle. Sandy's head dropped to the ground and she munched away on sporadic tufts of coarse grass while I wiped grimy sweat from my hairline with the back of my hand and rested my buttocks on a large rocky outcrop. The silence was eerie but calming so I closed my eyes and slowed my breathing.

'Time to get some perspective,' I whispered, and took in the views over the city to the barren plains beyond. The tranquillity of this spot was cathartic, the cat's cradle of jumbled thoughts rotating in my head gradually unravelling as the Indian subcontinent washed over me like Highland mist.

I was now seven months into my health project, and the WCHS was established in five districts of the Punjab, with newly trained health workers beginning to take up their posts in remote villages and towns. It had been slow going, but local Punjabi women were starting to gain confidence in attending the clinics and I was hopeful that infant survival rates would improve from our efforts.

'So why am I permanently angry?' I demanded of my surroundings.

Without prompting, my thoughts turned to my personal life. I pictured Frances and Jim laughing together in her quarters at St Saviour's and my heart ached. An image of Ruby and Vijay linking arms as they stood on their terrace caused my stomach muscles to tense. Jonathon's voice waxing lyrically about his beloved Henriette dragged me deep into a pit of despair. What was causing me so much angst was nothing more than pure jealousy.

I longed for the same things Frances, Ruby and Henriette had as young women, and I lamented the lack of a man in my life, like a widower lamented the absence of his wife.

Although I was enjoying the challenges of my medical career by day, by night I was constantly tortured with exotic sexual dreams of encounters at sea or intimate rendezvous in luxurious hotel suites, leaving me utterly frustrated and depressed on waking. What I wanted was someone who would love me, care for me, satisfy my sexual desire and be there when I needed support. Most of all, I wanted to stop feeling isolated and alone and this dilemma was beginning to affect my ability to function.

Subconsciously, I had tried to fill the void by caring for Lamis, but that was unfair on her and could never counter the empty hole in my heart. I had ignored the problem for months, burying my head in the sand hoping for the best, but my choices were clear. Either I abandoned my profession and all it entailed, or accepted the consequences of working in a man's world trying to compete on their level. Deep down, I yearned for a lover like Tom Wallace, but it was not reality and the sooner I accepted that the better.

I stared through the hazy orange glow blurring Delhi's rooftops, and in the stillness of the dawn I finally faced my demons. No-one else was to blame for my predicament, so there was no point in taking my frustration out on others. I was single with emotional needs, but I had chosen to be a career woman and I had to learn to wear my yoke like a shroud if I wanted to remain independent.

Sandy shook her mane and neighed. The pony was right. There was no point in sitting here getting maudlin over something I could do nothing about. Better to learn the lesson, accept the inevitable and be thankful for small mercies. I picked up the reigns, pulled myself back into the saddle and made tracks back along the ridge.

Sandy carefully picked her way down the incline and once on flat ground, my thigh muscles clenched, I rose from the saddle, pushed down on my heels and we galloped back to the Civil Lines, leaving my melancholy far behind on the ridge.

A postcard of the Trevi Fountain arrived some days later. Ruby and Vijay were in Rome and Ruby's staccato message seemed to imply that they were married.

Arrived Rome last night. Quick visit to Monaco Town Hall last Saturday from Cannes. Local mayor did the honours. All rather rushed. Been drowning in bubbly ever since. Will be bathing in ass's milk tonight after doing the sights. Wish me luck. R x

I telephoned Frances immediately to give her the news.

'Oh, Mac, I don't know whether to laugh or cry. Do you think it will turn out alright?'

'Heaven knows, Frances. The Rajmata is going to have apoplexy when she hears the news, and I wouldn't want to be Vijay when Lord Irwin finds out either. Maharajas marrying British showgirls give the government the jitters. I doubt Ruby will ever be invited to formal gatherings, Maharani of Jhalanpur or not.'

'I shouldn't think that will bother Ruby. One thing she hates more than curry is socialising with pompous, superior British aristocrats. According to her, they are all cross-eyed, pigeon-chested, interbred toffs.'

Frances had a point. 'I rather think Vijay agrees with her.'

'Do we know when they will be back?'

'Not exactly. Ruby did say she wanted to see what I looked like tripping down the aisle as an aging bridesmaid dressed from head to toe in crepe georgette, but I think that was a joke.'

'Joke or not, I'd better include them in the guest list, just in case.' Panic was making her vocal cords tremble.

'Do you really want Ruby upstaging you on your big day?'

'Better Ruby than Sybil Wetherington.'

'Sybil? I had no idea the Wetherington's were coming to the wedding.' An image of Sybil's large bosom draped in yards of taffeta and netting made me titter.

'Well, you do now. They were the first to accept our invitation and Sybil even suggested Archie as the father of the bride.'

'Lord Wetherington?'

'The very same. Sybil seems to think that they are almost family, and as my parents can't be there, Archie, being a Lord, would give the wedding party an air of grandeur.'

I couldn't stop laughing.

'I tell you, Mac, I wish I had never agreed to this wedding.'

'Well, it's too late now, and as I've never been a bridesmaid, let alone a Maid of Honour, don't you dare bottle out.'

'Even if I dress you in violent pink organza and voile?'

'Don't push it, Trotter.'

The British exodus to Simla was well advanced when Lamis and I left the dak bungalow in Patiala and climbed into a tonga.

'Patiala Railway Station,' I announced, watching our luggage being loaded into a second tonga by the guesthouse mali. 'Be careful with that trunk,' I shouted, as my monogrammed leather chest balanced precariously on the edge of the wagon.

'Yes, Memsahib,' he said, bowing from the waist.

'Hasan,' called the housekeeper from the entrance steps. He stood to attention and the trunk rocked alarmingly. 'Be careful with the Memsahib Doctor's luggage.' She waddled down the garden path and handed him my medical bag.

'I'll take that,' I said, my heart in my mouth.

A loud scraping, then a thud delivered the trunk to the floor of the flatbed, and I sighed with relief. I looked at my watch. 'We only have twenty minutes to catch the train, Lamis. I suggest we go ahead and hope the luggage follows in good time.'

Lamis's quick retort to the gardener in Urdu was too fast for me to understand but there was a noticeable surge in his loading.

The station was like an ant's nest of activity, and we had to push our way to the platform where the train to Kalka was standing, steam rising from its stack.

'Your compartment, Memsahib?' asked the stationmaster, moving the locals out of my way.

'B6,' I replied and eased Lamis ahead of me, then followed the uniformed officer along the train carriages. He flung open a door and helped me inside, ignoring Lamis, who dutifully stood back and waited. I glared at the Indian, stepped back off the train, took Lamis's hand and helped her climb the step. 'That will be all,' I said pointedly. 'Please make sure our belongings are loaded in the baggage wagon before we leave.' I handed him two annas and slammed the door shut in his face.

'Umi, you were not very kind.'

'An eye for an eye, Lamis,' I replied, ushering her into the compartment.

'I no understand,' she replied, placing her bonnet in the hat rack.

'I do not understand.' I repeated, sounding like Frances.

'Sorry. I do not understand.'

'Then I will explain once we are on our way.'

Four hours later we were in Kalka and Alastair Galbraith was standing, as large as life, on Platform 2 waiting for us.

'Good day, Mr Galbraith. This is Lamis Abbas, my ward.'

'Doctor Stuart MacKenzie, I'm pleased to see that you're looking much more rosy-cheeked since our last meeting.' He turned and tipped his hat to Lamis. 'And Lassie, it's a pleasure to meet you.' He bent to shake her hand, and I winced, praying he hadn't crushed her metacarpal bones. She, however, seemed delighted with the greeting.

'The pleasure is mine,' she announced in perfect English.

'Well, I'll be.' Alastair looked at me, his eyes twinkling, and I smiled.

'If you'll give me ten minutes to put this young lady safely on the train to Simla, along with most of our luggage, I'll be free to join you to inspect your salt mine.'

I led Lamis down the platform and across the track to the other side where the narrow-gauge steam train and brightly painted carriages stood waiting to leave. Affectionately named the toy train, this quaint mode of transport traversed the foothills above the Kaushalya River on its sixty-mile journey to India's famous mountain retreat, providing passengers with spectacular views of the Kaushalya valley and the far Himalayan mountains as it climbed to over seven-thousand-feet above sea level. It felt good to be back in the fresh mountain air, luscious vegetation and stunning scenery which attacked the senses from all directions.

'Now, Lamis, you have your ticket?'

'Yes, Umi.'

'And your tiffin box?'

'Yes, Umi.'

'Good. Doctor Iris will be in Simla to meet you and I'm sure the students from last year will be eagerly awaiting your arrival at Reading Hospital.'

'Yes, Umi.'

'I'll be back within the month. The Maharaja of Jhalanpur has kindly offered us the use of his guesthouse at Mallards, but you will stay with the other girls at the hospital and take your meals there until I return.'

'Yes, Umi. You have said so, many times, Umi.' She looked up at me from under her long black eyelashes and I couldn't help feeling amused at her irritated reprimand.

'Very well. I know I'm fussing but this is the first time I have let you travel alone. Don't speak to any strangers and when you see Miss Frances tomorrow, tell her I promise not to be delayed.'

'Yes, Umi.' She was now fidgeting so I let her go and stood by the window waiting for the train to depart.

Out of the corner of my eye I caught sight of our baggage being loaded by two turbaned station coolies and two minutes later the train's whistle blew, steam shot from the engine stack and the wheels slowly began to turn.

'Bye, Lamis. Take care and work hard at your studies.'

Her hand, behind the glass, waved madly at me and I felt myself blink. 'Must be the dust,' I mumbled, and waved back until the rear of the baggage wagon disappeared from view. Coughing to clear my throat, I made my way back to Alistair standing by the exit.

'Well, Doctor, I suspect that young lassie has an interesting history.'

'She does that, Mr Galbraith. Perhaps I can tell it as we make our way to Jalandhar.'

Chapter Eleven

We spent the night on the outskirts of Jalandhar and made an early start to cover the final fifty miles to the mine. The roads were nothing more than potholed tracks and when we finally arrived it was dusk, I was travel-sore and wondering if this has been such a good idea.

'What we need is a snifter to wet our whistles,' announced my companion as he carried our luggage into a weather-beaten wooden boarding house which needed some tender loving care.

My back creaked as I climbed the veranda steps, and I was never so glad to see a wicker bathchair in all my life. Sinking onto the rather threadbare cushions, I stretched out my legs and took in the magnificence of the snow-capped Himalayas catching the last of the day's sunrays which were turning the white peaks to a deep burnt amber. Night shadows chased the sun from the valley floor, steadily rising over the crags and across the higher snow fields, reminding me of my days in the Khyber Pass.

'Here, lubricate your larynx with this.' Alastair handed me a ginger ale laced with rum. 'That should revive your spirits.'

Fermented sugarcane hit the spot perfectly and I sighed. 'This is liquid velvet, Alistair. You're a life saver.'

'Aye well, I'll not argue with you there, Doctor, but perhaps you'd go easy on the compliments or Mrs Galbraith will be wanting to know why, and no mistake.'

I pictured Mrs Galbraith as an expansive hipped lady with greying hair and kind eyes. 'I hope I have the pleasure of meeting your wife one day.'

'Aye, she'd be delighted. You two would get on famously, Doctor. Pamela was a bit of an adventurer herself in her day.'

'Really? Tell me more.'

He settled into the adjoining bathchair and loosened his collar. 'My Pammy grew up fascinated by tales of the Northern Lights, but living in the borders, she was not best placed to get a good view. At fifteen, she hitched a ride to Ullapool on the back of a lorry then stowed away on a freighter going to Svalbard. The crew eventually found her covered in coaldust and in need of the lavatory.'

'Did she manage to see the Aurora Borealis?'

'Aye, she did that, and got a spanking from her Pa for her trouble.'

I recalled my own attempt at leaving home. 'I tried to run away to stay with my cousins when I was eleven, after Ma chastised me for getting caught scrumping in Reverend MacDougal's orchard. I got as far as Glenelg before my Pa caught up with me boarding the little ferry across to Skye.'

'What happened then?'

'I was sent to my room and had to apologise to Ma in front of the whole congregation the following Sunday. I was mortified and never did it again.'

'There you go. You and my Pammy would hit it off just fine.'

The sun dropped behind a precipice and a chill wind set in.

'Time for supper,' he added. 'You must be starving.'

He eased himself from his seat and wandered inside. I followed, my nostrils picking up the aroma of tandoori chicken pervading the walls of the rustic resthouse, leading me straight to the dining table.

Another early start followed, and by mid-morning, our dust-covered truck arrived at the entrance to what can only be described as Dante's inferno. Not a blade of grass was visible in this stark, rock-strewn landscape, where men in grubby dhotis and turbans, bent double from years of hard labour, were being swallowed up by the huge mouth of a mountain, the craggy edges glimmering with pink crystals illuminated by the dimly lit paraffin lamps within.

I climbed down as an explosion shook the ground under my feet and a cloud of pink dust erupted from the bowels of the earth like the breath of a giant fire dragon. I backed away as if shot.

'What in the world was that?' My ears were ringing.

'Gunpowder,' replied Alistair, covering his mouth with his arm as the dust settled all around us. 'There are five levels to this mine going down hundreds of feet, and they blast the rock salt to get at it. They've been mining here since the early eighteenth century.'

'It looks like it,' I said, trying to keep my footing. 'Is the whole mountain made of salt?'

'Most of it, and the process of extracting it hasn't changed in all that time. The miners drill holes into the rock with hand augers, then pack the holes with gunpowder and light the fuse. There are many deaths, as you can imagine.'

He led me on, my view blocked by a massive, eight axled tractor and trailer which appeared from the tunnel piled high with boulders of rose-coloured blocks. The transporter reminded me of a gaudy fairground ride, but in this bleak, pitted and scarred landscape it looked incongruous with its bodywork painted blue, pink, green and yellow, with white Punjabi writing splashed across it and decorative badges, rosettes and coloured ribbons hanging from every metal edge.

Rounding the trailer's bulky rear end with my head reeling, I took in the scene on the other side and thought my eyes were deceiving me. There, forming a long straggly conger line, were Indian women of all ages, dressed in ragged saris of every hue, their heads covered and their skin resembling rose alabaster from the constant dust. They were handing large lumps of rock salt from one to the other, the last women handing her load to a dhoti-clad skeletal man who threw it onto an ever-growing pink pyramid.

I was horrified at the dangers these women were in. Apart from obvious physical accidents, ingesting so much salt dust, especially for those who were pregnant would, at the least, cause high blood pressure and at the worst, preeclampsia, kidney failure and possible heart disease, to say nothing of life-threatening damage to the unborn child.

'How can this be allowed, Alistair?' I yelled above the noise of the tractor reversing towards the line. 'It's not only inhuman; its tantamount to second-degree murder.'

'Aye, I couldn't agree more, Lassie, but mineral wealth takes precedence over human life in India and local women are cheap labour. What is more, our Imperial masters condone it.'

If Lord Irwin had appeared at that moment I would have shot him. 'I need to examine every pregnant woman in this line, Alistair,' I shouted, pulling my camera from my bag and bringing the women into focus. 'Where do I find the man in charge?'

'He'll be in his office down by the entrance, but you could have a struggle on your hands. For a start, his English is none-existent, and he won't take kindly to being confronted by a woman. He will probably try to ignore you.'

'We'll see about that.' I felt my Stuart-MacKenzie backbone stiffen.

By the time the office came into view, I had donned my laboratory coat, pinned my WCHS metal badge to its lapel and was holding my medical bag prominently in front of me. I knocked on the wooden hut door and without waiting for an answer, stepped inside. The look on the manager's face was a picture of utter bewilderment.

'Good morning, Sir,' I announced in Hindi, hoping he understood. 'My name is Doctor Stuart-MacKenzie from the Women's Community Health Service and I want to examine any women working here who are with child.' I plonked my medical bag on his desktop and took my stethoscope from the interior.

Alistair towered over the man like a rugby prop-forward over a scrumhalf as I pulled an official document from my pocket and slammed it down in front of him.

'What is this?' he demanded; his Punjabi accent very prominent.

'An order from the Director of Public Health in Calcutta.' I prodded an official government blue stamp at the bottom of the document and before he could react, retrieved the paper and returned it to my pocket.

Alistair opened a door to my left. 'Will this do as an examination room?'

I poked my head inside, ignoring the manager. It was full of metal filing cabinets but I noted a rickety metal desk against the far wall. 'It will have to. I'll use that desk as a bed.' Turning back to the supervisor I continued our one-sided conversation. 'Where can I get some fresh water?'

He walked outside and pointed to another shack close by. As I approached, the smell of raw sewage was intense, and I gagged.

'Doctor Mac, leave that to me. You go with our friend here,' he glared at the man cowering against his office door, 'and gather the pregnant women together.'

Placing my stethoscope around my neck, I headed back up to the mine wondering how I was to get the women to understand me. I needn't have worried. As I appeared, they all stopped what they were doing and one stepped forward, placed her righthand in front of her eyes, palm inwards, her fingertips almost touching her forehead, bent from the waist and said, '*Aadab.*'

'*Tasleem,*' I replied, surprised that none had their faces covered. Must be Sikhs, I decided, and frowned as she shied away from me, her eyes lowered to the ground at the sight of the manager.

My arm telescoped sideways, stopping him in his tracks, and I deliberately stepped in front of him. 'Please. Who is pregnant here?' I indicated my meaning by drawing an arc in the air with my hands from my waist to my groin.

For a few seconds nothing happened, then one younger woman dropped her lump of salt on the ground, held her hands over her abdomen and stepped away from the line. Another followed. When the third woman joined them, I turned to the manager and pointed back down the rugged track. His eyes oscillated madly, his head constantly rocking, but he obviously didn't want to lose face in front of these women so he nodded and led the way.

With lots of coaxing and reassurance, I examined each girl in turn. One was hardly showing, one was about six months pregnant and the third in danger of going into premature labour at any moment. I permitted the first girl to remain at the mine but insisted that the other two were to stop work immediately and return to their village.

'Alistair, I should speak to their village elder. Is that possible?'

'I don't see why not, Doctor.'

'Good. How much are the girls paid?'

Alistair shrugged, ushered the manager into his office and closed the door, reappearing as I was helping the heavily pregnant woman climb into the back of the truck. He nodded in my direction and climbed in behind the wheel.

'Do you have any annas?' he asked, as we drove away.

The village was close by, and we caused great excitement as our passengers were helped down from the backseat and stood motionless beside the vehicle's bumper.

'Where do you live?' They pointed to some mud huts and led the way.

I was amazed to see how clean their huts were inside. The dirt floors had been recently swept, tin pans and utensils hung from hooks in the rafters and straw bedrolls were suspended in rope mangers attached to the circular walls.

I dug in my bag for my purse and extracted a pile of annas.

'No work until your baby is born.' I said, handed each girl some money. I then held my hands in prayer. '*Rab rakha*,' I said, bowing my head and stepping away. 'May God protect you.'

Alistair had found the village elder who seemed delighted to have an English lady in her white coat from the government in Delhi come to see him. We sat cross-legged in his mud hut with the rest of the villagers hovering outside, and with Alistair acting as mediator, I told him no woman was to go to the mine if she was pregnant. He constantly bobbed up and down from the waist, repeating the word '*Hanji*.' More annas were handed over for his trouble and we departed the village with me feeling rather righteous.

'I'd say that went well, Lassie,' Alistair remarked, as we made our way back to our lodgings.

'For today, maybe, but will it last?' My mind was buzzing. A clinic was definitely needed in the area, and I could only achieve that with the help of the local mission hospital. 'Alistair, I need to send a cable to my Chief Sanitary Inspector.'

'Maybe the local train station will have a telegraph office.'

'Then let's try there? I want these women to have a maternity clinic in the area with fresh running water, better sanitation and an offer of free baby food.'

'And the British mine owners? How do you propose to stop them using pregnant women in their workforce?'

'Gosh, I've no idea. It will take someone higher up the pecking order than me to achieve that, Alistair, but a report to my boss in Calcutta should help.'

'Not to mention that official document from the Director of Public Health.'

I shuffled in my seat and bit the side of my lip.

'It was from the Director of Public Health, wasn't it?' Alistair peered at me sideways, sounding suspicious.

'Not exactly.'

'What do you mean, not exactly? Who was it from?'

'The clerk of the Family Court in Delhi.'

'Say that again.' Our vehicle ground to a halt in a cloud of brown dust. 'Are you telling me it had nothing whatsoever to do with Public Health?' Alistair's expression match that of Ma when I told her I was going to India.

'I'm afraid so.'

'Then, in the name of heaven, what has it to do with?'

I swallowed hard. 'It's an official summons for me to attend a hearing at the Office of the Guardian in October. I'm hoping to become Lamis Abbas's legal guardian.'

'Well, I'll be.'

'Sorry about that, Alistair, but it arrived just as I was leaving home, and as it was written in English and had a rather large official stamp on the bottom, I thought it might come in useful.'

'It certainly did that, Doctor, and there's no need to apologise, but what will the Public Health Director say when he finds out?'

'He won't say anything unless you tell him, and what he doesn't know can't concern him.' I winked and we both burst out laughing.

'Do you use these covert tactics often in the WCHS?'

'Only when the situation demands it, and to be honest, Alistair, I can't take all the credit. I happen to have had a very good teacher when I arrived in India.'

Lord Cottesmore would be tickled pink at my ruse, I thought, as the train station hove into view.

By the end of the month, Jonathon and I had achieved the impossible. We had three clinics set up in the Jalandhar region each with running water and proper drainage. It had not been easy, and Jonathon had spent most of his time arguing with intransigent ICS staff who constantly put obstacles in his way. Finally, a genuine official order from Viceroy's House in Delhi, instructing the Province's Commissioner of Public Works to co-operate, did the trick. Meanwhile, I was busily organising local training courses and the Missionary Sisters took over running the clinics and persuading indigenous birthing attendants to join the call to become health workers.

It had been a long, arduous few weeks and I couldn't wait to return to Simla and the comfortable, lush surroundings of Mallards's guesthouse after days of creaking beds, cold water showers and poor sanitation. But before that, I had to write my report to Sir Peter about our progress in Jalandhar. With my photographs spread out across the bed, each highlighting the enormous injustice of female manual labour in deep and opencast mining, my pen shot across the page, the content becoming more impassioned by the sentence. As my anger grew, Aunt Karr's lilting accent echoed in my ears.

It's no good getting intense about this, Elizabeth. Men the world over have treated women as second-class citizens for generations. Your protest will be a cry in the wilderness, dear. Mark my words.'

'But I can't just sit back and do nothing, Karr?'

'Then leave, dear.'

'That's ridiculous. I can't walk away after seeing such female abuse. It's not right.' I stared again at the photographs. 'Men should not be allowed to use us in this way, then leave us holding the baby.'

'Are we talking about men in general or Tom Wallace in particular?'

'That's enough!'

Chapter Twelve

The screeching of metal against metal dragged me from my fragmented slumber as the toy train slowly pulled into Simla station. I stretched up to the hat rack to retrieve my valise and medical bag and caught sight of my dishevelled reflection in the bulkhead mirror. It was not a pretty sight. My hair stood on end, dark shadows ringed my bloodshot eyes and my skin was decidedly pasty.

Stepping onto the platform on a balmy early September evening, I looked around, smiling at the familiar scene of lush vegetation, Colonial architecture and abundant, fragrant blossom.

'Over here, Mac,' called Jim, waving his topi above the throng. I made my way to where he and Frances were standing. She took one look at my face and tutted.

'What you need, my girl, is a dose of Sanatogen tonic and a good night's sleep. Where's your luggage?'

She wrapped her arms around me, gave me a hug and sent Jim off to locate my trunk. 'Here, let me take that.'

I handed over my medical bag and followed her out onto the station forecourt, my valise slung over my shoulder and my topi held by its chinstrap. It felt so good to have her take control, which she did with her usual quiet authority.

Frances was not the headmistress of a well-run private girl's school for nothing, I thought, and knowing how stressful my weeks in the north had been, she was the ideal person to take me under her wing.

Jim appeared moments later, striding across the concourse ahead of two dhoti-clad coolies struggling with my trunk, their progress constantly hampered by a crush of bodies pouring out onto the street like a disturbed nest of ants.

'Right, Doctor Stuart-MacKenzie,' he announced as he opened the door of Ruby's small cream Hillman, let's get you to Mallards.'

I was grateful for some well-sprung seating and relaxed back as Jim took the wheel. The Mall was busy with people on their way out to dinner, all dressed in their finery, making me feel decidedly out of place. Climbing to the Ridge at ten miles an hour, Frances decided to get down to business.

'Mac, the money has finally come through for the Lady Irwin science laboratory at St Saviour's.' She was beaming at me from the other side of the car. 'How you managed to persuade Lady Irwin to raise the funds is beyond me, but Year 6 has never stopped pestering me to get the laboratory up and running before our autumn term begins.'

My mind immediately switched to Poona, and I recalled how fascinated and enthusiastic the students had been about my life as a doctor when I stayed there the previous year. At the Viceroy's Garden Party here in Simla, Lady Irwin had asked me if there was anything else she could do as President of the Countess of Dufferin's Fund before she and Lord Irwin finally left for England. I had suggested raising funds for a laboratory at St Saviour's in her name where the students could be taught biology and chemistry with a view to becoming medical clinicians. It had been a long shot, particularly as girls from the "top-drawer" were expected to grace the drawing rooms of colonial India as wives and mothers, not doctors, but Lady Irwin had thought it a splendid idea and, true to her word, had motivated the charitable ladies of the Home Counties to raise the money for this good cause.

'Quite right too,' said Jim from the front seat, referring to Frances's last comment.

'That's all very well for you to say, Jim Hamilton, but deciding where to locate the laboratory has been a real headache for me.'

'Why?' I asked, trying to work out where Bunsen burners, petri dishes and microscopes could be purchased in India.

'Because I fear the girls will blow the whole school to smithereens during one of their covert scientific experiments.'

'Oh, surely not, Frances?' I pictured Dorothy Wainthrop, Cecilia Stamford and Penelope Abraham, imitating the three witches from Act 1 of Macbeth, bubbling up some dangerous concoction in a cauldron in the dead of night. The thought rather amused me.

'You may jest, Mac, but I'd rather be safe than sorry, so I've decided to locate it as far away from the main building as possible, in the old stable block.'

'But that's Trotter's territory. What does the school mascot think about being blown-up instead?'

Frances sniffed. 'Trotter is being re-housed in the old pump room, whether she likes it or not.'

'Poor Trotter,' muttered Jim, under his breath.

'What do you mean, poor Trotter?' Frances was having none of Jim's asides. 'She's a sow for goodness's sake, not one of the school Governors.'

'If you say so, Fran, but do the students known you are about to evict the poor animal from her pigsty?'

'Oh, for the love of . . .'

We had arrived at the gates of Mallards, which was fortuitous, as any more chuntering from Jim could well have put an end to his pending nuptials. The car skirted the main house and veered to the left down a long gravel drive to the guesthouse, nestling in the trees some four-hundred yards further on. Mrs Appleby and Lamis were standing outside awaiting our arrival and I was delighted to see Lamis in her Reading Hospital sari, looking for all the world like a young nurse.

I was just climbing out of the car when I looked up and gasped. There, strolling down the drive as if he owned the place was Duncan Fitzpatrick, his khaki jodhpurs, bottle green polo shirt and brown leather riding boots showing off his physique to perfection.

'What the hell is he doing here?' I complained through the side of my mouth.

'I'll tell you later,' whispered Frances, turning to Jhalanpur's veterinary surgeon and smiling diplomatically.

'Cailin, you're back. I thought I might have missed you. I must leave tomorrow for Bombay.'

Pity my train wasn't delayed, I thought, as his arms wrapped me in a bear hug and the heady scent of bergamot from his eau-de-cologne overwhelmed my senses. 'Duncan, what a surprise.' I pulled back and saw my reflection in his familiar emerald-green eyes. 'Are you in Simla on business or pleasure?'

Frances nudged my arm.

'Business. I'm organising a race meeting in Jhalanpur this October in honour of the Maharaja's homecoming with his new Maharani.' He winked, using Vijay and Ruby's formal titles in front of Mrs Appleby and Lamis. 'I've been holding meetings all week with various dignitaries and equestrians here in Simla to finalise the plans.'

'Interesting,' I said, walking towards Lamis, leaving Jim to continue the conversation.

'Good evening, Umi.' She rose on tiptoe to peck my cheek.

'Good evening, Lamis, how is life at the Reading Hospital?' Her nose twitched and she shrugged. 'Then you are no doubt pleased to be staying here with me from now on. Mrs Appleby, how was your stay with your sister in Lucknow?'

'Oh, very nice, Doctor Mac, but far too hot. The mountain air is much more to my liking, and may I say, it's good to have you back again.'

'It's good to be back, believe me. Was everything in order at the guesthouse when you arrived?'

'It was Doctor, and dinner is ready when you are. I suggest you go and freshen up after your journey and I will attend to your guests.'

I didn't need to ask, but I did. 'Duncan, will you be staying for dinner?'

'Do the Irish drink Guinness, Cailin?' I raised one eyebrow. 'To be sure I'll be joining you. Your housekeeper kindly invited me when she heard that I was to eat alone at the Corstorphine Hotel tonight.'

Liar, I thought.

'I hope that was alright, Doctor Mac.' Mrs Appleby was fiddling with her apron. 'Mr Fitzpatrick here told me that you have been close friends since your university days and haven't seen each other for some time.'

'That's fine, Mrs Appleby. The more the merrier.' There was not a lot else I could say to this without causing offence. 'Perhaps you would act as host, Jim, while I change for dinner. Lamis, Mrs Appleby will need help with the drinks and Frances . . .' my friend's head cocked like an obedient sheep dog, 'perhaps you'd help me unpack?'

She led the way to the first floor, opening the door to the master bedroom and inviting me inside, closing the door firmly behind us.

'OK, fill me in. How long has Duncan been staying at the Corstorphine?'

'About a week.' Frances was opening my valise and pulling out dusty skirts and jackets and dropping them into the laundry basket. 'Good Lord, Mac, wherever have you been staying?'

'A long story,' I replied, running water into the bathroom's mottled green washbowl. 'So, what's the gossip on the grapevine?'

'How long have you got?'

I rubbed my face with a wet flannel. 'That bad?'

'Worse. In addition to a long line of Fishing Fleet lovelies cluttering up the hotel lobby since Duncan arrived, the buzz around town is that Lady Crawford has suddenly found a new lease of life.'

'Really. Then I imagine he hasn't been eating all alone at the Corstorphine after all.'

'As he said, do the Irish drink whisky?'

'Guinness.'

'What?'

'Nothing.' I reappeared, combing my tangled locks. 'How did he manage to wind Mrs Appleby around his little finger?'

'That was Jim's fault. He mentioned that your housekeeper was in residence here awaiting your arrival. The rest is history.'

I opened the closet door and pulled out a freshly laundered day dress which had preceded me to the Ridge. 'Will you be emasculating your future husband for me, or should I do it myself?'

'Good Lord, Mac, that's a bit harsh. Do you want my honeymoon to be a complete disaster?'

'Frances Trotter, you're sounding more like Ruby Tavener every day.'

'Speaking of Ruby, have you heard anymore from her since Rome?'

'No, not a word, but then I haven't been easy to locate during the last month.'

'Which is why Lamis had to come to me for advice.'

'Advice? On what?' I was busily buttoning the dress from the waist up.

'On what she should do about her period, which she started two weeks ago.

'What?' My fingers stopped mid-button.

'You heard me. The poor girl didn't want to ask Mrs Appleby for help, and as you hadn't made any contingency plans, she had to ask me.' She pushed my stained laboratory coat into the laundry bin with more force than was absolutely necessary.

'Oh hell, what did you do?'

'What any mother would have done in the circumstances. I took her to the local pharmacy and bought the necessary supplies.'

My day was going from bad to worse. 'Well, I'm back now and I will make sure she is well supplied in the future.'

'That's not all, Mac. She also asked me if she could now have children.'

My heart stopped. 'What did you say?'

'I told her she should ask you, as her doctor.' The barb hit home.

'Then I'll speak to her as soon as we get back home.'

'See that you do. Lamis may only be fifteen, but she is no different to any other girl of her age regarding her hormones. Relying on her awful experiences of the past to deter her from liking boys would be foolhardy in the extreme.'

I applied some lipstick and pinched my cheeks. I wasn't looking forward to my evening in Duncan's company, but after Frances's implied criticism of my efforts as a surrogate mother, even he seemed a reasonable option. 'Right,' I announced, checking my reflection in the mirror, 'let battle commence.'

'Just be careful Lady Crawford doesn't find out you've been entertaining her latest conquest or she'll be putting arsenic in your tea and I'll be minus a Maid of Honour.'

'Fat chance,' I said and held open the bedroom door.

I visited the tailoress in the Mall for a fitting after breakfast the next day on Frances's instruction. Which was why I was standing on a table surrounded by bolts of silks and satins with a young Indian girl, her mouth full of pins, kneeling at my feet when Ruby unexpectedly breezed through the door.

'Oh, you're back then?'

'No, Mac, I'm a figment of your imagination.'

'Very droll. How was the trip, Mrs Kumar Singh II?'

'Life changing. And its Maharani Manika Devi, if you don't mind.'

'Manika?'

'Correct. It's Hindi for Ruby.' She paused as the seamstress grovelled on the floor making a namaste. Ruby's eyelids lowered in acknowledgement, then she flicked her fingers indicating that the girl should continue with her work. 'If your backside wasn't so close to the ground, Mac, there would be no need to raise the hem of your bridesmaid's dress.'

I gave her one of Agnes Scott's withering looks. 'Thank you for pointing out my shortcomings, Ruby, I can see that you haven't lost your acerbic wit since becoming a Maharani.' Her large yellow diamond ring caught the sun's rays through the bow window of the fitting room.

'Just stating the obvious.' She touched the rose-pink, full-length gown with her fingertips, rubbing the silk material. 'Uhm, nice.'

'Nothing but the best for Frances,' I said, turning another twenty degrees as the young girl pressed my left ankle. 'So, when did you get into town?'

'Late last night.'

'How did you know where to find me?'

'Mrs Appleby told me.' She circled the table, her forehead creased. 'Isn't that the same colour as the camisole I bought you in Cairo?'

'Is it really necessary to remind me of that garment?' She was referring to the camisole that I had worn for Tom Wallace during our romantic nights at the Taj Mahal Hotel. The very same camisole that got me pregnant.

'Well, am I right?'

'Damn it, Ruby Devi. YES, it is. Now can we change the subject?'

'If you're so uptight about the colour connection, why did you allow Frances to suggest it?' Ruby was now sitting crossed legged on a cream damask sofa fingering a fashion magazine.

I sighed, irritated at being pressed on the point. 'I could hardly object when our bride-to-be has no idea why the colour is so significant.'

'Ah, that would explain it.'

'Exactly. Frances thinks the colour suits my complexion.'

'And she's right. Why do you think I chose it in the first place?' She peered at some article in the magazine. 'Is Tom going to be at the wedding?'

'Christ, I hope not.' The thought had never entered my head. 'I'm told he's somewhere in Africa.'

'Mozambique to be precise.'

'How on earth do you know that?'

'The Senior Surgeon at St Thomas's Hospital told Vijay when we were in London. Your ship's doctor has been there researching elephant . . . something.'

'Elephantiasis?'

'Yes, I think so. Sounds about right. What is it?'

'Gross swelling of parts of the body.'

'I've never heard sex called that before.'

'Ruby, really.' My chin dropped to the seamstress who pretended not to understand. 'Actually, its swelling from fluid retention, caused from mosquito bites.' I turned another twenty degrees and thought back to the chapter on elephantiasis in Ronald Ross's book on tropical diseases. 'A sufferer's arms and legs swell to several times their normal size and resemble the thick round appearance of an elephant's leg.'

'Good God, it sounds horrendous.'

'It is, and very painful.' I was intrigued as to why Tom was researching this particular disease.

'Is there a cure?'

'Not that I know of.' I was beginning to fidget, and a pin pieced my ankle.

'Oh, so sorry, Memsahib, Doctor. You stand very still please.'

'Vijay reckons that it's rife in Jhalanpur,' announced Ruby,' her magazine snapping shut. 'Could I catch it?'

I tried to bring Ronald Ross's supposition back into my mind. 'You'd have to be bitten a number of times by mosquitoes, Ruby, and they would need to be infected with roundworm larvae.'

'Ugh! What do I do to avoid them?'

'Sleep under a mosquito net at all times and wear long-sleeved tops and tapered trousers.' I made my final twenty-degree turn. 'Now can we change the subject?'

157

Ruby brushed my peevishness away with her fingers and returned to her magazine. 'Where is the future Mrs Hamilton, anyway?'

'In the next room, having her bodice taken in. She's lost some weight since arriving in Simla.'

'Wedding nerves?'

'Probably. Why don't you join her?' I was ever hopeful. 'No doubt she would welcome your seal of approval on her choice of wedding dress. It really is lovely.'

Ruby didn't need asking twice. 'What colour is it?' she asked, moving towards the door.

'Oyster white,' I replied, climbing down from my perch. 'And Ruby.' She turned, her hand on the door handle. 'Congratulations on becoming the Maharani of Jhalanpur, it suits you.'

'Let's hope Vijay's mother thinks so.'

'I'm sure your alluring charm will win her over, eventually. As for Frances, she'll be delighted to know that you made it back in time.'

'Me too. Wouldn't have missed it for the world.'

An hour later, Ruby strode across the tiled floor of the Wildflower Hotel lobby looking like Greta Garbo in her calf-length, beige linen suit, fox fur stole, seamed stockings, matching two-tone Oxford heeled shoes and chocolate brown slouched hat.

'Did anyone book a table?' I asked. Frances and Ruby shook their heads. 'Then we'll probably be out of luck.'

The maître d'hôtel met us at the restaurant door. 'Your Highness, Ladies, how can I help you?' His English accent was straight out of Dagenham.

'Good morning, Billings, we were hoping you could find us a table for lunch. We don't have a reservation.'

I scanned the room and found every table occupied by the great and good of colonial England.

'Leave it to me, Ma'am.' He crossed the expanse of varnished flooring to the window overlooking the hotel's expansive gardens and whispered in a diner's ear. The lady, in a flouncy day dress and matching hat looked in our direction and immediately nodded.

'Being a Maharani seems to have its advantages,' remarked Frances, watching the lady and her companion being squeezed into a corner alcove, the table invisible behind a large stone pillar while the vacated table was immediately re-laid for our use.

'If you've got it, flaunt it,' announced Ruby, sashaying through the dining room, ignoring the eyes of other diners following her progress.

'I feel like the lady's maid,' I whispered, zigzagging between the tables.

'Good practice for the church next weekend,' quipped Ruby, positioning herself in full view of the restaurant and milking the audience for all she was worth.

'Once a showgirl, always a showgirl,' I countered, as Billings pulled out her chair and she sank onto the plush regency-striped upholstery.

'A bottle of chilled champagne,' she ordered. He nodded and backed away.

'What are we celebrating?' asked Frances innocently, placing her pashmina on the back of her chair.

'Your wedding, you chump, next Saturday.' Ruby smiled at some-one across the room. I turned to see Lady Crawford standing by Billings looking very put out.

'Oh dear, we seem to have taken the last table,' remarked Frances.

'Then she should try the Corstorphine Hotel,' I replied. 'We have it on good authority that Duncan would be delighted to have some company. Is that not correct, Frances?'

'Really, Mac, you're impossible.' She blushed and turned to see if anyone was in earshot.

'So, is everything ready?' asked Ruby, losing interest in Lady Crawford.

'I think so.' Frances didn't sound too sure.

'Who's giving you away?' Our Streatham Maharani was now digging in her handbag for her cigarettes and lighter.

'Would you believe it, Lord Wetherington.'

Ruby paused. 'Did Archie have any say in the matter?'

'None whatsoever. Sybil was very insistent.' Frances puffed out her chest and imitated Sybil word for word. *"Now my dear, of course we'll be at your wedding, we wouldn't miss it for the world. As for the matter of giving you away, I've told Archie he must step into the breech. No arguments Frances, it's the least he can do."*

Ruby disappeared behind her menu, I dabbed my eyes with my hankie and Frances looked pained. Her impersonation was perfect, and I could well imagine the scene as she tried vainly to get a word in edgeways.

'Time for a toast.' Ruby lifted a glass from the waiter's tray. 'To the future Mrs Hamilton. God bless her and all who sail in her.'

'Hear, hear,' I added and also drank deeply.

'For goodness's sake, I'm not a ship.'

We both ignored her. 'Speaking of the wedding,' I said, 'who is Jim's best man to be? Do I know him?'

Frances's face resembled the deep plum colour of the dining room drapes. 'I'm afraid you do, Mac.'

It's Tom, I thought, in panic.

'Sadly, Jim's original best man has gone down with a bout of malaria, so he's had to ask Duncan.' Ruby's expression matched my thoughts. 'I know you'll groan, Mac, but he is an excellent raconteur and fortunately available.'

I gulped, not sure if I was relieved or mortified. The fact that Tom was not going to be present was one thing, but dealing with Duncan's wandering hands in my rose-pink, figure-hugging bridesmaid's dress as we ventured onto the reception dance floor, hardly made my day.

'But I thought he was in Bombay?' I said, ever hopeful.

'He is,' announced Ruby, but he'll be travelling back with Vijay on Wednesday.'

'Does that mean Vijay will be at the wedding too?' Frances looked as if she'd won the football pools.

'He'd better be Frances. I don't fancy sitting alone on one of those cold church pews, like some aging spinster aunt.'

'Ruby, you could never resemble an aging spinster aunt.'

'Do you think so?' Ruby loved compliments. 'I must say, with Lord Wetherington strutting his stuff in full dress uniform, and His Royal Highness the Maharaja of Jhalanpur looking on, it will be the wedding of the season.'

'A bit like chalk and cheese, wouldn't you say,' I noted, 'comparing Archie to Vijay.'

'Try telling Sybil that. They may have fallen on hard times after the Wall Street crash, but she can still hold her own with the aristocracy.'

'On a lighter note,' I said, changing the subject, 'what will our Maharani be wearing on Saturday?'

'Since my gold sequinned Cleopatra costume was ruined in the ship's fire, Mac,' lamented Ruby, 'I thought I would give my Manika Devi sari its first outing.' She tapped the side of her nose. 'With some adjustments you understand.'

'What sort of adjustments?' Frances sounded stressed.

'Knowing Ruby's penchant for the theatrical, Frances, I imagine she will have a bare midriff with a real emerald in her navel and a tiara stuck on her head bristling with diamonds.'

'Don't be crass, Mac. If there's one person I won't be upstaging on Saturday, it's the bride.'

'Thank goodness for that,' muttered Frances under her breath.

'Although I doubt Sybil will show such restraint when it comes to the big day. Surrogate mother of the bride and all that.'

'I need another drink,' groaned Frances.

'Good idea.' Ruby's yellow diamond glinted as it shot into the air. 'We haven't toasted me yet.'

Chapter Thirteen

S aturday dawned bright and clear, and it was all hustle and
bustle in the guesthouse. Ruby had insisted on Frances
staying with us at Mallards while Jim remained at the
Corstorphine Hotel. This way, he wouldn't see his bride until
she appeared at the church accompanied by Lord
Wetherington.

Ghalib was to act as chauffeur to the wedding party using
Ruby's Lincoln Sedan which arrived at the steps of the
guesthouse, with its sand-coloured canopy retracted. The door
handles and silver Lincoln greyhound mascot were all tied with
oyster-white bows, and a profusion of white roses and green
trailing eucalyptus leaves were strung in garlands hanging from
the dark green bodywork.

Ruby appeared from the main house after breakfast dressed
in a sapphire blue silk kaftan which cascaded to the floor in
luxurious folds. She proceeded to take charge of the constant
flow of dressmakers, hairdressers, photographer, and the
florist, the latter wanting to know where to put the various
posies and Frances's bouquet to keep them cool.

'Has anyone seen Lamis?' she shouted as she pointed the
florist in the direction of the kitchen.

'In the bath, being scrubbed from top to toe by Mrs
Appleby.' I called back.

'She's so excited,' added Frances, wandering through the
hall with her hairdresser in tow.

'Then, when she's finished abluting I have something for her.' Ruby walked into the drawing room holding up a delicate silver chain and pendant forming the word Lamis in Urdu.

'Gosh, this is beautiful.' Frances had backtracked and was holding the fine necklace up to the light.

'I found it in the souk,' explained Ruby, dropping it back into its velvet pouch. 'After what that kid has been through, I thought she deserved something special for today.'

Ruby was all heart, I reflected, as I leant on the banister rail and called Mrs Appleby. Her head appeared at the bathroom door. 'When Lamis is out of the bath, the Maharani would like a word with her.'

Minutes later, Lamis, her hair wrapped in a snowy white towel and body swathed in a matching bathrobe, stood on the landing looking pensive.

'Don't be shy, Lamis, Her Royal Highness won't bite.'

This pint pot of a girl, her eyes fixed on Ruby, descended in bare feet and bowed low. '*Assalam u alikum, Huzoor aliiii.*'

'Good morning, Lamis.' Ruby didn't do languages. 'To celebrate being Miss Frances's flower girl today, the Maharaja and I wish to present you with a small gift.' She held up the necklace and slid it around her neck. Our eyes met over Lamis's head and she winked.

Frances helped her flower girl step up onto a chair by the armoire so she could view her gift in the gilt wall mirror.

'Oh, Umi, this gift, it is beautiful.' Mrs Appleby was standing at the top of the stairs wiping her eyes on her apron.

'Grammar, Lamis,' chided Frances, ever the teacher.

'The gift is beautiful, Miss Frances,' corrected her student and received a hug for her effort.

Ruby held out her hand to help Lamis back down. 'Off you go now and get ready or we will all be late for church.'

Lamis bowed once more, thanked her profusely and ran up the stairs into Mrs Appleby's open arms.

'OK, where's mine then?' I asked, walking back into the drawing room.

'Your what?' asked Ruby, checking that the photographer had taken a shot of the presentation.

'My gift for being the Maid of Honour.'

'All you have to do is walk down the aisle without tripping over your feet and take charge of the best man. Hardly an earth-shattering event.'

'I'll have you know it is in my life, having never been a bridesmaid before.' I sounded peeved.

'Then buy your own gift. Better still, get the best man to buy you one.'

'Duncan? Any gift from him would have been purloined illegally.'

'That is sour grapes, Miss MacKenzie, and you know it. Duncan may be a womaniser, but I hardly think he's a criminal.'

'Humph.'

'Stop sounding so cynical and go and get your hair done.' Ruby was now looking at her watch. 'You have precisely one hour before your great debut.' She headed for the main house, shouting over her shoulder, 'I'll see you all in church.'

I stepped out of the Lincoln to rousing cheers from a group of St Saviour's Old Girls.

'Good morning, Doctor Mac,' shouted Cecilia Stamford, as Ghalib helped Lamis out of the Sedan. 'You look lovely, both of you.' Lamis beamed with delight.

'Thank you, Cecelia. When did you get here?'

'A group of us came up on the train yesterday for the weekend to attend the wedding. It's not every day that one's headmistress gets married, is it?'

'I guess not, and I'm sure Miss Frances will be delighted to know you are here.' We approached the church, and I sensed movement to my right. Dorothy Wainthrop was busily hiding hockey sticks behind a large hibiscus bush.

'For the guard of honour when Miss Frances leaves the church,' whispered Cecilia.

I winked at Dorothy. She winked back and put her forefinger to her lips.

'Right girls, off you go, or you'll miss the grand entrance.' They squeezed past, full of feverish excitement and disappeared into the nave to occupy their seats at the back.

'Nervous?' I asked Lamis as I plucked a fallen petal from her shoulder.

'Yes, Umi,' she replied.

'Don't worry, I'll be right behind you. Just remember to keep Miss Frances's veil straight and off the ground like we practised yesterday.' I recalled walking up and down the guesthouse hall with a cotton bedsheet knotted around my waist and Lamis following on behind hanging onto the other end. I bit my upper lip trying not to giggle and hoped I wouldn't be the one to upset the apple cart by tripping over the hem of my dress.

Jhalanpur's open landau appeared to a crescendo of 'oohs' and 'aahs' from the crowds of well-wishers now gathered out in the square, and I watched with interest as the coachman brought the horse-drawn carriage to a standstill exactly opposite the entrance. Lord Wetherington helped Frances to alight and she stood in a pool of soft morning light like some ethereal vision, the shoulders of her long lace dress draped in yards of fine, translucent, gossamer tulle, cascading to the floor like a mantle and held in place by a delicate diamante tiara.

She nervously touched her freshwater pearl necklace as soft natural curls framed her face. 'Will I do, Mac?' she asked, walking towards me on Lord Wetherington's arm.

All I could do was nod and gently squeeze her hands in mine before we gathered together in the church porch with cameras flashing from all sides.

The nave was full, most of Simla having come out to celebrate the wedding of the season, and I caught sight of Jim and Duncan in the distance resplendent in their silver-grey morning suits.

Now, don't make a fool of yourself, I prayed, as I followed Lamis down the aisle. She glided along in her rose-pink sari, her small arms outstretched, the gossamer train between her fingers, her long black hair gathered in one thick plait entwined with lilies of the valley lying across her shoulder. She looked adorable.

I nodded to Ruby and Vijay as I passed by, the Maharaja and Maharani looking imposing and regal adorned in

Jhalanpur's magnificent jewels and as we approached the altar, a shockwave of sensual pleasure surged through me as Duncan undressed me with his eyes. For a split second I wondered if I could recapture the adoration I had felt for this Irish veterinary surgeon in Edinburgh years before, but looking at the love in Jim's eyes for his bride, I knew that this was fanciful. Duncan's gaze was pure lust.

The church bells rang out across the foothills of the Himalayas as the newly married couple made their way down the aisle. Duncan slid his arm around my waist in a very proprietorial manner and whispered sexual endearments into my ear as we followed them, causing Vijay to nudge Ruby knowingly in the ribs while she raised her eyes to the vaulted ceiling.

I was about to respond in kind when I was distracted by the sight of a far too familiar figure standing at the end of the rear pew. Tom's bearded countenance towered above the congregation, a wistful expression on his handsome face and his eyes locked onto mine like a magnet on metal.

'NO!' I screamed internally. 'Dear God, no. Not here. Not now.'

Duncan propelled me through the porch and beneath twelve St Saviour's hockey sticks locked in an arch before deposited me on the grass verge, oblivious to the reason for my inability to function.

'Cailin, can you hear me? Are you alright? You look as if you've seen a ghost.'

'There you are, Mac. Can I have a word?' Ruby eased me from Duncan's clutches and propelled me to the rear of the church, plonking me on a headstone and checking we were alone. 'Right. Now breathe.'

'I . . . I can't.'

'Yes, you can.'

I smacked my chest with my fist and swallowed hard. 'Christ, Ruby, when did Tom arrive?'

'Halfway through the wedding service. I only noticed him when you all went into the vestry. Apparently, Vijay ordered Ghalib to pick him up at the station after receiving a cable from him earlier today. Poor man only arrived in Bombay yesterday afternoon. He's been travelling for days.'

I began to shake.

'Here, drink this.' She pulled a small silver brandy flask from her purse and stuffed it in my face.

The liquid burned my throat on its way down and I began to cough. Ruby's flat hand pounded my spine then insisted I took another gulp. I shook my head, but she insisted.

'Why didn't you warn me?'

'How could I? Vijay didn't tell me until we were inside the bloody church.'

'Jesus. It's bad enough having Duncan pawing me at every turn without Tom watching from a distance.'

'I know, but we can't do anything about that now. We have a wedding breakfast to go to.'

'Oh, FUCK!'

'Do you feel better now?'

'No.'

'Look, Mac. It's a shock. I understand that, but it's not the end of the world. Tom has moved heaven and earth to be at

Jim's wedding and I'm sure he's gutted that he couldn't get here in time to be his best man. Nevertheless, he made it against all the odds, and if this causes you a problem you'll just have to live with it. Now, stop acting like some Hollywood diva and get back to the wedding party. The photographer is probably already searching for you.'

I looked from left to right but the graveyard was empty. 'You'll have to stop me from getting drunk, Ruby, because I won't answer for what I might say to Tom if I do.'

'Then stick to water. Now, are you ready?'

I stood, brushed dried moss off my bridesmaid's dress, grabbed my posy from the grass and squared my shoulders. 'How do I look?'

'Beautiful.'

'Are you sure I can't just slip away quietly?'

'No, Mac, you can't, so show some MacKenzie backbone and start enjoying the fact that you have two desirable courtiers competing for your favours.'

'Bloody hell, Ruby, you make me sound like Anne Boleyn.'

'A bad analogy, Mac. She ended up without her head.'

Chapter Fourteen

Trying to detach Duncan from my side was like trying to extract a leech from a patient's skin, but finally, I managed to get Archie to engage him in conversation about polo horses and escaped to the lavatory where I bumped into Sybil.

'Doctor Mac, isn't it amazing?'

'It is, Sybil. The service was wonderful.' She blocked my progress into the toilet with her parasol.

'No, dear, I mean about Doctor Wallace making it all the way from Africa for the wedding. You must be thrilled.'

I eased the parasol to one side and escaped into a cubicle, ramming the door closed with the words, 'Certainly surprised, Sybil.'

'Just think, if he'd been here earlier, he could have been Jim's best man.'

I closed my eyes. 'Exactly, Sybil.'

'Still,' she continued as I emptied my bladder, 'better late than never, eh?'

'Better late than never, Sybil. Better late than never.'

I reappeared as the Master of Ceremonies was banging his gavel and asking the guests to take their seats. The top table seemed miles away and I could see Tom and Jim in deep conversation to my right. I moved left and made a beeline for Lamis who seemed to be a bit lost, standing alone by the wedding cake table.

'Over here, Lamis,' I said, ushering her ahead of me aware of deep blue male eyes following my progress. We edged along the top table looking at the name plates and I was relieved to see that Lamis had been seated between Duncan and I with Lord Wetherington on my other side. Frances tapped me on the shoulder as she made her way passed.

'Are you OK, Mac?'

I nodded, not daring to open my mouth and kept myself busy pulling out a chair for Lamis as Jim showed Tom to his seat next to Ruby.

I really don't remember much about the meal other than hardly eating anything. Lamis kept me going with a myriad of questions, interrupted at times with champagne toasts, speeches from Archie, Duncan and Jim, thunderous applause and the ceremony of cutting the cake.

Eventually, with the tables cleared, the hotel musicians took their seats on the rostrum and their singer commenced proceedings with Hoagy Carmichael's *"Stardust"*. Jim led Frances onto the ballroom floor to another round of applause and we watched as they swayed to the strains of this well-known popular song until Frances had had enough of the limelight and beckoned us all to join in.

Duncan's hands encircled my waist and I was ushered onto the dance floor where he pulled me towards him, brushed his lips against my neck and led me off in a fox trot. I could see Tom leaning against the far wall and prayed he wasn't thinking what I thought he was thinking. A quickstep followed, Duncan refusing to let me go, then came the inevitable waltz. Duncan smiled, I inwardly groaned, and the strains of Gus Khan's *"It had to be you"* filled the room.

'Excuse me, but I think this one's mine.'

Before Duncan could object, Tom had me in his arms and it was as if we were back on the hurricane deck of the ss Narkunda, me in my emerald-green evening dress from Simon Artz and Tom in his 'all whites' uniform, dancing under the stars as our ship made passage along the Suez Canal.

'Hello, Mac.'

'Hello, Tom.'

Nothing more needed to be said. Our bodies moulded together as if twinned, his hand rested on the centre of my back, and I felt my hair brush his cheek as we became lost amongst the crowd of couples.

When it ended, he held me at arm's length and took in the full length of me.

'You look beautiful, Mac.'

My cheeks burned and I fumbled with my hair. 'I think we should go.'

He walked me back to my table where Lamis was waiting patiently, her young face beaming with delight.

'Umi, you can dance?'

'Don't sound so surprised, dear. Tom, may I introduce Lamis Abbas, my surrogate child.' I felt him stiffen, but he quickly recovered. 'Lamis, this is Doctor Wallace, a colleague of mine from England.'

Tom bowed. '*Assalamu' allaikum,* Miss Abbas.'

'*Wa-Alikum-Assalam, Sahib,*' she replied, making a namaste.

'May I say you look very lovely in your bridesmaid's sari.'

'Thank you, Sir. My Umi chose it for me.' Tom stiffened again as Lamis looked lovingly into my eyes.

'Hello stranger.' Frances was standing behind us, waiting patiently.

Tom turned, smiled and wrapped her in his arms. 'Florence Nightingale, I don't recall giving you permission to marry that Bedouin imposter from the ss Narkunda.'

'Heaven forefend, Sir Richard, but this particular Bedouin assured me that he was your closest defender and ally, who had advised you of his marital intentions.'

Lamis's eyes were nearly popping out of her head, and I couldn't help chuckling, amused at the reference to our fancy dress characters at the ship's gala ball.

'Just make sure the scoundrel treats you with the respect you deserve, or he'll find himself run through with my sword.'

'Who will?' asked Jim, appearing by my side.

'You will, dear, if you don't know your place in this marriage,' said Frances, taking Lamis by the hand. 'Come on flower girl, Lady Wetherington wants to see your new necklace.' They disappeared into the throng leaving the three of us alone.

'How does it feel to be married again after all these years, Jim?' Tom kept me firmly in his line of sight.

'Like all my Christmases have come at once, Tom.'

'Then you're a lucky man. Women like Frances don't come along very often.'

'My wife may look as if butter wouldn't melt in her mouth, Tom, but she can be quite the tyrant when she wants to be. Isn't that right, Mac?'

'Oh, I don't know, Jim. If you will act like some of her students, what do you expect?'

'Cheeky monkey. Any more of that, and I'll put you over my knee.'

'Promises, promises, Mr Hamilton.'

'I tell you, Tom, it's been an uphill battle keeping these three in check,' he nodded to Ruby and Frances conversing with Sybil. 'They were always a force to be reckoned with onboard ship, but since arriving in India they've become impossible.'

'Have they indeed?' Tom gave me a sideways stare. 'What they need, Jim, is a firm hand.' A wry grin crossed his face.

'Perhaps you could start with this one. I suspect she's the ringleader.'

Before I could object, Tom had placed his hand on my back and I was manoeuvred between the other guests and out onto the terrace. We passed Duncan on the way, but he was busy chatting up one of the hotel waitresses and never even noticed.

'I see Mr Fitzpatrick enjoys the company of the ladies.' Tom's sarcasm spoke volumes.

'Sour grapes, Doctor Wallace?' The retort appeared sharper than I intended. 'Actually, it's the ladies who enjoy the company of Mr Fitzpatrick.'

'Sorry, Mac, I didn't mean to offend.' He sounded contrite.

'You haven't. But it's a long story and not one I wish to go into right now.'

Tom lifted two bubbling champagne flutes from a waiter's silver tray and carried them down the terrace steps to the garden. I could have escaped right there and then, but curiosity kept me by his side. We stood in the shade of a Neem tree neither knowing how to begin the conversation until his eyes travelled to my wrist and he pointed to my malachite and ivory bracelet.

'You kept it then?'

I tried to hide the beautiful beaten silver and precious stone bangle with my hand, wishing it was still lying in my jewellery box. 'As you gave it to me for services rendered, Tom, I thought I deserved to keep it.'

My remark had cut him to the quick and he recoiled in shock, but there was no pleasure in my sarcasm after all this time and I immediately regretted what I had said. It was too late to retract it so I did the next best thing and moved away, trying to put distance between us. He let me go, then changed his mind, halting my progress with his next question.'

'How is India treating you, Mac?'

I stood rooted to the spot trying to forget how much this married man had meant to me. 'Not too well I'm afraid. Our colonial masters don't take kindly to having their customary ways challenged.'

He walked across the grass and linked his arm in mine, determined to keep me close and did his best to keep the conversation professional. 'And your Ph.D research?'

'Cancelled.'

'Then that is the CSTM's loss.'

'My thoughts entirely, Tom, but having decided to criticise the IMS hierarchy in the national press, I'm afraid I became *personae non grata*.'

He led me to an ornamental concrete bench and as I sat, I covertly drizzled my champagne onto the grass.

'I imagine you had just cause to criticise them.'

'I did, but it didn't help, and if it hadn't been for Sir Peter Bonham-Cavendish intervening on my behalf, I would have been back in England months ago.'

As the afternoon sun began to merge with the Himalayan peaks, the beauty of my surroundings helped to ease the tension gripping my body, and gradually my nervousness dissipated.

'I understand from Ruby that you have been travelling for days to be at the wedding. Mozambique wasn't it?'

'Yes. A pretty exhausting journey one way or another, but I couldn't let Jim down, even though I couldn't make it any sooner.'

'Why Mozambique?' I asked.

'Another long story, Mac, and one for another day, but when I heard that Vijay wanted me to assist him with his hospital project, I immediately packed my bags and hightailed it to India. Mozambique is an interesting place and research on tropical diseases challenging, but India is where my heart is.'

I felt my stomach cartwheel. 'Then, no doubt, our paths will cross again in the future.' I wasn't sure where this was going so decided to close the conversation down. 'Perhaps we should join the others before they send out a search party.'

Tom refused to budge. 'Are you happy, Mac?'

I hesitated, knowing exactly what he was referring to. 'I have my work, Tom, which keeps me busy and, right now, my main concern is caring for Lamis and getting her trained as an obstetrics nurse.'

'She certainly adores you.' He stood and took my empty glass.

'I have high hopes for her. Once India is given home-rule, that young lady could be at the forefront of female emancipation.'

'Tell me more.'

'Another long story for another time.' We entered the ballroom as Duncan and Frances were tripping the light fantastic in a rumba.

'I look forward to it.' He bent closer, his whispered breath warming my skin. 'Perhaps the next time we meet, you will feel less nervous about being in my company.'

I turned, my eyes widening. 'Tom, I'll admit it was a shock seeing you today, but life has moved on. The past is the past and that is where it should stay. I hope you agree.' I waved to Ruby who beckoned me over giving me the excuse to escape.

'Well, that put him in his place, Elizabeth.'

'Leave it alone, Karr.'

'If you say so, dear, but don't blame me if that charming man marries someone else.'

'He's already married, Karr.'

'Ah yes, I forgot that, but seeing the way he looks at you, things could change.'

'Oh, for goodness's sake.'

'Ruby, that outfit of yours is absolutely stunning.'

Chapter Fifteen

S leep was out of the question. I paced backwards and
forwards trying to get my head together as the moon
tracked across the clear, starlit, indigo sky. My bridesmaid's
dress was discarded in a heap on the chaise longue, my shoes
dumped below, and my posy rammed into a glass flower jar
minus any water.

My head kept insisting that I had handled the encounter
with decorum, but my heart just relived the feel of Tom's
broad hand on my back and his warm breath on my neck in a
never-ending loop.

'Oh, for Pete's sake, stop torturing yourself, Mac.'

I flung open the balcony doors and walked over to the
balustrade, breathing in the fresh night air as a shooting star
flashed across the heavens. My whole being was in turmoil, not
helped by the fact that Tom was about to work with Vijay in
Rajputana. I was hopelessly in love with him and what I needed
right now was a good dose of Ma's common sense.

I closed my eyes and wondered what she would say if she
knew the predicament I was in. It was easy to picture her sitting
at the scullery table in the Vicarage, her flowery cotton pinafore
dusted with flour, a cup of tea in her hand and a very cross
expression on her face.

*'I'm disappointed in you, Elizabeth. I thought you had more sense
than to get mixed up with a married man. You were never this foolish
when you lived in Riveldene.'*

'I know, Ma, but Riveldene is hardly the centre of the modern world.'

'Then all I can say is thank the Lord for that. I can only assume your head has been turned by that awful woman from Streatham, seeing the mess you are in right now. My advice, child, is for you to cut all ties with this Tom Wallace, pack your bags and get back home as quickly as possible. We may be a backwater, but we still believe in the ten commandments and good old-fashioned morality.'

And there it was. Ma's answer to all my angst. A pot of tea, a life of tedium and virtuous living in Northumbria and the prospect of sliding into old age as a barren spinster.

'Bugger that for a game of soldiers!' I groaned and went to bed.

I woke with a splitting headache and assumed that this was caused by over-indulgence the day before. It was Sunday and I needed to be back in Delhi by Tuesday for a meeting with Sir Peter and Agnes and saw no point in delaying my departure, especially as Frances and Jim were about to leave Simla for their short honeymoon in Kashmir, before the start of the new school term. Lamis also needed to be formally enrolled in the Lady Hardinge student midwifery programme. Then there was the pending hearing at the Office of the Guardian which I needed to prepare for, to say nothing of my responsibilities at work.

Mrs Appleby was preparing breakfast as I walked into the kitchen and the aroma of smoked haddock turned my stomach. I made a dash for the lavatory to retch over the toilet pan. Memories of morning sickness reverberated through my head, and I gripped the toilet pan, reminding myself that this was impossible unless I believed in the immaculate conception.

'Doctor Mac, are you alright?' Mrs Appleby was tapping the lavatory door as I flushed my stomach contents into the drain and staggered to my feet.

'Yes, thank-you, but I think I will forgo breakfast if you don't mind.'

'Should I make you some porridge instead of kedgeree if your stomach's upset?'

'No, don't bother. I'll just have a cup of chai and let nature take its course.' I appeared in the hall, sweat dripping from my forehead.

'Goodness me, you don't look at all well. Why don't I send a message to the main house and ask the Maharani to call the doctor?'

'I'm sure I will be fine, Mrs Appleby. Probably something I've eaten. I think I'll go back to bed for a couple of hours. Maybe I will feel better later.'

Later turned out to be mid-afternoon. By now my temperature was raging, I had violent pains in my stomach and my muscles ached all over.

'It's no good, Doctor Mac, I'm sending for help.' Mrs Appleby handed me a glass of water, laid a cold wet flannel across my forehead and sent Lamis to the main house with a message for Ruby.

Much to my humiliation, fifteen minutes later Tom walked through my bedroom door, shooed Lamis and Mrs Appleby out onto the landing with instruction to boil a kettle then threw his medical bag on the chaise longue, rummaged through it and slapped a thermometer in my mouth.

'Don't talk.'

As if I could. I sat there, water glass in hand, thermometer stuck under my tongue and my nightdress splattered with vomit. Very nice I thought and glared at Tom as if it was his fault.

He was concentrating on his watch as my pulse banged away under the pressure of his fingers.

'Which area of the Punjab have you been working in over the past month?'

I frowned, trying to follow his line of questioning. Surely this was simply a bout of food poisoning? He pulled the thermometer from my mouth and held it up to the light.

'Jhalandhar District,' I said, clearing my throat with a bout of coughing.

'Where's that?'

'North-West of here in the foothills of the Himalayas.'

'Christ, Mac, you're burning up. Your temperature is off the scale.' He pulled my eye sockets down and checked for anaemia. 'I assume you were in and out of some remote villages during that time?'

I lay back, feeling weak and bit my lip. 'Yes, quite a few, including a salt-mine.'

'Right, I want to take some blood. Where is the nearest laboratory?'

'The Lady Reading has one, but I have my own microscope in the trunk over there.'

'Excellent.' He walked onto the landing and called out. 'How are we doing with the hot water?'

'Just coming, Doctor,' shouted Mrs Appleby. She arrived seconds later with a steaming kettle in her hand.

'Thank you, dear. Doctor Stuart-MacKenzie is to remain isolated in this room until I say otherwise. Everything she uses,' he handed over my water glass, 'is to be sterilised and I need to take a blood sample from both you and the child.' He turned to me looking for help.

'Lamis,' I said and began to panic.

'Yes, Lamis. I'll be about thirty minutes here so don't leave the house.'

'No, Doctor. We'll be downstairs when you need us.'

'Fine Mrs . . .'

'Appleby.'

'Mrs Appleby. There's no need to be alarmed.' My housekeeper looked terrified. 'This is all just a precaution. I imagine Doctor Stuart-MacKenzie ate something that didn't agree with her yesterday, but I need to check she is not suffering from anything more sinister. You do understand, don't you?'

'I do, Doctor, and I'm so grateful you were staying at the main house and could get here so quickly.'

'So am I.' His eyes met mine across the room. 'Off you go now, and I'll be down shortly.'

Tom scrubbed his hands in the wash-hand basin then pricked my finger and took blood, smearing it on to a microscope slide. When he'd finished he turned, his legs astride, his right hand holding a swab. 'Right, Mac, roll over.'

'Oh, God, is this really necessary?'

'You know it is. Now, on your stomach.'

I lay with my chin on the pillow and felt him pull my nightdress above my buttocks.

'Spread your legs.'

I closed my eyes, trying desperately to forget that I was exposing myself to the one man in the world I wished was still in Mozambique.

Professional to a fault, he swabbed my anus then covered me up and walked over to the trunk while I endeavoured to regain some composure, my mind tracking through symptoms for enteric fever, dysentery and cholera. 'The microscope is at the bottom of the trunk on the ride-hand side.'

'Yes, I've got it.' He set up the instrument on the occasional table by the window, dragged a chair alongside and went to work.

Minutes passed then he looked my way. 'Do you want to see for yourself?'

I nodded, feeling queasy. He placed the microscope on my lap and stood by the window staring out across Mallards's grounds. I pressed my right eye to the ocular lens and twiddled the rotating screw on the side of the instrument to bring the image into focus. Staring back at me on the glass slide was a smear of my blood and swimming amongst the red erythrocytes and white leukocytes cells were long, tubular, hairy *Salmonella typhi bacterium*. 'No! No, it can't be.'

'I'm afraid it is, Mac.'

I quickly moved the second slide into position smeared with traces of my faeces. There they were again. I slowly raised my head fighting against reality.

'But this is typhoid fever.'

'Exactly.'

'I can't afford to have typhoid fever, Tom. I've got too much to do.'

He turned and looked at me as if I was an irritable child refusing to eat my greens. 'Don't be ridiculous, Mac. This could kill you unless you're treated with infusions and enema decoctions of Neem bark, echinacea and camomile. I assume you were never immunised against typhoid before you left England.'

'No. I know the British army lads were routinely immunised against it in the war, but all I was told was to be careful what I ate and drank.'

I could hear Tom's teeth grate together. 'Then the fever must run its course, however long it takes, and you're not going anywhere until it's passed. Nor am I.'

'But surely the Assistant Surgeon at Reading Hospital can deal with this, there's no need for you to delay your plans.'

'Keen to get rid of me, are you?'

'No . . . I mean . . . yes. Oh, drat. You know damned well what I mean.'

'Mac. We are talking killer disease here. I'm sure the Assistant Surgeon is very good at tennis injuries and the odd myocardial infarction, but I imagine his experience with typhoid is a little rusty up here in Simla.'

'She.'

'What?'

'The Assistant Surgeon is a woman, Tom.'

'Then I'm definitely staying.'

'Doctor Wallace, you are not my keeper.'

'More's the pity, but there is no use arguing with me, Mac. For better or worse, I'm the best chance you have of getting better. Now, give me a detailed rundown of how you are feeling right now.'

'I'm feeling weak, my muscles ache, I'm sweating, my head feels as if it's being chopped in half with a hatchet, my stomach aches and . . . oh hell, I've got the runs.' I felt by bowels turn to liquid and made a dash for the bathroom. Tom was waiting for me as I came out. I took one look at him and my knees buckled.

I've no idea what happened after that. Drifting in and out of sleep in a constant state of delirium, I think I was given cool bed baths, recalled choking on some foul-tasting concoction morning, noon and night, and heard male and female voices some way off, but couldn't make any sense of the words. If I tried to focus on anything, the room began to spin and I immediately felt sick.

Not knowing how long I would be in this state, the world moved on without me, until the day my body finally rid itself of the *Salmonella typhi bacteriam* and I surfaced, a stone lighter and feeling like a rag doll. I opened my eyes and found Agnes Scott half-reclining on the chaise longue reading a medical journal.

'Agnes, what are you doing here?'

'Good evening, Elizabeth. You've finally condescended to join us then?'

'What time is it?'

'Half-past eight, on Friday evening.'

'SIX DAYS! But what about our meeting with Sir Peter? Where is Lamis? What's happening at the WCHS?'

'All in good time, young lady. Right now, you have to get better and the first thing you need is some decent food inside you.' Agnes was checking my vital signs as she spoke. 'Now stay there and don't you dare move. That's an order.'

I was a mass of questions but now talking to an empty room. There was quite a commotion downstairs then Lamis suddenly burst through the door.

'Umi!' She rushed to my side and was about to give me a hug when Agnes's firm voice stopped her in her tracks.

'Get back here, Lamis. Doctor Mac may still be infectious.'

The poor child hovered on tiptoe neither moving forwards or back.

'Go and stand by the door, Lamis,' I said, easing myself up against the wrought iron bedstead. 'I'm fine, but the last thing I need is to infect you with typhoid.'

She backtracked to Agnes and hovered at the doorframe. Agnes ushered her from the room and closed the door. My heart went out to the child, but Agnes was right. I might well have been a carrier of the disease and the fewer people who came near me for the next week the better.

'Where's Doctor Wallace?' I asked, curiosity getting the better of me.

Agnes handed me a glass. 'Drink that. Doctor Wallace left for Himachal Pradesh the minute I arrived.'

My heart sank. 'What's in Himachal Pradesh?'

'The Vaccine Research Institute in Kasauli. He's gone to get some typhoid antibody proteins. We are all about to be immunised.'

My spirits instantly rose and the freshly squeezed orange juice tasted so good, I polished off the whole glass in one glug. Do you know if anyone else has contracted typhoid?'

'Yes, unfortunately you're not alone. I understand Alistair Galbraith and Jonathon Davies are both down with it, but they were inoculated so they are both on the mend.'

'We must have eaten something contaminated in Jhalandhar District.' I struggled to stay upright so Agnes re-arranged my pillows.'

'Mr Galbraith was not sure of the cause when Doctor Wallace spoke to him on the phone, but he has notified the Public Health Director about what has happened. Meanwhile Doctor Wallace has taken blood samples from everyone you have been in contact with since arriving back in Simla and, thankfully, no-one else is infected.'

'Including Frances and Jim?'

'They were the first people he contacted as soon you collapsed.'

'Oh goodness, Agnes, that's the last thing the Hamiltons needed just as they were going on their honeymoon.'

'The Maharani told me that Doctor Wallace had their results within minutes, thanks to your microscope. He did double check the slides down at the Reading laboratory after they departed, but the result was the same.'

A tap on the door announced my food. 'Thank you, Mrs Appleby. Perhaps a nice pot of chai wouldn't go amiss either.'

'Right you are, Doctor Scott. I'll bring it straight up.' A steaming bowl of vegetable soup was wafted under my nose.

'Can you manage or do you want me to help you?' Agnes was hovering again.

'No thanks, I can manage. Were you able to cancel Sir Peter's visit to Delhi?'

'He was on his way back to Calcutta from Mussoorie, so he needed to stop-over in Delhi anyway for meetings at Viceroy's House. He sends his regards and hopes you make a full recovery sooner rather than later.' That sounded ominous seeing as he was a senior immunologist by profession. 'He also asked me to pass on a message. Lady Stewart-Symes has accepted his invitation to take on the honorary role of President of the WCHS.'

'Oh, that's great news, Agnes. Geraldine will be another string to our bow when it comes to lobbying the Institute.'

'My thoughts entirely, Elizabeth. Now finish your soup and get some rest. Your body has been through the wringer this week and you need to build up your strength.'

'And Gloria?'

'Handling the department perfectly well in your absence. In fact, I think she's enjoying being the boss for a while.'

My spirits seemed to be rising and falling like a proverbial hotel lift. 'Then the sooner I get back to work the better.'

'Rubbish. Gloria may be a good organiser, but she does tend to rub people up the wrong way. Sadly, she doesn't have your management skills.'

I felt relief like a productive enema. 'Good to know,' I said, and made headway with my soup.

Two days later, I was sitting on the bedroom balcony watching an osprey rising on a thermal when Tom reappeared.

'How's my patient?'

'Skeletal, but alive. Mrs Appleby is on a mission to turn me into one of Vijay's elephants.'

'Well, at least the fever didn't ruin your sense of humour.'

He checked my pulse, grunted, nodded and removed his jacket.

'Will I live?'

'Probably, but I would appreciate it if you would stop trying to die on me every time we meet.'

'It's not intentional.'

'I'm pleased to hear it. Now, I've managed to get some vials of anti-typhoid serum, so the minute you are back on your feet, you need to be inoculated. I'll be dealing with the others here at Mallards tomorrow morning.'

I smiled. It felt so good to have him in charge.

'Be careful, Elizabeth, you know what your Ma said.'

'Yes, Karr'

'When are you leaving for Jhalanpur, Tom?'

He sat on the adjoining wicker chair and rubbed his forehead. 'Vijay is intending to leave on Sunday and I imagine he'll want me to go too. He's keen to introduce Ruby to his subjects and get Puttaker Lodge shipshape before the Hindu Festival of Diwali on the twenty-first of October.'

'Gosh, that's only three weeks away. According to Ruby the whole place needs a thorough revamp. She was planning to take Madame du Bois with her.'

'Who's she?'

'The French interior designer from Delhi. She did up my house in Alipore Road thanks to Vijay's generosity, and I have to say, she certainly turned my sow's ear into a silk purse.'

'Well, not that I know all the ins and outs of Ruby's plans, but I think Vijay is intending to stay at the Jhalanpur Palace until the renovations are complete.'

Chilly fingers playing with my vertebrae caused goosebumps.

'Are you cold? Do you want my jacket?'

'No, Tom, I'm fine. It's just the thought of Ruby and Vijay's mother living under the same roof.'

He patted my arm. 'I think a four-hundred and fifty-roomed palace will give them plenty of space to avoid each other.'

'Let's hope so or Vijay could find himself between a rock and a hard place.'

'A bit like me then?'

Before I could cut him off from further reference to our past relationship, Agnes strode through the door.

'Elizabeth, I've been thinking.'

I had learned early on not to argue with Agnes once she had made up her mind, and she had been doing a lot of thinking over the previous twenty-four hours. What she had decided took me completely by surprise.

'Elizabeth, I am going to take Lamis back to the Lady Hardinge on Sunday. I will enrol her myself in the midwifery course and she can stay in the student's dormitory until Mrs Appleby returns to Alipore Road. Meanwhile, you will remain here at Mallards and continue to isolate until you are non-contagious, with your housekeeper looking after you and sterilising everything you touch. Once you're clear, you will be off to Jhalanpur for three weeks.'

'Pardon?'

'The Maharani and I have discussed it and we agree, you will recuperate far quicker in the comfort of the Jhalanpur Palace than you will back in Delhi with all its distractions. I will take the reins at the WCHS in your absence, and I don't want to see you back at your desk until after Diwali.'

I seemed to have lost control of my life. 'But Agnes . . .'

'No buts, Elizabeth. I need you fit and well to carry this project through the winter and the last thing I need is for you to have a relapse just as you are about to go before the Institute's board. Don't you agree, Doctor Wallace?'

The corners of Tom's lips lifted. 'Indeed I do, Doctor Scott, and Mac can do regular blood tests herself to check for *Salmonella typhi* while she's here.'

They were both ganging up on me, that was obvious, but I had one last go at shattering their plans. 'There's one small point you seem to have overlooked, Agnes. I must appear before the Office of the Guardian next week regarding Lamis's legal status.'

'Then you must write to them immediately explaining your present circumstances and requesting a postponement until November. I'll take the letter back with me to save time.' That was it. All done and dusted.

Charming, I thought, but reluctantly capitulated, deciding to use the time to finish my overdue report to Sir Peter and take some long mountain walks.

Agnes was keen to leave the room but I needed to ask her a favour. 'Agnes, can I have a word in private?'

'I'll be at the main house if you need me,' said Tom and left us alone.

'What is it, Elizabeth?' I could see that her mind had moved on to more pressing matters.

'It's Lamis, Agnes. She started her period while I was working up in Jalandhar District. Frances told me that she was asking if she could now have children.' I suddenly had my boss's attention.

'What did Frances say?'

'She told Lamis to speak to me about it.'

'And have you?'

'No, I contracted typhoid fever instead.'

'Well, this conversation needs to take place sooner rather than later, Elizabeth.'

'Exactly, Agnes, and as you are now taking Lamis back to Delhi on my behalf, I was wondering if you could broach the subject with her.'

'There are times when I despair of you, Doctor Stuart-MacKenzie.' The timbre of her voice had dropped an octave. 'My answer is, no I won't. You were the one who decided to take the child under your wing even though I advised against it, and as her protector and provider it is your job to tell her that her physical disabilities will cause major problems if she ever gets pregnant. Now, if there is nothing else, I'll be on my way.'

Before I could argue further, she had left the room, intent on setting in motion all her plans. As the day progressed, trunks were packed, train tickets were booked and local transport was organised. I was to be left alone in Simla, bar Mrs

Appleby and Ghalib, while the rest of Mallards dispersed across the continent.

Maybe, I'll get to see some of the sites I planned and failed to see last year, I mused, waving madly from the landing window as everyone departed. That's assuming I can escape from under Mrs Appleby's beady eye, I thought, and returned to bed.

'Right, Doctor Mac,' said my housekeeper, poking her head around my bedroom door two hours later. Your dinner is on a tray on the landing and I've moved the laundry basket out there as well. If there's anything you need just ring this bell.' She placed a brass hand bell by the door frame. 'Now, what do you fancy for your breakfast?'

Chapter Sixteen

The early autumn mornings in the mountains were a delight. Free from constant health checks by Tom or Agnes, I settled into a regime of regular meals, copious glasses of fresh fruit juice, long mountain walks and regular self-administered blood tests for lingering signs of typhoid. The British hill-station was quickly emptying of colonials, all heading back to Delhi for work and the polo season, which was their next main focus of interest.

On the seventh day, I announced that I was out of danger to both myself and others, so Mrs Appleby and I were driven to Kalka by Ghalib in Ruby's Hillman and the East India Railway Mail deposited us at Delhi Junction some hours later, ready to go our separate ways.

'Now, Doctor Mac, I've sterilised all your clothes, shoes and instruments and added a few packets of Neem bark, echinacea and camomile in case you need it in the desert. Don't worry about Lamis, I'll take good care of her and make sure she gets to college every day on time.'

'Thank you, Mrs Appleby, I don't know what I'd do without you.'

'Don't mention it, Doctor. Now, you just get better, dearie, under the watchful eye of that wonderful Doctor Wallace, and come back fit and well at the end of October.'

The mention of Tom's name did nothing for my peace of mind. After a week apart, I had given myself a severe talking to and had every intention of keeping him at arm's length during my stay with Vijay and Ruby.

'Mrs Appleby, could you ask Lamis to give this report to Doctor Scott.'

'Certainly, Doctor. Now, I must dash if I'm to get to the market before it closes.'

'Give Lamis my love and tell her I'll write.' I bit my knuckle remembering my failed promise to her in the library at the Lady Hardinge the previous autumn. It seemed like a lifetime ago. I waved and went in search of my overnight train to Jodhpur.

Tom was waiting on Jodhpur's station platform as I stepped down from my carriage on that cool, sunny morning, with a zephyr of breeze coming off the arid, alluvial Rajputana plain. I looked about and saw Vijay's private train in a siding, grey smoke curling upwards from the engine's smokestack.

I was still feeling weak and underweight, but I had slept well in my second-class cabin and was looking forward to some breakfast. Tom ushered me into the station restaurant where trays of pastries, warm samosas and fresh fruit lined a long trestle table, the steaming, chrome tea-urn on the counter above hissing softly.

'I was not expecting to see you here, Tom.'

'I had little choice, Mac, Ruby insisted.'

Did she, I thought, deciding to have words with Miss Tavener when I arrived in Jhalanpur. I helped myself to slices of fresh watermelon and mango. 'What was the general reaction when she appeared at the palace for the first time?'

'Mixed,' replied Tom, biting into a sweet pastry. 'I think you could describe it as muted.'

'Crikey. How did Ruby take that?'

'With her usual East-End aplomb. You would never have suspected her of being nervous. Must be her stage experience.'

'And Vijay. How did he handle the situation?'

'Vijay doesn't have to handle anything. He is a God in the eyes of his subjects and gets an enthusiastic welcome wherever he goes around Jhalanpur. You will see quite a different side to him here in his realm. It's so easy to forget that he is the King when he is amongst westerners, but put a regal pagri on his head and suddenly you are in the presence of a supreme being.'

'I know what you mean. I felt the same way at the Viceroy's summer garden party last year in Simla.'

I was finishing my second cup of Darjeeling tea when the stationmaster came to inform us that our train was ready to depart.

'How long does it take to reach Jhalanpur?' I asked, walking along the platform.

'Six hours. Plenty of time for us to fill in the gaps since our disastrous parting in Bombay.'

If I could have found a train leaving for Delhi right at that moment I would have been on it. Instead, I clenched my jaw, crossed my fingers and kept Ma's opinion of affairs with married men firmly in the front of my mind.

The scenery as we travelled west reminded me of our passage through the Red Sea, the same miles of sand and scrubland extending to the horizon on all sides. I settled back in the comfort of the plush day carriage, placed my feet on a pouffe and let the chilled air cool my legs and lower body as it rose from the huge ice block below the grating. Tom requested coffee from Vijay's steward then sat himself opposite me and picked up a paperback novel. Obviously, he was in no rush to fill in any gaps, I concluded.

'What are you reading?' I asked for something to say.

'Gandhi's autobiography.' He raised the book to show me the cover. *My Experiments with the Truth.* 'He serialized it in his Gujarati newspaper in the Twenties, but they have since been combined into a book.'

An unusual choice for someone not planning to stay long in India, I thought and changed the subject. 'You were going to tell me why you went to Mozambique.'

He hesitated, chewing the inside of his cheek, then placed the book on his lap. 'The Royal Society of Medicine was looking for someone to head a team of researchers who had been given funding to investigate the causes of elephantiasis in Africa. As I felt like a change of scenery and had a personal interest in the subject, I put my name forward.'

'What type of personal interest?' I sounded rather nosy, but I couldn't remember Tom ever mentioning it in the past.

'My twin brother was posted to Mesopotamia during the war. The British army had been tasked with safeguarding the Basra oilfields from the Ottoman Empire and his regiment fought in this area for nearly four years. During that time he contracted elephantiasis, and without a cure, he faced living with one leg three times the size of the other for the rest of his life. It affected him mentally, as well as physically.'

'Gosh, I'm so sorry, Tom. Have you and the team been successful in finding a cure?'

'Sadly not. It will take years to crack that nut, but we will continue our research no matter how challenging. Vijay tells me that the people of Rajputana also suffer from this affliction so he has agreed to fund a research programme in Jhalanpur as well.'

'Very commendable,' I said, realising that Tom was to be in India for some considerable time.

He sipped his coffee and went back to his book.

Being alone with Tom with no means of escape reminded me of my train journey from Peshawar to Bombay with Duncan, on our way back from the North-West Frontier. At that time, a long-overdue argument about our eighteen-month affair in Edinburgh had hung in the air like a bad smell, but Duncan had casually read his newspaper from cover to cover, pretending that nothing was amiss. It didn't last, of course, and within the hour, we were having the mother of all rows.

I lay my head on the leather upholstery and closed my eyes. Two can play at that game, I thought, and promptly fell asleep. I woke with a start as we pulled up in the middle of the desert.

'What's going on?' There was not a building in sight.

'We're stopping for lunch.' Tom opened the carriage door and helped me down on to the rough parched earth. Heat burned the soles of my shoes and singed my lungs. We were in another siding off the main track and when I shielded my eyes from the intense sunlight, I could see a large white canvas tent with the Jhalanpur crest embroidered in dark green and gold on the side, erected some fifty yards further on.

'Lunch, out here in the wilderness?'

'Follow me.'

Camels surrounded us in a disorderly fashion, sitting on the hot sand chewing their cud, grunting and noisily breaking wind. I gave them a wide berth and stepped into the interior. I was met with a Hollywood film set.

The floor was covered in large Persian rugs, the walls hung with faded tapestries of hunting scenes, a huge, suspended fan was swaying back and forth from a complicated set of pulleys and ropes and four uniformed staff in white pagris, white tight-fitting trousers and bottle-green long sherwani jackets stood to attention either side of a long ebony table crammed with platters of food.

'I've died and gone to heaven,' I whispered, as one steward pulled a heavily engraved ebony chair out and I took my place at the end of the table. Tom seemed miles away at the other end and I was convinced we were about to be joined by the cast of some Cecil B. DeMille extravaganza.

'Penny for them, Mac?'

'Did you slip hashish into my coffee on the train?'

'Not a chance. Why?'

'Because, either I'm having an out-of-body experience or this . . .' I stretched both arms out straight, 'is some desert mirage and I'm delirious with another bout of typhoid fever.'

A steward poured chilled pomegranate juice into a tall pewter goblet by my right hand. I acknowledged him with a nod and drank deeply.

'Get used to it, Mac. This is par for the course in His Royal Highness's life.' He pointed to a platter of freshly grilled fish. 'I hope you're hungry.'

After my breakfast in Jodhpur, all I wanted was a light lunch, but I did my best and when my dessert plate was finally removed, the stewards melted away leaving Tom and I alone.

So much liquid had expanded my bladder and I desperately needed the lavatory but as one wasn't evident. I shuffled on my chair and rammed my ankles and knees together.

'Something wrong, Mac?'

'A slight bladder need,' I said, trying to whisper and throw my voice across the full length of the table at the same time. 'Do I crouch against the tent side or is there a lavatory around here somewhere?' I swear Tom's laughter could have been heard in Bombay. 'It's all very well for you,' I whined, 'but this could become embarrassing.'

'Don't worry, Mac, all your possible needs are taken care of in this Princely State. Do you see that tapestry of rutting stags on your left?'

I nodded, recalling such a tapestry in the great hall at Wentworth Woodhouse in Yorkshire.

'You'll find a tent flap behind it leading to the ladies room.'

'You've got to be joking?' I now looked as if I'd been goosed by a frisky orangutan.

'Go see for yourself.'

I did, and wished I'd had my camera handy. 'Ma and Pa would never believe this,' I muttered, taking in the cream silk drapes, the brown marble washstand, gold taps reflecting the lamplight from two huge, beaten copper lamps on marble plinths and a full-sized marble lavatory encased in an ebony wooden box. I'm hallucinating, I decided, as I relieved myself, imagining the contents of my bladder seeping slowly into the desert sand.

Tom was pouring amber liquid from a crystal decanter on my return. 'Well, how was it?'

'I was wrong, it wasn't hashish you put in my coffee, it was pure opium.'

'Brandy?'

'No thanks.' I pointed to the huge rectangular fan in the eaves and frowned.

'There's a punkah wallah sitting outside operating the pulley with his feet,' said Tom, dragging his chair closer to mine.

'Oh. I hope he's not getting sunstroke.' I sensed trouble and helped myself to brandy after all.

'Are you and Duncan Fitzpatrick having an affair?'

I slowly placed the decanter back down on the polished surface and picked up my brandy bowl. You devious bastard, I thought, recalling my assumptions of Duncan earlier and wondered how I should respond.

'How's your wife?' I was rather pleased with my retort.

'Living with some local insurance man, and according to my lawyer, asking for a divorce.'

Brandy dripped from my chin onto my skirt. 'And your nephews?' I choked.

'Upset, but Enid has made it quite clear that I am not to interfere.'

I was back in the lavatory, rubbing the brandy stain for all it was worth with a wet napkin, my peace of mind in flux.

'OK, Aunt Karr, what the hell do I do now?'

We were back on the train with another two hours to go and a battle royal was in progress between my heart and my head while I searched for a way to deal with the shock of Tom's news.

'Sorry, Mac, I didn't mean to blurt it out quite like that, but you did ask.'

'Only because I was countering your question about my private life.'

'Then, I apologise. It was never my intention to push you into a corner, but the thought of that womanizing bastard playing with your feelings makes me see red.'

'That's rich coming from you, Tom Wallace. The man who curled me around his little finger until I was putty in his hands only to announce he was a married man who would never leave his wife.'

'That's unfair.'

'No, it isn't. At least Duncan was single when he pulled the wool over my eyes.'

'When did he do that?' His jawbone crunched.

'In Edinburgh when I was an under-graduate. He used me for near on eighteen months to boost his own ego, then buggered off to India on a three-year sabbatical without even a backward glance. I was left dealing with a broken heart, nearly failing my medical degree, and swearing that no man would ever do that to me again. Then I met you.'

'I had no idea, Mac, you never said.'

'Why would I? I don't make a habit of broadcasting my personal rejections to all and sundry.'

Tom smacked his fist against the wooden seat arm. 'Well, unlike Fitzpatrick, I did love you, and you knew it, even though you wouldn't give me the opportunity to explain.'

I clamped my hands together in my lap and refused to back down. 'What could you have said that would have made any difference?' My sarcastic remark spattered out at him like shrapnel. 'That last day, at our picnic overlooking Bhor Pass, I was convinced you were going to propose and frankly, I had no idea how I was going to reply.' My upper lip curled. 'What a bloody fool I was.'

Tom remained seated, his blue eyes piercing mine with laser precision. 'Mac, for the love of God, will you let me explain?'

'There's no need Tom, Frances told me all about the death of your twin brother when she stayed with me in Calcutta that first Christmas.'

He sprang to his feet and slammed his back against the compartment bulkhead, making tramlines through his hair with his fingers. 'Why didn't you tell me? I've lived in torment for nearly two years believing you were under the misguided impression that my marriage was harmonious.'

I was on the cusp of telling him the truth and needed to stop this discussion before it went any further. 'I didn't write, Tom, because there was no point. You would never have left Enid, you're far too principled, and I could never have lived with you in sin. I'll admit, it was hard at first, but work kept me sane, and I came to accept that it was all for the best in the end.'

'And now? What do you say now, knowing that my brother's wife has left ME without a backward glance?'

'What Enid has done to you is despicable, Tom, but it changes nothing. I'm afraid there is no way back for us, that ship sailed a long time ago.' I felt light-headed as words poured from my mouth. 'Believe me, we would be on a fool's errand if we tried.'

'I don't believe you, Mac, but if what you say is true, then I have no choice but to accept it.' The catch in Tom's voice clawed at my emotions. 'Obviously there is nothing I can say to change your mind so I won't mention it again. All I can hope is that we can remain friends.'

My heart was in bits as the train rattled on towards Jhalanpur. 'Tom, we were colleagues before we were lovers and I, for one, will always treasure that relationship. As for the rest, I suggest we erase it from our memory and get on with our lives.'

'Very well.' He didn't sound optimistic. 'Just one last thing, Mac, and don't jump down my throat.' He hesitated and I held my breath. 'I still need you to tell me exactly what your relationship is with Duncan Fitzpatrick. I don't want to say anything in the future which will be misconstrued.'

My sigh was audible. 'Tom, Duncan is a highly respected veterinary surgeon who is good at his job and superb with animals. That's why I recommended him to Vijay in the first place. But he's also a narcissistic egotist and, as you rightly said, a womanizer. Add to this his good looks and charismatic Irish charm and you have a potent cocktail that no woman in her right mind would ever take seriously.'

'So, I won't offend you by treating him with contempt?'

'Men like Duncan should be pitied, Tom, not scorned. In my opinion, he is destined for a very lonely old age. We go back a long way so I probably know him better than most and I will always respect him as a friend. But he is not, and never will be the man of my dreams.'

'Thank God for that . . . Oh look, there's Puttaker Lake.' Tom pointed to a large expanse of water below a sandstone escarpment. My eyes travelled to the top of the plateau where an imposing sandstone fort dominated the skyline.

'Is that Ruby's new home? How could anyone call it a lodge?'

'It's all relative, Mac.' Tom was now standing behind me, our bodies almost touching. 'Having only one-hundred-and-fifteen rooms, it's referred to as the Maharaja's hunting lodge.'

'Then I'd better get some rifle practice in. I wouldn't want to let the side down at the tiger shoot.'

He slowly turned me to face him as Puttaker Lake faded into the distance. 'Just remember, if you ever need me, all you have to do is ask.'

'I'll remember, but after years coping on my own, I think I'll be fine, Tom, but thanks anyway.'

Chapter Seventeen

The Rolls Royce Silver Ghost cruised up the hillside and halted at the base of a wide expanse of sandstone steps leading to the Jhalanpur Palace porticoed entrance. Vijay's seat of power was a mausoleum of a building, its domes, turrets, towers and colonnades not dissimilar to Viceroy's House in Delhi. I should have been impressed, but after a day of earth-shattering revelations and intense emotions, I couldn't raise the energy.

Tom preceded me into the entrance hall, a gigantic oval space lined with cream marble where animal heads peered down from a great height and hundreds of rifles, pistols and swords in geometric formations hinted at past campaign glories and oozed wealth beyond imagination.

The immense central dome rose hundreds of feet above my head letting in protracted light to the floor below, and on either side of this vast space two sweeping staircases curled upwards, joining at first floor level where a wide, arched entrance led to the main body of the building.

My footsteps echoed across the space like Arapaho drumbeats, and I knew instantly why this was not where Vijay wanted to be. It was soulless.

Climbing the stairs was like tackling the lower slopes of Ben Nevis and I was in danger of having a seizure before ever reaching Ruby's private quarters in the West Wing of this royal pile.

Uniformed staff were everywhere, seated at ornately gilded desks, standing like toy soldiers in doorways or huddled in alcoves talking in whispered voices. A world away from Mallards and the informal atmosphere of Vijay's home in Delhi.

The walk took forever. The long colonnades of carved circular sandstone pillars, separated by recurrent views through fretted marble screens of formal gardens and desert vistas beyond, seemed to never end.

With my knee joints creaking, we arrived at an immense door, intricately inlaid with lapis lazuli, topaz, turquoise, amethyst, jade and crystal precious stones in flowing floral designs, where two more uniformed guards blocked our path.

'Please inform the Maharani Manika Devi that Doctor Stewart-MacKenzie and Doctor Wallace are here and request an audience.'

'Please, you wait, Sahib.' The staffer moved beyond the opulent barrier, leaving us standing there kicking our heels like two miscreants outside the headmaster's office. My MacKenzie hackles were rising.

'An audience?' I whispered, becoming more incensed by the second.

'Shhh, Mac, you're not in Mallards now.'

'Well, I bloody well should be. This is all positively ridiculous.'

'You're fractious after your long journey but trust me, it does get better.'

The door ceremoniously opened revealing Ruby standing in the centre of a silk Persian rug, her feet and hands embellished with henna tattoos, her tall, slim frame swathed in the most exquisite sea-green and silver silk sari and her fingers and toes adorned in a mass of silver and gold rings. She looked like something out of One Thousand and One Nights.

'Practising for a part in Aladdin, are we?' I sniped and breezed past her on my way to her inner sanctum. I had now lost it completely and craved for some normality to my day.

'Wrong time of the month, Mac?' she quipped, following me through yards of cascading brocade drapes to a vast circular room with an arc of more fretted marble screens, more tapestry wall hangings and a surfeit of Persian carpets.

I flopped into a velvet, broad-armed chair and kicked off my shoes. 'What's it like living in the Natural History Museum?'

'Ignore her, Ruby. Our Northumbrian doctor has had a long day and needs time to adjust to Rajputana life.' Tom moved over to a leather Chesterfield sofa and wiped his forehead on his handkerchief.

'Don't patronise me, Tom Wallace. It was you, Ruby and Agnes who dreamed up this crazy idea to bring me here to recuperate, so here I am, though heaven knows why, when I have a perfectly comfortable home in Delhi.'

'And hello to you too.' Ruby clapped her hands and turned as Sanjay appeared from behind a voile screen, bowing low. 'My guests need refreshment.' He backed away, bowing and nodding as he went. She turned back to me. 'So, how are you really, after that brush with death?'

'I'll tell you when I've quenched my thirst, had a long warm bath and changed into something light and casual. This desert sand certainly knows how to creep into every nook and cranny.'

'Then your suite awaits. Tom, how about you?'

'Likewise, Ruby. We've had a rather intense and stressful journey.'

Ruby spied me from the corner of her eye. I shrugged, thinking how unfair it was of me to take out my fragmented emotions on her when she had enough problems of her own. All I could hope was that a couple of hours pampering would ease my body, bring some perspective to my mind and transform me from being the guest from hell.

My trunk was already unpacked when I entered my suite and I found my medical bag, microscope and pith-helmet stored on shelves in the walk-in dressing room, my rifle box leaning against the wall. A huge white cast-iron bath on clawed feet was filled with warm scented, rose-petalled water reminding me of the one at the Taj Mahal Hotel. I quickly zapped all reference to Bombay from my mind, undressed, lowered myself up to my chin, closed my eyes and wallowed in regal extravagance.

There was a knock on the bathroom door. The lady's maid had already departed so it could only be Ruby, I surmised. 'Come in.'

Her head appeared around the door. 'Do you want some company?'

'Not really, but that's not going to stop you.'

'Correct. Now what did Tom mean about an intense and stressful journey?'

'Exactly that. Following your match-making attempts, we found ourselves opening up old wounds, he asked if Duncan and I were having an affair and I found out that his wife, Enid, had left him for an insurance salesman and wanted a divorce.'

'Bloody Nora.' Ruby was now sitting on the end of the bath looking like Hollywood's answer to Rudolph Valentino's paramour in *Son of The Sheik*.

'Your covert plan to bring us together failed miserably, I'm afraid.'

She had the grace to look embarrassed. 'Why?'

'Because turning the clock back would only drag up too many bad memories.'

'Like what?'

'Room 52 at the Metropolitan Hotel, or had you forgotten?' I sank beneath the waterline and breathed out, hoping to close the conversation down. So much for recuperation, I thought. When I surfaced Ruby was sitting on the window seat, her arms crossed, her facial expression determined.

'I don't understand you, Mac. Why on earth do you have to tell him about the abortion?'

'How the hell could I spend the rest of my life with that hanging over my head?'

'Other women have and survived.'

'Well, I'm not other women. Now, leave well alone, Ruby. That part of my life is over. As for your life, how do you cope surrounded by all these grovelling minions who don't understand a word you say?'

'With difficulty, I'm afraid. Vijay is often absent and I hate leaving these apartments for fear of bumping into his awful mother. She could give Laura Henderson a run for her money.'

'Have you met Princess Dashwanabai yet?'

'If you mean Rani Dashwana Devi, the answer is no.' All these name changes were making my head spin. 'I was hoping you would introduce us, now you're here.'

'You do know she doesn't speak English either.'

'Then I'll just have to mime. There's no way I'm learning Hindi.'

'This I have to see.' I rose from the bath and stepped out. Ruby dragged a bath towel from a shelf and threw it in my direction. 'Alright, first thing tomorrow morning I'll pay a visit to the royal zenana and arrange a meeting. I'm sure you and the Princess . . . I mean Rani, will find some common ground, even if the Rajmata is set against you.'

'That would be my hope, Mac. I could do with someone in my corner right now.'

'Then leave it to me.' I slipped into my kaftan. 'If there's nothing else, do you think you could let me rest. I'm supposed to be here recuperating, not running some agony aunt personal advice service.'

'Fine.' She pulled out the bath's plug and water gurgled noisily down the drainpipe. 'Perhaps a short nap will also improve your mood, because from where I'm standing, it's you who needs an agony aunt, not me.'

It was Prince Kapoor Dhawan's wife who met me as I walked into the Jhalanpur zenana at ten-thirty the following morning, and the smile on her face said it all.

'Doctor, Memsahib. So wonderful you come back to us.'
My spirits rose like an erupting geyser, and I made a
namaste. 'How are you and my patient after all this time?'

'I am well for my age, Doctor Memsahib, and my niece is
so happy to know you are here.'

'Then we must go to her immediately,' I said, conversing in
Hindi, 'but first, with your permission, I would like to arrange
for Rani Manika Devi to visit the zenana.'

The aunt hesitated, not sure how to proceed.

'She is one of my closest friends from England and hopes
to become a friend to you all, in time.'

'A friend of you, Doctor Memsahib, is welcome to visit the
zenana at any time.'

'Then there is no time like the present.' I walked to the
zenana entrance and instructed my lady's maid to fetch Ruby
who was waiting nervously in her apartment. She arrived fifteen
minutes later, by which time I was sitting cross-legged on a pile
of silk cushions surrounded by zenana women with Dashwana
Devi explaining to those I had never met before, how she had
transformed me into Scheherazade aboard the ss Narkunda.

'I felt like my sister's rag doll,' I was explaining. 'Bodice on,
bodice off, trousers on, trousers off, hair up, hair down, rings
on, rings off, until your Rani and her aunt decided that I looked
perfect.' The room exploded into laughter, Dashwana's aunt
chastised me for exaggerating the truth and then the screen
parted and Ruby was announced.

The change in atmosphere was palpable as all sound
stopped and, except Vijay's first wife, the women bowed low in
subservient respect. It was if the room had been frozen in time.

Ruby looked at me in utter bewilderment and I needed to act quickly if I was to break the ice. I turned to Dashwana, now standing amongst her entourage, her silk sari flowing, like liquid gold, across her bejewelled toes, her defiant head rigid above her erect spine.

'Your Royal Highness, may I present Her Royal Highness the Maharani Manika Devi from England. She and I have been close friends for many years,' Ruby's right eyebrow arched, 'and she has been anxious to meet you since first arriving in Jhalanpur.'

Dashwana, still only twenty-two years old, her thick black hair cascading down her back and her deep ebony eyes peering over a fine silk veil, placed her hands in prayer, her slim fingers pointing to her forehead then bowed her head. 'Maharani Manika Devi, you honour us with your presence.' I translated each word. 'We know little of your world beyond India, but we hope you will enjoy being part of our world here in Jhalanpur and invite you to visit the zenana whenever you are at the palace.'

Ruby swallowed hard, trying to retain her composure as I finished translating. With her manicured fingernails touching, she repeated the Rani's gesture, bending more from the waist than the neck and then spoke in soft, affectionate tones, her words so unlike her usual acerbic asides. 'Your Royal Highness, I wish you to know that I am also honoured to meet you and the ladies of this zenana.' Dashwana hung on my every word while Ruby laid her crossed palms against her chest. 'You and I are both deeply loved by His Royal Highness the Maharaja

Vijay Kumar Singh II, and it would give me great pleasure if we could become close friends.'

Vijay's younger wife, much smaller in stature yet equally regal in bearing, offered her hand to Ruby and led her to a cobalt blue leather pouffe panelled in intricately painted miniature desert scenes, and helped her sit.

'Memsahib, Doctor MacKenzie, please tell our honoured guest that she is very welcome amongst us today, and we would be fascinated to learn about her life in your country.' She clapped her hands and refreshments magically appeared from nowhere while her aunt stood to the rear of the group, nodding benevolently with a gentle smile on her lips.

Ruby's bland expression hid a multitude of ribald comments now flashing between us in the ether. Obviously, the Windmill Theatre in Soho was not going to be part of the conversation, but the ice was broken and for the next two hours the translations went back and forth, question following question, each louder than the last, as Ruby warmed to her audience and I did my best to give her answers justice in Hindi.

It took some doing. Ruby had become very creative, spinning yet another far-fetched, elaborate tale of her life in London, like the one she had fed to the first-class passengers onboard ship about her dearly departed husband who had died fighting for the British at Passchendaele in the Great War. There was no mention of a first husband in this version, only glamorous tea dances at the Ritz, summer afternoons enjoying polo at Smith's Lawn and Christmas's spent in the glens of Scotland with her darling Ma and Pa. Her fictitious story gained enormous respect from the ladies of the zenana and I could only hope that Ruby remembered everything she had said, because I had lost the plot.

What she now needed was a confidential female translator who could accompany her whenever she left her apartments, enabling her to live amongst these people without feeling at a disadvantage. I must have words with Vijay, I thought, as we returned to her apartments and put our feet up, my head spinning from all my linguistic acrobatics.

'Owning a large houseboat on the Thames, Ruby? Where the hell did that come from?'

'Elsie Thompson's biography. The second Maharani of Tikari owned one in Kashmir to entertain her lovers. I thought it was a nice touch.'

'I hardly think Dashwana Devi would think so. Taking lovers in this zenana would result in you being banished from the kingdom.'

When Vijay and I arrived to view the groundworks of the Dhyan Kumar Singh General Hospital later that day, I spotted Tom standing under an acacia tree in deep conversation with some site official. His khaki tropical suit and gabardine topi made him look like some Egyptian archaeologist leading a dig in the Valley of the Kings, and his handsome bearded features, covered in fine desert dust, only added to that impression as he joined us at the car.

'Morning, Mac, I hope you slept well?'

'I did, and I have since visited the Princess, I mean Rani Dashwana Devi in the palace zenana.'

Vijay seemed more interested in his groundworks and wandered off to find his architect.

'How is she?'

'Blooming, Tom. It was such a delight to see her again.'

He checked my pulse and pulled down my lower eye socket to peer inside. 'And you? Surely this heat is too much for you right now?'

'Oh, stop fussing. I think I'd know if I couldn't handle the heat. I am a doctor, after all.'

'Just don't overdo it. Typhoid is not to be treated lightly.'

'No, doctor.'

We moved across the extensive site heading for a marquee set up by the proposed hospital entrance as the sun began its westward descent into the Rajputana sand. Sets of architect's plans were spread out across a trestle table and it soon became obvious that Tom's eye for detail was in evidence as he explained the general design and pointed out various changes in red ink where he had made alterations.

The hospital was to have four wings, each with a Nightingale Ward of sixteen beds on the first floor for added ventilation, the operating theatres and other medical units located below. Each wing joined at a central concourse above which was a colonnaded circular balcony, the atrium lit from on high by natural light cascading through a domed glass ceiling. It was impressive.

St Thomas's, eat your heart out, I thought, staring beyond the marquee. 'And the Women's Hospital?'

'That will be situated on the far side of the site,' announced Vijay. I turned to find him at my side. 'Here let me show you.'

More scrolls of architect's plans were pulled from under the table and rolled out on top of the others. 'It will be a scaled-down version of the General Hospital, with fifty beds, but there will be an extra entrance below ground and securely patrolled to ensure my female subjects can remain in purdah.'

'You seem to have thought of everything, Vijay.'

'Well, I would like you to study the detailed plans while you are here and make whatever changes you think are necessary.'

'I'll be delighted. Perhaps the plans can be taken to my suite in the palace and I can burn the midnight oil.'

Vijay rolled them up, called to the site official and handed them over. We followed him out of the marquee as a dust cloud appeared on the other side of the site and seconds later Duncan rode up with two male companions and a spare horse.

'Your Highness.' He nodded to Vijay and jumped from his mount. 'Cailin, how do you fancy an early evening gallop through the desert to blow away the cobwebs?'

'I don't think so,' said Tom, holding onto my arm. 'Doctor Stuart-MacKenzie is still rather weak, and I would not want her to lose control of her horse.'

'Take my word for it, Doctor Wallace, Mac is more capable of handling a horse than any Cossack on the Russian Steppes, even after a bout of typhoid, and I will be there to catch her if she falls.'

'That, Mr Fitzpatrick, is what I'm afraid of. As her doctor, I strongly advise against it.'

I could feel Tom vibrating with anger. Gently removing his hand from my arm, I walked over to the gelding and took the reins. 'I suggest a sedate trot would be more to my liking, Duncan, but you are right, it would be good to blow the cobwebs away.' I mounted and looked down on Vijay and Tom, both standing in my path like centurions.

'Your Highness, do I have your permission to return to the palace on horseback, if I promise to be careful?'

'Far be it from me to stop a determined Highlander, Mac. But Tom is right, you are still weak, and I really do not want you breaking your neck before the tiger shoot.'

'Then I will be especially careful. My mother has already made room above the mantlepiece in Riveldene Vicarage for the tiger's head.' With that, I pulled on the reins and led Duncan and the other riders out onto the plain.

'Bloody woman,' I heard Tom say, as he made his way back to the marquee.

We crossed a dry riverbed and climbed to the scrubland on the other side. Duncan signalled for the others to return to the stables, leaving us alone as the waning sun turned the sky the colour of turquoise and the underside of the clouds burnished coral. I was beginning to regret my impetuous decision, but the damage was done and all I could do was enjoy the ride.

We were out for well over two hours and my muscles ached and my throat was parched as we trotted under the arched entrance of the palace stud with night enveloping the stable complex and the milky way meandering across the starlit sky.

'Beautiful, isn't it?'

Duncan was helping me slide from the saddle, his powerful hands gripping my waist and rubbing his chest against my mine as I descended. I pulled away, handing my crop to him as I passed by. 'It certainly beats Northumbria for clarity. Now, how do I get back to the palace?'

'Don't you fancy a sundowner before dinner, Mac? I have a bottle of Jameson's in my quarters.'

'You never give up do you, Duncan?'

'Can you blame me, Cailin? It's not every day I have you to myself.'

'And it's not every day that I can upstage Lady Crawford, but all things considered, I'll opt for a nice bath and a sundowner on my own balcony if you don't mind.'

'As you wish, Cailin, but you don't know what you're missing.'

'Oh, I do, Duncan. Believe me, I do.'

The pony and trap dropped me at the Palace entrance and as I hobbled up the imposing sandstone steps, I caught sight of Tom standing on a West Wing balcony looking at his watch, his body partially in shadow.

'Bugger,' I whispered and made my way to my room.

Chapter Eighteen

P uttaker Lodge put me in mind of Bothal Castle in Morpeth. Its position on the edge of the escarpment gave superb views across the lake to the distant Aravalli Range and I was surprised how verdant the Rajputana desert was at this point.

Ruby was in her element explaining how her home was to be revamped and modernised, as a constant breeze kept me cool from the open windows of the Rolls Royce.

Madame du Blois had already returned to Delhi with copious notes and photographs and was, apparently, already emptying the city's emporiums of European paintings, fabrics and art deco furniture while an army of Indian workman were knocking seven bells out of the building's interior.

It was cool within the thick stone walls and Ruby led the way through a myriad of rooms, up and down numerous staircases and along substantial ramparts and fortified battlements. After an hour I was crying out for a pause.

We halted on the south parapet and took stock of events since my arrival.

'Don't you get a bit tired of all this abundance?' I asked, watching three Indian Spotted Eagles circle on a thermal above my head.

'Actually, Mac, I wouldn't say this to Vijay, but I would die for a pot of jellied eels or some cockles and winkles.'

'You can take the girl out of the East End,' I quipped, 'but you can't take the East End out of the girl.'

'Very funny.'

'Just saying. What did you think of Dashwana Devi?'

Ruby took her time answering. 'She's very beautiful, isn't she?'

'In a very Indian sort of way, yes. Does that make your relationship with Vijay more complicated?' I couldn't understand how Ruby could share him with anybody.

'Not really. I've known from day one that he was married, that he was a Hindu and could have as many wives as he liked. Seeing Dashwana was a bit of a shock, but you had warned me of her age and beauty months ago, and now I've seen her with my own eyes, it only emphasises how much Vijay must feel for me.'

It seemed an odd justification for her relationship, but I wasn't Ruby or deeply in love with Vijay. 'When will you be back in Delhi?'

'Two weeks' time. After Diwali.'

'Ah, Diwali. I can never understand what the Hindus do for five days.'

'Eat, drink, dance, light candles and pray to their Gods at the start of their Hindu New Year. It's all to do with light over darkness and good over evil, apparently.'

'A bit like the Druid's worshipping the sun god on the summer solstice at Stonehenge then?'

'No idea. I've never been to Stonehenge.' Ruby was being obtuse.

'Do you have to attend the whole thing?'

'No. Only day three. That's when families visit each other with food and gifts. Vijay's subjects will bring offerings to him at the Palace, and he will hand out gifts to them.'

I walked over to the crenelated tower and pulled open the cracked wooden door. 'Perhaps a jar of jellied eels as a Diwali present for the Rajmata would cement relationships between you and your mother-in-law.'

'Don't jest, Mac.'

'I wasn't suggesting you should poison her.' We were now descending a steep, circular, stone staircase with daylight slits every fifth step making it difficult to see my feet. I pressed my hands on either wall to keep my balance.

'I wish.' Ruby's voice bounced off the tower and echoed around the interior.

'Oh, come on, Ruby, she can't be that bad, surely?'

'She's worse, and now lining up suitable third wives for Vijay's delectation.'

'Did he tell you that?' I walked out into bright sunlight and had to pause while my irises adjusted.

'He didn't have to. One of the Rajmata's chambermaids is related to Vijay's chaprassi, who mentioned it to Sanjay.'

'And Sanjay mentioned it to you?'

'Correct.'

'Then the sooner your husband gets back to Delhi the better.' We wandered down to the entrance where Ghalib was waiting.

'A little bird told me you were out riding alone with Duncan yesterday evening.'

That stopped me in my tracks. 'Jesus, Ruby, does the chaprassi have relatives in the stables as well?'

'I couldn't say, but Vijay was rather amused watching Duncan and Tom sparring with each other out at the hospital site in the afternoon.'

'Then the sooner I get back to Delhi, the better for me too.'

'To say nothing of Gloria.' Ghalib held the door for Ruby, and she climbed inside.

I waited for him to open my door, then settled back onto the cream leather upholstery. 'What's Gloria got to do with anything?'

Ruby tapped her nose.

'Fine. It's probably nothing to do with me anyway.'

Ruby chuckled. 'Let's just say Gloria knows Tom very well, and she happens to think he's very good looking.'

'When did Gloria meet him?' My fingers were making a mess of my linen slacks.

'When he was on secondment to St George's Hospital during the ss Narkunda's refit. She was working at Bombay's Cama Hospital at the time. Small world, isn't it?'

Poisoned jellied eels suddenly seemed to have any number of beneficial properties.

A soft knocking on my bedroom suite door interrupted a letter I was writing to Frances. I crossed to the door and found Dashwana Devi standing on the other side. I'm not sure who was more surprised. After a quick namaste, I ushered her inside and checked no-one else was loitering in the outer lobby.

She removed her veil and waited by the sofa. I poured two glasses of chilled Lassi, handed one to her and invited her to sit.

'Your Royal Highness, what a lovely surprise.'

'Memsahib, Doctor, I am so happy you are here.'

'How are you, my dear?'

'I'm well thank you, Memsahib Doctor.' She hesitated. 'At least I think I am well.'

'Please call me Doctor Mac as you did before. Now, how can I help you.' Something was worrying her and I suspected I knew what it was.

'Did my miscarriage stop me from having any more children, Doctor Mac?'

As I thought. 'Normally, no. However, there are certain problems that can stop you getting pregnant, which can all be remedied with medical procedures.'

'What are these problems?'

I grabbed my pen and some paper from the desk and drew a diagram. 'Well, there could be a blockage in your fallopian tube here,' I pressed my finger into the left side of my abdomen, 'or pelvic inflammatory disease.' I circled the whole diagram. Her eyes widened. 'Do you have any pain in your abdomen?' She shook her head.

'Pain when you empty your bladder?' Her head continued to shake.

'And your courses, are they heavy or irregular?'

'Only irregular, Doctor Mac, but I would not say heavy.'

'Then I think we can rule out pelvic inflammation. Has there ever been a time when you thought you were pregnant since the miscarriage?'

Her head shook again and tears welled in her eyes. 'No, never. What is wrong with me?'

I held her small hand and lightly rubbed the soft olive skin. 'Your Highness, there is probably nothing wrong with you, but would you allow me to examine you in the privacy of this suite so I can put your mind at rest?'

Like a timid fledgling hovering before its first flight, Dashwana scanned the suite. 'I do not have long.'

'It will only take a few minutes. The sooner we get started the better.'

We moved to the bed, and remembering my examinations onboard ship, she lay on her back, lifted her skirt above her waist and pulled down her silk trousers. Fifteen minutes later she was back on the sofa fully clothed, and I was examining a sample of her vaginal fluid and blood under the microscope.

'Your Highness,' I placed my hand on my heart, 'I am delighted to tell you that you are a perfectly healthy young woman. Rest assured, the only thing that is stopping you from getting pregnant is up here.' I tapped my head. 'Take my advice, stop worrying and try to relax. You are young and have many happy years ahead as the Maharaja's first wife. Let nature takes its course and I'm sure you will be a mother very soon.' I mentally had my fingers crossed.

'Will you look after me when this happens, Doctor Mac?'

'You have my promise. Nothing would give me greater pleasure than being at the birth of your next child, and you already know what my instructions will be.'

She wrinkled her nose and giggled. 'No caffeine, no spicy foods and plenty of rest.'

'If all my patients were as good as you, Your Highness, I would be out of a job.'

'Doctor Mac, I will return to the zenana with a happy heart.' She stopped by the armoire. 'Is riding out of the question?'

I remembered my aching buttocks and thighs from my ride across the plain. 'Once you are pregnant, definitely, so make the most of your freedom while you can.'

'I will, Doctor Mac, and thank you.'

I cleaned my instruments and went back to Frances's letter.

. . . to add to everything else that has happened to me since your wedding, I now find that Gloria Hodgson is besotted by Tom and, according to Ruby, is rather anxious to have me out of here. Apparently, they became friendly when they were both working in Bombay after I left for Calcutta.

What is so frustrating is that I'm irritated with this news when I should be relieved, and don't quote the adage — "I don't want him, but I don't want anyone else to have him." I already know that!

What you don't know is why I'm not dancing in the aisles at the knowledge that Enid wants a divorce. Suffice to say, my reasons are sound but not ones to put on paper. Hopefully we will get together for Christmas and I can tell all then.

I'll be back at Alipore Road in two weeks so send your reply there. I'm anxious to hear all about the honeymoon.

Much love

Mac

xxx

The tiger shoot was arranged for the Saturday before Diwali, so I spent the next few days taking pot shots at tree stumps with my rifle.

Duncan had suggested that I sit in a howdah strapped to the top of a rock pile to get an idea of height, and two stable hands had been set the task of building this while I finished studying the plans for the Stuart-MacKenzie Zenana hospital. A bamboo ladder was leaning against the stack of rocks when I rounded the corner at the back of the stables and Duncan was on hand to give me a leg-up, which was fortuitous as an elephant was a great deal taller than I had imagined.

'How do I mount an elephant,' I asked, scrambling into the wooden howdah and looking down at my ex-lover standing below me, a riding crop in one hand and his emerald-green eyes twinkling from his unfettered view of my posterior.

'With difficulty, Cailin, you being a woman.'

'Oh, very droll, Fitzpatrick, but not helpful.'

'I mean it, Mac, mounting an elephant is not the easiest thing to do in a skirt.'

'Why?'

'Because the elephant will lift you onto its back using its trunk.'

'Good God! Where does it put its trunk?'

'Under your right foot. You hang on for grim death until you reach the top, then crawl over its ears.' His comment was deadly serious.

'Then I'll be opting for a pair of jodhpurs.'

'Shame.'

'Duncan Fitzpatrick, you're unbelievable.'

'That's what all the girls say.'

If I allowed anymore of this banter to continue, I'd be practicing my shooting skills in the dark, so I ignored him, balanced my rifle barrel on the front edge of the howdah, tucked the curved stock under my armpit, closed one eye, sited the tree stump some two-hundred-yards away and pulled the trigger. The rifle butt nearly shattered my scapula and a puff of sand rose from the scrub, yards from my target.

'Well, that went well,' tutted Duncan, peering through his binoculars. 'You just annihilated a snake.'

I reloaded the rifle with some difficulty and tried again, angling more to my right.

'Fire,' shouted Duncan and I shattered a rock twenty yards past the stump. He cocked his head and shielded his eyes. 'At this rate, every tiger in Rajputana will have run to the hills.'

'Have faith, Gunga Din.' I loaded again and this time I lowered the barrel a couple of inches, took my time lining up the ground in front of the stump, countered to five, breathed out and tried again. 'Yes!' I shouted, as the bullet ripped into my target.

'Well done, Cailin, but as you'll only have one shot at a tiger, I suggest you keep practicing.' With that, he rotated his heels in the sand and strode away, leaving me to climb down the rickety ladder on my own.

'Charming,' I shouted and rammed another bullet down the barrel.

Ruby was waiting for me when I arrived back in the West Wing, my hands and face covered in black powder residue and a broad grin on my face.

'You look like an East End chimney sweep?'

'I tell you, Ruby, this rifle is amazing.' I placed it against the wall, leaving a black smudge. 'It can kill someone at four-hundred yards with practice. Those Pashtuns really knew what they were doing.'

'Fascinating.' Ruby handed me a gin and tonic, noting the mark on the expensive wallpaper. 'Could you take a pot shot at Vijay's mother from your balcony, that would be about four-hundred yards?

'Why, what's she done now?' I lubricated my parched throat.

'She's refusing to allow me access to the zenana. Our illustrious Rajmata is convinced I'll be a bad influence on her son's first wife.'

'And she's probably right.'

'Thank you, Mac. You're a great help.'

'My pleasure.' I rubbed black soot from my glass with my thumb. It didn't help. 'Ruby, whatever the Rajmata says, it won't stop Dashwana Devi doing exactly what she likes. She may be under that woman's influence, but I can assure you she has a mind of her own. Do you want me to have a word with her?'

Ruby grabbed my sleeve, about to reply, but ingested black powder residue and disturbed dust instead and headed for the window, coughing. 'Christ, Mac, why can't you act like other women?'

'I do.'

'Don't be bloody silly. If I didn't know you had a womb, I'd be the first one to think you were a man in disguise.'

'Rubbish, and for goodness's sake keep your voice down.'

'Well, really. Just look at you. What possesses Tom Wallace or Duncan Fitzpatrick to find you attractive is beyond me.'

I caught sight of my reflection in the large ornate wall mirror and groaned. 'I'm off for a bath.'

'What about Dashwana Devi?'

'I'll deal with her when I've re-discovered my feminine side.'

Chapter Nineteen

I thought I looked rather fetching in my cream jodhpurs, umber leather riding boots, khaki safari jacket, red silk neckerchief and gaberdine topi. My rifle had been cleaned and oiled, my bullets prepared and lying in their ammunition pockets across my chest and a beaten-up army issue water cannister was hanging in its canvas holder from my hip. A glass of wine at breakfast had coloured my cheeks and brightened my eyes and I was ready and eager to get on my way.

'Right, Mac, go show these men a thing or two about hunting.' My reflection saluted and I strode out of my suite with butterflies ambushing my stomach.

The all-male shooting party stood in a group at the bottom of the main entrance steps with a line of cars drawn up behind. Each turned as I appeared, and Vijay stepped forward and held out his hand.

'I trust you are well rested, Mac. It's going to be a long day.'

'Where are we going, Vijay?'

'Puttaker Forest. One of my villagers spotted fresh tiger scat by the dry riverbed and one of his oxen is missing.'

'Then I look forward to the hunt.'

We arrived in a clearing thirty-minutes later where Indian beaters in loin cloths and turbans milled around a large canvas tent. To its right, a group of mahouts were tending their elephants and to the left, the British Political Agent, Major Snellings, was leaning against a tree trunk smoking a pipe.

'Good morning, Snellings,' shouted Vijay across the clearing. 'Let me introduce Doctor Elizabeth Stuart-MacKenzie, my honoured guest. Mac, this is Major Snellings.' The agent tipped his pith helmet, looking me up and down with disgust and excused himself to go and talk to Duncan who was already checking on the animals.

'I guess he got out of bed on the wrong side this morning?' I whispered. Vijay smiled and led me into the tent where a steward stood with a tray of nimbu panis.

'Would you prefer something stronger?'

'No,' I replied, following Tom with my eyes as he crossed the clearing. 'This will be fine.'

'Then if you'll excuse me, I'll go and check on progress with my shikari.'

I wandered outside sipping my drink and stood under the tent canopy surveying the scene before me. It was hardly a forest, I thought, the ragged, gnarled branches of acacia trees providing some shade amongst the tall grasses and bent arak shrubs but giving little in the way of a forest canopy. I recalled a lecture I had listened to in Edinburgh Medical School about the healing and antiseptic properties of the arak tree and how the ends of its fibrous twigs had been chewed for centuries by indigenous Indians to use as oral toothbrushes. I watched, fascinated, as one of the beaters plucked just such a twig from the bush alongside him and stuck it in his mouth.

A tall man with a mass of greying facial hair under a large white pagri, his cotton safari jacket and gathered pantaloons looking well worn, approached and addressed me in Hindi.

'Memsahib.' With his hands together, he bowed his head. 'Please, you come now. We are ready for shikar.'

I grabbed my rifle, donned my topi and followed him towards a thicket of scrub where the elephants stood chewing rough vegetation while their handlers busied themselves checking the wooden howdahs and tightening the straps encircling the elephants' bellies, foreheads and tails. 'You ready to climb, Memsahib?' asked my mahout.

I locked eyes with Duncan, handed my rifle to the shikari, walked around the front of my elephant, placed my right foot in its curled trunk and wrapped my arms around its thick, bristled appendage. 'I'm ready.'

'Up,' shouted the mahout, sitting cross-legged on the elephant's head and with that I left the ground like a rocket to the sound of a trumpeting roar and scrambled unceremoniously across the back of the mahout before clambering over the howdah's side.

Phew, I thought as I stood up. At least I didn't make a complete fool of myself.

Duncan raised his hand in a wave, winked then turned and said something to his mahout. I watched in disbelief as his elephant went down on its rear knees, stretched out its front legs along the ground and rested on its stomach. A short wooden step ladder was placed against its flank and Duncan casually walked up the animal's side and sedately entered his howdah.

You bastard, I thought, as I leant over to grab the stock of my rifle from the shikari. Duncan refused to make eye contact as I made a very rude finger gesture.

'May I join you?' said a familiar voice from below. I peered
down to find Tom looking up. For a split second I didn't know
what to do, but Vijay, eyeing me from the top of his own
elephant, his black eye patch visible below his dark green pagri,
briefly nodded his head.

'Of course, Tom. There's certainly room for two.'

The mahout acknowledged Tom's raised hand by giving his
elephant the order and the howdah swayed alarmingly as our
elephant sank to its knees to allow Tom to mount, which he
did with ease, then instantly grabbed my waist to stop me
losing my balance as the animal stood up.

'OK?'

I brushed small wood splinters from my jacket and counted
to ten. 'Yes, fine.'

'No, really, Mac. Are you OK?'

By now, I was short on pleasantries. 'For the love of God,
Tom, stop fussing. I'm fine. Now let me enjoy my day.'

We set off with eight elephants forming a well-spaced line. I
leant forward to ask our mahout the name of our elephant.

'Babar, Memsahib. Elephant called Babar.'

I looked from left to right noting who was where. Vijay
with his shikari and two armed guards led from the centre, the
shikari shouting instructions to the beaters and pointing with a
long stick. To his left was Duncan and the architect. We were
on Vijay's right and beyond us were Major Snellings and the
Colonel of the Jhalanpur Guard. I had no idea who the other
guests were sitting atop of their elephants as they tramped
through the undergrowth, but I could feel excitement
mounting all around me as Babar used his long tusks to push

aside trees and shrubs, causing wild peacocks to fly from their
perches, their long tail feathers streaming behind as a
cacophony of high-pitched, shrill cries exploded across the sky.
A panicked group of Rhesus monkeys suddenly leapt from
branch to branch, their camel-furred bodies and pink faces
flashing past in every direction, only adding to the mayhem
with their ear-splitting shrieks of alarm.

We continued ahead in regular formation, and I quickly got
used to swaying with Babar's gait as we went along. At one
point, emerging from a thicket of trees, I spotted Chital deer
and Black Buck vaulting across our path in a long balletic line,
making me sigh at the beauty of God's wild creatures, but this
emotion was quickly extinguished when a commotion up ahead
caused much shouting and signalling and we went forward
slowly, each hunter raising his rifle in expectation.

Babar trumpeted loudly, smelling danger and the beaters
spread out wide, banging the ground with their sticks while
ululating.

'Look,' shouted Tom, pointing at some deep claw marks
dug vertically into a tree trunk on our right.

'Tiger,' called out the shikari and bellowed more
instructions. My heart was now in my mouth, my fully loaded
rifle barrel resting on the front of the howdah, my finger on the
trigger.

Babar pushed an acacia tree aside and there, lying dead on
the ground, its stomach ripped open and its guts spilling out
across the rough, blood-stained ground, was an ox.

'Quiet,' shouted Vijay. We all held our breath.

Coming from the long grass up ahead, we could hear a low guttural growl. Whatever was there was well camouflaged. The shakiri pointed his stick left and right without saying a word and the beaters melted into the undergrowth.

'Where are they going?' I whispered.

Tom moved closer, his hot breath in my ear. 'They want to encircle the tiger and push it towards the guns.'

I closed my eyes, feeling the fear of the animal we were about to kill as Babar shook his large head and flapped his enormous ears then moved ahead. Only the crunch of dead grasses under the animal's feet and a low grumbling growl in the undergrowth could be heard as each elephant slowly advanced, then the beaters' ululating trills reached us on the wind.

A bone-chilling snarl sixty yards ahead prompted a sudden flash of yellow and black in the undergrowth as a tiger bolted across the parched earth to my left, a gun went off and a bullet ripped a swathe diagonally through the grass where the animal had just been hiding. I looked up to see white smoke rising from Major Snellings rifle.

'Let's hope that idiot hasn't wounded the animal,' hissed Tom through gritted teeth, scanning the scrubland.

Like a well-formed military platoon the elephants veered left and stood, fifty yards apart, waiting. I grabbed my water bottle to quench my thirst and handed it back to Tom as I realigned my rifle. The beaters were getting closer, their shouts louder, heightening the tension all around as my gut sensed danger straight ahead.

Instantly my world shrank to a pinpoint and appeared to slow right down. It was as if I was standing in a time warp, my brain pouring all its energy into my eyeballs as they locked onto an enormous tiger in full technicolour. It rose from the grass, fifty yards away, its head down, its teeth barred, its fangs dripping saliva as it bounded across the gap at breakneck speed, heading straight for Babar. With powerful rear leg muscles, the animal then leapt into the air, its forelegs outstretched, the claws of its huge paws fully extended, and a baying roar curdled my blood. I fired.

'Get down,' yelled Tom.

I felt the impact of the animal smack into Babar's head and lost my grip on the rifle which went flying. I could hear the tiger's claws rip into the elephant's leathery skin and smell its breath as a wild human scream rent the air. There was a shot, a thud and all went quiet. Tom rammed his pistol into its holder while I peered over the howdah at our mahout, lying across Babar's head, blood pouring from his arm.

'Quick, we must do something.' Before I could move, another heart-stopping roar came from my left.

'Mine,' shouted Vijay, standing, legs apart, his rifle held rigidly above his chest. I froze, transfixed. Charging from behind a thicket came a second tiger, blood oozing from its hind leg as it thundered across the ground creating a dust cloud. Vijay's rifle bullet hit it smack between the eyes, lifting the body in a twisted death spiral before dropping it to the ground like a sack of potatoes.

'Tom,' I shouted, dragging my kerchief from around my neck and climbing out of the howdah. He held onto my waistband as I tied the scarf tightly around the mahout's upper arm forming a tourniquet and we dragged him bodily back into the howdah and laid him on the floor.

Babar's ears lifted to the sound of the shikari's command and the animal stepped forward, raising its right leg. It then kicked the fallen tiger three times with its colossal, padded foot, sending the limp carcass rolling across the dirt while Vijay, rifle still cocked, ordered his elephant forward to do the same with his kill.

I couldn't take my eyes off what was happening.

'Mac, I need some help here.' Tom was fighting to stop the mahout from bleeding to death.

I guiltily knelt and pressed down hard with my hands on the deep wounds as Tom ripped his shirt apart and used it as a bandage. Our eyes met across the mahout's trembling body. 'You killed it, Mac, straight through the heart. My shot only ended the beast's muscle spasms.'

I picked up my rifle from the dirt and we left the scene with our mahout laid out on a roughly assembled stretcher, his arm sterilised with brandy, rebandaged and held across his chest with a leather strap. The two dead tigers looked huge and magnificent, hanging by their feet, lashed to rustic poles and carried by beaters. One had a bullet through its forehead and a rifle wound in its hind leg, the other with a hole through its heart and a pistol shot to its temple.

I felt gutted as Babar, with weeping claw marks scaring his head and upper body, carried Tom and me back to the clearing where I insisted on cleansing and sterilising the elephant's wounds while trying to deal with my guilt for causing the death of such a beautiful wild animal.

Back at the palace, I shut myself in my suite and cried tears of deep remorse. What had started as a wickedly exciting adventure had ended in an indefensible blood bath, all to satisfy men's desire for sport, and I knew whatever danger might befall me in the future, I would never again lift a gun in anger.

'Cailin, can I come in?' Duncan's concern was touching.

'It's open,' I called and rubbed my eyes with my knuckles.

He stood inside the door, all jocularity gone from his face and waited for me to open the conversation. I just stood there, rooted to the spot, my blood-spattered jacket evidence of the day's carnage.

'It was a clean shot, Mac. Death was instant. All Tom Wallace did was sever his nerve endings.'

I turned away and walked onto the balcony. 'How do you do it, Duncan? How do you men justify killing such magnificent beasts for sport? Those animals didn't stand a chance.'

'No, they didn't, but the only reason Vijay shot the other one was to put her out of her misery.'

'Her?'

'Yes, I examined the carcass and found she had been lactating. The Maharaja and I searched the area for hours after you left and found three tiger cubs cowering in a depression at the side of the dry riverbed.'

I swung round, my heart about to break in two. 'My God! Where are they now? How old are they?'

'We brought them back to the palace. They are about four months old, and I'll rear them until they can fend for themselves in the wild and then I'll set them free.'

'And that makes you feel better, does it?'

'No, Mac, and you should know better than to think I would condone hunting any wild animal unless it was endangering human life or was badly injured, but this is India and game shooting is embedded in the male psyche, just as it is in Scotland.'

I gripped the sandstone balustrade. 'Then, all I can say is, I'm glad I'm a woman. What I did today was unforgiveable, but I will just have to live with it.' I sounded cynical. 'However, I'll never forget the smell of that tiger's fear and never, ever, do such an evil thing again.'

'Come here.'

He came up close and held me tightly in his arms, trying in vain to shield me from the images revolving around my head. 'Don't torture yourself, Cailin. The animal would have killed you if he could. What you did was kill in self-defence.'

It didn't help, but I saw no point in telling Duncan that, and I knew, deep in my own psyche, that the cubs would be given the very best chance of survival under his professional care.

Chapter Twenty

I spent most of my remaining days at Jhalanpur in the tiger cub enclosure, feeding them, playing with them, loving them, while the rest of the Princely State celebrated Diwali.

Dashwana Devi came by most afternoons, and we sat, cuddling the three bundles of fur and speaking of our lives and what the future held. Ruby joined us when she could. It was the perfect opportunity for them to get better acquainted without the Rajmata's interference and they quickly grew to trust and respect each other.

On the third day of Diwali it was hot with little breeze, and I felt for Ruby as she stood alongside Vijay on the steps of the Jhalanpur palace watching him giving and receiving New Year's gifts. I sat with Dashwana Devi and her entourage sipping chilled lemonade on the first floor above the main entrance, hidden behind a fretted marble screen.

Ruby looked stunning, her blonde hair and curvaceous frame barely visible beneath the same cream silk sari she had worn at Frances's wedding. The Rajmata, veiled in deep green, stood to one side and slightly to the rear of her son never taking her eyes off Ruby, her spine rigid. The hatred in her eyes was obvious. She detested the very idea of Vijay exposing his wife's features to all his subjects in such a western fashion, but Ruby was oblivious to this. She played her role to perfection, smiling broadly as each chosen family mounted the steps, made their deferential namastes, and laid their meagre offerings at the feet of their king.

It all seemed to take forever, but finally we adjourned to the zenana for more refreshments and food, leaving Ruby and Vijay to return alone to their quarters.

For the first time in days, I was able to relax, socialising with the Jhalanpur women and making them laugh at my expense over my time with the Khyber Rifles in Landi Kotal. My story of Lamis had them enthralled, and they insisted on making up a parcel of sweetmeats, lotions and scented candles for me to take back to her in Alipore Road, making me promise to bring her on my next visit to the palace.

Great excitement then ensued when Dashwana's aunt announced that Vijay would be visiting the zenana for the night and her niece was to prepare herself accordingly. The ladies immediately busied about readying the queen for her husband's delight, giving me the excuse to slipped away. Ruby would be on her own trying hard not to feel rejected, I thought, and I was right.

'Would you like some company?' I asked, as I gained entry to her apartments.

She was reclining on a sofa dressed in a mink-coloured silk kaftan and flicking through the pages of a high society magazine. She laid the magazine aside and clapped her hands. Sanjay instantly appeared. 'We will be two for dinner, Sanjay.

'Very well, Your Highness.'

I raised my eyebrows at such formality in her private suite and flopped onto the paprika-toned leather chesterfield. 'So, how did it go?'

'You should know if you were watching from the zenana's prison cell.'

'Actually, I was behind a fretted, marble screen, with a pleasant breeze keeping me cool, but I couldn't see much, other than you bowing like a nodding donkey and your mother-in-law aiming virtual daggers in your direction.'

'To be honest, Mac, I found it all rather boring, but we only have to do it once a year so I'm sure I'll cope.'

'At least it's now over for this year and you can get back to Delhi. Thankfully I can too. I can't imagine what problems Gloria has stored up for me at the WCHS.'

'I assume you know Vijay is with Dashwana Devi tonight?'

'Another Hindu custom?' I asked, not sure how to respond.

'Yes and no.' She looked at me from under her long, blackened eyelashes. 'He loves her you know, in his own way, and now I've got to know her, I don't feel quite so bad about sharing him.'

'But what about you?' This whole scenario was way beyond my comprehension. 'What are you supposed to do while he's enjoying the delights of his first wife?'

'Enjoy the company of a certain Northumbrian doctor, eat wonderful western cuisine and drink a very expensive bottle of French wine.'

'What's on the menu?'

'Beef Bergin whatsit, with new potatoes, green asparagus, and creamed mushrooms.'

'*Boeuf Bourguignon,*' I corrected.

'If you say so. Now, how about some bubbly to start the evening off with a swing?' She moved across to the gramophone player and the strains of Duke Ellington's *Mood Indigo* rippled through the apartments. I found myself swaying in time to this popular American rhythm and longed for my own home.

The night sky was aglimmer with stars as we sat on Ruby's spacious balcony after dinner, looking out across the palace grounds to Jhalanpur city, twinkling with Diwali lights from every veranda, balcony and garden, the strains of soft Indian sitar music captured on the evening air. The meal had been sensational, and I lay back on the wicker bathchair and let the cool breeze wash over my perspiring skin.

'By the way,' Ruby announced, sipping her thick, sweet Moroccan coffee, 'Vijay has fired his Political Agent.'

'Major Snellings?'

'Is that his name? All I know is that steam was coming out of Vijay's ears when he returned from the tiger hunt, and he didn't have a good word to say about the man. Exactly what did happen out there in Puttaker Forest?'

'Major Snellings is a pompous old codger with an ego the size of Duncan's. He couldn't resist showing his prowess as a shooter when the tiger cubs' mother tried to escape from the guns. He was aiming for a kill, of course, but missed and wounded her badly in her hind quarters. If Vijay hadn't put her out of her misery, she would have died a very slow and painful death, as would her cubs.' The Diwali lights seemed to prism through my watering eyes.

'Blimey, no wonder Vijay was so angry. He can't stand cruelty to animals.'

I bit my tongue. This was not the moment to point out that the whole idea of a tiger shoot was cruel.

'Are you still upset about what happened?'

I blinked. 'Of course, Ruby. I took the life of a majestic wild animal whose only crime was to kill one of the villager's oxen for food. Expensive and exotic animal skins may be your idea of posh furnishings, but killing a healthy animal to get them is indefensible.'

'Are you saying I'm two-faced?'

'In a word, Ruby, yes, just like the rest of Europe's nobility.'

'That's unfair and you know it. Their skins are not the reason these animals are hunted.' She poured more coffee. 'Do you want some?'

'No thanks, it's far too strong for me.'

'Fine, but there's a lot wrong with your argument, Mac.' We were both tipsy and she was like a dog with a bone. 'How about explaining away that poor mouse you mutilated to find out if you were pregnant? It may not have been a majestic tiger, but it was a living, breathing, healthy creature all the same.'

I had no way of defending myself. Ruby had extinguished my argument as quickly as dousing a match in water. That didn't stop me feeling affronted however, so having no retort, I got to my feet, wished her a good night and weaved my way back to my bed. As for my good night's sleep, after the reference to the dead laboratory mouse, I could kiss that goodbye before I even lay down.

At three in the morning I was still awake, reliving my pregnancy test at Elsie and Arthur Thornton's bungalow in Calcutta when the sound of heavy banging interrupted my thoughts. I staggered across my suite, pulling my kaftan over my head and trying to get my brain to function when I heard a heavy thump and someone whimpering. Wrenching the door open, I found Ruby lying in a heap at my feet, panting and staring up at me, her eyes full of fear.

'Ruby, what's wrong?'

'I . . .' she smacked her chest.

'Sanjay,' I screamed and went into clinician mode. He appeared instantly.

'Fetch Doctor Wallace immediately and tell him to bring his medical bag, then wake up the compounder and get the palace dispensary open.'

'Yes, Memsahib, Doctor.'

I grabbed my stethoscope as my medical mind searched for answers. Ruby's heartbeat was rapid and very irregular, and she was beginning to heave. I pulled her to her feet and helped her to the bathroom where she sank onto her knees and grabbed the lavatory pan. Ramming my fingers down her throat, I tried to make her vomit. She wretched and wretched but little came out.

Tom rushed in, his striped pyjama bottoms and silk dressing gown far too familiar from our nights at the Taj Mahal Hotel. 'What's happening?'

'I'm not sure. Her heart is racing, it's very irregular and she's trying to be sick. And, Tom, I can't get a pulse.'

He dropped his medical bag and knelt beside her. 'Ruby, can you hear me? We need you to tell us what's happening.' Her hand gripped her throat and she shook her head.

'OK, nod if any of the following applies. Do you understand?'

She nodded, heaved again and I began to tremble violently.

'Do you feel dizzy? . . . Have you got stomach-ache? . . . Do you have a headache? . . . do you have a burning sensation in your mouth? . . .' To my horror, Ruby nodded to all of Tom's questions.

'What is it, Tom? What's wrong?' I was now standing by the wash-hand basin, gripping the edge.

'She's been poisoned, Mac. Cardiac glycosides are attacking her heart. We need to give her an emetic urgently to empty her stomach or she'll die.'

'How, Tom? She can't vomit.' I needed to get a grip. 'Salt water, that should do it.'

'Ipecac syrup would be better, and we need ground charcoal to soak up the toxins.' Tom was now pushing his fingers down Ruby's throat.

'I'll get some from the dispensary. What's the poison?'

"Probably crushed oleander. It's very common in India.'

"Then, thank God you're here.' I had never seen anything like this.

'There's not much time, Mac, so be quick. And bring plenty of water.'

I don't remember reaching the dispensary or getting back to the West Wing, but I rushed through the door carrying ipecac syrup and activated charcoal and began mixing the latter in a tumbler of water. Ruby was still retching and groaning but Tom didn't hesitate. He grabbed the syrup, threw her head back and poured the contents straight down her throat.

'Be careful, Tom, or she'll choke.'

'Better that than dying.' My blood ran cold.

We waited in silence, me with my fingers crossed and Tom studying the minute hand on his watch as Ruby continued to groan and tremble. Finally, her shoulders shot up, her head disappeared into the lavatory pan and a blackened kaleidoscopic of stomach contents erupted from her mouth.

'There goes our evening meal,' I murmured, feeling relief like a shot of morphine.

'Sadly, the toxins might already be in her bloodstream,' replied Tom, ominously. 'Let's get her onto the bed and get some charcoal down her.'

She lay back on a mass of cushions, her eyes oscillating from side to side. 'Mac, I can't see.'

'That's because your blood pressure has dropped,' said Tom, his voice calm but firm. 'Don't worry about that now, the important thing is to drink this medicine.'

I placed my hand on her back and brought the glass to her lips. As the black liquid went down, she coughed and spluttered, jettisoning most of it over my kaftan. 'For Christ's sake, Ruby, don't do that,' I shouted, in frustration. Her forehead creased, she rubbed her abdomen and shook her head.

'Come on, Ruby, you must help me. Your life depends on it.' I tried again, more slowly, and watched the contents slide down her oesophagus. 'Good Girl.'

'Mac,' her hand gripped mine, her knuckles white. 'Don't let me die.' Her words devastated me.

Tom placed his stethoscope bell on her left breast and shook his head. 'We must wait for the charcoal to do its job,' he said, keeping Ruby calm. I spun away, clawing at my hair and shaking my head in sheer terror. What the hell had she eaten, I thought, probing my memory for a clue. Tom must have been thinking the same thing, because he waltzed me out of the bedroom and sat me on the sofa.

'Where's Vijay?'

'Spending the night with Dashwana Devi.' His teeth ground together. 'I joined Ruby for dinner to keep her company.'

'What did you both eat?' I went through the list. 'And were you served from the same dish in each case?'

I nodded, remembering Sanjay bringing the tureen to the table and serving from there.

'What about drinks?'

'We both had champagne and then French red wine.' I looked into his deep blue eyes. 'The bottles were opened before my eyes and the contents poured directly into our glasses.'

'And, after the meal?'

'I had a small brandy and Ruby had her usual Moroccan coffee.' My hand hit my mouth.'

'But you didn't?'

'No, she offered it to me, but I don't like strong black coffee.' I felt blood drain from my face. 'Tom . . . I could have been . . .'

'Don't go there. We need that coffee pot as evidence.'

I ran to the kitchen. 'Sanjay,' I screamed, 'have you thrown the Maharani's coffee away?'

'No, Memsahib, Doctor. I throw away in morning with rubbish.'

'Where is it?' I was now shaking his arms violently.

'Here, Memsahib Doctor.' He lifted the long-handled metal pot from the stove and handed it over.

'Where does the coffee come from?'

'The bazaar, Memsahib. The emporium in the bazaar.' He looked terrified, and no wonder, but I didn't have time to explain.

I returned to find Tom standing by the window looking out into the black Rajputana night and Ruby laying against the pillow, her gaunt face devoid of colour.

'Is she dead?' I touched her skin which was still warm.

'Not yet, Mac, but she's collapsed. Where's the nearest hospital?'

'I've no idea. Jodhpur? Jaipur?' . . . Jodhpur. Windom Hospital.' It was as if a light had gone on in my brain.

'We need to get her there as fast as possible if she has any chance of staying alive.'

'Then we must tell Vijay. I'll go to the zenana. Can you raise Vijay's chaprassi and get him to organise the royal train?' I felt more in control now that we had a plan and ran through the palace as if my heels were on fire. I shoved my way passed the zenana guards with strength I didn't know I had.

'Vijay,' I screamed, having no clue where Dashwana's private apartments were. 'Vijay, where are you?'

'I'm here, Mac.' He stood in a doorway in a long white kurta.

'The West Wing. NOW!' I didn't wait to explain but charged back through the East Wing with him following in my wake.

He headed for his own apartments, but I grabbed his arm. 'No, this way.' We entered my bedroom together and the sound that came from his throat sounded like a wounded animal in excruciating pain. He rushed to Ruby's side.

Tom reappeared, dragged him bodily off Ruby and spun him around. 'Vijay, she's still alive, but she's been poisoned. I'll explain everything on the way, but right now we must get her to Jodhpur Hospital, and we need the train.'

'I'll fetch more charcoal,' I muttered, half-talking to myself.

'And ipecac, Mac,' added Tom.

'We'll need to warn the hospital,' I said, looking from Tom to Vijay. Tom, facing the door, repeated my words, in Hindi.

'I can do that, Doctor Mac.'

Dashwana was standing behind me, her face uncovered, her eyes locked onto Ruby's face and her small, graceful hands plucking at her nightdress.

I grabbed them in mine and spoke slowly and clearly. 'Ring the hospital and tell them that Manika Devi has been poisoned and needs atropine. We don't have any here in Jhalanpur.'

'Atropine.' The word sounded strange coming from her lips.

'Yes, that's right. Atropine.' I grabbed my pen and a sheet of paper from my notepad and wrote it down, then stuffed it into her hand. 'Tell them we think it is oleander poisoning. They'll know what to do.' She backed away, constantly repeating the word as Vijay picked up a large glass vase from the dresser and threw it at the wall.

'Vijay!' Tom shook him vigorously by the shoulders. 'You need to get a grip, man. This isn't helping.'

The man I had loved for years nodded to me as he left the room with Vijay in tow leaving me alone with Ruby, her body fighting against enormous odds to stay alive due, in my opinion, to her mother-in-law's vicious intent.

'Don't die, Ruby,' I pleaded, wrapping the coffee pot into a pillowcase and putting it in my valise. 'Don't allow that evil woman to murder you in cold blood.'

Chapter Twenty-One

The toxicologist had been briefed and was waiting for me as I entered the hospital laboratory with samples of Ruby's blood and stomach contents. I handed them over with the coffee pot, disinterested in the formal diagnosis. Whatever the cause, Ruby had fallen foul of a culture she didn't understand and was probably about to pay the ultimate price.

'How is the Maharani doing?' he asked.

'Badly,' I said and left him to his work. There was nothing more I could do but hover in the background. Ruby had only just survived the journey and she was still critically ill. We had given her more ipecac and charcoal on route and the clinicians had done their best, administering atropine and monitoring her hourly for atrial fibrillation and bradycardia. Vijay, meanwhile, flatly refused to leave her bedside as the long hours went by.

I needed to get back to Delhi and Agnes needed to be told what had happened so she could field any questions. I asked where I could make a telephone call and was directed to the Senior Surgeon's office.

'Elizabeth, is that you?'

'Yes, Agnes. I'm at the Windom Hospital in Jodhpur with Vijay Kumar Singh and Tom Wallace.' I filled her in on everything that has happened and told her I would be leaving for Delhi that afternoon.

'Are you sure, Elizabeth? Don't you want to stay to see this through, whatever the outcome?'

'No, Agnes. Ruby is in good hands here and I need to get back to work. I will ring you again as soon as I reach home.'

'Very well dear. Take care and I'll see you in a day or two.'

Tom saw me off at the station. Just a hug and a quick peck on the cheek. I had no idea if or when I would see him again, but I didn't care. Since leaving Delhi, I had contracted typhoid fever, killed a tiger and one of my closest friends had been poisoned. I was an empty shell on two legs and all I wanted was to get home, hug Lamis and try to mend under Mrs Appleby's tender care.

She met me on the veranda steps, took my valise and led me into the drawing room where a tray of sandwiches, a pot of Darjeeling tea and my mail were waiting on the table.

'Lamis is in her room, Doctor Mac, and I've told her not to disturb you until you have had time to rest.'

'That's fine, Mrs Appleby. I'll read my mail then have a shower before dinner. I'll pop up to see her on my way to the bathroom. Has there been any news from Jodhpur?'

'Nothing as yet, dear, but Doctor Scott called by earlier to explain what had happened and she left you some reports to read before you go back into work.'

I poured some tea and picked up the first letter in the pile, recognising Frances's familiar hand.

Dear Mac,

Your long letter, full of exciting and challenging events left me breathless. I hope you are now fully recovered with no lingering side effects from the typhoid fever and ready to continue your work at the WCHS.

As for Gloria and Tom, I shouldn't read too much into Ruby's words. Gloria may be fancy free, but I doubt Tom would be ready for a new relationship so quickly after being spurned by his ex-wife. That said, I am truly relieved that Enid finally decided to release him. That marriage has been failing for years, if it ever got started in the first place. No matter what your reasons for spurning his advances are, and I can't wait to hear about them at Christmas, I hope his future is far brighter than his past.

As for the Hamiltons, we had a wonderful honeymoon in Malabar. The mountains were spectacular, and the long unspoilt beaches reminded me so much of Ireland . . .

The second letter was from Virginia Cottesmore with a three-page spread from the Calcutta Statesman on the wedding of Henriette and Jonathon. It had also been the social event of the season and I had completely forgotten about it. I made a note to ring Virginia the first chance I got to apologise for being so remiss, then turned to Agnes's reports.

Things had progressed smoothly at the WCHS in my absence. We now had forty-eight clinics around seven Punjab districts and a new class of welfare workers were about to qualify and take over from the missionary sisters in various locations. Gloria had been remarkably subdued in her attempt to expand our services and I could only assume that she was more fearful of Agnes's temper than she was of mine. There had been one dispute with the Public Health Commissioner in Sialkot over funding, but Agnes had asked Sir Peter to handle that from Calcutta, which he had done with his usual diplomatic aplomb, and all had ended amicably.

I guess I'm dispensable, I thought, as I climbed the stairs to Lamis's bedroom and was instantly smothered in loving hugs. She was full of news about her new course and the myriad of other students in her class and the time flew by. I heard Mrs

Appleby call from the hall that dinner was nearly ready so I rushed away for my shower, comforted to be back in the bosom of my family and praying that Ruby's heart was strong enough to counter the cardiac glycosides.

My working days seemed irrelevant as I waited for news from Jodhpur and I insisted on remaining in the Delhi office until Ruby either survived or died, so that I was by the phone.

The news came one Tuesday morning while I was holding a meeting with Fatima Patel and the Head of Midwifery from the Lady Hardinge.

'Doctor Mac,' said my assistant, popping her head around the door. 'I have Doctor Wallace on the telephone wishing to speak with you.'

My feet dragged as I walked to my office and quietly closed the door. As I picked up the telephone my hand shook violently, and I lowered myself into my office chair with a sinking feeling in the pit of my stomach.

'Tom, Mac here.'

'Mac, I've just been handed the latest toxicology report on Ruby. It would appear our efforts in Jhalanpur have saved her life.' My spirits soared. 'She is weak, but the atropine is now maintaining a good heart rate, her blood pressure is back to normal, and her breathing is more stable. The arrythmia is going to be a long-term problem but at least her heart has come through the ordeal in one piece and her eyesight is restored.'

'And Vijay? How is he holding up?'

'It's hard to say. His relief that Ruby is going to live is obvious, but he still refuses to leave Jodhpur and I understand the atmosphere in Jhalanpur is one of accusation and mistrust. Prince Kapoor Dhawan has been appointed to head an investigation into the poisoning, and the Commissioner of Police in Lahore is helping with the interrogations. The emporium in Jhalanpur's bazaar has been closed and the proprietor arrested.'

'Is Ruby able to talk? Can I speak to her?'

'She's hardly functioning right now, Mac, understandably. I suggest you wait until the weekend then have a word with the Senior Surgeon here. Vijay has asked me to return to Jhalanpur to monitor progress on the hospital development but if I can be of help over the next few weeks, all you need to do is call.'

'Thanks, Tom, I appreciate that.'

'How are you doing?'

'Surviving but having bad dreams.'

'About Ruby, or what might have happened to you?'

'Both. I have a natural aversion to coffee now and every time I see a yellow oleander bush on the roadside I get a panic attack. That plant was the cause, wasn't it?'

'Yes. The plant's seeds were crushed and dropped into the fresh coffee grinds. There were enough in there to slay a herd of buffalo, so our fast action was really the only thing that saved her.'

'And Sanjay? What has happened to him?' There was a deafening silence at the other end. 'Tom, are you there?'

'Yes, Mac, I'm here. Sanjay was found hanging from a rope in his room two days ago. He had committed suicide.'

'But it wasn't his fault.' I yelled, choking on my words.

'I know, but his part in the poisoning played on his mind. He knew Vijay would banish him from the Royal Household and he could see no purpose in going on.'

I couldn't take any more. 'I must go, Tom, I'm in the middle of a meeting. Please give Ruby my love and tell her I will be here the minute she gets back to Delhi.'

'Will do. And Mac?'

'Yes, Tom.'

'Stay safe.'

The meeting was almost over when I returned. Fatima hung back wanting to speak to me, and what she had to say in private only made my day worse.

'Doctor Mac, I am very worried about the statistics coming from Jalandhar District.'

My mind tracked back to Alistair Galbraith and the salt mine. I took the paper from Fatima's hand and studied the columns of figures. 'What am I looking at, Fatima?'

'The discrepancy between overall births recorded by the health workers and death rates of babies under two months old.'

I looked more closely and could see an imbalance between deaths of female and male new-borns. 'What are you suggesting, Fatima?'

Her eyes dropped to her hands, and she hesitated to answer. 'I suspect that female infanticide is still being practiced in this region, Doctor Mac.'

I froze. 'Are you telling me that mothers are deliberately killing their new-born babies because they are girls?' The very idea made me question my sanity.

'Not the mothers, Doctor Mac.'

'Then the fathers?' She nodded and I could feel my heckles rise against this constant male domination. 'In heaven's name, why?'

'In our culture, Doctor Mac, girls must have a dowry to get married. Most poor families cannot afford this dowry. It is simpler to remove the problem at birth.'

I threw my hands in the air in horror and slumped onto the edge of my desk. 'Leave it with me, Fatima.' My head felt pulverised from endless bad news. 'I promise to look into it further as soon as I've had time to clear my desk.'

'I'm sorry, Doctor Mac. Perhaps I should not have mentioned it right now.'

'No Fatima. You were right to speak out. Infanticide is a crime against humanity and it must be stopped.'

At the lunchtime break I left the office and took a rickshaw to Ruby's mansion. It felt strangely empty, but I needed to find some peace to gather my thoughts and find some perspective. I wandered over to the fountain and sat on the stone surround, watching the koi carp swim lazily through the clear blue water, their gentle meanderings easing my anguish. From this position, I scanned the mansion's veranda where Sanjay had spent so many of his days serving Vijay, Ruby and me lunchtime aperitifs or pre-dinner cocktails and I sensed a panic attack threatening.

'Why, Sanjay? What inherent cultural obligation drove you to take your own life.' Only the sound of leaves fluttering in the trees answered me and, for once, I understood why a man, whose whole life had been in the service of his master, would fear an uncertain future alone, cast aside, banished from Vijay's employ. 'God go with you, Sanjay. You deserved better from your land and its people, but rest now in peace.'

I wandered down to the tall hibiscus tree where Ruby and I had buried my child. That tiny embryo in its bejewelled metal box, lying peacefully within the safety of the tree's roots, gave me some solace. I sank to the ground and thought more of infanticide. I failed to understand how any father could smother his female child, but was his action any worse than mine? Was infanticide worse than abortion? I simply had no idea, but my resolved stiffened as my hand brushed across the mossy grass. It would take a higher court than that on earth to judge me, I thought, but that wouldn't stop me fighting tooth and nail to end the barbaric Indian practice of female child murder.

'Enough, Elizabeth. Your habit of becoming maudlin when life deals you a body blow was never one of your better attributes. Be thankful for small mercies. Ruby is alive and so are you. Now get on your feet, dust yourself down and get back to work.'

'Karr, why can't you ever give me some sympathy?'

'Because you wallow in enough of it on your own, dear. That's why.'

A note from Gloria was waiting for me on my desk.

Mac, can we chat after work? I'll be at the printers till five, chivvying them along with the new pamphlets on pre-natal hygiene, but I'm free after that. How about a drink in the Patiala Peg bar at the Imperial Hotel? I could do with some old-world charm after the day I've had.

Gloria

The wooden panelling, dark green leather upholstery, hunting prints, glass mirrors, brass fittings and varnished oak flooring smacked of a British Gentleman's Club when Gloria and I propped our bottoms on two bar stools and ordered some drinks from the steward behind the bar. I looked around noting the absence of any other women in the room, then turned my attention to my deputy.

'How's Ruby?' she asked. I filled her in on my conversation with Tom earlier that day.

'You must have been relieved that Tom was there when it happened.'

Her use of his first name jarred. 'In my opinion, Gloria, if Tom Wallace had not been there, Ruby would be dead. I've never come up against yellow oleander poisoning before, and frankly, had no real idea what we were battling against.'

'If it makes you feel any better, Mac, nor would I, but I guess Tom has more general experience of India that either of us.'

'You seem to know him well?' It was out before I could stop it.

'Not as well as you from all accounts, but we did have a couple of dinners together in Bombay when he was at St George's. Personally, I think it's a great shame he's married, but then, let's face it, all the best men are.'

I gritted my teeth and hoped she would not find out the truth about his divorce for some considerable time to come. 'Gloria, have you ever come across infanticide in your Indian travels?'

She didn't seem to have noticed my deliberate change of topic. 'No, why?'

I repeated Fatima's concerns. 'I'm not sure what we can do at the WCHS, but we need to do something. If those statistics are correct, there is wholesale murder going on up north in the privacy of Indian homes.'

'Well, perhaps we should gather up the unwanted little girls and bring them under our care and tutelage as future health workers.' She smiled at this jocular quip while her eyes followed a tall, impeccably dressed European entering the bar, who nodded as he passed her stool.

She's a female Duncan Fitzpatrick, I thought, as he joined a group of male friends over in the corner. 'Actually Gloria, that's not such a daft idea. If there were orphanages set up, allied to the WCHS, which could care for these infants, we would potentially have our own homegrown work force, which in time would become a genuine asset to the country instead of a dead statistic.'

'Maybe, but that would take years. Meanwhile, someone has to pay for their upkeep, and I doubt your cash-strapped government would stump up the funds.'

'But our upper-class ladies might, and I know just the person to get the ball rolling.'

'Who?'

'Lady Geraldine Stewart-Symes, our imminent Honorary President.' I needed to find out from Sir Peter when she and Sir George were leaving Aden for India so I could have a proposal written and ready for her when she arrived.

'But how would we persuade families to hand over their infant daughters without some compensation?' Gloria was having difficulty concentrating on me.

'We don't. Our health workers would spread the word that families with too many female mouths to feed could apply to have them join the Junior Health Corp.'

'Sounds a bit like the Girls Scouts to me.'

'In England it's called the Girl Guides, Gloria, but yes, similar. We could even name it after Geraldine. That should get her motivated.'

Gloria still had one eye on her admirer. 'OK, let me get this straight. Female infants who are surplus to family requirements would be gathered into a colonial children's corps by the WCHS and grow up as cloned health-workers, paid for by charitable donations from the well-heeled upper classes in England.'

"Umm? When you put it like that it does sound a bit far-fetched. Still, it's certainly got some merit. All we need to do is refine it over the next few months and put it as an addendum to my annual report for future consideration. You're always saying we should expand our operation.'

'Yes, but think about it, Mac,' Gloria swivelled on her stool so the man in question had a good view of her long legs. 'If the Catholic Mission hears of your idea, they might decide to adopt it to boost their missionary numbers.'

'I doubt indigenous families will to be too keen on their little girls being converted to Catholicism, Gloria.'

'Oh, I don't know.' She was now totally distracted and I was getting tetchy.

'Either way, I need to dash. I promised Lamis I would take her through the process of human gestation before her test tomorrow.'

'Will you also be warning her about the dangers of getting pregnant?'

I was half off my stool. 'Bugger, I knew there was something important I had to do. Thanks for reminding me, Gloria. This might be the ideal opportunity to bring it up.' With that, I was out of the Imperial Hotel and heading home with infanticide and Lamis's query on pregnancy uppermost on my mind.

Chapter Twenty-Two

As the weeks passed Ruby gradually improved, but the aftermath was shocking. Her heart had been permanently damaged by the poison, and she suffered with arrythmia which often caused her to feel weak and breathless when doing anything strenuous. Her asthma didn't help and hot weather only exacerbated the problem. However, these physical ailments were nothing compared to what the poisoning had done to her mind. For months, she refused to leave the mansion, only eating food she had prepared herself or drinking liquids that came from sealed bottles.

Things were no better for Vijay. Prince Kapoor Dhawan's investigation proved that the emporium owner's wayward son had been bribed by the Rajmata's chaprassi to spike Ruby's Moroccan coffee and he was so stupid, he'd delivered the doctored packet to Sanjay himself.

Both the son and the chaprassi were executed in front of the palace entrance in full view of Vijay's subjects and the Rajmata was exiled to the family's palace in Ooty where she was under house arrest and never allowed to return. Vijay added insult to injury by informing her, as she stepped onto the royal train with her entourage and a mass of luggage, that she would never lay eyes on her son again. Dashwana Devi later told me that she became a shadow of her former self and was hardly ever heard of again.

I spent the weekends with Ruby trying to coax her out of the mansion, but her resistance was so strong I eventually gave up.

Apart from occasional visits to Alipore Road, she insisted on eating at home. She also refused to consider her future in Jhalanpur.

'I'm never going there again,' she would say if the subject came up. 'Vijay will just have to visit Jhalanpur alone, and Dashwana Devi can be the one to satisfy his libido.'

Vijay tried and tried to get her to change her mind, but he too finally gave up and accepted the inevitable. He would be living two very different lives in the future, lives which would never again intertwine. All work on Puttaker Lodge ceased and Vijay only visited Rajputana for official palace business. Dashwana, the Jhalanpur court and Vijay's people suffered the ignominy of knowing that their Maharaja hated being anywhere near his Princely State.

'If only Dashwana Devi would get pregnant,' remarked Ruby, one Sunday as we sat on the veranda shortly after Christmas. 'Everything would be so much easier if she produced an heir.'

I could tell she was thinking of what might have been, and I questioned her on it. 'Would you go back to Jhalanpur under those circumstances?'

'I don't know, Mac. It's all too raw, but the pressure would be off Vijay, and I would be left alone if the court had a young prince to concentrate on.'

She was right, of course, and I was convinced Vijay would be a much happier man if he had a child of his own to love. 'Then let's both keep our fingers crossed. Now, what do you want me to do in the kitchen?'

As I stood peeling potatoes, I ran through the events of the previous couple of months . . .

My conversation with Lamis had been easier than I thought regarding her problems over pregnancy. We studied her X-rays from the Lady Hardinge and she could see for herself how small and malformed her pelvic structure was. We read books from the library on similar cases in pregnancy and both agreed that gestation would be dangerous for both Lamis and her baby. She seemed to take it all in good part.

'Of course, you could always adopt a child, Lamis, if you really wanted to,' I suggested, trying to be positive.

Her reaction was rather ambivalent. 'It wouldn't be the same though, would it, Umi? Having your own child is a bond that an adopted child could never replace.'

'What about us? We have bonded, haven't we?'

'That's different?'

I peered at her over my reading glasses. 'How?'

'When you found me, I was broken. You were the one who put me back together. That is a bond only we can understand.'

Lamis's arguments were well beyond her age and she always made me feel so proud when she came out with such statements.

'Have you heard any more about the Family Court hearing?' she asked.

'No, I haven't. When I wrote to them from Simla I suggested postponing it until November but, so far, they haven't replied.'

'Do you think there will be a problem?'

I wasn't sure how to answer. Her story was now well known around the WCHS and I had no idea if her parents in Old Delhi had heard about it or even objected to the suggestion that they had been guilty of neglect. 'If there is a problem it will be because your father refuses to give up his right to parental control.'

'Should I talk to my mother?' She never used the familiar word "Umi" when referring to her biological parent.

'I'm unsure. It may do more harm than good if she tells your father how you think about him. It could make him even more intransigent.'

'What's intransigent?'

'Pig-headed.' My fingers touched my lips, realising I had just insulted her Muslin faith. 'Or should I say hard-nosed, or more determined, or digging in his toes?'

'I get the picture.' She went back to the X-rays. 'Could I use these in court as evidence of neglect?'

'You won't be there, but there's no reason why I can't use them. In fact, I think it's a very good idea.'

'You could also point out that due to this neglect, I will never be able to have children.'

I looked at her as Aunt Karr used to look at me when I said something profound. 'Lamis, would you like to rethink your future and study to become a lawyer instead?

The legal notice arrived shortly after our conversation and the hearing had been re-scheduled for early November. I was to attend Court 2 thirty minutes prior to the hearing and bring whatever evidence I had to justify my claim for Guardianship. I felt on edge as I read the official document, but having set the wheels in motion, I knew Lamis would never forgive me if I backed out at the last minute.

My courage deserted me as I sat alone on the long wooden bench outside Court 2. I was far too early and having been too uptight to eat lunch my empty stomach rumbled loudly which didn't help my nerves. By the time my name was called I didn't think my legs would carry me into the courtroom.

'Get a grip, Mac,' I muttered, as I took my seat at the large oak table in front of the bench. It reminded me of my interview with the Board of Governors at the Calcutta School of Tropical Medicine and I longed for Lord Cottesmore to appear and work his magic. Sadly, he was miles away in Calcutta with no knowledge of this hearing.

Judge Boothroyd made his entrance dressed in his judicial wig and gown, nodded to his court clerk and sat.

'Doctor Elizabeth Stuart-MacKenzie,' he said, peering down at me from a great height.

'Yes, Your Honour.'

'I understand you would like us to grant you guardianship of one . . .' he paused and flicked through some papers, 'one Lamis Abbas of 208 Alipore Road, Delhi, previously of the house of Abbas in the Dariba Kalan District of Chandni Chowk. Is this correct?'

'Yes, Your Honour.'

'I see.' He aimed his next question at the clerk. 'Are the parents in court?'

'No, Milord.'

'Are they still alive?'

'We have been assured that they are, Milord. They were served with official papers but we have heard nothing in response.'

I visibly sighed, convinced my application was a foregone conclusion.

'Very well. Doctor Stuart-Mackenzie, please tell the court why you wish to apply for guardianship of this child.'

I drew breath then started at the beginning, giving a graphic account of how I had found Lamis.

'The child had been so badly abused sexually she needed an urgent temporary colostomy operation and constant medical care to allow her bowel and back passage to heal. It became clear on exploratory investigation that her sphincter muscles around her anus had been torn to shreds and she needed an operation to reattach these muscles if her digestive system was ever to return to normal. During her months of hospitalisation, her father never came to see her once, never enquired about her welfare or showed any concern for what she had been suffering. I also have it on good authority that her mother was banned by her husband from visiting the hospital. Meanwhile, I reported this illegal child marriage and associated injuries to the Chief of Police in Old Delhi. The husband, Jusuf Abbas, was arrested, duly tried and given a ten-year prison sentence under Sections 375 and 377 of the Indian Penal Code 1860 and the Child Marriage Restraint Act 1929. The marriage has since been dissolved and I have taken over personal responsibility for Lamis Abbas's education, her subsequent student training for midwifery at the Lady Hardinge Medical College and I am providing her with shelter at my own home. Therefore, I would respectfully ask this court to grant me the legal right to be her guardian.'

I handed over various medical documents and photographs to corroborate my statement then sat down.

'Thank you, Doctor Stuart-MacKenzie. Very concise. Now, could you please answer the following questions, with yes or no answers.'

I stood to attention once more.

'Are you in gainful employment?' He was obviously reading from a script.

'Yes. I'm the head of the Women's Community Health Service under the auspices of the Women's Health Service.'

'Do you have children of your own?'

'No, Your Honour.'

'Have you ever had children?'

I swallowed. 'No, Your Honour.'

'But you are married?' His eyes pierced my soul.

'No . . . Your Honour . . . I am single, but I have a permanent housekeeper who takes care of Lamis when I am at work.'

His eyebrows knitted together, and he drew a line around his question. 'Are you intending to marry in the near future?'

Oh, hell, I thought, this is where it all goes down the drain. 'No, Your Honour.'

He shuffled his papers together and raised his head. 'This concludes the hearing. I will now deliberate on the matter and the court will write to you with my judgement in due course. Good day, Doctor Stuart-MacKenzie.'

I staggered down the Family Court steps feeling as if I'd been hung out to dry. 'Damn, damn, damn!' How I was to tell Lamis that his Lordship was not impressed with my marital status was beyond me, so I delayed the confrontation by visiting the local souk.

She came running through the door full of expectation and stopped dead when she saw my face. 'Umi? No!'

I tried to explain but she wouldn't listen, shouting about how unfair the judge was, that she was going to write to him and threaten to kill herself if he made her go back to Chandni Chowk, then flew up the stairs and sent shockwaves through the house by slamming her bedroom door.

I had never seen her so angry. Mrs Appleby peered around the kitchen door and puckered her lips.

'Leave her be, Doctor Mac. She's hurting, and no wonder. I'm sure she will calm down eventually and you can then make her see sense.'

'I hope so, Mrs Appleby.'

'Will the judge really send her back to Chandni Chowk?'

'Over my dead body, Mrs Appleby. Over my dead body.'

That evening I rang Frances who was as shocked as I was over the judge's reaction.

'Mac, if marriage is the only stumbling block, then Jim and I will apply for guardianship. The judge can put that in his pipe and smoke it.' She was spitting bullets.

'It's good of you to offer, Frances, but hardly practical when you're in Poona and Lamis is here.'

'I know, but really. What does that man think he is doing? Of course Lamis is not going back to her father in Old Delhi.'

'Exactly what I said to Mrs Appleby. If all else fails, Frances, Lamis will go and live in the students' quarters at the Lady Hardinge and come here at weekends.'

'Have you spoken to Agnes about it?'

'Not yet. She will refrain from saying "I told you so," but she won't have to, it will be written all over her face.'

'Oh, Mac, can anything else go wrong?'

'You could discover that Jim was having an affair with Gloria Hodgson,' I joked.

'She'd kill him. Seriously, what are you going to do now?'

'I'll wait to see what the court says and then decide from there. My main worry is stopping Lamis from doing something stupid.'

'Would you like me to have a word with her?'

'It may be better if you wrote her a letter instead. Right now, she is not interested in talking to anybody.'

'Poor child. I tell you, Mac, I could swing for that judge.'

The court judgement arrived in the post a week later. By then Lamis had calmed down but I had become angrier by the day.

We opened and read it together. As suspected, Judge Boothroyd had rejected my application on the grounds of marital status, but as Lamis had been in an illegal child marriage arranged by her father, the judge had ruled that she would become a Ward-of-Court until she reached the age of sixteen.

'Does this mean I can stay with you?' Lamis resembled an orphaned puppy.

'I believe so, but we need to check. I imagine you will be appointed a Guardian-of-the-Court who will inspect this house, assess your educational ability and manage any money that you may have or inherit in the future, until your birthday next year. Then you can do as you please.'

'That's alright then. This house is a palace, Miss Frances said I was a star pupil, and I don't have any money.' She swung me round then went off to give Mrs Appleby the good news.

The following Wednesday an official appointed as Guardian-of-the-Court came to inspect the house, interview Lamis and me, and speak to Frances by phone. His report could find nothing wrong with any of the legal issues and he left, rather disgruntled at having wasted his valuable time. Needless-to-say, we heard nothing further.

'I should think so too,' chuntered Frances, who had now lost all faith in the justice system.

By December, Lord and Lady Stewart-Symes had arrived from Aden, were settling into the Metropolitan Hotel and busily deciding on where they should live. Geraldine immediately insisted on making a tour of the health clinics around Punjab before pouring praise on my efforts, which she ensured went straight to the top. We met over lunch at the hotel and the subject of infanticide came up.

'We need to do something about this, Geraldine, it simply cannot be allowed to go on.' I handed her my detailed proposal for a Stewart-Symes Junior Health Corps. She was tickled pink, and before the lunch was over, had already made up a list of suitable ladies from England's top drawer who would be commandeered to begin a campaign to raise funds for such a worthwhile cause. It would be years before the WCHS saw any benefit but I came away feeling cock-a-hoop for the first time in months and invited Ruby to join me for dinner at Alipore Road to celebrate.

She agreed on the understanding that she watched Mrs Appleby at every stage of the preparation, which I thought might cause tension in the kitchen. Fortunately, my housekeeper knew of Ruby's phobia, took it all in her stride and even taught her how to make treacle steamed pudding.

Frances and Jim came to stay for Christmas and the New Year and on a quiet afternoon, while Jim was off playing tennis with friends, I finally told Frances of my secret abortion.

'Mac, was that why you were so sick on the morning after the New Year's Gala Ball at the Calcutta Club?'

'I'm afraid so, Frances, although I didn't know that at the time.'

'You must have been mortified when you found out. All alone in a strange city with no support.'

'If it hadn't been for Ruby, Frances, I think I might have thrown myself off the Calcutta Hooghly Bridge. I admit, I did think about it.'

'Oh, Mac, the very thought sends shivers down my spine. As for Tom, if he'd known what you were going through, he would have been beside himself with worry and guilt.'

'That's why I never told him. What good would it have done anyway. Enid would never have divorced him, and I could never have lived in sin.'

'Indeed, but don't you think he would want to know, now?'

We were standing under a copse of silver birch trees with the sound of leather on willow reaching us from a local cricket field. 'Frances, believe me, I have thought about this over and over since he told me about his divorce, but I killed his one and only biological child. He would never forgive me.'

Frances was having none of it. 'What were you supposed to do, Mac, lose your career? Have the baby out of wedlock and try to bring it up on your own? That's ridiculous, and if Tom couldn't see that, he's not the man I think he is.'

'Maybe, but my decision is to let bygones be bygones. I know it's sad, but I have come to terms with it after all this time, and like Ruby, you should too.' She squeezed my arm and no more was said.

Jonathon and Hettie arrived in Delhi fresh from their extended honeymoon in Tanganyika in early January and settled into a lovely house in New Delhi's bungalow district. My social circle was expanding by the day and life for all of us settled into a pleasant routine. For the first time in ages, I was able to make new friends and spend quality hours with my ward-of-court, but the end of March was quickly approaching, and that appointment with the All-India Institute of Hygiene and Public Health in Calcutta began to loom large. I had no idea how the board would react to my presentation, but after the disasters of the past six months, I was somewhat pessimistic.

Chapter Twenty-Three

'Pages of statistics are all very well,' announced Geraldine, sitting at the head of our boardroom table with Agnes to my right, Jonathon and Gloria to my left and Sir Peter opposite, as we thrashed out a plan of action for the Institute presentation scheduled for Tuesday, March 31st. 'We all know that the board will have had a good lunch before Elizabeth gets to her feet,' she continued, 'and the last thing she needs is to send them to sleep with columns of figures.'

'I agree,' said Agnes, scratching her head, 'but trying to rouse that lot after their lunchtime tipple is about as successful as waking the dead.'

'Agnes.' objected Sir Peter, scowling, 'I know you have little time for the All-India Institute, but this attitude is not helping.'

'My apologise, Sir Peter, and you are correct. I find the Heads of Government Departments difficult in the extreme. Still, what we need is to find something eye-opening that will prick their interest.'

'Exactly,' agreed Jonathon. 'How about a film detailing what we've achieved in a year.' We all looked a bit stunned at this off-the-wall suggestion. Geraldine glanced my way hoping for a response.

'Do we have the facilities for showing a film at the Institute, Sir Peter?'

'I've no idea, Mac, but I can ask.' He scribbled a note on his pad.

'It would be even more relevant if we could get a village elder, a health worker and a local mother to give an interview in

278

front of the camera, with sub-titles,' Gloria mused. 'That way, the board would hear first-hand what villagers and staff thought of the scheme, without them having to leave their seats.'

'Gloria has a very good point, Geraldine.' I was already planning the questions. 'If Pathe News can produce newsreels, so can we.'

'Yes, but who's going to pay for it?' asked Sir Peter.

'Initially, we will.' Geraldine was also scribbling. 'I'm sure we have a creative accountant somewhere in the WMS who can cobble together a budget.' Agnes's eyes widened. 'We can pay them back once we get our own permanent funding. How much is it likely to cost?'

'That depends on who we use and how long it takes,' replied Jonathon. 'I'm sure a quite word in the ear of the Muslim League might produce a cheap camera crew.' He winked in my direction.

'Then leave me to have words with Fatima Patel. If anyone can magic up a camera crew locally, then she can,' announced Agnes, glancing in my direction. I remembered Fatima getting my Kodak film of Lamis's injuries printed within hours from the local camera shop.

'Maybe the Cow & Gate Company will cough up some cash as well,' suggested Gloria. 'We buy enough of their powdered baby milk to give away free in our clinics, and if we get the green light to expand across India, we'll be buying a whole lot more.'

I could see that Sir Peter was becoming rather impressed with Gloria.

'They could even sponsor some of our clinics,' I added. 'That way the Institute could reduce their costs and we would all be happy.' Sir Peter nodded enthusiastically, while Gloria remained tight-lipped.

'Elizabeth, that's a wonderful suggestion,' remarked Agnes, 'and should help get the board onside.'

'So, are we all agreed that we produce a newsreel of what we are, why we exist and what the benefits have been?' said Geraldine. 'Can I have a show of hands?'

Jonathon's hand shot into the air followed more reservedly by the rest of us.

'Then that's unanimous,' she confirmed, clapping her hands together. 'So, what's the next step?'

Nothing more could be done until we knew we could screen the newsreel at the Institute. Sir Peter reported back the next day with good news. The major-domo of the Institute had confirmed that they had a movie projector and screen for use on cinema nights for their members, and that he saw no reason why it could not be utilised for our presentation.

With the first hurdle overcome, we needed to decide on who should be interviewed and the locations where they would be filmed. Gloria appointed herself as casting director, Agnes had the job of finding WMS finance for the project and corporate funding from Cow & Gate, Jonathon and Fatima were to locate a cheap film crew who could take on the work and my job was to project manage the newsreel and write the script.

Having never done anything like this in my life, I turned to Ruby for help. She warmed to the idea and within days I was being introduced to Theodore Peterson from America who had been with Gandhi on his salt march two years earlier, filming the whole event for American audiences. We met at her mansion and I explained our intention, our limited budget and our lack of experience in the movie world.

'What you need is a film director,' he said, pulling out a small pocketbook, 'and I know just the chap.'

I bit my lip, crossed my fingers, and with a large dose of apprehension went to meet a Walter Smith from Los Angeles. He turned out to be a charming young man. Born in India while his father was working as the Asia Correspondent for Reuters in Bombay, he had been educated in Los Angeles and had dabbled in film production from an early age. Now back in India and hoping to work for the Imperial Film Company in Bombay as a fledgling director, he was keen to expand his curriculum vitae.

Walter's enthusiasm for our project was infectious and before I knew it, this all-American boy, with a set of perfectly aligned teeth, hazel eyes, short wiry auburn hair and a grin the size of the Mississippi, had taken the reins, organised a shooting schedule and was off searching out suitable locations.

'He makes my head spin, Ruby,' I said for the umpteenth time.

'How old is he?'

'I've no idea, but probably mid-thirties.'

'Good looking?'

'In an American sort of way.'

'Short, tall, middling?'

'Middling. About the same height as Vijay. Where is Vijay, by the way?'

'Jhalanpur. It's the Hindu festival of Holi.'

'What are they celebrating this time?'

'Spring, love and new life. A festival of fun where the locals sing, dance and throw powder paint and coloured water over each other. You must have seen it?'

'Oh, that festival,' I said, making a mental note never to go anywhere near Holi.

'So, single?'

'What?'

'This Walter Smith. Is he single?'

'How the hell should I know?'

'Well, does he wear a wedding band?'

'Ruby, I can't say I've noticed.' Mrs Appleby interrupted me, wanting to know when I would like lunch. 'In about half-an-hour, Mrs Appleby. We're waiting for Mrs Harrington-Davies to arrive. Now where was I?'

'Proving how unobservant you are.'

'For goodness's sake, Walter is directing my film, not auditioning to be the future Mr Stuart-MacKenzie.'

'How would you know; you never make any effort to find out.'

'Oh, give it a rest, Ruby. You never were cut out to be a matchmaker.'

'Hi, Girls, how's life in Alipore Road this week?' Henriette breezed through the door looking a picture of loveliness in her pink organza dress and matching slouch hat. She even put Ruby to shame.

'Troubling,' remarked Ruby, giving her a theatrical peck on both cheeks.

'Ignore her, Hettie, Ruby is trying to marry me off to Walter Smith and I'm having none of it.'

'Well, I must say he seems to be quite a catch, Mac. Jonathon is well impressed and now that Walter has asked him to appear in this epic newsreel of yours, I can't do a thing with my husband.' She duly pecked me on both cheeks, removed her hat and flopped into a chair. 'What's for lunch?'

'Mrs Appleby's famous pork and chicken terrine with tabbouleh salad and onion relish.'

'Umm, sounds scrumptious.' Hettie kicked off her shoes and stretched her legs over the arm of the chair. 'What about you, Mac, are you to star in this community health epic?'

I suddenly realised that Ruby hadn't insisted on joining Mrs Appleby in the kitchen. 'Apparently, I'm to introduce the film, sitting in my office dressed in my laboratory coat with my stethoscope around my neck, giving forth to all who will listen on the benefits of the WCHS.' I handed a chilled ginger ale to each of my guests and continued. 'Geraldine is to close the film with her usual panache, staring straight into the camera and speaking directly to Reginald Townsend through the lens.'

Ruby rearranged her long legs on the pouffe. 'What's she going to say?'

'Stuff about how much the clinics are needed in this country and why it must remain within the auspices of the Women's Medical Service.'

'That should go down like a lead balloon with Reginald,' remarked Hettie, obviously well-briefed by Jonathon.

'Maybe, but Geraldine has been told that he might object and won't hesitate to point out how clueless he is in the matter of women's health if he tries to take the department away from Agnes Scott.'

'And if he ignores her insult?'

'She will take him to one side and remind him that he's never even seen his own wife naked, and they've been married for thirty-five years.'

'What?' Ruby choked on her ginger ale.

'Absolutely true, Ruby. Mrs Reginald Townsend happened to drop this little pearl of wisdom out during one of Geraldine's female bridge parties.' Hettie nearly fell of her chair laughing.

'Lunch is served,' called Mrs Appleby from the kitchen. Ruby still didn't react, simply taking her seat as my housekeeper gave me a knowing smile and went to stand by her chair. 'Now, Your Highness, what can I get you?'

After the girls had left, I went to find Mrs Appleby in the scullery. She was on her knees washing the floor.

'Well, that went well, didn't it?'

She beamed. 'Doctor Mac, it was a joy to see Manika Devi tuck into everything on offer without questioning me on how I'd made it or where I'd bought the ingredients. Let's hope it's a sign of the times and the Maharani can get back to being her effervescent self.'

'I rather think she's already found her acerbic wit, Mrs Appleby, but I agree, it was a joy to see her eat without that constant need for reassurance.'

'Is she fully recovered from the poisoning, Doctor Mac?'

'No, sadly. Her heart will always be weak, but as she has no intention of running a marathon, I doubt it will be life-threatening. Not until she's much older, anyway.'

'She looked as if she'd put on a few pounds today.'

'Then, that's all to the good. She was like a bag of bones at Christmas. Keep fattening her up, Mrs Appleby, our Maharani needs her vitamins.' I strolled back into the lounge wondering how Dashwana Devi was doing and whether she was fit and well.

On March 4th, and I was sitting behind my desk with a camera stuffed in my face, some woman constantly dabbing my forehead, and arc lights blasting my eyeballs.

'No, Doctor Mac,' shouted Walter from behind the camera. Don't shuffle your papers, it gives the sound engineer apoplexy. Just relax, keep your hands still and speak normally. Now let's try it again, and this time, forget about the camera crew and imagine you are talking to one of your patients.'

I nodded, finding it hard to act normally with Ruby hovering in the background wrinkling her nose at my efforts.

'Right, quiet now everybody. On the count of three.' Walter's fingers counted down the numbers, I took a deep breath and waited for the cue. 'Action!'

It took fifteen takes, but by then I was word perfect and convinced that the movie industry was not for me. I escaped when Gloria arrived to tell me we had a visitor.

'Who is it?' I was intrigued and walked into her office trying to think who would be calling without an appointment.

'Good morning, Elizabeth.'

'Well, I never. What brings you to our neck of the woods, Lord Cottesmore.'

'Official business with the Viceroy, so I made time to pop by and see how your little film project was coming along. How are you, dear? Hettie is full of praise for your efforts with the WCHS.'

We left Gloria looking rather dumbstruck at the sight of the Governor of Bengal and strolled out into the Delhi sunshine, parking ourselves on a bench under a eucalyptus tree. I explained everything that had happened since the start of the project, knowing full well that he already knew everything there was to know from either Jonathon or Sir Peter. Nevertheless, he listened in silence then patted my hand.

'I always knew you had leadership qualities Elizabeth, but don't you miss being at the coalface getting your hands dirty?'

'I do, Lord Cottesmore, more and more as the months go by. All this management stuff takes up so much of my time I've forgotten what it's like to treat a patient.'

A shadow darkened his features and I sensed his visit wasn't only to pass the time of day.

'When will you be in Calcutta, Elizabeth?'

'The end of the month. Why?'

He twisted his wedding ring and looked beyond the lawn. 'I'm a bit worried about Virginia and I'm hoping you can talk to her.' His sombre tone was so unlike him.

'What do you suspect is wrong with her?'

'I don't know and she won't say. All I get is bravado and bluster when I ask, but whatever it is, Virginia is in pain and she's losing weight.'

'How old is Lady Cottesmore?' Not a question one should ask the Governor of Bengal, I thought, but I was a medic and medics needed to know these things.

'Sixty-eight.'

'Has she seen a physician about the pain?'

'No, she's burying her head in the sand, just like her mother, and refuses to believe there is anything wrong. That's why I have my hopes pinned on you. She trusts you after what you did for Hettie,' he turned and smiled, 'and anyway, you're part of our family.' He squeezed my hand.

'What was wrong with Virginia's mother?'

'She had gastric cancer. Died of it when she was sixty-nine.'

I could see why Virginia was worried. 'How long do you think Lady Cottesmore has been suffering with whatever is ailing her?'

'Hard to say, Elizabeth, but she seems to have been in pain on and off for some months.'

'Then it's imperative she sees a consultant quickly. Cancer can be genetic, as you well know, but in my experience, only ten percent of stomach cancer patients fall into this category. Lady Cottesmore is naturally associating her symptoms with her mother which is understandable, but her problem could be something else entirely. I don't want to wait until I get to Calcutta. I need to talk to her now. Do you think she will be angry with you for telling me?'

'She won't be best pleased, Elizabeth, but her health is more important, and I'd rather be sent to the doghouse for a spell than end up a widower.'

'Then, I'll ring her straight away. I take it she is at home right now?'

'Yes, she still takes her morning ride on Sapphire but has cancelled most of her social engagements recently. I imagine she will be having a quiet afternoon.'

I left him sitting there staring at his hands, a man who had the power to move mountains in his working life yet resembling a lost child at the thought of losing his wife.

'Hello, Virginia, Doctor Mac here.'

'Elizabeth, what a lovely surprise. How are you?'

'I'm well, thank you, but I understand you are not.'

I refused to allow her to trivialise the matter with comments about James making a fuss about nothing. I wanted to know when her symptoms started, what symptoms she was having and how much weight she had lost. As the conversation progressed, any animosity towards her husband was replaced with relief at being able to talk about it in confidence.

'A problem shared is a problemed halved, Virginia, and these symptoms could be anything from gastritis to a stomach ulcer. Now, I know your mother died of gastric cancer but that doesn't mean you will. I'll be in Calcutta at the end of the month but I don't want you to wait that long. I'm going to ring the gastroenterologist at Calcutta's Medical College Hospital this afternoon and discuss your case with him. What is essential right now is for you to have some preliminary tests before I arrive.'

'Is this really necessary, Elizabeth?'

'Yes, Virginia, it is. We need to know what we are dealing with.'

There was a pregnant pause, then an audible sigh, then another pause.

'Virginia, stop trying to run away from the problem. You are a fit, healthy woman. Instead of sleepless nights worrying about what might be, do exactly what I say and leave the worrying to me. Now, do you understand?'

'Yes, Elizabeth, I do, and thank you for being there.'

'Where else would I be right now? I'll ring you immediately I have spoken to the consultant, and I will be monitoring your symptoms daily until I reach Benningtons.'

I was put through to the Medical College Hospital gastroenterology department and asked for the senior physician on duty. A junior doctor came on the line and agreed to get Professor Samuel Hutchinson to ring me back once he was out of theatre. James Cottesmore was still where I had left him on my return.

'I've managed to get her Ladyship to agree to having some discreet tests and I've been in contact with the MCH. Professor Hutchinson will call me later this afternoon.' I repeated my conversation with Virginia and explained that I had registered myself as her doctor and would be kept fully advised.

'You will be staying with us at Benningtons, won't you?'

'Try keeping me away, and Lord Cottesmore, it goes without saying, as her doctor Virginia can rely on my professional confidentiality.'

'Then, I'll leave you to your afternoon, but I expect you at the Metropolitan Hotel tonight for dinner. Hettie and Johnathon will be joining us, and now you are taking control, I think I will get through the evening without putting a damper on proceedings. It's a relief, I can tell you. The thought of Hettie becoming hysterical over terminal cancer is more than I could stand right now.' His doleful eyes searched mine for reassurance, but I was not prepared to promise something I couldn't guarantee.

'What time should I arrive?'

'Shall we say, seven.'

'Seven it is.' I stood and looked down at this man who had come to my rescue two-and-a-half-years earlier and it was high time I repaid that debt. 'Lord Cottesmore, sleepless nights are not good for you either. Your wife will need your full support over the next few weeks, so no fading away like some withering wall flower. Chin up, my Lord, we are in this battle together.' I gave him a strong hug and walked him to the entrance.

Back in my office, I found Walter alone, busily writing.

'All in the can, Doctor Mac.' He tapped the large circular aluminium cannister. 'I'm off to Bombay tomorrow to start the editing.'

'Why Bombay?'

'Lady Stewart-Symes persuaded the Imperial Film Company to lend her their cutting room on the understanding that they are mentioned in the credits.'

I smiled. Geraldine knew that Walter was hankering for a job there so Imperial Films had been her first point of call. I was about to wish him luck when he cut in.

'How about a drink tonight to celebrate, Doctor Mac. Just you, me and a bottle of the best bubbly.' His sudden attempt at flirtation took me completely by surprise. My eyes fixated on his ring finger. It was empty.

'Another time, Walter.' I replied, the blood vessels around my neck and cheeks expanding. 'I have an important dinner engagement with the Governor of Bengal this evening.'

'My, my, such posh friends. Well, I certainly can't compete with the Governor of Bengal, so I'll just have to hope that Gloria is free instead.'

'I'm sure she would love that.' I now felt guilty for name-dropping. 'When will we meet up again?'

'In Calcutta on the twenty-ninth for the preview before your big day. Where will you be staying?'

He's not giving up, I thought, but I had no intention of adding insult to injury. 'I'm not sure right now, but I'll keep you posted.'

'You do that, Doctor Mac. See you on the twenty-ninth.'

I walked into Alipore Road feeling drained. What I needed was for Tom to put his reassuring arms around me and tell me that Virginia was going to be alright, but much as I wished it, that was certainly not going to happen. Mrs Appleby, on the other hand, seemed to have a sixth sense when it came to my moods and met me in the drawing room with a large Bloody Mary.

'Here, drink this, Doctor, and put your feet up. You've got at least an hour before you leave for the Metropolitan Hotel. The taxi will be here at six-forty-five. I've taken the liberty of steaming your silver evening dress, I assume that's the one you plan to wear tonight.

'It is, Mrs Appleby, and thank-you. You're amazing.'

She picked up my attaché case and headed for the hall. 'That's not what my sister in Lucknow reckons, but then, she doesn't get invited to dine with the Governor of Bengal, so what does she know?'

Chapter Twenty-Four

Virginia looked very drawn standing at the entrance to Benningtons waiting patiently as Ronald, their chauffeur, helped me from the car. The palatial mansion, set in its own extensive grounds had been the Cottesmore's family seat for years and it felt so good to be back in such familiar surroundings. I looked about me, reminiscing about my first months in India, then made my way to where she was standing and checked for signs of exhaustion.

'Have you been sleeping?'

She shook her head and gripped my hands in hers. 'Come on, let's get you settled then we can have a long chat.'

The results of her tests lay hidden in my valise. They were inconclusive and Professor Hutchinson had recommended a more specific exploratory procedure to get to the bottom of the problem. It had fallen to me to break this news to Virginia.

Ronald took my bags to the guestroom and I followed. My back ached from being so long on the train and although I knew my hostess was desperate for answers, I wasn't sure I was in the right frame of mind to provide them.

I stood on the bedroom balcony for a long time, searching for the right words but nothing seemed appropriate which wouldn't cause her even more stressed.

'It's no good standing there cogitating, Elizabeth,' remarked Aunt Karr, back in my brain. *'Better to get it over with.'*

'That's all very well for you to say, Karr. You're not the one delivering the bad tidings.'

'But you are, and as I recall, you were very cocky about being capable of imparting bad news to patients when I questioned your choice of career before you went up to Edinburgh.'

'I didn't expect then to be dealing with someone so close.'

'Beggars can't be choosers, dear. Now get yourself downstairs and put Lady Cottesmore's mind at rest. Exploratory procedure is what is says it is, exploratory. No need to be wearing black just yet.'

I tapped on the drawing room door and entered. Virginia was sitting in her usual chintz chair by the fireplace, her hands clasped in her lap and her head held high. This was not going to be easy for either of us, but it was my job to make sure she understood all her options and Karr was right, we were a long way from terminal cancer at this stage. Right now, my job was to be positive and supportive in equal measure.

She was over her tears and approaching the situation with a modicum of stoicism by the time Lord Cottesmore arrived home. I hadn't sugar-coated the test results but neither had I allowed her to wallow in pessimism. She was on a journey, one with many twists and turns and I was determined to see her through them whatever the prognosis. Agnes had been appraised of the situation before I left Delhi, but I promised to be back at my desk within the week and planned to travel to and from Calcutta every weekend thereafter.

Lord Cottesmore listened attentively as I repeated everything I had said to Virginia, then I left them and returned to my room to read up on the procedure for the new semiflexible Wolf Schindler gastroscope which Professor Hutchinson planned to use to examine the inner lining of Virginia's upper digestive system. I intended to be present for this procedure but there was every chance I would be refused. My reputation as a divisive figure was infamous in the corridors of Calcutta's Medical College Hospital, and I had everything crossed that my fracas with the ex-Surgeon General of the IMS would not stand in my way of gaining access to the operating theatre.

Virginia was admitted to the MCH on the day before the film preview and I was invited to join Professor Hutchinson in his office while she was being prepared for her intrusive investigation.

'Good morning, Professor, perhaps you could tell me if you are going to sedate Lady Cottesmore before you begin the gastroscopy?'

He looked up from his desk and invited me to sit. 'Doctor Stuart-MacKenzie, there is something I want to get off my chest before we go any further, and it's in regard to Sir Charles Ponsonby-Pritchard.'

Here we go, I thought, and dug my thumbs into the leather upholstery of my chair. 'I assume you believe I was irresponsible and out-of-order in writing the article for the Delhi Times.'

'I do, Doctor, and it did nothing to help the rest of us retain the respect we deserve when trying to do our work within the IMS.'

'I am sorry that you think that, but I stand by every word I wrote. If you are implying that you condone the attitude of Sir Charles to the Lamis Abbas case, then there is little point in continuing this conversation.'

'Allow me to. . .'

I refused to let him interrupt me. 'However, Lady Cottesmore is my patient, whether you like it or not, and I insist on being present at the gastroscopy and ask you again if you intend to sedate her for the procedure?'

The Professor sat back in his chair and placed his clasped hands across his chest. He reminded me of George Philpott in the Military Hospital in Peshawar who used to take the same superior pose when we faced off against each other regarding the benefits of female clinicians.

'I can see why you have a reputation for being headstrong, Doctor.' I sniffed. 'However, if you had let me finish, I was about to say that I too decry racial prejudice amongst my fellow surgeons and, although your action in bringing Sir Charles Ponsonby-Pritchard's failings to light was a little extreme, I can see that you had no other choice under the circumstances. Which is exactly what I have said on more than one occasion when discussing the matter with my associates.'

'Close your mouth, Elizabeth, the professor is not interested in the lining of your oesophagus.'

'Well, I'll be damned,' I spluttered, emptying my lungs. 'Are you telling me, Professor, that you agree with me?'

'I do, Doctor, and I would like you to know that a number of other Senior Surgeons do too. In answer to your other question, Lady Cottesmore will not be sedated for her procedure as I believe simply numbing the back of her throat with a local anaesthetic will suffice to stop her gagging.'

Virginia walked into the theatre to a wall of scrubbed and gowned theatre staff and students, was introduced to the Assistant Surgeon and led to a reclining chair, illuminated from above by a large surgical lamp. I knelt by her side, took her hand in mine and told her to relax. My presence seemed to calm her and she lay back, opening her mouth as the Assistant Surgeon lowered the back of her chair still further then swabbed the back of her throat with a liquid anaesthetic.

'Can you feel this, Your Ladyship?' Virginia shook her head as a surgical probe rubbed against her throat a few minutes later. 'Good, now try to keep your head still and close your eyes.'

Professor Hutchinson began slowly pushing the gastroscope passed her tonsils and down into her oesophagus while giving a running commentary to his students in a clear, concise and calm tone. Virginia squeezed my hand and I stroked her arm, indicating that all was well. It looked horrendous but once the tube reached her stomach, Professor Hutchinson peered through the lens at the other end and thoroughly examined the area under suspicion.

'I shall now extract the gastroscope in stages,' he announced, closely checking the rest of the upper gullet as the tube slowly reappeared. Minutes later Virginia was upright once more and swallowing a glass of water. Rather wobbly on her feet, she was wheeled away to the ward for a rest.

We removed our theatre gowns and returned to his office to discuss the instrument's findings. I broke out in a cold sweat convinced he was going to tell me he'd seen a cancerous growth.

'Well, Doctor Stuart-MacKenzie, it would appear her Ladyship is suffering from a gastric volvulus.'

'A twisted stomach,' I repeated flabbergasted, all fear dissipating.

'Exactly, and I doubt this is the first time it has happened to our patient. Are you aware of any other occasions when her Ladyship has complained of such symptoms?'

'Lord Cottesmore did say that she had mentioned difficulty keeping her food down and had suffered some stomach bloating on two or three occasions during the year, but it had gone away so she had put it down to indigestion.'

'As I suspected, chronic gastric volvulus. She could have been suffering from it for years. If it is now getting more frequent it could become acute. We don't have a moment to lose. I must untwist the stomach then permanently anchor it to stop further rotation.'

'Do you propose keeping her in hospital tonight?'

'I do. The sooner we do this the better. Shall I inform Lady Cottesmore, or will you?'

'I will, Professor Hutchinson. Our patient is terrified that she has stomach cancer like her mother, so facing an operation for gastric volvulus will be a welcome relief, I'm sure.'

'Then I suggest you tell her straight away. I don't want her stressed before her general anaesthetic tomorrow.'

'Will she make a complete recovery with no possibility of recurrence?' I asked.

'You assume correctly, Doctor. You can assure her that she will be up and about within the week, but I'll be insisting that she take things easy for some time. No horse riding for at least a month.'

I arrived on the ward to find the Governor of Bengal sitting by her bed and the nursing staff acting rather nervously around their prestigious visitor.

'Lord Cottesmore, Virginia, I have good news. Perhaps we could go somewhere a little more private while I explain exactly what is causing your affliction?'

I left them in a side room wrapped in each other's embrace, Virginia with tears pouring down her cheeks and Lord Cottesmore patting her back and muttering, 'Now, now, Ginny, no more tears. You'll be as right as rain before you know it. I did say you were getting yourself into a dither for no good reason and I was right, you silly chump.'

Out in the forecourt, I leant against a tree and let all the pent-up tension drain from my body before going to find Ronald, waiting patiently in the parking area.

'Could you take me back to Benningtons please, Ronald. Her Ladyship is fine but she needs a small operation tomorrow so will be staying in hospital tonight. The Governor will get his office to arrange some transport for him once his wife is settled for the night.'

'Is she really on the mend, Doctor Mac?'

'She is, Ronald, and will be needing your services regularly after she's had time to convalesce.'

'Lord, be praised, Doctor. Now you jump in and we'll be home before you know it.'

While Ronald garaged the car, I went over to the stables to find Sapphire, Virginia's horse. He was in his stall, banging the wooden door demanding long-overdue attention.

'It's alright, old boy, your mistress is going to be OK. Now, how about you and I go for a short canter around Rabindra Sarovar Lake to blow the cobwebs away?' He shook his sleek black head and loudly neighed. 'Right, give me ten minutes to change and I'll get you saddled up.'

Back in my room that evening after a rather lonely dinner, I began to wonder what was wrong with me. I should have been delighted to know that Virginia was to make a complete recovery, but something I couldn't put my finger on was niggling me inside.

'I'll tell you what it is.'

I could always rely on Karr to interrupt my thoughts. 'Out with it then. What's bugging me?'

'You are, dear.'

'Me?'

'Yes, Elizabeth, you. The thought of spending the next few years stuck behind a desk expanding the WCHS is an anathema to you, when what you really want to do is get back to doctoring.'

As usual, she had hit the nail on the head.

'Now that Professor Hutchinson has removed the very obstacle you thought existed between you and the IMS, there's nothing stopping you returning to what you do best, and that's being a doctor.'

'But I can't abandon Geraldine and Agnes after only one year, what would they think?'

'You'll never know unless you ask them, but I'd stake my reputation on Agnes Scott welcoming you back into the WMS as a clinician with open arms. She never wanted you to leave in the first place.'

'What reputation is that Karr?'

'No need to be cheeky, Niece, or I'll take my sound advice elsewhere.'

If only she would, I thought.

'I heard that, Elizabeth!'

Next day, having stabled Sapphire after our morning ride, I walked into the dining room to find Henriette and Jonathon sitting there, eating breakfast.

'When did you two arrive?' I asked, helping myself to a bowl of porridge, liberally covering it in honey.

'Late last night,' replied Jonathon, tucking into a bowl of kedgeree. 'We came down with Ruby.'

'Ruby? What's she doing in Calcutta?'

'She's insisting on seeing the film preview today. Something about her being the one to get the ball rolling in the first place.' Henriette was being much more abstemious with her plate of fresh fruit.

'Is that right?' asked Lord Cottesmore as he joined me at the armoire.

'Actually, yes,' I said. 'She introduced me to Theodore Peterson who told me I needed a director and put me in touch with Walter Smith.'

'Then it seems to me Ruby has every right to be present.' Hettie went over to her uncle and hugged him.

'How's her Ladyship,' I asked, sitting opposite Jonathon.

'Comfortable, under the circumstances. I left her at nine-thirty last night being given a sedative by the staff nurse to ensure she got a good night's sleep.'

'What's wrong with Aunt Ginny?' Henriette was out of her chair and pacing the floor.

'She's having surgery at the Medical College Hospital today,' I said. 'Nothing serious, Henriette, so stop pacing. I'm sure she will be delighted to see you once she has recovered from the anaesthetic.'

'But what's wrong with her?' Hettie insisted.

I gritted my teeth. There was only one way to close this conversation down, I thought, looking at Lord Cottesmore's pained expression, and that was to suggest it was a feminine issue. I oscillated my eyes between the two male members in the room and glared at her. It worked.

'Oh. Oh yes, I see. Perhaps you can fill me in later Doctor Mac.'

'I'll be delighted, Hettie. Now, what time do we have to be at the preview, and more importantly, where in the world is it being screened?'

'The Great Eastern Hotel, at four-thirty,' announced Jonathon. 'Lady Stewart-Symes is organising an informal reception to celebrate. I understand, Uncle, you and Aunt Ginny have received an invitation from Sir Peter.'

'We have. However, Virginia will not be able to make it,' he turned to face me, 'although I will certainly try.'

I smiled. 'I won't be offended if you miss it, Lord Cottesmore. I can't imagine it will be that amazing anyway.'

'Mac, how can you say that?' Jonathon had his kedgeree fork pointing at my nose. 'This film will revolutionise the way we spread the word in the future. Gloria is already planning to send copies of it around the provinces to generate interest.'

'Is she indeed. Well, let me remind you both that I haven't been given permission to expand this project across India yet, and there's every chance, film or no film, that the Institute

Board will thank me for my efforts and send me away with a flea in my ear.'

'I don't think so,' said Henriette, locking eyes with her uncle. 'Not if the Governor of Bengal has anything to do with it.'

My palms shot out. 'Don't tell me. I don't want to know what devious plans are going on behind my back. I'll never get through the meeting if I think there's some covert operation afoot.'

Lord Cottesmore's face was a picture of innocence. 'As if there would be, Elizabeth.'

Gloria met me on the steps of the Grand Eastern Hotel. She had travelled down overnight and was looking rather weather worn. I assumed she hadn't slept well and said so.

'Troop changes in Lucknow and a body on the line at Varanasi,' she complained. 'It all made for a very disturbed night.'

I felt for her, having been on a number of similar journeys myself. 'Everything running smoothly back at headquarters?'

'Yes, I think so. By the way, Tom sends his regards and hopes things go well tomorrow.'

'Oh, did he ring the office?'

The hotel porter pulled the ornate, heavily carved entrance door open with its polished brass doorhandle and waited.

No.' She breezed into the foyer. 'By letter. We've been corresponding for some months now.'

'Really? I had no idea.' Suddenly, I couldn't care less if Gloria had been stranded in Varanasi all night.

Geraldine was holding court in the middle of a multitude of people, two-thirds of whom were complete strangers to me.

'There you are Elizabeth. Come and meet the Production Director of Imperial Films. He is interested to learn about your plans for the WCHS's future development.'

Why a production director had any interest in my plans was beyond me, but I allowed Geraldine to lead me across the lobby where a rather short, rotund New Yorker stood waiting, chewing on a cigar.

I had spent the morning with Virginia in her private room at the hospital. She had been given nothing to eat or drink since the previous evening and was feeling fractious. Nerves were the root cause of this irritation but, having brought a medical journal with me from the college medical library, I was able to explain in diagrams what Professor Hutchinson was about to do to her which appeared to allay her fears.

Her operation was planned for twelve o'clock and would take about two hours, so I stayed until Lord Cottesmore turned up in his full Governor regalia. He'd been attending a military award ceremony at Fort William barracks and looked magnificent. I assured Virginia that I would return immediately after the film preview and that I was confident she was in very good hands.

I was not surprised, therefore, when I heard a collective intake of breath as the Governor appeared in the foyer of the hotel still in his ceremonial dress. Geraldine was ushering everyone into the conference room at the time so I held back and waited for him to join me.

'How did it go?'

'Very well from all accounts. When I left Virginia, she was awake but groggy. Hopefully, she will be more alert when we get back there later. I can't tell you how grateful I am for all you have done, Elizabeth. This could have gone on for months if I hadn't said anything to you.'

'Well, you did, and Lady Cottesmore is now on the mend, so let's here no more about it.'

We walked through into what was a converted cinema. A large white screen was suspended from the ceiling at one end of the room and a film projector centred on a table at the other with Walter standing to attention by his projectionist. The audience were taking their seats as if for the first night of some Drury Lane musical and a hotel staffer was poised by the door ready to douse the lights. I caught sight of Ruby sitting in the back row and suggested to Lord Cottesmore that we join her.

Geraldine walked to the front and clapped her hands for silence. 'Now, Your Lordships, distinguished Ladies and Gentlemen, it gives me great pleasure to welcome you to the premier of the Women's Community Health Service's documentary film . . .'

Fortunately, our Honorary President was not one for long speeches and within minutes the room went dark and all that could be heard was the whirring of the projector spools as white flickering lights bounced around the screen. These were replaced by a numerical countdown. 5 . . . 4 . . . 3 . . . 2 . . . 1, sitar music set the scene and we were off.

I gasped as my face filled the screen, the camera panning out to a shot of me sitting at my desk, my familiar voice with its hint of Scottish accent, filling the auditorium as the music faded away.

Ruby nipped my arm, leant in and whispered, 'Star of stage, screen and radio, Mac. Not bad for a shy, retiring Northumbrian doctor.'

Lord Cottesmore chuckled. I grunted and was severely 'shushed' by a gentleman sitting in front of me. When my introduction concluded I also faded away and the WCHS logo took my place with the film's title superimposed on top.

Making a difference, one clinic at a time.

We were now taken on location where Jonathon was directing operations. A dhoti-clad farmer was walking across the dusty ground dousing for water using a coconut. Cheers could be heard from bystanders as the coconut upended and Jonathon ordered his Indian workforce to begin digging, while a group of squaddies erected a large army issue tent close by.

'I bet Hettie is proud,' Lord Cottesmore muttered. I smiled, imagining her inflated chest as she sat alongside Jonathon, three rows down.

The story now began to unfold. Walter had decided to highlight the plight of Sarika, a Hindu girl from the remote village of Alampur in the Fatehgarh Sahib District of Punjab. She had already lost three children, one to miscarriage, one a stillbirth and the third to pre-natal asphyxia. With a voice-over in English, she explained that by getting health care at a central WCHS clinic in her area, she now had a healthy, bouncing, six-month-old little boy called Akash. She held him up for all to see. When asked what she prayed for in the future, the camera zoomed in on her face. 'For Allah to give all women in India health clinics like mine.' There wasn't a dry eye in the house!

We now cut to Gloria, standing inside the tent, handing out free packs of Cow & Gate milk powder to sari-clad mothers, while pregnant women were seated around a trained health worker, learning about postnatal hygiene and being handed graphically designed posters to hang in their huts. As the chatter decreased, the camera's focus curved towards Geraldine standing alone outside the tent holding Akash in her arms. She began to speak to camera, the background misting.

'This child's life is the reason the Women's Community Health Service exists. Healthy children grow into healthy adults, and healthy adults can fend for themselves and work for the benefit of their country instead of being a burden on the state.' The camera concentrated on Akash's deep ebony eyes. 'If this little boy is to have any real chance of survival, then India needs the WCHS, and it is the job of the British Imperial Government and its commercial partners to support it.' Even I found her words moving.

Sitar music overlaid Akash's gurgles of joy and the credits began rolled. Finally, the screen went black and the auditorium was plunged into silence, only the sound of the projector spool could be heard spinning as it ran out of film.

The lights came on, the audience rose as one, and a cacophony of applause rent the air.

'Speech,' shouted Jonathon, pointing in my direction.

'Oh, my Lord.' I looked at Lord Cottesmore who nodded.

'Come on, Elizabeth, it's time to take a bow,' he said and walked me to the front.

Chapter Twenty-Five

T he East India Mail train rattled passed Agra on its way into New Delhi as Ruby and I sat in her private carriage eating breakfast, trying vainly to ignore the aftermath of our previous evening's argument.

My decision to leave Calcutta early had been at Virginia's insistence. She had come through her operation with no complications and when Lord Cottesmore and I arrived to see her after the film preview, she was sitting up in bed with no pain and longing for some coddled eggs.

'Now Elizabeth,' she said, 'there's no need to hang around Calcutta after your meeting tomorrow. You have plenty to be getting on with in Delhi and I shall be well looked after here at the MCH for the next seven days.'

'Are you sure, Virginia?'

'Absolutely. Henriette is staying on to keep me company and exercise Sapphire, and James will be in and out between engagements and will keep you regularly posted on how I am doing.'

'Then, if you don't mind, I will get back to the office, but you really must follow Professor Hutchinson's advice once you get home. Any excessive exercise could tear the stomach anchors so riding is definitely out of the question. You must get plenty of rest and keep your feet up whenever possible until the wound has healed. You do understand don't you, Virginia?'

'Yes, I do, Elizabeth, and I know I can call you the minute something doesn't feel right. Now on your way. It's getting late and you have a lot of preparatory work to do for that important presentation at the Institute.'

The meeting lasted two hours and once it was over, I had joined Ruby at Calcutta Station where we were escorted to her private carriage by the stationmaster, coupled to the rear of the East India Mail. Having hardly sat down, I found myself being cross-examined about my day.

'How did it go?'

'You'll be pleased to know that the Women's Community Health Service is to be expanded across all of India.' I replied, nonchalantly.

'Then the film worked?'

'It did, and I take my hat off to Walter Smith. He certainly knows how to pull the heartstrings. Even the Chairman was dabbing his eyes by the end.'

'What about Reginald Townsend?'

'He wasn't there.'

Ruby's night attire hovered, half out of her case. 'What do you mean he wasn't there?'

'Exactly that. He's been shunted off to Hyderabad as Commissioner of Public Health after some transgression over his department's finances.'

'He's been nicking company funds?'

'It would seem so.'

'And I imagine Lord Cottesmore exposed him.'

'I have no idea.' What I believed and what I was prepared to acknowledge were two very different things.

'So, which chinless wonder from the army medical corp has replaced him?'

'Would you believe, George Philpott.' I placed my valise in the hat rack.

'THE George Philpott. The colonel who tried to get his hands inside your knickers up at Landi Kotal?'

'The very same.'

'Bloody hell!'

'As it happens, he's a sensible choice for the role. George is a superb physician and a great military administrator. He will be a far better Director of Public Health than Reginald Townsend.'

'Well, you should know having worked with him for weeks. But how did you react when he walked in the room?'

'I took a leaf out of your book, Ruby. I smiled, congratulated him on his promotion and kept my fingers crossed that he was still oblivious to our little incident outside the Sergeants' Mess. After all, he was blind drunk at the time.'

'Little incident,' gasped Ruby, stuffing her silk nightdress under her pillow. 'The bloody man wanted to rape you.'

'Well, he didn't, Duncan Fitzpatrick saw to that with a right upper cut to his jaw. It would appear George has no recollection of the night and seems to think that I'm the best thing since Disraeli. He made it quite clear to the rest of the board that they should back me, hook, line and sinker.' I giggled at the serendipity of my life. 'Anyway, how do you know about Landi Kotal? I never told you.'

'Walls have ears, Doctor.' Ruby was being her usual devious self.

'Gloria told you, didn't she?' Her silence spoke volumes.

'Was Lord Cottesmore instrumental in George Philpott's appointment too?'

'Don't answer a question with a question, Ruby. Who else would be the bearer of gossip, if not Gloria?'

'Tut, tut, Mac, you're showing your claws, and we all know why that is, don't we?'

'I've no idea what you are talking about, Ruby.' I stretched up and pulled a bottle of Bollinger from my valise. 'Time to celebrate. It's not every day you share a train carriage with India's most celebrated departmental head.'

'Great Scott! Whoever did you purloin that from? I know your salary, pal, and it doesn't stretch to Bollinger.'

'James Cottesmore gave it to me as he dropped me at the station. I've even got a bucket of ice to go with it.'

'Then, get it open. I'm parched.'

We sat enjoying our celebratory drink while West Bengal flashed passed the carriage window. With my project now secured, I again mulled over my own future and knew I wouldn't sleep until I had set some wheels in motion.

'Ruby, is Vijay back from Jhalanpur yet?'

'No, he gets back on Sunday. Why?'

'I need to speak to him.'

Ruby peered at me from over the rim of her glass. 'Why?'

My inner lip caught between my teeth. 'What would you say if I told you I wanted to spend the next six months in Jhalanpur getting the Stuart-MacKenzie Zenana Hospital up and running?'

'I would say that Dashwana Devi has told you she is pregnant, and you want a reason to be around to see her get through her confinement.'

'Don't joke. My question was serious.'

'So was my answer. It's as true as I sit here, Mac. Vijay told me on the phone yesterday. I understand our young Rani is three months up the duff.'

'Honestly?' My emotions oscillated between great elation and fears for the embryo. 'Then that settles it. Vijay will just have to speak to Sir Peter and make sure I'm released as soon as possible.'

Ruby tutted again from her corner of the carriage.

'What's wrong with you now? I would have thought you'd be delighted to know that I was in Jhalanpur to monitor Dashwana as she goes to full term.'

'Correct. If anyone can turn Vijay's first wife into a mother, you can, but that's not the point. You have a career to think about, Mac, and swanning around Jhalanpur dishing out pills and potions to Dashwana Devi for the next six months is not a great way to advance it.'

'Ruby, this was not an off-the-cuff comment I made just now. I've been thinking about my future for some time and running the WCHS does not feature strongly in my preferences.'

'Then what does, for pity's sake?'

'Spending my days as a doctor and surgeon, not an administrator.'

'Can't you do both?'

'Hardly, when the WCHS keeps me chained to a desk for days on end.'

'But what about Tom? What about working alongside him day after day, to say nothing of bumping into Duncan every five minutes? Are you seriously considering going back into that ménage à trois?'

'It wasn't a ménage à trois,' I shrieked, indignation pumping through my veins, 'and suggesting otherwise is insulting.'

'Temper, temper, Elizabeth. Methinks the lady doth protest too much.'

'Not about a ménage à trois, I don't. Jesus, if my Ma could hear you now, I would be disowned.'

'I'm still waiting for your answer. Do you really want to manage two men with only one thing on their minds, and that's you?'

'You're being ridiculous, Ruby. Duncan already knows I have no interest in us getting back together and as for Tom, his interest seems to have shifted to Gloria Hodgson. Did you know they've been corresponding for months?'

'Yes, but why does that bother you so much? I thought you insisted that Tom was merely a work colleague.'

'He is, damn it!' I was shouting again, but my angst ran off Ruby's back like melting ice off a glacier.

'OK, Mac, let's put this all into perspective. You intend to abandon the WCHS after spending fifteen months burning the midnight oil, shedding blood, sweat and tears building it up, only to bury yourself in a gigantic sand dune running a zenana hospital and watching the only two men who have ever meant anything to you, find happiness in the arms of other women?'

'Yes.'

'And you think my life with Vijay is weird.'

'If that's the last word you have to say on the subject, I'm off to bed.' I grabbed my toiletries and slammed the lavatory door behind me.

So here we sat over breakfast in an atmosphere you could cut with a knife. I needed to clear the air or this quarrel would fester. 'Perhaps we should start where we left off, last night.'

'Fine.' Ruby put down her knife. 'As I recall, I was saying that you thought my life with Vijay was weird.'

'Well, it's certainly not usual, and you know it. But it seems to work for you and Vijay so that's all that matters.'

'And you think practicing medicine in Jhalanpur will work for you too, despite the disadvantages.'

'Yes, I do. Being back in the operating theatre with Professor Hutchinson at the MCH only confirmed something I've known for months. I belong in medicine, Ruby, not public health. That's what I trained for and that's what I'm good at.'

'But what happens to you after six months? How do you earn a living then? Having burned your boats with the Women's Medical Service after upsetting the whole of the IMS, what's left? Private practice? I can't see you putting up with that for long.'

'Too right. Dealing with Elsie Thornton's haemorrhoids in the first few weeks of being in India was enough to put me off private practice for life. However, by this October, we will have been in India for three years and it is high time I had some furlough back in England. Aunt Karr is on her last legs, to say nothing of Pa's back and Ma's arthritis. It's time I made an appearance in Riveldene, if only for a few months. After that, who knows?'

'You do intend to return, don't you?' Ruby's voice tremored.

'Maybe . . . probably . . . and when I do, I'll ask Agnes for a job back with the WMS.'

'But I thought you said . . .?'

'I know what I said, but I was wrong. Professor Hutchinson told me that most of his peer group actually agreed with me about Ponsonby-Pritchard, it's just that they weren't best pleased with the way I went about exposing him.'

'You're kidding me?'

'No, I'm not.'

'Then, rushing back to England in a fit of pique last January was all for nothing?'

'So it seems.'

'And now you want me to organise a meeting between you and Vijay so you can give up the very job that brought you back from Aden?'

'Yes. With Dashwana Devi pregnant, time is of the essence.' I buttered a warm roll. 'But let's keep my plans to ourselves for now, Ruby I don't need Gloria moving into my office before I've had time to vacate it.'

Vijay appeared to have found a new lease of life since becoming an expectant father and was all hail-fellow-well-met as he greeted me outside his office door at the mansion the following Monday afternoon. We went for a walk around the gardens and I filled him in on Calcutta.

'Vijay, would you employ me for the next nine months on the same pay I am getting now, so I can monitor Her Highness's pregnancy and get the maternity and neonatal units up and running at the Zenana Hospital, just in case?'

'You know very well, I will, but why so long? Dashwana is already three months pregnant and the Zenana Hospital is well ahead of schedule. All we're waiting for is the equipment to go into the building and my excellent agent in London is sourcing all of that as I speak.'

'So Ruby told me, but the fact is, Vijay, I want to go back to England for three month's furlough after your baby is born and the little savings I've managed to make may not tide me over until I get back to work. I need to keep Alipore Road and retain Mrs Appleby for my return, and there's also the ongoing costs for Lamis.'

'Then, rest easy, Mac. My son will be in your hands, as before, and there is no price on earth that is enough to compensate you for that responsibility. Where do you want to stay while you're in Jhalanpur? I imagine the palace will be out of the question.'

'I'm afraid it will, Vijay. Does that upset you?' We'd arrived back at the terrace so went to sit opposite each other on the familiar ochre linen sofas. A new butler appeared from the hallway and I involuntarily gasped. Vijay had his back to him but knew instantly what the problem was and dismissed him without turning around.

'I miss Sanjay too, Mac. He was part of my household since I was a young boy and, with the exception of Ruby, his suicide is probably the worst thing that has happened to me for many a year. As to your question, I can fully understand why you wouldn't want to stay at the palace, believe me.' The pain in his eyes reminded me of his distress on board ship when he'd learned that his first child had died. 'There are times, Mac, sitting alone in my apartments late at night, when my anger gets so intense I want to pull the whole building down with my bare hands.'

'Oh, don't do that, Vijay. It's not the building's fault, but the people in it.'

'I know, but I'm back living a double life which my marriage to Ruby was supposed to stop.' He rubbed his forehead and I assumed he was back suffering from headaches. 'But enough about me. You will have your own villa on site once the hospital is finished and meanwhile, the Bhupendra Singh hotel in the city centre is very comfortable. When do you expect to arrive in Jhalanpur?'

'That will depend on Sir Peter and Agnes Scott. They won't want to be left in the lurch, so I will probably have to commute between both locations until a suitable successor is found.'

'Umm, that's not going to be easy.' He frowned, stared at the ceiling fan then suddenly shot up from the sofa. 'Ruby,' he shouted, 'where are you?'

'Here,' she replied, hanging over the first-floor balustrade.

'What's the name of that company you used to get down to Bombay after my polo accident?'

'Silver Wing Air Transport,' she called out.

'Then get me their telephone number, I've got an idea.' He turned back to me. 'Mac, have you ever flown before?'

Chapter Twenty-Six

G halib drove us through the gates of Willingdon Airfield and pulled up outside the small Delhi Flying Club building. Vijay pointed to a silver-coloured light aircraft appearing from the hangar, its wings folded, being pushed by four chaps in khaki shorts and white shirts, each wearing sunglasses.

'That's our plane, Mac.' He sounded excited. My heart was in my mouth as I concentrated on the Silver Wing's logo painted on the tail.

I climbed from the Lincoln Sedan and followed him over to where a tall, hazel-eyed European was standing watching the biplane rolling to a stop. He nodded to us as he slung two bits of wood under the front tyres.

'Don't want the Fox Moth running away from us now do we?' His accent was pure Home Counties and, as he turned to shake my hand, I noticed that his face was badly scared from burn marks. 'Patrick Simmonds,' he announced. 'I'll be flying you down to Jhalanpur today.'

'Nice to meet you, Captain Simmonds. Elizabeth Stuart-MacKenzie, but please call me Mac.'

'Pleasure to meet you, Mac, and I only answer to Pat. Is this your first flight?'

'It is, and I have to admit, I'm terrified.'

'Don't be. This little beauty,' he brushed his hand across the wooden, strutted wingspan, is a doddle to fly and as safe as houses. You'll be in Jhalanpur before you know it.' Vijay appeared amused. 'Your Highness.' They shook hands and he left to help the crew unfold and bolt the wings in place.

'It's not very big, is it,' I commented, as Vijay walked me to the side of the aircraft, opened the passenger cabin door and told me to, 'hop in and have a look around.'

I stepped onto the wing and entered. It was rather luxurious inside. Brown leather seats faced each other, two at the rear and one at the front, with plenty of room below and above to store bags. On the rear cabin bulkhead was a small circular glass porthole giving hand access to the cockpit. 'I guess the pilot sits in there,' I said, undoing the brass screw clasp and peering through.

Pat's face bobbed up at a cabin window. 'Yes, that's where you pass me my sandwiches.' He bobbed down again. I liked Pat Simmonds.

We had been at the airfield for about an hour when Pat announced that all was ready, asked if either of us needed the lavatory, then helped me climb aboard, insisting that I sat in the rear seat while Vijay faced me. 'Must make sure the plane's trim is balanced,' he explained. 'Once we're airborne you can sit side-by-side.'

'How long will it take?' My heart was thumping as I fastened my seatbelt.

'Five hours, depending on the wind. There's a couple of canteens of coffee and a bag of sandwiches under your seat, along with some water and ginger biscuits in case you feel a bit sick. Paper bags are in the side pocket if you need them. Just throw the used bag out of the window.'

My eyes rolled at the thought of some poor unsuspecting Indian farmer being covered in my stomach's contents. 'Right. Any other rules I should know about?'

'Yes,' said Pat, a broad grin on his face. 'Don't wander around on the wing.' He pulled his cockpit canopy open, climbed in and waited for the ground crew to remove the tyre chocks, slowly turn the propeller blade then back away. There was the sound of a starter motor, the blades began to rotate and the engine coughed into life, drowning all conversation. As the noise intensified, the plane began to move ahead, the Fox Moth bouncing across the dusty ground leaving the hangar in our wake.

'How are you feeling, Mac?' Vijay was studying me with interest.

'Nervous but exhilarated.'

'Me too.'

We reached the end of the grass runway, turned and paused. The glass porthole opened and Pat's voice filled the cabin. 'All well in there?'

'Yes,' shouted Vijay. 'All strapped in and ready to go.'

'Right oh! Jhalanpur here we come.' The window snapped shut and the cabin began to shake.

'Oh goodness,' I muttered and grabbed the leather strap hanging above my right ear. We gathered speed, Willingdon Airfield flashing past at a rate of knots and suddenly we were floating, the wings rocking in a thermal as we skimmed the treetops and the ground disappeared below me.

'Look down there,' said Vijay seconds later, pointing to a large building in its own grounds on our left. 'Viceroy's House.'

There it was, like a child's sandy-coloured toy house, its central dome sliding by as if on runners. I was too interested in what was happening to feel sick and when we parted a fluffy white cloud, like a whisk parting whipped cream, I was like a child at a funfair, 'oohing' and 'aahing' for all I was worth.

'Five hours,' I said, as I sat back and watched the familiar fields of Delhi morph into a flat, arid landscape, the Fox Moth now on a westerly heading, following the railway line towards Rajputana.

'It took me eleven hours to reach Jhalanpur in October, not including our lunch stop after Jodhpur.' I couldn't believe it.

'That's why we're doing this, Mac. It will be so much easier for you to commute between Delhi and Jhalanpur in one of these, and I could find many other uses for it if I had one of my own.'

'Are you serious?'

'Why not. If the Prince of Wales can have one, why can't I?'

'What speed are we doing?' I watched a train far below pull into a station and crowds of people mill around the platform.

'I've no idea. Ask the pilot, Mac, he should know.' Vijay was now sitting alongside me drinking coffee and reading the Delhi Times as if he had done this sort of thing regularly. I opened the glass porthole. 'Pat, what speed are we doing?'

'Ninety miles an hour, Mac. You should see Jaipur on your right in about twenty minutes.'

'Do you want some coffee?'

'Yes, that would be good. Just don't spill it on the instruments.' I carefully manoeuvred the tin mug through the hole then helped myself.

Sure enough, the famous pink city glowed in the sunlight as it appeared over the forward horizon, and when we drew closer Pat detoured over the city skyline to give us a bird's-eye view of the City Palace and the Hawa Mahal with its five storeys of ornate latticed windows adjoining the Jaipur Royal zenana.

'The Palace of the Winds,' I whispered, imagining the ladies of the zenana watching processions and festivals behind the seclusion of their unique screen. Vijay smiled. 'Magnificent, isn't it?'

The Man Sagar Lake was next with the Maharaja of Jaipur's Water Palace rising from its centre, the glassy surface of the lake reflecting our aerial passage. It brought back images of Puttaker Lodge and Ruby. Intuition told me that Vijay was having similar thoughts.

'I'm sure she'll return to Jhalanpur one day, Vijay. It will take time, but Ruby is becoming more confident as the weeks pass.'

Vijay, his eye patch absent, focused on my face. 'I have my doubts, Mac.'

'Don't lose hope. Once your son is born, Ruby will feel less threatened in Jhalanpur and can begin to enjoy her status as Manika Devi. I firmly believe Puttaker Lodge will become your home and that you will both be very happy there.' I dragged the picnic bag from under my seat and offered him a sandwich and a napkin.

We were approaching Jhalanpur's recently cleared landing strip when Pat opened the porthole once more. 'Please tighten your seatbelts as the landing might be a bit bumpy on this rough ground, and make sure everything in the cabin is tucked away where it can do no damage. If you don't mind, Your Highness, I would appreciate it if you would return to your take-off position.'

Vijay placed the coffee flasks back into their stowage and moved forward while I used my heels to push the picnic bag into the recess behind my calves. I could see the dusty landing strip straight ahead beyond the city and grabbed the leather strap once more. Five hours had flown by, literally, and I would always be eternally grateful to Vijay for giving me yet another amazing experience that I would be able to recall in my dotage.

The wheels touched terra firma and we bumped along the ground with a cloud of dust billowing out behind, creating a small sandstorm. A myriad of wild birds rose into the air squawking madly and minutes later we were parked by a pile of fuel cannisters and Pat cut the engine.

'Well, that went well, Mac,' announced Vijay, unclipping his seatbelt and checking his watch. 'Five hours and ten minutes. I won't be travelling any other way from now on. The cabin door opened and he climbed out, offering me his hand as I stepped down from the wing.

'So, how was it?' asked Pat, as we all walked across to the Rolls Royce.

'Fantastic, Pat, particularly our detour over Jaipur. When do you return to Delhi?

'Tomorrow morning. His Highness wants me to meet with his advisers at the palace later this afternoon and I'm not allowed to fly in the dark.'

'Then I'll say cheerio now as I won't be at the palace tonight. Thanks for getting me here safely, Captain. My parents will be forever in your debt.'

His gravelly laugh rang in my ears as Vijay and I departed, our feet firmly back on God's earth.

Prince Kapoor Dhawan was standing at the entrance to the zenana waiting patiently. I could feel my cheek muscles lift at the sight of this wonderful Hindu royal aristocrat who had helped me through all manner of emergencies in the past.

A tall man, his Jhalanpur green pagri nearly touching the top of the marble door surround, his grey beard hiding a large dominant chin, and his deep brown, penetrating eyes so familiar and so warm. He bowed and smiled, exposing perfectly aligned white teeth.

'We meet again, Doctor Mac. This time in more auspicious circumstances.'

'Long may they last, Your Highness. How is your niece today?'

'Delighted to know you are here and anxious to see you, but first I would like a word.' He drew me into a side room off the corridor and quietly closed the door. I could see the airstrip from our elevated position through the room's fretted window, the Fox Moth sitting shimmering in a heat haze with sunlight reflected of its glossy, silver wings and fuselage. It looked like a mirage. 'Would you care for any refreshments?'

'No thank you, I had plenty during the flight.'

'Then let me get straight to the point. My wife is very concerned that you might think she had something to do with Maharani Manika Devi's poisoning and that you would not wish to be in her company ever again. We would both quite understand, but I need to hear it from your own lips. Is she correct?' The taut lines on his forehead showed the strain he was under at that moment, and I had to be sure my words could not be misconstrued.

'Your Highness, the politics in this palace are as complicated and intriguing as any other Royal Palace in the world, and I am far from qualified to know where such political power lies or how it corrupts. All I know is that your wife seemed genuinely pleased when I introduced Manika Devi to Dashwana Devi and she never once stood in your niece's way when she wanted to spend time with Vijay's second wife. It was the Rajmata who banned such visitations, believing that the Maharani would corrupt your niece to our western ways and values,' I paused to get my breath, 'so by allowing these meetings, your wife was placing herself in a very difficult position. If you tell me that she was not involved in the poisoning, I will accept your word against any other. You are not a man to be swayed by opinion and, I believe, an excellent judge of character.'

'Then I give you my word, and I know my wife will be greatly relieved. May I ask her to join us.' He clapped his hands on my nod and his wife glided through the side door, her long flowing midnight blue sari giving grace to her otherwise aging frame.

She moved forwards, her rheumy eyes never leaving mine. 'Doctor Mac, you honour me with your presence.' She bowed low, placing the hem of my dress to her lips.

I quickly brushed my dress from her light grip, lifted her up and took her hands in mine, placing them together against my heart. 'I would never question your loyalty to Rani Dashwana Devi, Your Highness, but neither would I believe you could do any creature harm, no matter how foreign or threatening. Be assured, you have my utmost respect and friendship, and I will need your help in ensuring your niece delivers a healthy son and heir to His Majesty.' Throwing care and royal protocol to the wind, I took her in my arms and hugged her, as a daughter would hug a sick mother in a time of crisis.

'I will take great pleasure in following your instructions, Doctor.' She stepped back and gave me her Hindu blessing. 'Now, perhaps we should go to Dashwana Devi without delay, or she will faint from over-excitement.'

Prince Kapoor Dhawan did what he always did when in serious thought, he twisted the large ruby ring on his little finger.

'There's something else, Your Highness?'

'Only that I would ask you to extend my family's sincere concerns to Maharani Manika Devi regarding her state of health. We pray every day for her full recovery, and please assure her that we will be her constant protectors should she ever decide to return to Jhalanpur.'

'On her behalf, Prince Kapoor Dhawan, I thank you from the bottom of my heart, and I pray that one day the Maharani will find the strength to overcome her fears and accept your assurance personally.'

'Then that is all I can ask. Now, away with you or I will have the unenviable task of informing His Majesty that his first wife has passed away from nervous anxiety.'

My patient was pacing her apartment, raising her blood pressure and doing untold wear and tear to the Persian rug under her feet.

'Good afternoon, Your Highness.'

'Doctor Mac,' she exclaimed, 'where have you been? I've been waiting for hours.'

'A slight exaggeration, my dear, but after sitting in that small aircraft for five hours, I needed time to relieve my bladder and wash the desert dust from my face. However, I do apologise for keeping you waiting. Now let me look at you?'

She did a quick twirl, fanning out her long black hair and turning her heavy Rajputana embroidered skirt into a bright cerise silk lampshade swirling around her matching tight silk trousers. I eased her onto the nearest brocade couch and checked her pulse.

'Your pulse rate is far too high for the baby,' I announced and turned to her aunt. 'No more sweetmeats for Dashwana Devi until she learns to take her pregnancy seriously.'

The aunt raised her hands in exasperation. 'I will try, Doctor Mac, but I'm afraid my niece has a mind of her own these days, and the palace is not like the ss Narkunda.'

I looked at Dashwana and chuckled. She was now three years older than when we had first met, and was used to holding sway over the palace servants. Stopping her doing anything she wanted was going to be a challenge. 'Then we will just have to send her to the maternity unit at the zenana hospital for the duration of her pregnancy. I'm sure Matron will keep her under control.' Matron didn't yet exist, but Dashwana didn't know that.

'Please, Doctor Mac, I promise to do everything you say if you will let me remain in the palace.' She seemed desperate. Her aunt nodded and quickly turned away as laughter lines creased her temple.

'Very well, Your Highness, but never forget, I have spies everywhere in this building and I'll know instantly if you fail to do as you're told. We don't want a repeat of the past, now do we?'

Goosebumps appeared on her exposed arms as her expression darkened. 'What are the chances of this baby . . .?' She couldn't finish the sentence and I felt instantly angry at causing her distress.

'Your body has had plenty of time to repair since the crossing. You are young, healthy and fit, and the palace is a far better environment for you than the hot, humid atmosphere onboard ship. There is no reason why this child shouldn't go the full term.' I tried to think of a way to bring her out of her melancholy. 'Besides which, I have made a promise to the Maharaja that he will be the proud father of a son and heir by October, and if I fail I'm sure he'll want my head on a spike above the battlements.' I rubbed my neck and stared at her from under my eyelashes. She giggled and a sparkle came back into her eyes. 'Now let's start at the beginning. I want you to tell me everything medically that has happened to you since your last menstrual cycle.'

With the help of her aunt, she told me all I needed to know. We then transferred to her bedroom and I gave her a thorough examination. She was understandably nervous, her pulse rate thumping away at 95 beats a minute, but the foetus sounded untroubled in its sac and her general health appeared normal. We returned to find Prince Kapoor Dhawan and his wife relaxing by the window.

'I'm pleased to say, Your Highness, your niece is in excellent health and her baby very content. It is important for Dashwana Devi to keep her blood pressure down and I suggest some daily meditation and gentle exercise would help here, but otherwise all is well.'

'I will relay that to the Maharaja immediately and organise morning Dhyana sessions with the palace yoga master.' His niece wrinkled her nose but he ignored her. 'Doctor Mac, you must be exhausted after your long journey, is there anything else you need to do at the palace, or should I arrange for a car to take you to your hotel?'

'A car please. I will return again tomorrow.'

Vijay's chauffeur was standing to attention by the Rolls Royce when Prince Kapoor Dhawan and I descended the palace steps. My escort moved closer, lowering his voice.

'Perhaps tomorrow, we can have lunch together and discuss how things are in Delhi and, more importantly, how you think His Majesty is coping with the situation he finds himself in.'

'I would like that,' I quietly replied, 'and you can tell me how our three tiger cubs are coming along.' I climbed onto the Silver Ghost's running board and dropped onto the expensively upholstered backseat, wondering why Vijay's uncle was so concerned.

My plan was to spend the rest of the afternoon catching up on my correspondence and writing a long letter to Frances. A great deal had happened since my last communication with her and an update was long overdue, but as the car slowed at the hotel's porticoed entrance, Tom came striding down the steps in a khaki safari suit and was looking rather grumpy. He opened my passenger door and offered his hand.

I clenched my abdominal muscles in an attempt to stop butterflies invading my stomach. 'Good afternoon, Tom, your timing is impeccable.'

'Not really, Mac. I've been waiting here for two hours.' He escorted me into the lobby and waited while I checked in.

'Gosh, I'm exhausted after leaving Delhi so early this morning,' I said, hoping he was going to invite me for a drink.

'I can see that you are, so I won't keep you, Mac, but this can't wait. The hospital site foreman can't go any further with the interior of the maternity unit until you have decided where you want all the power points to go.'

It felt as if he'd kicked me in the stomach. 'No, I suppose he can't,' I replied, trying to sound interested. 'I'm not sure I know either.'

'That's why I thought I would forewarn you. Perhaps you could think about it overnight then have a word with him in the morning. I've told him to bring the drawings over at nine o'clock. Does that suit you?'

'Yes . . . I guess so . . . whatever is best.'

'Good, then I'll leave you to your afternoon.'

'I was wondering if you would like to . . .'

He was already at the entrance door. 'Oh, and congratulations on your success with the Institute. Bye.'

'. . . join me for dinner?' He was gone, leaving me standing there like a prize lemon. I gritted my teeth, angry at being made to look a fool. 'And goodbye to you too, Doctor Wallace.'

Dear Frances,

I've just had an experience of a lifetime, flying in a light aircraft, called a Fox Moth (apparently the Prince of Wales has one) from Delhi to Jhalanpur with Vijay. It was amazing. We flew straight over Jaipur and Jodhpur, and it only took five hours to get here. The pilot, Pat Simmonds, must have been a flyer during the Great War because he has severe burn marks on his face and hands, but he certainly knows how to fly that passenger plane. He followed the railway line straight across the desert and Vijay is now hell bent on buying one for himself. I hope Captain Simmonds ends up as his private pilot as he's a really nice chap. As for Dashwana Devi. She's in rude health and pregnancy is certainly agreeing with her . . .

I brought her up to date with all my news and finished by telling her that Tom had been corresponding with Gloria for months and that I suspected they were now in a relationship.

. . . I'm not sure what my schedule will be over the next few months, but I do plan to go back to England after the Rani has had her baby and spend the Festive Season with the family in Riveldene. Are you and Jim planning a visit back home, if so, we could travel together?

Much Love

Mac

x

When Pat Simmonds picked me up the following Friday, he told me Vijay had contacted the manufacturing base of *De Havilland* in England and had already placed an order for a Fox Moth in Jhalanpur's colours. Pat was to take delivery of it then fly it out to Delhi, having been offered the job as Vijay's private pilot.

'That's fantastic news, Pat. You must be delighted?'

'I am, Mac and I was hoping you would celebrate with me next weekend? I understand the Delhi Gymkhana Club does a great Saturday night dinner dance.' He seemed rather shy about his invitation. 'I won't be upset if you turn me down. I know I'm not the most handsome man on the block, but I understand you have some celebrating to do yourself, so I just thought . . .'

'That's really nice of you, Pat, but I have a prior engagement next weekend so I'm afraid I will have to decline.' I felt really sorry for him but I had enough on my plate, one way or another, without any more complications.

'That's OK, another time.'

The passenger cabin door closed, I strapped myself in, pulled out a huge file on the Zenana Hospital project and settled back for five quiet hours checking equipment lists as the Fox Moth lifted me to eight thousand feet and carried me back home.

Chapter Twenty-Seven

'So, what did you think of flying?'

Ruby was back on my peach and powder blue sofa searching in her handbag for her cigarettes and cigarette holder.

'It was fabulous and so quick. I assume you know Vijay is buying one of his own?'

'Yes, which means I can get to Calcutta or Bombay in a day. Now that's what I call progress.'

'What's in Calcutta and Bombay,' I asked, trying to punch holes in a WCHS report from Agnes to go into my ring binder.

'I not sure right now, but there must be something.'

I looked up. 'Ruby, I imagine the plane will be spending so much time going backwards and forwards to Jhalanpur that you won't get a look in. And would you put that damned cigarette out.'

She sauntered over to the bay window seat and blew smoke into the front garden 'How were things in Jhalanpur?'

I repeated Prince Kapoor Dhawan's message to her.

'Do you believe him?'

'Yes, I do, Ruby. Vijay has cleared the palace of anyone remotely associated with the Rajmata, and I'm quite sure Prince Kapoor Dhawan and his wife had absolutely nothing to do with your poisoning.' I waited for her to respond but she remained quiet. 'If you're wondering if you should go back, you might like to know that Vijay is building me a villa in the hospital grounds and I will be taking Mrs Appleby along if she'll go, so you could always stay with me.'

'Is Tom getting one too?'

'He is, but I think he's quite happy living at the palace right now, so there's no rush to get his built.'

'Did you see much of Tom and Duncan during your visit?'

The ring binder dropped into my attaché case and I joined her by the fireplace. 'You'll be pleased to know that both of them reacted around me as if I had the plague. Duncan disappeared to Lahore for most of my visit.'

'And Tom?'

'What can I say? He was extremely civil, included me in any discussions regarding hospital matters and kept me at arm's length the rest of the time. I tell you, Ruby, it felt weird after our five exotic nights at the Taj Mahal Hotel.'

'Speaking of that, Gloria let it slip two days ago that she would be meeting Tom in Bombay next week.'

Another body blow pummelled me into my seat. 'Is she? Well, good luck to her. That could have been me but I chose to turn him down so I can hardly complain now, can I?'

Ruby let the matter drop and asked how Lamis was doing on the Lady Hardinge midwifery course.

'Very well, according to Agnes. She's the youngest in the class and yet consistently gets the highest marks. As soon as she breaks up for the summer, I'm taking her down to Jhalanpur with me. She'll make a great addition to the maternity ward until I can permanently fill all the posts.'

Jonathon popped his head around my office door to say hello.

'How's Lady Cottesmore, Jonathon?'

'Fine, Mac. She's being a real trooper following the rules set by her surgeon and the hospital are very pleased with her progress.' He pulled out a chair.

'Do pass on my regards and tell her I will ring Benningtons the next time I get a free five minutes.'

'That bad, eh?' He rocked back, his feet crossed on the edge of my desk.

'Worse. I don't know which way is up right now.'

'Has Agnes found anyone to replace you yet?'

'Not that she's said, but then Agnes always keeps things close to her chest. Has Sir Peter dropped any hints?'

'No, he's just back from Madras after attending a conference on yellow fever with a group of scientists and medics specialising in tropical disease control, so we haven't spoken.'

I doodled on my pad, wondering if I would have been there if my Ph.D research funding hadn't been cancelled.

'Meanwhile, some bloke was asking after you the other day,' continued Jonathon, on another tack.

'Oh, who?'

He scratched his head, trying to remember the chap's name. 'Salim something . . . Tariq . . . That's it, Lieutenant Salim Tariq of the Afghan Rifles. Said you treated him up in Landi Kotal. Does the name ring a bell?'

My face exploded with joy. 'Yes it does. How did you come to meet him?'

Jonathon took out his Swiss army knife and started sharpening my pencils all over the desktop. 'He's applied to be a Sanitary Inspector in the Rawalpindi District. Got discharged from the army on medical grounds. Breathing problems, apparently. Took a bullet through the chest from an Afridi sniper. Nasty.'

'It was. I was the one who stopped him falling to his death off an escarpment during the attack in the Khyber Pass. It was Colonel Philpott and me who kept him alive during our long climb to Landi Kotal on horseback in a snowstorm.'

'That was Salim Tariq? The chap you got your bravery medal for?'

'Yes, and my Jezail. If I were you, Jonathon, I'd snap him up pretty damned sharpish. According to his unit, he's the best Indian officer they've ever had.'

He was out of his chair instantly and on his way down the corridor, shouting as he went, 'Ahmed, get me Salim Tariq's application form, I need to speak to him, now.'

A small world, I thought, as Gloria walked passed my window on her way to the canteen. Agnes said she had requested a week's leave some days earlier, and although work was piling up, Agnes had been unable to refuse after all the time I had spent away from the office. I took in Gloria's curved figure, slim hips and long legs as she crossed the quadrangle and couldn't help imagining Tom's large hands wandering all over them.

'God, will this ever get any easier?' I thought and picked up the phone. 'Operator, Delhi Flying Club please.'

'DFC. Can I help you.'

'Yes, is Captain Simmonds around at the moment.'

'No, Miss, he's doing some circuits and bumps with a trainee pilot right now. Can I get him to call you back?'

'No need. Just tell him that Doctor Stuart-MacKenzie is unexpectedly free this Saturday.'

'Doctor Stuart-MacKenzie . . . free . . . Saturday.' He was obviously writing it down. 'I'll make sure he gets the message, Doctor.'

'Thank you. Have a good day.'

Lamis wanted to know everything about Captain Simmonds as I dressed for the evening. We had gone together to Connaught Place Shopping Mall to buy me a new evening dress and I had splashed out on a rather risqué, backless ensemble in cobalt-blue silk crepe de chine, with a matching stole.

It seemed to please Lamis that Pat was disfigured. Perhaps it made her feel less embarrassed about her own deformity, I thought. When he rang the doorbell she beat Mrs Appleby to the door.

'Captain Simmonds, my name's Lamis. Please come in.'

I could hear them chatting in the hall and Pat didn't flinch when I told him she was my surrogate child.

'What a great kid,' said Pat, as we drove away. 'Where did you find her?'

'I'll tell you over dinner, Pat. It's a very long story.'

The evening passed far too quickly and it was a relief to feel so relaxed in a man's company. He was a great raconteur, keeping me entertained with amusing stories of his years in the Royal Flying Corp, only briefly mentioning his crash in a Sopwith Camel in northern France when it caught fire. I had treated a number of airmen with burn injuries back in Northumbria after the war so already knew the trauma he must have gone through.

Pat was quite a nifty dancer too, twirling me around the Gymkhana Club's dance floor as the band played swing and jazz rhythms well into the early hours. When he dropped me back home just before dawn, my feet hurt, my back ached and I felt on top of the world.

'Pat, that was the best night I've had in years. How I'm supposed to stay awake for Lamis's visit to the zoo later I've no idea, but I wouldn't have missed this for the world.'

'My pleasure, Mac. You're a real sport. Perhaps we can do it again sometime?'

'If I ever get my breath back, I'd be happy to oblige.'

Lamis crept into my bed as a distant cockerel announced the new day. 'Did you have a good time, Umi?' she whispered, cuddling up close.

'I did, Lamis. Now, do me a favour and let me get some sleep.'

'Next time Captain Simmonds flies you to Jhalanpur, Umi, can I come too?'

'We'll have to see, but can we talk about it in the morning?'

'It is the morning, Umi.'

Lamis and I flew to Jhalanpur at the beginning of July. The zenana hospital was finished, the grounds were being landscaped and my villa was already at roof height. Vijay had asked how many bedrooms I thought I needed and cheekily I had said four, suggesting that it would be more convenient to host visiting paediatric and obstetric physicians at the house rather than them travel backwards and forwards to the city's hotel. He seemed to think that was sensible and instructed the architect to base the villa's design on Mallards's guesthouse in Simla, but bigger.

Agnes had waved us off at the Delhi Flying Club knowing we would not be returning to India until after the New Year, but she had been successful in filling my post at the WCHS with a highly qualified female administrator from the pharmaceutical industry in America which made me feel less guilty at leaving. I had spent my final weeks tying up loose ends while interviewing female doctors, nurses, midwives, and auxiliary staff, ready for the zenana hospital's forthcoming inauguration.

Our flight to Jhalanpur had not been Lamis's first flight either. Pat had taken her up twice on joyrides above Delhi, so she was a well-seasoned traveller by the time she climbed aboard Vijay's Fox Moth for our five-hour flight west.

Lamis had become firm friends with Pat over the months and, much to my disgust, announced that she wanted to be a pilot rather than a doctor as we sat having dinner one evening at Alipore Road with Jonathon and Hettie.

'Why can't you be both?' I asked, looking to Jonathon for support.

'Yes, you could be a flying doctor,' he said, 'like the ones in Australia.' He wasn't being very helpful to my plans for her future.

Lamis wanted to know everything there was to know about flying doctors while I racked my brains trying to think of a more negative viewpoint. When she realised her life might be cut short as a pilot she had second thoughts on the matter, and I quickly moved the conversation on.

Pat and I had been out a few times by then and on each occasion he had been the perfect gentleman, leaving me at the door with a friendly peck on the cheek and a cheerful wave. I began to wonder if there was something either wrong with me, or wrong with him, but had no way of broaching the subject.

One evening as we were strolling through New Delhi after a quiet dinner at the Imperial Hotel, he plucked up the courage to tell me that he was a homosexual. I wasn't sure how I should react, so I used my professional veneer to overcome any embarrassment.

'That must have been very difficult for you, Pat, especially in the career you had chosen.'

'It was, Mac. Pilots are supposed to be hair-raising womanisers not sexual deviants, but flying was my passion, so I ignored my physical needs and concentrated on my career hoping for a change in homophobic attitudes in the future. Sadly, the war intervened and since my injuries I'm neither use to man nor beast. Nevertheless, I've accepted the hand I've been dealt and now enjoy life the best way I can.'

'What other injuries did you sustain in the crash?'

He hesitated, obviously reliving the disaster. 'I seem to have a neurological screw loose, Mac. That's what I've been told anyway. I was in a coma for weeks, having been knocked unconscious on impact. When I came round, I was not only badly disfigured but impotent too, if you get my meaning?'

'I know what impotent means, Pat.'

'Sorry, I keep forgetting you're a doctor.'

'Did the neurosurgeon think the problem would eventually right itself?' We paused by a small lake.

'He couldn't say, but he had never known it happen before.'

'So you decided to run away to India instead?'

'You're very perceptive, Mac.' His smile crinkled his facial scars. 'I'm afraid the English are not good at dealing with other people's physical disabilities, they tend to stare, and there were too many memories of what might have been for me to feel comfortable back home. Here in India, disability is common so I can go about my business without feeling like a freak, and I get a real buzz being able to fly around this continent with no-one telling me what to do. When I'm up in the clouds with the wind in my hair, I can forget what I am and just remember who I am.'

'Well, you're a bloody good pilot, that's for sure.'

'And you're one of the best friends I've ever had.'

We continued on our way. 'When did you realise you had sexual feelings for other men?' I asked, genuinely interested.

'When I was courting a girl from Potters Bar. I found I was more attracted to her brother than I was to her. It was a shock, I can tell you.'

'Well, I'm glad you confided in me, Pat, and you can rely on my confidentiality as a close friend and a medic.'

'Thanks, Mac, and if you ever need a shoulder to cry on, I'm your man.'

Lamis and I made a grand tour of the zenana hospital with all its state-of-the-art equipment and long corridors and we travelled up and down in the zenana lift feeling like naughty schoolboys. I was now solely responsible for the smooth running of this medical facility and I felt a surge of pride as I saw my name emblazoned above the concourse entrance.

Leaving Lamis with my new neonatal staff nurse, Siobhan, I headed to the palace to check on Dashwana and the baby.

She was now seven months pregnant and with the weather turning hot and humid from monsoon rains, she was beginning to suffer swollen ankles and severe back pain as the baby grew in her womb. With each month that passed she became more and more anxious, gripping my hand as I went to leave and asking me over and over if the birth would kill her. I constantly reassured her but with each conversation I was becoming convinced her agitation had roots far deeper than that of her previous miscarriage.

Having managed to overcome my anxiety at being in Tom's company, I was again enjoying discussing my cases with him and had invited him to dine with me at the hotel that evening to discuss my concerns about Dashwana. Once Lamis had gone to bed I brought up the subject of Vijay's young wife.

'I can't put my finger on it, Tom, but Dashwana Devi is in a state of constant hypertension. Her blood pressure is a little high but not excessively so and the baby is perfectly happy, but she needs constant reassurance from me and can't seem to believe that she will survive the birth.'

'Is this not a normal reaction to what happened before?'

'Difficult to say, Tom, every woman reacts differently to miscarriage. Some of the women I knew in Northumbria treated it as an everyday event but, let's be honest, Dashwana wouldn't survive five minutes in the back streets of Newcastle. What I do know is that she is worrying unnecessarily, and I am loathe to give her a sedative in case it complicates her pregnancy in some way.'

'That's very wise, Mac, but could she not take some natural herbal remedy for anxiety, like lemon balm or valerian?'

I considered his advice and agreed. Camomile tea was not working. She needed something stronger and valerian root was probably the best option to help with her sleepless nights and exhaustion. It would also go some way to lowering her blood pressure. 'Thanks, Tom. I'll try her on valerian and see what happens.

'Have you written your speech yet for the hospital inauguration?' He helped himself to more coffee.

'No, I haven't had the time. My days are filled with staff rosters, seniority lists, training schedules and management meetings in addition to visiting Dashwana on a daily basis. By the evening I can hardly stay awake let alone write a speech.'

'Would you like me to write it for you? I think I know you well enough to draft something suitable.'

That's an understatement, I thought, but kept my thoughts to myself. 'If you could at least give me some pointers. Having never opened a hospital before I certainly don't want to say something that will embarrass Vijay in front of his dignitaries and subjects.'

'Then leave it to me. I'll drop something off in a couple of days.

'Tom,' I focused on his Nordic blue eyes. 'Thanks for being there. I really appreciate it.

'You're welcome, Doctor Stuart-MacKenzie. The feeling is mutual.'

Chapter Twenty-Eight

When the day came I was a bag of nerves. My hair seemed to have a mind of its own, flying around my head full of static, and it was so hot I felt like a limp lettuce leaf. Added to this, I had lost Tom's speech in the rush to move into the new villa and Lamis and Mrs Appleby were now searching from attic to basement looking for it.

'Here it is,' shouted Mrs Appleby coming into the drawing room with it held above her head. 'It was in the laundry basket.'

'Oh, thank goodness for that. Lamis, you are to wear the pale blue midwives' uniform. I take it we have one in her size, Mrs Appleby.'

'Right here, Doctor Mac, made especially for her last week down in the bazaar.'

I looked at my watch. 'Crikey, we need to get a move on or the Maharaja will be there before we are.' We left the villa and drove the few hundred yards to the hospital entrance with mechanical fans spinning madly all around the car's interior.

A large canopy had been placed over a rostrum in front of the concourse entrance with a deep green carpet leading from it to the drive. A second larger canopy was shielding the audience area and a microphone was being tested by a chap who looked very similar to the sound engineer of the WCHS documentary.

'Penny for them?'

I turned and found Tom standing behind me, looking very professional in his hospital scrubs and laboratory coat.

'Aren't you hot in that?' I pointed to his coat.

'Sweltering, but we've got to keep up appearances. How are the nerves?'

'Like a set of violin strings. You could play Beethoven's Fifth on me, I'm so tense.'

He coughed and changed the subject. 'Did you know that Ruby is here for your opening?'

My jaw dropped to my chest. 'When did she arrive?'

'She flew down with Vijay yesterday.'

'But where is she staying? Surely not the palace?'

'No. Prince Kapoor Dhawan has set up a royal tent enclosure on the outskirts of the city for them both, with guards every three feet and food tasters to check anything she eats and drinks.'

'Well, if it's anything like the tent we had lunch in, she will be very comfortable. I can't tell you how pleased I am to know that she's finally here.'

'Me too. Needless to say, Vijay is delighted.'

With fifteen minutes to go, I found my seat on the rostrum and looked down on Lamis and my other hospital staff, all sitting in their different coloured uniforms, to one side of the aisle. Tom and his staff sat opposite and members of the palace staff sat behind. The front two rows were filled with the great and good of India, while most of the city's residents stood in large groups, out in the open, their white and cream umbrellas shielding them from the hot sun, the gold and silver edging of the women's saris shimmering in a kaleidoscope of colour.

A trumpet fanfare announced the Maharaja's arrival and the Silver Ghost cruised to a stop at the edge of the carpet. Lightbulbs flashed as Ruby, in a bottle green sari, her neck, ears, fingers and ankles adorned with Jhalanpur jewels, alighted from her side of the car and the royal couple progressed passed a sea of bowed heads. It was quite a sight, and when Ruby arrived at the rostrum, she crossed her fingers, wished me luck and sedately occupied the smaller of two heavily embellished gold-leaf thrones.

Dignitaries had come from far and wide, Indian Princes, senior clinicians, government representatives and Jhalanpur sporting celebrities, all playing their part in making this a very special occasion, and when I stood to give my speech the applause, rising in a crescendo, must have been heard in Jodhpur. I saw Pat standing at the back with his ground crew, clapping for all he was worth and as the applause died away, his hand came up, his thumb pointing skywards.

'Your Majesty, Your Highness, members of the Royal Families of India, dignitaries, ladies and gentlemen, it gives me great pleasure to welcome you here today for the official opening of this,' I turned, indicating to the building behind me, 'the Stuart-MacKenzie Zenana Hospital. None of this would have been possible without the generous patronage of Maharaja Vijay Kumar Sing II, who has had a life-long dream to provide all his subjects with the very best medical facilities in India. This zenana hospital, with its larger neighbour, the Dhyan Kumar Singh General Hospital are the result of that dream. From today, all women and children of Jhalanpur will be able to access medical treatment from highly trained doctors, nurses and auxiliary staff who will maintain a standard of excellence second to none . . .

Two of my theatre nurses, each in crisp white uniforms, their breast pockets emblazoned with the Jhalanpur crest, held a wide green ribbon as a barrier across the hospital's double doors. With cameras whirring and flashlights popping, Vijay drew a gold engraved Pathan sword, its blade viciously curved and highly sharpened, from its scabbard by his right hip and handed it to me, pommel first. I took it, stepped forward and raised the glittering weapon aloft.

'I declare the Stuart-MacKenzie Zenana Hospital of Jhalanpur open.'

The blade came down and sliced through the ribbon like a guillotine, the two sides of the ribbon fluttering away to cheers and applause from all around. Returning the sword to its sheath, Vijay threw open the glass doors and invited everyone inside.

'Quite a day, Cailin.' Duncan took my elbow and eased me away from the other guests, all mingling in a sea of humanity across the atrium concourse. 'I bet you never expected this when you left Riveldene in '29?'

'Duncan, this was unimaginable in '29. In fact, I need to pinch myself to believe it even today.'

'I guess none of us know what fate has in store for us, do we?'

'Life is certainly stranger than fiction, and we should know, Duncan, we've both lived it.'

'Any regrets?' His emerald-green eyes held me in their magnetic grip.

'A few, Duncan. And you?'

'Only one, Cailin. Only one.'

History had taught me not to buckle under the force of his charisma. 'It never does to look back, Duncan.'

'Then let's look forward. How about joining me for a ride at sunrise tomorrow. You never know where it might lead.'

We were interrupted by Lamis tapping my arm. 'Umi, a journalist from the Delhi Times wants to speak to you.'

'Sorry, Duncan, duty calls.'

Dashwana was lying on a pile of cushions alongside one of the marble fretted windows of her apartments with a long curtain of plaited jasmine hanging from a perforated lead gutter above her head. Cool water slowly dripped onto the leaves and flowers and when the wind blew, the wet foliage chilled the air and gave off a wonderful perfume which filled the room. I checked her temperature and pulse and asked how she was.

'Hot,' she said, 'and uncomfortable.'

'Has the valerian root helped you sleep?'

She eased herself onto her elbows, her bump now expanding her loose kaftan like an inflated balloon. 'Yes, but the baby kicks so hard, he wakes me up.'

She had hardly got the words out when a hernia-shaped mound stretched her left abdomen then retreated. I placed my hand on what must have been the baby's foot and waited. Seconds later it kicked again. 'Well, you could have a budding football player in there,' I said.

'That or a wrestler. How much longer do I have to put up with being a punchbag?'

'Another four weeks, assuming your child is not late.'

She groaned and lay back on the cushions. 'And when do I move to the hospital?'

'That will depend on when the baby's head engages.'

'Do I have to go, Doctor Mac? Can't I stay here and have the baby in comfort?'

'How many times do I have to tell you, Your Highness, comfort is not my priority. Yours and your baby's welfare are. Now, lift your kaftan and let me listen to its heartbeat.' I pulled my stethoscope from my bag and stuck the ends in my ears, wondering if the little mite was male or female and not daring to think of the consequences if it was a girl.

'I saw you out riding early this morning.'

'Then you must have been awake early. I left at dawn.'

'When will I be able to get back on a horse?'

'Not for some weeks.' I was counting the heartbeats and listening to all the other gastric gurgles emanating from Dashwana's gut.

'I really miss feeling the wind in my hair. No-one told me how restricting this being a mother would be.'

'Get used to it, Your Highness, motherhood is a vocation I'm afraid.'

'Have you ever had children?' An innocent enough question which shattered my concentration and left me stunned.

'No, never.' I replied, crossing my fingers and mentally apologising to my maker.

'Then how could you know what it feels like? I wish I could change my mind.'

'Dashwana Devi! What a thing to say. You're carrying the future Maharaja of Jhalanpur. What do you mean, you wish you could change your mind?'

'I don't really mean it, Doctor Mac, but I get so bored lying here day after day.'

My heart went out to her. Pregnancy in the height of the summer was certainly not a joke, especially in the middle of a desert. 'Would you like me to arrange a cool lavender bath to refresh you?'

'Umm, that would be nice.'

'Then I'll get your aunt to organise it. But don't stay in there too long. We don't want you getting wrinkly.'

Vijay was studying some papers at his desk when I was ushered into his office. It felt strange to be back in the royal apartments without Ruby in residence and the memories of our mad dash to the Windom Hospital in Jodhpur made me shudder.

'Good afternoon, Mac, how are my wife and child?'

'Your child is destined to replace Jack Allen as Newcastle United's centre forward. As for your wife, she's unhappy at being used as a punchbag.'

'I didn't know you were a football fan, Mac.'

'I'm not,' I said, helping myself to some water from a crystal jug. 'But you don't get far in Northumbria unless you follow the Magpies.'

'The Magpies?'

'Yes. Newcastle United's colours are black and white, so the fans refer to them as the Magpies.'

'Then perhaps I should start a football team here in Jhalanpur in honour of my son.' He came over from his desk and we sat under the slowly rotating ceiling fan. 'With our dark green and white kit we could call ourselves the Jasmines.' He began to chuckle.

'Hardly a suitable name for a football team, Vijay.'

'Perhaps you're right. Anyway back to business. Is everything running smoothly at the hospital?'

'Yes it is, and the maternity wing is all ready for Dashwana Devi as soon as the baby's head has engaged.'

'When will that be?'

'Hopefully, in about four weeks, assuming there are no complications.' I could have bitten my tongue.

'Complications?' Vijay had turned white. 'What sort of complications?'

'There's no need to panic, Vijay, it's just a medical term. Dashwana Devi may well have got her dates wrong, or the baby could have heard you talking about a football team named the Jasmines and decided to remain where he is.' My joke fell on deaf ears. 'Vijay, stop worrying. Your wife and baby are both fine and I have no reason to think that this birth is going to be anything other than normal. Now relax, you will be the proud father of a son and heir before you know it.'

'I hope so, Mac. I really hope so.'

The post had arrived when I got back to the office, a letter from Frances visible on top. I looked at the postmark. It had been posted on the twelfth of August.

Dear Mac,

Jim has been promoted. He's going to run the India Maritime Coastal Service based at Viceroy's House, so we'll be relocating to Delhi. He's put in for some furlough before he takes up his post so we could well be travelling to England at the same time as you. There's a departure on the eighteenth of October from Ballard's Pier. I think it's the ss Rawalpindi.

Are you taking Lamis with you and, if so, do you want us to book two double cabins at the same time?

As for my teaching plans, the Board of Governors here at St Saviour's are now advertising for a new head. I wander if Beaky Beckinsale will try to apply? With Jim's salary increasing I have time to decide where I would like to work in the capital, so I could end up being a lady of leisure for a while, like Ruby.

How is she getting on? Jim heard from Tom that she had gone back to Jhalanpur for your inauguration. You must have been delighted to see her.

Not much to tell you on the 'Gloria' front. Jim doesn't seem to know anything, but then he is a man, and I don't have any contacts other than you and Ruby in regard to our Doctor Hodgson. What I do know is that Tom's divorce was finalised in July. Enid wrote to Jim asking for Tom's address as she wanted to let him know . . .

I read the rest of the news, then folded the letter and put it in my desk drawer. If only their marriage had ended before I'd left Tilbury in '29, I thought, how different my life would have been then. Seeing Tom was not getting any easier and my nights were again being disturbed by strange erotic dreams.

I was about to head back to the villa when Siobhan knocked on my office door. 'Sorry Doctor Mac, but we have a problem in reception.'

I looked at my watch, it was half-past six. 'Can't one of the other doctors handle it?'

'No, the father is demanding to see you, and you alone.'

When I arrived at the concourse, Vijay's new Political Agent rushed over and insisted we went somewhere private to discuss his dire circumstances. I led him to my office and sent Siobhan away.

'Now, Mr Cuthbert. What emergency brings you here tonight?'

'Doctor Stuart-MacKenzie, what I'm about to tell you MUST be kept strictly between ourselves. Is that understood?'

I was rather taken aback by this superior attitude and after Frances's letter, I was not in the best of moods. 'Mr Cuthbert, if this is a medical emergency, then I will decide what is confidential and what is not. Is that understood.'

The man deflated like a burst balloon. 'I apologise, Doctor, I did not mean to question your judgement, but my wife and I are beside ourselves with worry.'

'Then, out with it, Man. Whatever is the matter?'

'It's our daughter, Doctor. She is fourteen years old and our only child. In June, we had a social function to go to at the Bhupendra Singh hotel and left our daughter in the care of our Sikh housekeeper. When we arrived back, Poppy was hysterical, and the housekeeper could do nothing with her. It took my wife days to calm her down and when she finally told us what had happened, we were horrified. You see, the housekeeper had been paid to allow her uncle to gain access to Poppy and rape her.'

I could now see why he was so upset.

'Naturally, I advised the police of this, the rapist was apprehended and he is now in jail awaiting trial for this vile deed, along with the housekeeper for aiding and abetting.'

'So, how can I help?'

'Poppy is pregnant. My wife confirmed to me this afternoon that my daughter has missed two of her monthly cycles. I need you to terminate this pregnancy immediately,

Doctor. Poppy cannot be subjected to such a degrading pregnancy.'

I sat back, my arms resting on my desk and tried to think of a suitable response to this news. 'Mr Cuthbert, I see clearly why you would ask for the assistance of the S-MK to undertake such a termination, but I'm afraid this procedure is frowned on by the medical profession unless there is some major medical or mental reason to justify it.'

He crashed his hands on the desktop and my pencil pot leapt into the air. 'Mr Cuthbert, please control yourself.'

'For Christ's sake, woman, we do have a major medical and mental reason.' He could be heard in the hospital grounds. 'Poppy was born with mongolism!'

I now found myself between a rock and a hard place. The rock was that Poppy needed to remain in her own familiar surroundings due to her mental state, which meant that she would be having the termination at home. The hard place was that Mr Cuthbert was insisting I carried out the procedure to ensure that there was no possible leak into the community regarding this horrific case.

The last time I'd had anything to do with a Manual Vacuum Aspiration procedure was when Fatima Patel had used it on me in Room 52 at the Metropolitan Hotel in Delhi and repeating it on Poppy was going to play havoc with my sanity.

I agreed to visit the Cuthbert family the following day and left for the villa convinced that fate had dealt me yet another blow.

Poppy's flattened face, almond shaped, upwardly slanting eyes, small ears, hands and feet, a short neck and poor muscle tone, all pointed to John Langdon Down's description of mongolism.

The teenager was terrified, screwed up in a ball in the corner of her bedroom refusing to allow me anywhere near her. I had to resort to mild sedation to get anything done at all, while Mrs Cuthbert spent the whole time wringing her hands and apologising to her daughter for failing her as a mother.

The atmosphere was tense, but I eventually managed to take some blood, urine and vaginal samples, went back to the hospital laboratory and two days later confirmed to the Cuthberts that their daughter was indeed with child.

I was facing my own demons. Being in a constant state of flux, I was not convinced I would get through the procedure without having a panic attack. Mrs Appleby, sensing that something was wrong with me, kept asking if I was alright. I could hardly tell her the truth, so I brushed away her concerns with some inane excuses.

It was essential that Poppy was kept calm, so I took Lamis to one side, gave a brief outline of the case and told her I needed her help. Realising that my patient had been abused by an Indian man, Lamis grew very cold, her voice dropped an octave and she insisted on befriending Poppy. It worked. She spent that night sleeping in Poppy's room at the Cuthbert's, chatting about anything apart from the morning's procedure and assuring the teenager that she was not alone.

I arrived after breakfast, having decided that laudanum was my only chance of getting through the day in one piece. I disguised the MVA equipment the best I could at the side of Mrs Cuthbert's bed and laid out some hospital sheets and towels on the mattress. Closing the net curtains to dampen the light, I thoroughly scrubbed my hands and took a last look around. All was ready. I took ten very deep, slow breaths and went to find the girls, bringing them both into my makeshift surgery.

Lamis was amazing. She had, of course, seen Gloria's lecture on MVA at the Lady Hardinge and had even attended one such case earlier in the year, so what I was about to do to Poppy did not concern her at all. She sat by her head, held her hand tightly and never stopped talking, Her English was now fluent, so Poppy spent the whole procedure hearing vivid descriptions of strange Indian temples, snow-capped Himalayan mountains, Fox Moth aircraft flying through the air like a bird and the joys of decorating her home for the festive season.

As I worked, I listened, and came to realise that this must have been how Lamis had survived Jusuf Abbas's violent abuse. She had mentally taken herself off to beautiful places where that flea-infested room couldn't penetrate, and by doing so, she had managed to maintain her sanity. If I loved Lamis before, it was nothing to the feeling our now had for my surrogate child.

After the MVA was completed, I walked Poppy back to her room and left Lamis with her for another night, quietly instructing her to check for any signs of excessive bleeding and to send someone to tell me straight away. Mr Cuthbert handed me a large glass of whisky as I descended the stairs.

'Here, Doctor Stuart-MacKenzie, drink this. I'm sure you need it.'

'Thank you, Mr Cuthbert.' I downed it in one gulp. 'Poppy is now in her own room and being monitored by Miss Abbas.'

'Can we rely on Miss Abbas's confidentiality, Doctor?'

I bristled. 'Sir, Miss Abbas is one of the most loyal members of my team and would never divulge a confidentiality. If you are implying otherwise, then perhaps you should ask the same question of me. Goodnight, Mr Cuthbert.'

Placing the MVA case back in the boot of my car, I revved the engine in sheer anger, kicked up a shower of gravel as the back wheels spun on the drive and shot out onto the road like a bat out of hell.'

Mrs Appleby was waiting for me when I arrived home, and so was Tom. I looked from one to the other and realised that I was to face a third degree before I would be allowed any peace.

'Mac, Mrs Appleby is worried about you.'

'Obviously.' I sounded tetchy.

'Don't be so sarcastic. She's concerned for your welfare, and she tells me that you are suffering from panic attacks.'

Bugger, I thought, feeling cross that I had failed to fool my housekeeper. 'Yes, I've had one or two, but they come and go, usually triggered when I am taking on too many problems.'

He pulled my lower eyelid down. 'Are you sleeping?'

'Sort of.' I was going to have to acquiesce to his examination or I would make him even more suspicious.

'What you need, my girl, is rest. Your last few months have been manic and your body is trying to tell you to slow down.'

Actually, I thought, I've been manic ever since you got me pregnant. I dug my thumb into the palm of my hand and tried to remain calm. 'What do you suggest, Tom, a three-month sabbatical relaxing by Lake Geneva?'

'Stop it, Mac. This is serious. He rammed a thermometer under my tongue. 'You can't go on trying to run the world as a one woman show. You have to delegate.'

'I do delegate.' I mumbled, trying to keep the thermometer in place. There were some criticisms I simply could not allow to go unchallenged.

'Oh really. So where have you been until this late hour. Certainly not to a bridge party looking at that MVA case in the hall.'

Oh, shit! I cursed under my breath. Locking eyes with Tom, I removed the thermometer, shook it and checked my temperature. 'Normal,' I announced and handed it over. 'As for my movements tonight, I had my reasons and you will not question them.' I knew from his expression that my professional dagger had reached its mark.

'So be it, but take my advice. Find a way to pace yourself, or the S-MK will find itself devoid of a Senior Surgeon.'

He stormed out, leaving me to deal with Mrs Appleby. She was in the kitchen pretending to scrub my smalls. I put her at ease and promised to slow down, then climbed the stairs and slid the MVA case under my bed until the morning.

My head hurt. I had ended yet another healthy baby's life and my guilt was palpable, but this was part of my job, and I knew it had been the right thing to do in this instance, no matter how much it hurt.

'I don't need you questioning me, Tom Wallace,' I complained. 'Just disappear into the sunset with Gloria Hodgson and leave me alone.'

Chapter Twenty-Nine

L amis arrived back home in time for supper, dropped her midwifery bag at the bottom of the stairs and collapsed in a heap in the drawing room.

'How is Poppy doing?'

'Not too badly, Umi. I gave her another dose of pain relief, as you recommended, and I have left her to sleep. I will call again tomorrow to see how she is, but I think she will need a psychiatrist if she is ever to overcome her fear of men.'

'You did an amazing job yesterday, Lamis. I couldn't have been prouder.' I blew her a kiss. 'As for psychiatric help, I'll need to have a quiet word with Doctor Wallace to see if we can get some home visits organised. How is her mother coping? It seems to me she also needs counselling.'

Lamis nodded and went to change. I sat alone, imagining how my conversation with Tom might go after his abrupt departure. I'd be walking a tight rope, whatever I said, but I had no choice. The S-MK didn't have a psychiatric unit, whereas the Dhyan Kumar Sing General Hospital did.

He was in Theatre C checking the newly installed operating equipment when I found him.

'Tom, may I have a word?'

He raised his hand, gave some ongoing instructions to his Assistant Surgeon, then led me to his office. It was more spacious than mine, more masculine in design, but identical in the quality of fixtures and fittings. His oak desk and chocolate brown leather chair were positioned at one end of the room in front of a first-floor view of the hospital compound while, at the other end, a large oak boardroom table and eight chairs stood before a full-length oak bookcase. The area between had been set out as a sofa area with an ebony coffee table and two chocolate-brown leather settees, which is where he sat and suggested I did the same.

'Tom, I need your hospital's help with psychiatry.' I filled him in on exactly what had happened over the past days at the Cuthbert's. He listened in silence until I had finished, his facial muscles rigid.

'So, both the mother and daughter need counselling?'

'Yes.'

'And the doctor. Does she need counselling too?'

My heart skipped a beat. 'You mean me? Why would I need counselling, Tom?'

The pain in his eyes needed morphine. 'I know what you did, Mac. I know about the MVA at the Metropolitan Hotel.'

I leapt from the settee. 'How? Who told you? That was my secret, my body, and nothing whatsoever to do with you,' I screamed defensively.

'It had everything to do with me, and you know it,' he countered, his voice rising. 'That's why you could never contemplate a future with me, isn't it? No wonder you're suffering from acute mental stress.'

While my heart bled to death, my head demanded answers. 'Who was it, Tom, Ruby or Frances? Which one of them broke their promise to me?'

'Does it matter?'

'Too damn right it matters. What I told them was in confidence.'

His voice cracked. 'And the only reason they broke that confidence was because I told them you were about to have a nervous breakdown and I now know why. This has been eating away at you for years, Mac, and it's the worst news of my life.'

'YOUR LIFE!' My sneer was straight from a hyena's playbook. I felt gutted that he finally knew the truth, but my head didn't care, it underlined the truth in thick black pen.

'Yes, I aborted your child. Yes, I made the decision alone. No, I had no choice, and what is more, I have paid for it every day of my life since. I was twenty-nine years old, pregnant, single, and about to lose the very career which had brought me to India in the first place, so take that 'holier than thou' look of your face, Tom Wallace. It wasn't me who was married, it was you.'

The dam had burst and all of my years of angst poured out. 'Has being told made any difference to YOUR life? Will you be walking around in sackcloth and ashes from now on?' He didn't answer. 'I thought not, so don't stand there like some bloody priest taking confession. The foetus may have been yours, but it was me who was facing the consequences. Does that sound cathartic enough for you? Why don't you add insult to injury, Tom, and bugger off to your girlfriend now you're divorced, while I continue to live with my guilt.'

Tom was on his feet, pressing his back against the office door barring my chance of leaving. 'Girlfriend? What girlfriend?'

'Oh please, spare me the righteous indignation. We all know that you and Gloria Hodgson are as thick as thieves.'

'Gloria Hodgson? What has she got to do with this?'

'For Christ's sake, Tom, I'm not stupid nor mentally unhinged. You were seen socialising with Gloria in Bombay after I left, you've been corresponding with her for months and you've just been back to Bombay with her on a week's R&R. Where did you stay? At the Taj Mahal? In the same suite?'

'You really have gone out of your mind if you honestly believe all that drivel.'

'Really?' I was now leaning against the windowsill, my arms firmly crossed against my chest, rage oozing from every pore.

'Yes, really. Gloria and I did meet after you left Bombay and we did have dinner together, not because I desired her, but because she was hankering for a job with the medical team at St George's Hospital and wanted my help. As for corresponding for months, that's a complete and utter fabrication of the facts. We have exchanged letters three times. Once when she advised me that she no longer wanted my help to get into St George's because she had been offered a job by you at the WCHS, a second to tell me that your film preview was to be held in the Great Eastern Hotel in Calcutta and did I want an invitation, and the third, to invite me to her engagement party.'

'Engagement party?' I was losing touch with reality.

'Yes, Mac, her engagement party. Walter Smith asked her to marry him while they were in Calcutta. That's why she went to Bombay. Not to meet me in some clandestine sexual tryst, but to spend quality time with her fiancé after months of working her socks off.'

I refused to be placated. 'And you, why were you in Bombay?'

He exploded, striding across the office, taking me by the shoulders and shaking the living daylights out of me. 'Because I had to sign some bloody divorce papers for Enid in front of a notary and get them back to England on the next ship. If you don't believe me, then ring Thackery Burgess Solicitors, and speak to Wallace Whitfield.'

He bounced off the walls, incapable of standing still. 'Christ Almighty, could this get any worse? I married my brother's wife out of duty, then fell deeply in love with a P&O passenger and got her pregnant. I've spent three years not knowing that I had a child or that this child's life was terminated because I was a married man, and then the woman who was my wife decided to leave me for some bloody penniless insurance man. When I finally thought I could find some happiness in my life with the only woman I have ever loved, I'm accused of screwing Gloria Hodgson in the same bed, in the same suite at the same hotel where my child was conceived. If it wasn't so fucking serious it would be laughable.'

His final bounce took him out of the office and down the stairs. I followed, not sure what I thought I was going to do to right this, but fate never gave me the chance. The emergency bell shattered the silence of the concourse and Tom suddenly had other things on his mind.

I stood there, alone, with my world collapsing around me, and longed for home, Pa's unwavering ministry and the peace and tranquillity of his house of God.

The Scottish Presbyterian Church sat proudly in its churchyard next to the Christian Mission on the other side of the city, its tall spire and solid construction offering solace to any tortured soul who happened to pass by. I lifted the rusty metal latch and pushed the warped wooden door aside and entered. The place was empty, only the dappled sunlight through the stained-glass window cast a golden glow on the cream embroidered altar cloth below.

I sat in the front pew, my hands in my lap and poured out my heart, begging forgiveness in prayer for the deaths I had caused and the deep scars they had left behind. Tom's child in my womb, the emaciated boy on the train, the tiny foetus of Poppy Cuthbert. I had never questioned my lack of faith back in Northumbria because, for me, God didn't exist, but all I wanted now was for that same God to show me compassion and understanding. In short, I wanted him to mend my broken heart, because I was incapable of mending it myself.

When all my guilt and anguish had been spent and the sun had set, I got up off my knees and walked out. The beauty of the desert evening was a balm to my pain as I wandered beside the gravestones, their solid presence making me homesick for Pa's Vicarage in Riveldene. The sky was crystal clear, the moon full and a zephyr of breeze cooled my perspiring skin as an eagle owl glided overhead. I tracked its dark body as it crossed the great white orb. It was like witnessing an ancient evil omen and I shivered.

'Jesus, Mac, you are having a nervous breakdown,' I muttered, and turned for the gate hoping I hadn't tempted fate.

A faint cry caught the air. I stood still and listened to the rustle of the leaves and the hoot of the owl. I must have imagined it, I thought, then it came again. A whimper of distress. This was not the sound of the night, this was a baby's plea for help. I searched between the headstones trying to locate the sound, but I seemed to be moving away from it instead of getting closer. I backtracked and tried again until I was standing above a newly dug grave, the dying flowers and limp wreaths shielding the sound.

I moved the grave's detritus away and exposed a tiny naked baby, abandoned and all alone. I carefully lifted it to my shoulder and looked about, trying in vain to find the person who may have left this innocent child in such an exposed location, but there was not a sound, not a snap of breaking twig nor the crunch of feet on gravel. Nothing.

I quickly wrapped the child in my pashmina then bent to the temporary wooden cross and read the scribbled inscription.

FREJA CHANDI

1915 – 1932

R.I.P.

'Is this your child, Freja?' I asked, but I received no answer.

All was quiet at the S-MK when I carefully eased the car down the hospital ramp, conscious of the baby lying on the back seat. I parked alongside the zenana lift and with him safely curled in my arms, I entered the cold, featureless cavity and waited for the doors to slide shut, as if closing on a dark chapter of my life.

Once inside the obstetrics department, I placed the baby on a towelling mat and checked for any injuries. Lying there still whimpering was an Indian child. A little boy, probably no more than a couple of days old, his tiny olive-skinned fingers holding onto mine like a limpet, his mouth sucking on my little fingernail as his deep brown eyes searched my face and his soft dark downy hair brushed against the palm of my hand like velvet.

'Well, young man, you appear to be hungry?'

Wrapping him in a small towel, I carried him to the staff kitchen where I knew we had some powdered baby milk, made up a bottle then walked into my office. It felt good to have this little miracle nestling in my arms as the rubber teat delivered warm sustenance to his tiny stomach. I sat in the dark, rocking him to sleep, trying to decide what I should do next.

If I was right, this poor mite's mother had died in childbirth, and my new foundling was probably an orphan. No doubt the Minister would be able to fill in the gaps, I surmised, but meanwhile I needed to keep the baby safe, and there was no better place than here at the neonatal unit.

He looked so peaceful lying in his hospital cot, with a hospital tag tied to his ankle.

Baby delivered last night – Mother died in childbirth. Weight six pounds, two ounces. Last fed at 11.15 pm. Dr E S-MK.

It was one o'clock in the morning when I climbed into bed still pondering on the events of the night. I knew it was ridiculous, but it did feel as if fate had deliberately placed me in that churchyard in order to find the child, as if I was being given some form of redemption for my sins. I slept soundly and was woken by Mrs Appleby with my morning cuppa.

'Good morning, Doctor Mac, what would you like for breakfast?'

'The usual, Mrs Appleby. Porridge and toast.'

'Will you be back for lunch?'

'No. I mean to go up to the palace to check on Her Highness so I will probably have something later in the hospital canteen.'

'Very well, Doctor. Lamis has already left for the day, so I'll see you both tonight.'

I quickly dressed and went to check on the foundling the minute I arrived at the S-MK. He was asleep, having been given another bottle at six o'clock. I hooked the medical chart back on the end of the cot and went to find Lamis. She was preparing the pre-natal clinic trolley and was rather surprised to see me.

'Lamis, can you come to my office?'

We sat at my desk while I described the events of the night.

'I want you to take care of the baby for me until I can find out if he has any family. I'm not hopeful but I must try. He's in the neonatal unit right now, but he is a healthy little chap, all he needs are regular feeds and fresh clouts. I'd leave him where he is for the time being. We can move him to the new-borns' dormitory soon enough. If anyone asks you where he's from, just say you're not sure.'

'Yes, Umi. By the way, Doctor Wallace left a message for you to contact him.'

'I'll do it later. Right now, I'm expected at the palace and I'm late.'

Any thought that fate had given me a helping hand was quickly quashed when I found Dashwana, as white as a sheet, hanging onto the end of the couch, clutching her abdomen and crying out in pain.

'How long has this been going on?' I demanded.

'Fifteen minutes ago, Doctor Mac,' said her aunt.' She was talking to my husband's chaprassi when she began to feel dizzy, then the pain started.'

I eased her into a lying position and checked the baby's heartbeat. 'Right, Your Highness, the baby's head has engaged. It's time to go. You're in the first stages of labour.' She didn't react, her eyes staring into a void, her mouth firmly clamped shut. I cocked my head towards the aunt. She just shrugged.

My labour plan had been practiced often enough in the zenana and when it went into action it worked like a charm. Within fifteen minutes, Dashwana, her face veiled, was being driven into the hospital's underground entrance and taken to her private room using the zenana lift. I stayed with her, checking her vital signs and watching the clock as its minute hand slowly rotated. Her labour pains were now every eight minutes and her cervix at three finger width. She was so tense it was exacerbating her pain, so I gave her some mild pain relief and went to check on my theatre staff, just in case.

'Is the anaesthetist here?' I asked my senior theatre nurse.

'Yes, Doctor Mac, but she's already dealing with another operation in Theatre B. A patient with a hiatus hernia.'

'Then let's keep our fingers crossed we won't need her services. Has the blood bank been told to stand by?'

'Yes, Doctor. They have supplies of AB negative blood ready for a possible emergency transfusion.'

'Excellent. Well done. Hopefully we will get through this royal birth without Her Highness suffering any complications. Once her waters break, I will move her to the labour ward, but I won't relax until I know the baby has taken its first breath. Until then, I want all the theatre staff to remain on duty. Is that clear?'

'Yes, Doctor Mac. Perfectly clear.'

I returned to Dashwana's side. Her contractions were coming every five minutes and her cervix had opened to a five-finger width. Anytime now, I thought, as I kept her calm with breathing exercises. She was still spaced out and uncommunicative, but I put this down to fear and kept my voice low and passive. Within the hour, her waters broke.

'Wheelchair, nurse,' I ordered and helped Dashwana off the bed. The fact that the baby was coming early didn't worry me, she could have easily miscalculated her dates, especially as her courses had never been regular, but her state of mind did.

'Try to relax, Your Highness, and keep taking deep breaths. The baby is in the correct position, and your body is going through the stages of labour perfectly normally. It won't be long now before you are holding your child in your arms.' I had everything crossed.

The midwife sat by Dashwana's head, wiping her brow with a damp cloth and making reassuring noises as I raised her feet onto the edge of the delivery bed, keeping her hospital gown draped across her knees to maintain some patient dignity.

At four-thirty in the afternoon, her cervix was fully extended and as the next contraction grew in strength I told her to push. Every muscle in her body strained against the pain as she bore down hard, forcing the baby along the birthing canal to my open hands.

'It's coming, Dashwana,' I said calmly, 'I'm about to see the baby's head. At the next contraction, push again as hard as you can.'

I felt her tense, she screamed as she pushed and I couldn't believe my eyes. To my utter horror, the baby's head stretched the opening of the vagina and I was staring at a pale pink cranium covered in copper red hair.

'Jesus, Mary and Joseph,' I blasphemed under my breath. I clamped my mouth shut and let my mind do the talking. This was not Vijay's child, it was Duncan's.

My brain scrambled trying to think of a way out of the dilemma when I caught sight of the umbilical cord wrapped tightly around the baby's neck.

'Don't push until I tell you,' I bawled, and slid my finger down the side of the baby's ear and tried to ease the cord over its head. It was too tight and with every inch of movement forwards, the child was turning blue from strangulation.

'Clamp and scissors, now.' I said quietly. 'Dashwana, short pants please.' The midwife thrust the instruments into my hand.

I immediately cut the vaginal skin to make more room, clamped the cord as my eardrums vibrated to Dashwana's violent screams and, seconds later, cut straight through the cord separating the baby from the placenta.

'Right, at the next contraction, push as hard as you can . . . PUSH!'

A little girl slid into my hands, her face screwed up like a dried prune, her body limp. I quickly released the severed ligature from around her neck, wrapped her in a towel, covering her head completely, and clamped the other end of the placenta.

'Nuchal cord' I mouthed to the midwife at the other end of the bed. She blinked her understanding as I backed out of the delivery room swing doors and ran to the neonatal unit.

'Lamis,' I called, I need your help.

I had lost the will to live as I stared at Duncan's lifeless child lying in front of me on the blood spotted towel. I had tried to resuscitate the child, but I had failed and all I could think about was how was I going to explain this to Vijay?

So many scenarios revolved in my mind. What would this revelation do to Vijay? What would happen to Dashwana? Who would pay the ultimate price for allowing her access to one of the world's most charismatic womanisers? Who would be the first in the firing line? Her Aunt?' God, I hoped not.

The inevitability of what was about to happen overwhelmed me and I had no way of moving on, nor any idea how I could move on. Then Lamis appeared in the doorway.

'Umi.' My surrogate child, dressed in her midwife's uniform stretched out her arms, the palms of her hands holding Freja Chandi's baby wrapped in a hospital towel, its dark brown eyes staring out from its cocoon. I shook my head violently. The very idea froze me to the spot. How could I take such a monumental step? I would be playing God with other people's lives, playing with fire in regard to my own. But Lamis just stood there, so placid, so collected, so sure of what she wanted me to do.

'It is best, Umi. Best for everybody, and this little boy deserves a better life.'

I trembled from head to toe as she placed the tiny, breathing being into my arms, bit down hard on my lower lip, and prayed for guidance. The baby whimpered, his eyes searching my face for some reaction, then he parted his baby lips and gave me the most beautiful gummy smile.

'Am I really going to do this, Lamis?'

'Yes, Umi, you are.'

With one final look at Dashwana's dead daughter, I walked out of the neonatal unit, stepped back into the delivery room, smiled at the midwife who was tying the last of three catgut sutures and walked to the head of the bed. With my stomach churning and my heart in traction, I laid my bundle of life into Dashwana's outstretched arms.

'Your Highness, meet Jhalanpur's new heir to the throne. From all of us at the Stewart-MacKenzie Zenana Hospital, may I extend our congratulations on the birth of your healthy and happy little boy.'

I heard her sobs of relief as her index finger pulled down the towelling cocoon below the baby's chin and she gazed at the child for the very first time. Her look of salvation when she raised her eyes needed no explanation. I patted her shoulder, instructed the midwife to take over and returned to the lifeless child who deserved more from life than having Duncan Fitzpatrick as her father.

Chapter Thirty

The nave echoed to my footsteps as I took my place at the back of the congregation. The Minister climbed the steps of the pulpit, adjusted his cassock and peered down to his flock.

'Fellow sinners, today we reinforce our belief in the Covenant, and on this third Sunday in August we turn to the Old Testament and Leviticus 19:11 where we are told not to steal, not to lie and not to deceive those around us . . .'

I couldn't have picked a better Sunday to attend my first church service since leaving Riveldene. I struggled through the tedious hour of religious retribution, knowing that the man in the pulpit relaying God's word was no better than me, but he did have information vital to my needs.

'Good morning, Madam. I don't think we have seen you at our church before?'

'You haven't, Minister, but I have been here alone.'

'Then welcome. Is there something I can help you with?'

'There is, Minister, but perhaps this can wait until the rest of the congregation have paid their respects'.

When his flock had dispersed, he followed me to Freja's grave, and I introduced myself, emphasising my status as a doctor.

'Could you tell me who Freja Chandi was and what the circumstances were which caused her death?'

'I can, Doctor, and it is a very sad case indeed.' My enquiry didn't seem to concern him. 'Freja was a Sikh who converted to the Christian faith when she was seventeen. She was devout. A child of Jesus who had become a novice nun at the Christian Mission next door, giving her life to the glory of God.' He genuflected. 'What we did not know at that time, was that she had been raped by a member of the Sikh community.' He paused and shook his head. 'Perhaps that is why she turned to the Presbyterian Church. She was pregnant, you see, and eight months later, she produced a child.'

I looked again at the wooden cross and prayed that she was now with her maker.

'Sadly, she died in childbirth, and I have no idea what happened to the infant. The nuns at the mission are bound to secrecy and would deal with this in their own way.'

Which they did, I thought, my bile rising. In my book, the nuns at this Christian Mission were anything but a force for good over evil. I remembered the baby lying there naked, exposed to the elements for any wild dog or snake to finish it off, and hoped the nuns burned in hell.

'Tell me, Minister, did Freja have any family?'

'Not that I know of, Doctor, but when a young novice decides to become a nun, she renounces all her worldly possession, devoting herself entirely to the service of God.'

'As I thought, Minister. Thank you, you have been very helpful. I'll leave you now to your Sunday ministrations.'

'Will we be seeing you at next Sunday's morning worship, Doctor?

Not if I can help it, I thought. 'Perhaps you will, Minster, if my work schedule allows. Good day.'

I slept badly and woke with an excruciating headache. Lamis kept her council at the breakfast table but I could tell she was keen to know what I had learned from the Minister. We closeted ourselves in my bedroom away from Mrs Appleby's hearing and I told her what I knew.

'Then Freja can rest in peace, Umi. Her baby will be loved and cared for throughout his life and, one day, he will return that love by taking care of all Jhalanpur's people.' Lamis was so good at seeing life in simple terms.

'Perhaps he will, Lamis. All we can do is hope and take his secret to the grave.'

'I am proud of what you did, Umi, and I will keep this secret locked in my heart for ever.'

She was totally unperturbed by what I had done, yet I was buckling under the weight of my deceit, struggling to come to terms with such an outrageous decision. I tried to tell myself that I had no other choice at the time, but I knew this was nonsense. If Duncan's little girl had lived, the scandal would have rocked Jhalanpur, leaving Vijay no choice but to divorce his first wife, even banishing her from court altogether to live in exile like her mother-in-law. He would then have married again to produce an heir, and I had no idea how that would have affected Ruby.

As it was, I had covered up Dashwana's sexual misdemeanour, put paid to a major scandal in this Princely State and left the world believing that Freja's son was the legitimate heir to the Jhalanpur throne. A heavy burden indeed, I thought, and one that was playing on my mind.

I needed to confide in someone I could trust and there was only person I knew I could truly depend on. I went to find Tom.

He was alone in his office as crowds of people gathered beyond the perimeter gate, cheering and letting off firecrackers as the news of the new prince's birth quickly spread. He looked up as I knocked and beckoned me in, the dark shadows under his eyes emphasising the tension he was under.

'You look as bad as I feel, Mac,' he said, pulling out a chair.

'I am, and with good reason.' I paused for breath trying to steady my nerves. 'Irrespective of the animosity we may feel for each other, Tom, I need to share a confidence with you as a fellow medic and a colleague, and I can only hope that you will understand the predicament I am in.'

'Go on.'

'Yesterday, I faced a medical dilemma of monumental proportions and the action I took to overcome it has probably created untold complications for the future of Jhalanpur. It wasn't an easy decision and it wasn't right, but it was the only practical solution available to me at the time.'

I relived events since we had angrily parted, every word shaking my foundation to the core. Tom walked round his desk and leant on the edge. 'Does Duncan Fitzpatrick know?'

I shook my head. 'I don't even know if I should tell him. Maybe letting sleeping dogs lie would be the better option right now?'

'That option didn't work in our case, did it, Mac?' The barb went deep. 'If you are asking for my opinion, then whatever the consequences, the father has a right to be told. You cannot allow him to die never knowing he had a daughter.' The inference was obvious. 'And I'm afraid it is imperative you speak with him without delay because he's lying in our intensive care unit right now with a bullet hole through his chest.'

I felt a hammer blow pulverise my brain and slipped from my chair into a deep black hole.

'Mac, wake up. Mac, can you hear me?' Tom's voice reached me through a long, dark tunnel. 'Mac, here, breath this.'

Astringent ammonia invaded my nostrils making my eyes water. I coughed, trying to clear my airways.

'Mac, are you with me?'

I heaved myself back into the chair and nodded my head. He waited until my colour returned then allowed me to speak.

'What do you mean Duncan is in intensive care with a bullet hole through his chest?'

'Exactly that.' He screwed the top on the smelling salts and placed it on the desk. 'He was brought into the emergency unit three days ago. You were there at the time. You must have heard the alarm?'

Images flashed through my mind of me running down the hospital stairs after Tom as a Klaxon bell rent the air and nearly burst my eardrums.

'That was Duncan?'

'Yes. He'd been shot from the rear with a rifle while out riding. The bullet went straight through his chest. They think it was poachers.'

'My God.' My hand smacked into my mouth. 'Has he survived?'

'It's touch and go, Mac. The bullet only just missed his heart, but it has severely damaged his left lung. He was suffering from major internal bleeding when he arrived at the hospital. Fortunately, I'm no stranger to battlefield bullet wounds so he was lucky. I managed to stem the haemorrhaging and he is now stable and in recovery, but I might yet lose him to infection.'

Suddenly everything became crystal clear. 'That's what Prince Kapoor Dhawan's chaprassi must have been telling Dashwana when I arrived at the palace yesterday. He must have told her that Duncan had been shot and the shock sent her into premature labour. Christ, Tom,' I stuttered, my eyeballs on stalks, 'I had no idea what I was dealing with. I could have lost her too.'

We sat in silence, both thinking of the possible repercussions of that statement.

'Thankfully you didn't, Mac,' uttered Tom, going to his desk drawer and pulling out a half empty bottle of brandy. Another firecracker ripped through the silence and I visibly shook. 'Do you want me to go with you?'

He handed me a hospital glass. Staring at the brown liquid I didn't even know if I could get out of the chair, let alone make it to the intensive care unit, but I shook my head anyway. It was my job alone to tell Duncan he was a father and that his daughter had died of asphyxiation in my arms. As the brandy glass trembled in my hand I made myself face the inevitable. Whatever the consequences, I could not repeat history. Tom was right, I had made the wrong decision once before and I must not do it again.

'But the news could kill him, Tom.'

'Not while I'm his surgeon, it won't. He's heavily sedated anyway and may not react at all.'

"I hope you're right.' I downed the shot of brandy in one go and waited for the alcohol to give me Dutch courage.

'I'll go and check on him now and increase his sedation if necessary. Meanwhile, you stay here and calm your nerves. The timing is terrible but none of this was your fault, and if I know Duncan Fitzpatrick he will leave Jhalanpur as soon as he is recovered, because he will want to save his own skin above all else.'

Duncan was attached to any number of tubes, all connected to the latest in thoracic medical equipment, when I entered his room. A nurse was sitting at his bedside monitoring his vital signs and taking regular readings off an oxygen bottle while he struggled to breathe through an oxygen mask covering his nose and mouth.

'It's alright, nurse,' I whispered. 'I'll monitor Mr Fitzpatrick and will call you immediately there is any change.'

Reluctantly she departed and I read through his medical chart, noting his blood group and number of transfusions. Tom was right, Duncan was in a critical condition and what I was about to tell him was only going to add to his troubles. I wanted to feel sorry for him, but having gained some composure in Tom's office, all I could think about was how he had abused Vijay's trust for the benefit of his own ego.

'Can you hear me, Duncan?' My voice was devoid of emotion.

He acknowledged my question with his eyelids and I stepped up to the metal bedframe and gripped it with both hands.

'I have something to tell you and I imagine you already suspect what it is. Yesterday afternoon, Rani Dashwana Devi gave birth to a child. Your child, Duncan. A little girl.'

He could have been a tailor's dummy lying there, his eyelids retracted, his emerald-green eyes fixed on a spot beyond my head.

'During the birth, the umbilical cord was wrapped around the baby's neck and although I did everything in my power to save her, she succumbed to strangulation and never regained consciousness. I am so very sorry, Duncan.' I stretched for his hand and squeezed it tightly. 'I would give anything not to have to tell you this sad news, but as a veterinary surgeon, you know only too well that these things happen during birth and there is often nothing we can do about it.'

He continued to look past me, remorse, like a grey mist, descending around him. 'Where is she, Cailin, where is my daughter now?' His words were so faint I had to lean in to hear him.

'Hopefully with God, Duncan, having paid the ultimate price for your folly.' I couldn't help myself. 'You can do nothing for her now, but if you have any feelings at all for her mother you will bury this information so deep it will never see the light of day.'

His eyes finally locked onto mine. 'What's the point, Cailin? Somebody in the palace already knows the truth.'

'Are you saying that somebody wanted you dead? That the bullet was no accident?'

He tried to answer but was struggling to breathe and becoming agitated. I checked the oxygen bottle gauge.

'No-one but you and I know the truth, Duncan, and even though your daughter died, you didn't. Providing you stay calm and follow Tom Wallace's instructions, you will live to see another day, although I doubt that will be here in Jhalanpur.'

He raised his head off the pillow. 'And Dashwana?' he wheezed. 'What will happen to her?'

You should have considered that before you got her pregnant, I thought, but kept it to myself. 'Dashwana doesn't know, Duncan.' I clenched my jaw and lied through my teeth. 'Fortunately, she produced two children yesterday, a girl and a boy. Twins, but fertilised by different fathers. It's a phenomenon we refer to in the medical profession as heteropaternal superfecundation. The boy survived. Vijay and Dashwana are now the proud parents of a son and heir.' I could faintly hear the fireworks penetrating the hospital walls and wondered if Duncan could hear them too.

Every muscle in Duncan's body tensed. 'Jesus, Mary and Joseph!'

Tom was hovering outside the room and I beckoned him in. 'Perhaps some more sedative,' I whispered, then left. Minutes later he joined me in the waiting room and nodded, indicating that all was well.

'How did he take it?' His question was hardly audible.

'Not well, but I think I have made him see reason. Once he's had time to assimilate what I've said, I'm sure he will do the right thing and leave Jhalanpur for good.'

'That would be best.'

I was about to tell him that Lamis had said the same thing that very morning, when the nurse's shouts of panic reached our ears.

'Doctor Wallace, Doctor Wallace, come quickly, it's Mr Fitzpatrick. He's spewing blood from inside his mask.'

There was nothing Tom could have done. Duncan had deliberately pulled his tubes from his chest cavity and a major haemorrhage in his left lung filled the organ with blood. He died on the way to the operating theatre.

I sat in my bedroom in the dark, trying to come to terms with his death and recalled the good times, in Edinburgh, when I had been infatuated with this complex character who I only really came to know later in life.

Had he deliberately killed himself? I wasn't sure. Perhaps he had hoped to make me feel guilty for being the bearer of bad news, gambling on Tom being able to pull him through.

But the simple fact was that I didn't feel guilty. It wasn't my fault that Duncan couldn't face a future without the pomp and kudos of being Jhalanpur's highly respected veterinary surgeon. Nor was it my fault that Duncan was full of hubris. In the end, it was hubris that had killed him.

I checked the time. Eight-thirty. Tom had told me to be at the DKS mortuary at nine, so I left the villa and strolled across the compound, my thoughts turning to Frances and Ruby. Why had they broken their promise? They knew how important it was to me and yet they had not hesitated to tell Tom when he questioned them. I was confused, but the damage had been done and now a barrier the size of the Great Wall of China was separating Tom and me emotionally.

The basement mortuary was dim and unwelcoming, just one single bulb giving light to an oak coffin resting on a trolley in the centre of the room, the lid with its brass plaque propped against the metal frame. Duncan looked so peaceful in death, his eyelids closed and his thick dark hair spread across the white taffeta lining. I stretched in and lifted a lock from his forehead, a gesture I'd done so often in the past, and then placed my fingers against his hard cold lips.

'I'll never forget you, Duncan. For better or worse, I will never regret knowing you.' I pulled a sealed bottle of Jameson's whisky from my pocket and laid it by his feet, sensing a presence behind me.

I turned to find Tom standing there holding Duncan's daughter swathed in a shroud. I took her from him, kissed the tiny forehead and carefully placed her in the crook of Duncan's right arm. Digging deep into my memory, I found myself reciting an Irish blessing.

'May the road rise up to meet you, may the wind be always at your backs, may the sunshine warm upon your faces, the rains fall soft upon your fields, and until we meet again, may God hold you both in the palm of his hand.'

Tom lifted the coffin lid and slid it into place, then sealed it with six brass screws. I brushed my hand against the heavily varnished oak, kissed the brass plaque and turned my back on my first love.

'When are you leaving for England, Mac?' asked Tom, as we came out onto the drive. The evening air was warm after the relative coolness of the mortuary.

'Immediately after the funeral. Pat Simmonds will fly Lamis, Mrs Appleby and me to Delhi, then, when I have tied up any loose ends and packed my housekeeper off to her sister in Lucknow, Lamis and I will take the Frontier Mail to Bombay.'

'Will you be returning to Jhalanpur in the New Year?'

I hesitated. 'I don't think so, Tom. Much as I have enjoyed running the S-MK, too many bad things have happened here.'

'What will you tell Vijay?'

'I'll leave that to Sir Peter Bonham-Cavendish. Right now, Vijay is in the middle of huge celebrations to honour the arrival of his son and heir. There's no need for me to rain on his parade.'

'Then there is nothing left for me to say other than to wish you fair winds and a smooth voyage. I doubt I'll get the opportunity to do so in the morning. Give my love to England, Mac, and have a happy festive season with your family up north.'

'Thank you, I will. You too.' There was something final about this parting, but I was too emotionally drained to do anything about it. As I made my way back to the villa I wondered, not for the first time, why my life was a series of painful goodbyes.

Chapter Thirty-One

Tuesday 18th October 1932

Lamis and I approached the ship's gangway to find Frances and Jim waiting for us. I hadn't spoken to Frances since finding out that she had broken her promise and I was not looking forward to discussing it face-to-face. The subject was still raw and I could tell Frances felt the same way. After hugs and greetings, we moved aboard and I was about to lead Lamis to our second-class cabin when a dark green Lincoln Sedan drove down the length of Ballard Pier's quayside and stopped below us. Ghalib moved to the rear of the car and opened the door for Ruby, who stepped out dressed in western clothes. Placing her gloved hand to her forehead, she searched the boat deck, caught sight of us all and headed up the gangway.

'Ruby,' I said, astounded, 'what are you doing here?'

'Heading for my first-class suite,' she said, handing her ticket to the purser. 'I couldn't leave you and Frances to have all the fun. And anyway, Vijay is deep in the desert enjoying parenthood right now so I thought I'd enjoy a couple of months buying up Harrods for Puttaker Lodge.'

'You're going to renovate it after all?'

'Naturally. I can't put up with a tent forever when I'm visiting Jhalanpur no matter how luxurious. I tell you, Mac, that sand manages to get into everything, including places it shouldn't.' She hugged Frances, winked at Jim then took Lamis by the hand and disappeared up to the hurricane deck to watch the hustle and bustle around the dock as the ss Rawalpindi prepared for departure.

'Is she serious?' I muttered into Frances's left ear. 'If I hadn't seen her with my own eyes, I would never have believed it.'

'You know Ruby. Never one for letting the grass grow under her feet, but I suspect it's an excuse. It can't be easy for her to take a back seat in the Royal household right now, and I imagine she's feeling rather lonely and abandoned in Delhi, although she'd never admit it. Still, it will be nice to have the three of us back together again,' she peered at me sideways, 'assuming we are not persona non grata.'

She picked up her valise and searched the crowds of passengers on deck looking for Jim. He seemed to have disappeared. Leaning out trying to see further down the deck she suddenly pulled back. 'Prepare to repel borders.'

I followed her finger pointing at the quay.

'Frances, Doctor Mac, over here,' shouted Sybil Wetherington, her beaming face staring back at us as she sat alongside Archie in a plush, new, open landau, waving her lace parasol like a sailor passing a message using semaphore.

'Goodness, have the Wetherington's come into money?'

'Search me, but no doubt we're about to find out.'

Time was pressing and I still hadn't made it to my cabin, but I could hardly ignore Sybil and had trouble keeping a straight face as she waddled up the gangway, elbows at right angles, pushing everyone else out of the way in her usual galleon ship style.

'Sybil, had did you know we were leaving today?' I pecked her on both cheeks and handed her rotund body over to Frances.

'Well, dear, it was like this. I happened to be in the shipping agent's office checking on the ss Viceroy of India's arrival later this week. My nephew and his wife are on board. Just married you see and wanting to start a new life here in India.' We both nodded. 'Anyway, while the agent was checking his ledger, I happened to see a reference to the Maharani of Jhalanpur travelling on the Rawalpindi, so I looked closer, and there you all were. Amazing isn't it?' Sybil could read Sanskrit up-side-down if she wanted to, I thought. 'So I said to my Archie, "We can't let them leave Bombay without a proper send off, it wouldn't be right." So here we are.'

Retracing our steps down the gangway against the flow, we all climbed into the landau and greeted Archie.

'How are you?' asked Frances, slipping her arm through his and giving it a squeeze.

'Better for seeing you, my dear. How is married life treating you?'

'I can't complain, Lord Wetherington, and you appear to have a new mode of transport.' She tapped the expensive upholstery with her fingers.

'Indeed, we have, Frances. My dear wife's brother sadly passed away with the pox and she has inherited all his estate. Isn't it wonderful?'

Not for Sybil's brother, I thought, remembering Henriette's cure for syphilis. 'Well, you certainly deserve some good news after the Wall Street crash, Lord Wetherington, and I'm sure your lovely wife will make the very most of her unexpected affluence.'

'Oh, I certainly will, Doctor Mac. But enough about us. We haven't got long before you sail so we just wanted to say, "Bon Voyage," have a wonderful time with your families in England, and come back refreshed and ready to tackle another three years in India.'

I gripped the edge of the landau, the underlying cause not lost on Frances.

'We will be back before you know it, Sybil,' she replied and wished them both an enjoyable festive season.

'Phew, that was unexpected.' Frances was leading the way back aboard and found Jim standing by the top step looking bored.'

'Was that the Wetheringtons?'

'It was Jim. Now can we get to our cabin before the whole of St Saviour's Sixth Form turn up to say cheerio.'

Ruby was waiting in Cabin 4 when I opened the door.

'Where's Lamis?'

'Being given a ship's tour by Jim while Frances organises their baggage.'

I dropped my medical bag on the floor and opened the starboard porthole window.

'Port Out, Starboard Home,' she pointedly remarked, lighting a cigarette with a rather smart gold Dunhill lighter.

'If you must smoke, Ruby, then go and do it in your own cabin.'

'Suite dear. Maharanis don't travel in mere cabins, and don't be so tetchy.' She rammed the cigarette end into a collapsible silver ashtray she was holding in her hand and laid it on my bedside table. 'And I'm not leaving this cabin until we've cleared the air over the Metropolitan Hotel debacle.'

'Do we have to?'

'Yes, we do. I have no intention of spending the whole of this voyage staring at your miserable face, so out with it, what is rattling your cage?'

I stood leaning against the wash hand basin, my fingers now digging into the rim of the ceramic bowl. 'Why, Ruby? What possible reason did you have for breaking your promise?'

'That's simple, Miss MacKenzie. Your sanity. Tom Wallace suspected there was an underlying reason for your total inability to function properly and he made it quite clear that you were heading for a nervous breakdown. When he informed Frances that you were unusually distraught after carrying out an abortion on a girl with mongolism, we both knew why.'

'But why didn't you discuss it with me first?'

Ruby leant back against the bulkhead and crossed her arms. 'We tried, Mac, believe me, we tried, but you had left instructions not to be disturbed.'

I frowned, trying to remember the night in question, then an image of Tom sitting in my drawing room when I arrived back from the Cuthbert's and my strict instructions to Mrs Appleby later not to allow anything to disturb me before the morning, sprang to mind.

'Mac, your health is more important to Frances and me than any grievance you might have with Tom Wallace over what you did back in Calcutta. If you had told him in the first place, as I suggested, none of this would have happened and you wouldn't be standing here like some lost soul alone, facing a lifetime of community service and personal celibacy.'

'I'm not a lost soul.'

'Cobblers, Mac. You're like an Israelite wandering through the wilderness looking for the Promised Land.'

'Have you quite finished?'

'No, not until you accept our apology for breaking a confidence and accept that we had no choice. Thanks to us, you can now face your future without that damned secret hanging over your head like . . .'

'The sword of Damocles?'

'No, that would be too quick. More like syphilis eating away at your brain.'

'Charming.'

'But true.' She came over to me and laid her hands on my shoulders. 'We're bitterly sorry for breaking a confidence, Mac, but we did it for all the right reasons, and the sooner you realise that the better.' She picked up her bag and opened the cabin door. 'Don't turn your back on us, Mac. Think about it, how many other friends do you have to lean on when the going gets tough? You need us, and we need you.'

Lamis woke to the soft lapping of the Indian Ocean against the hull as the ship's bow cleaved a path through the water, on course for Aden. She had been so excited on her first night aboard and it had taken me ages to get her off to sleep.

'Good morning, sleepyhead, are you wanting breakfast or should I leave you here all day?'

She jumped from her bed and grabbed her toothbrush, sitting with mine in the glass monogrammed tumbler.

'Umi?'

'Don't speak with your mouth full.'

'Umi,' she repeated, gargling and wiping her mouth on the monogrammed white towel. 'Did you know that the Chief Engineer on this ship is an Indian?'

'Who told you that?'

'Uncle Jim. He even took me to the engine room and introduced me to him. Apparently, they are great friends from when Uncle Jim was a ship's officer.'

'Don't tell me you've changed your mind again and want to be an engineer now?'

'Well, no, not exactly. But it is amazing, isn't it?'

'Not really, Lamis. If there is one thing your nation excels at, it's engineering, but I can't see you up to your armpits in axle grease, so we won't go there. Agreed?'

She giggled and started to rummage through her trunk.

'What are you looking for?'

'My tennis skirt. Uncle Jim is going to show me how to play quoits this afternoon. It is similar to tennis, isn't it?'

'No, Lamis, it's nothing like tennis. You have to try and throw a rubber ring over a spike from some way off. The winner is the one who has the most success.'

'Then I'd better start practicing.' She threw her silver bangle at the hook on the back of the door and missed.

'Come on, Lamis, I'm starving and if we don't get to the dining room soon, I will miss out on my porridge.'

'Sorry, Umi.' As her head popped through the neck of her yellow and white gingham dress she gave me one of her wonderful smiles. 'I almost forgot; Miss Frances told me to wish you a happy birthday.'

My heart skipped a beat.

They were all waiting for me as I strolled onto the foredeck in my swimming costume, a towel wrapped around my shoulders.

'Here comes the birthday girl,' remarked Jim, holding a slim package wrapped in gold paper with a wide silver bow.'

I gingerly opened it with Lamis jumping up and down by my side. There, lying in a wooden box, was a brand-new Leica Model II/D camera. 'Jim, Frances, you shouldn't have.' I lifted it out and examined the casing from front to back. 'This is far too generous.'

'Let's just say it's a peace offering,' replied Frances.

'Is there a film in it?' asked Ruby.

'Yes, I think so.' Frances glanced at Jim who nodded.

'Then I suggest we have a group photograph to celebrate Mac reaching the grand old age of thirty-two.'

'Thanks for announcing that to the world, Ruby, I was hoping to keep it to myself.' She chuckled as I asked the passing Serang if he would do the honours.

'Custard,' he shouted, having brought us into focus.

'Cheese,' corrected Lamis in a fit of giggles. This started us all off and the foredeck erupted in a cacophony of laughter.

'Umi,' said my ward-of-court once the hilarity had died down, 'Mrs Appleby baked your favourite Victoria sponge cake, and I helped her ice it before we left Delhi. I was supposed to keep it a secret but I just forgot.'

'Seems we are all having that problem, Lamis.' Ruby handed me a small white gift bag with black ribbon handles. It looked expensive and I'd seen something like it before. 'I suggest you open this in the privacy of your own cabin,' she whispered.

My lips pressed together as I handed it to Lamis and asked her to put it safely in my trunk with the camera. 'Am I allowed to have a swim now or do I have to stand here and let the sun turn me into an aging wrinkly.'

'You're already an aging wrinkly,' she replied and nodded to Jim.

The next thing I knew, Jim had picked me up bodily and thrown me into the canvas-sided pool.

'HAPPY BIRTHDAY, MAC!' was all I heard as I disappeared below the waterline.

Returning to my cabin after our celebration tea and birthday cake, my thoughts turned to Ruby's gift, and I dragged my trunk from under the bed. Carefully untying the bow, my fingers parted the thin cardboard packaging and, as I expected, the interior was filled with black tissue paper. A card was placed on top.

Happy 32nd Birthday, Mac.

It's never too late to start over, so here's a little something to help you get back in the saddle. Hope you like the colour. Decided rose pink was a bit old hat.

Much love

Ruby

xx

I was holding a beautiful ice blue and cream lace camisole up to the light when there was a knock on the cabin door. 'It's open,' I called, quickly tucking the gift under my bedspread.

The door swung back and my Goan steward stood in the corridor holding a full ice bucket in his hand, the gold foil neck of a Veuve Clicquot bottle jutting above the rim.

'Memsahib, Doctor, I have been asked to give you this.' He pulled a small white envelope from his breast pocket, placed it and the bucket in my hands and backed away bowing.

'No, this can't be happening?' A jolt of déjà vu left me dumbstruck as I remembered my steward, Salvador, doing exactly the same thing on my twenty-ninth birthday aboard the ss Narkunda. I crossed to my bed trying to comprehend what had just happened and felt the mattress slump under my weight.

Frances popped her head around the cabin door sometime later and found me still sitting there, Ruby's gift spread out on my pillow and the ice bucket at my feet.

'Just thought I would let you know that Lamis is on the promenade deck playing quoits with Jim.'

I must have resembled a half-wit, staring vacantly at the bulkhead.

'Hello, is anybody in there?' I didn't respond so she scanned the cabin wondering what was wrong, finally noticing the bottle of Veuve Clicquot. 'Wow, who's you're admirer, Mac?' She stretched across me and picked up the card. 'May I?'

Dear Mac,

I hope you will accept this as a peace offering and agree to share it with a certain fellow-medic on the hurricane deck at dusk. Sincere apologies for all that has gone before and

Happy Birthday

Tom

'Did you know he was on board?' When I found my voice, it sounded belligerent.

'No, Mac, I didn't, but I bet my husband did and we'll be having a few choice words about it later.'

'Well, obviously he is, and I don't know what I'm supposed to do about it.'

'Mac, stop vacillating. If I'm right, Tom has decided to bring this whole mess to a head and he's doing it the only way he knows how.'

'What here, in the middle of the India Ocean?'

'For goodness's sake, Mac, there are times when you can be very thick. The man's trying to recreate the best night of your life in the hope of reminding you of what you are missing.'

'But . . .'

'No buts, Mac. If Tom is trying to mend fences, then the least you can do is meet him halfway.' She opened my locker and rifled through my clothes. 'What have you got to lose? One night under the stars with a handsome doctor. It didn't stop you last time.'

'And look what happened then?'

St Saviour's headmistress just tutted and pulled my emerald-green silk evening dress out and held it up. 'When were you thinking of wearing this, Mac? It's hardly suitable for New Year's Eve in Riveldene.' She hung it on the back of the door and examined her handiwork on the hem. 'So, what do you say? Are you be going to the ball, Cinders, or will you be spending the next three weeks hiding in a closet?'

'Oh, bloody hell, Frances.'

'Temper, temper, Elizabeth, there's no need to swear.' She picked up Ruby's gift and dropped it on my lap. 'Time to find your inner femininity, Mac. I know she's in there somewhere, and don't try using Lamis as an excuse to get out of this. Your ward-of-court will be sleeping in Ruby's suite tonight.'

She opened the cabin door. 'What's your steward's name?'

'Paulo.'

'PAULO!' she bellowed down the corridor.

'Yes, Memsahib.' He staggered to a halt looking rather flustered.

'Take this, keep it chilled and place it with champagne glasses on the hurricane deck at seven-thirty.' She rammed the ice bucket into his arms.

'How many glasses, Memsahib?'

'Two, Paulo. Just two, and run the Doctor a warm bath. She'll be along shortly.' She swung back to me. 'Can I assume you won't be needing my tailoring skills on this occasion?'

'Hardly, Frances, unless I've shrunk since Port Said.'

My evening dress caressed my ankles as I climbed the third set of companionway steps leading to the hurricane deck. I'm getting old, I decided, as my lungs gasped for oxygen. I paused at the top to get my breath and stretched my neck to see the top of the ship's two black funnels against the night sky. The layout was different to the ss Narkunda and I wasn't sure which way I should go but a steward, appearing from the stern, pointed aft. I was convinced he could hear my heart thumping.

Moving at a snail's pace, I made my way along the ship's port side and caught brief glimpses of the Indian Ocean between the lifeboats hanging from their davits, the still waters far below rippling with starlight, contrasting sharply with the turmoil going on in my gut. 'This is ridiculous, Mac,' I mumbled under my breath, 'it's only Tom you're having drinks with, not King George V.' I halted by a life-jacket stowage and gave myself a strong talking to, checked my ivory and malachite bracelet was securely fastened, brushed a stray hair from my cheek and walked with purpose onto the stern deck.

Tom was standing by the rail dressed in an evening suit, his white tuxedo sporting a red carnation in the lapel and his black dance shoes reflecting the moonlight. He looked like a matinee idol. At the sound of my footsteps, he lifted the chilled bottle of Veuve Clicquot from the ice and deftly popped the cork.

'We meet again, Doctor Mac,' he said, as if we were accidentally bumping into each other on the street. 'May I say you're looking as lovely tonight as you did three years ago.' He handed me a glass and raised his own. 'Happy Birthday, Elizabeth.'

The champagne touched my throat and gave succour to my tense emotions as we stood in silence, neither knowing quite what to say next. As if on cue, the ship's orchestra struck up on the promenade deck, beginning their opening set with the *Blue Danube* waltz, the strains of the melody reaching our ears on the updraft. I closed my eyes, trying to ignore the memories of my twenty-ninth birthday and failed miserably.

'Why are you here, Tom?'

'I didn't mean to be, Mac, that's the truth, but the thought of you travelling back to England and maybe never returning was a gamble I was not prepared to take. Our parting at the DKS left so much unsaid. We deserve better than that after all we have been through. We deserve more than an abrupt formal goodbye.'

I concentrated on the ship's wake as it flashed like fire in a tumble of phosphorescence.

'If you disagree, I'll disembark in Aden and you will never hear from me again, but at least I will know that I tried.' He brushed his finger across my bracelet. 'I've had time to think about my reaction in Jhalanpur and how I must have hurt you. None of what happened was your fault and you should never have been made to deal with the consequences alone. I know it is too late to change the past because I can't give you back the years of pain and guilt which you have suffered, but I can make up for it, Mac, if only you'll let me try.'

We stood in a maelstrom of emotion which swirled around us as the ss Rawalpindi ploughed on through the waves.

'The choice has to be yours, Mac. If your feelings for me died with our child, then tell me here and now, because frankly, I'm having difficulty believing it.'

He was offering me a second chance of happiness and yet I had become so ingrained in believing I didn't deserve happiness, I was incapable of responding.

The music swelled as he left my side and walked to the centre of the deck.

'Don't think, Mac, just close your eyes and take a leap of faith. I promise, I WILL be there to catch you.'

Slowly, I walked towards him and felt his arms envelope me against his chest, the scent of his aftershave invaded my senses and my lips parted in expectation.

It felt so good to let go, so wonderful to know that I was loved and cherished, so safe locked in Tom's embrace, and as we swayed to the rhythm of the *Blue Danube*, all my pent-up anger, frustration and despair of the previous three years dissipated like the ship's wake, leaving me cleansed and feeling whole again.

When the music faded, Tom lifted my chin and ran his finger across my cheek. 'Your cabin or mine?' he whispered.

'Yours,' I replied, and our lips met once more. When we finally came up for air the steward was hovering by the life-jacket stowage, hesitating to step forward.

'Sahib, the band, they ask if you have other request for a tune.'

Tom, looking rather sheepish, handed him the ice bucket, and champagne flutes. 'No, thank you, steward, but please take these to my cabin. We will be along shortly.'

'I have a request,' I interrupted, focusing on Tom.

'Yes, Memsahib. Please, you tell me.'

'Ask the band to play *"It Had to be You"* by Gus Khan.'

He backed away, laughter lines creasing his olive face.

'I assume, Doctor Stuart-MacKenzie, you are insisting on leading me around the dance floor one more time before we adjourn below.'

'Well, Doctor Wallace, on the basis that there is no other attractive man on the hurricane deck for me to choose from, I guess I'm stuck with you.'

'Hussy,' he groaned and swung me around like a piece of flotsam before carrying me across the deck and down the companionway steps as Gus Khan's opening refrain filled the air.

Tom undressed me in the moonlight, its glow through the cabin porthole illuminating my naked skin as he caressed each erogenous zone from memory. Slowly, patiently and with controlled passion, his lips hardened my nipples, his soft beard, like velvet, stroked my abdomen and groin and when I felt the full weight of his body on mine, my back arched demanding more. I had yearned for this feeling for so long, and now that I had it, I didn't want it to ever end.

Without a care for the consequences, our bodies fused together in an act of sheer intensity and total abandon, pleasure being given and received with deep love and affection. It felt so natural, so right, so inevitable.

Lying with perspiration beading our skin, Tom's arm wrapped around my shoulders, my head resting on his chest, I blinked a tear from my eye and sighed.

'Penny for them?' Tom murmured.

'Thank you for loving me.'

In the silence of the cabin his words were hardly audible. 'Don't ever leave me again, Mac. I'm getting too old for all this excitement.'

I turned onto my side, stared into his deep blue eyes and smiled.

'Are you implying that your libido is in question, Doctor Wallace? If so, perhaps I should reconsider my position right now.'

He pulled me onto his chest and hugged me so tightly my ribs creaked. 'If that's the only reason you would leave me,

Madam, then a few nights spent in a five-star hotel in London should put your mind at rest. I'm confident my libido will be the last thing to be found wanting.'

I didn't need to answer, but I did thank my lucky stars that I would not be returning to England as one of the Fishing Fleet's "Returned Empty" lost causes.

'About time too, if you ask me.'

'I wasn't, Karr, so buzz off.'

-END-

MAC's Trilogy

BOOK 1
CALL ME MAC – PORT OUT

In the male dominated world of the Raj, female infirmity was treated with disdain. Only a woman of substance could bring about change.

Mac was feisty, courageous, accomplished, audacious, doggedly determined and single. Everything a woman was not expected to be in the late 1920's. Her chosen career was medicine, her speciality obstetrics, her goal to medically improve the plight of India's women whatever their religion, culture or status. It was a very noble cause, but first, Mac had to get there.

'Join the Fishing Fleet, dear,' suggested her aunt, which turned out to be an adventure in itself.

In Calcutta, a united front of pompous, misogynistic men of the India Medical Service stood ready to block her progress. To them, reducing female and infant mortality in an already over-populated continent seemed both illogical and absurd. As was, heaven forfend, allowing a female doctor into their ranks, no matter how well qualified.

Dr Elizabeth Stuart-MacKenzie was young and on a mission. Such out-dated opinions were irrelevant. Nothing was going to stand in her way. Not even sex!

Join Mac as she boards a P&O passenger-liner on route to Bombay. If she survives intact, her story will continue . . .

BOOK 2
MAC's INDIA

It was now 1930 and Mac had finally secured her Ph.D. post with the Calcutta School of Tropical Medicine. For the next 3 years, she intended to travel the length and breadth of India working for the Women's Medical Service and researching the effects of tropical diseases on mother and infant mortality.

To achieve her goal, Mac would find herself facing life-threatening action in the Hindu Kush, battling with the Delhi Police over the illegality of child marriage, putting up with unsolicited sexual advances from male colleagues and experiencing a concerted effort by her peers to undermine her progress. As for her private life, the least said about that the better!

Mac knew that fighting a rear-guard action against the misogynistic and racially prejudiced world of British Colonial India would be an uphill battle, fraught with setbacks and detrimental to her own career but she was determined to try. Would this feisty female medic succeed where others had failed? Only time would tell . . .

Acknowledgements

Alexandra Allden gets my sincere gratitude for her talented, patient and creative input as my graphics designer and Jenny Crickmore-Thompson, who professionally edited the first draft of the novel and whose critique helped move the story along.

To my close family and friends, whose reader critiques leading up to publication were invaluable, thank-you all for your input and support, it means a great deal. As for my husband, David, who argued his point of view with vigour and sound common sense and put up with my many moods whilst undertaking the extensive research, I can only reiterate, 'Like my previous novels, without you, this novel would never have seen the light of day!'

Finally, I pay tribute to the many long-suffering and doggedly determined female doctors, nurses and midwives throughout India whose dedication to their profession improved the plight of women and infants throughout this sub-continent and brought western obstetric knowledge and education to a country rife with female and infant mortality. They were the medical pioneers of their time and are owed a huge debt of gratitude. Your gender salutes you.

About the Author

Susie Baggaley was born in Nottingham in 1948 and by the age of nineteen had become an executive air-stewardess before starting her own successful company managing residential property for private owners working overseas.

Her passion for sailing became a lifestyle when, after twenty-three years, she sold her company, and went ocean-cruising with her husband, David, crossing the Atlantic Ocean four times and covering over 50,000 nautical miles on their private yacht. During the long hours at sea, Susie wrote articles for the sailing press and regular blogs for family and friends. Writing fiction was a natural progression beginning with her first novel, DEAD RECKONING, under her maiden name of Su Garcia, in 2015. Since becoming land based, Susie continues to write from her delightful home in Devon.

After a lifetime of travel, her wealth of experiences forms the basis for her intricate plots and characters. MAC'S DILEMMA, - IMPOSSIBLE CHOICES, is the author's latest novel to be published.

Review this Novel

If you have enjoyed reading the third novel in the 'Mac' series, and have purchased it on a digital book website, such as Amazon Kindle or Barnes & Noble, I would be most grateful if you could spread the word by uploading a review onto the relevant site for the benefit of others considering purchasing the novel for themselves, family or friends.

MAC's Dilemma – Impossible Choices

Thank you
Susie Baggaley

If you have not yet read Book 1 and 2
Call Me Mac - Port Out
Mac's India – In the Face of Resistance
they are available on digital websites in both ebook and paperback and through many High Street bookshops.

Author's Books

Fiction

The 'Mac' series of novels
Call Me Mac – (Book 1)
Mac's India – (Book 2)
Mac's Dilemma – (Book 3)
(by Susie Baggaley)

Dead Reckoning
Rum Punch
(by Su Garcia)

Non-Fiction

Islas Baleares Pilot Book
by David & Susie Baggaley

(published by IMRAY / RCCPF)

Baggatelle Publishers Ltd
www.baggatellepublishers.com

Printed in Great Britain
by Amazon

11900653R00234